The Creation
Chaos Rising

By
Art Gulley Jr.

THE CREATION: CHAOS RISING

First edition. November 18, 2024.

Copyright © 2024 Art Gulley Jr..

ISBN: 979-8230534761

Written by Art Gulley Jr..

Also by Art Gulley Jr.

Author's Note

My education in religion started when I was very young. My mother was Episcopalian, my grandmother a devout Catholic, and my father a Baptist. I spent grades five through seven in a Lutheran school, and grade eight in a Catholic. I myself eventually became a member of a non-denominational church and spent several years working at a Non-Orthodox Synagogue.

This extreme exposure to such varying religious doctrines left me with one burning question: What if God, the Angels, and everything in between are nothing like we think they are?

The following story is my imagination's attempt to answer that question. It is a work of fiction drawn from a philosophical "What if..." point of view and should in no way be taken as a criticism or denouncement of any particular faith or religious doctrine.

That being said...Enjoy!

For Traci, Ethan, Adam, and Jacob

The Starting Time

In the Beginning of all Beginnings there was the Event; a molecular cataclysm that spawned all that exists including the infinite expanse of Celestial Energy known as The Void.

It was from The Void that The Almighty drew forth the power to fashion The Creation; a system of three intertwining Realms to contain and nurture the myriad forms of lesser, sentient life developing around Him.

The first Realm He named Celestia, for it was home to all beings with the innate ability to manipulate The Creation's Celestial essence, thus granting great power and immortality. The second Realm He christened Sublimia, for it was a fluctuating expanse of sublime energy siphoned from The Void that served as bridge and buffer between the Real and the Ephemeral. The third Realm He named Mortalia, for within its dimensional boundaries dwelled all the beings and creatures whose lifespan, abilities, and intellects were finite, thus limiting their Creational stature.

To govern His Creation and maintain the delicate Balance He had achieved between the eternal forces of Order and Chaos, The Almighty set-in place a system of rules known as the Divine Tenets. These Tenets were enforced by a select group of Celestials within the Ruling Hierarchy known as the Divine Watch.

As the various Mortal Races matured, so did their push toward moral and spiritual disobedience, as many sought to supplant the Tenets with their own self-serving doctrines and decrees, thus threatening the Balance.

To combat these periodic Risings, The Watch would initiate specific Protocols to return the transgressing Race to the path of the righteous. During these times of Spiritual Reclamation, Members of the Watch would often call upon select Mortals to carry out specific Tasks within Mortalia in support of the Divine Effort. For the most part those selected, willingly served. But occasionally a Mortal would resist the *call. When that happened, Members of the Watch would be forced to use alternative measures to ensure cooperation.*

An excerpt from The Journals of the Archangel Michael

Emergence

Chapter 1

The first bullet hit with the force of a sledgehammer smashing bones and cartilage to bits as it tore its way through her shoulder. The second bullet impacted against her chest fracturing the breastbone. Curiously enough there was no pain. Only a dull ache and an overwhelming fatigue sweeping through her body as her life's blood seeped from the wounds.

"Why are you doing this?"

The answer to her anguished cry was the flash of the gun's muzzle and a resounding thunder as the third bullet found its mark through her carotid artery...

Nina Delcielo woke with a start, her silken gown drenched with sweat, her breath tumbling from her mouth in ragged gasps. She blinked several times trying to discern her surroundings then exhaled in relief when the bedroom's familiar furnishings filled sleep blurred eyes.

Nina pressed the heel of her hand against her forehead hoping to relieve some of its knotted tension. She tried once again to make sense of the bizarre scene that had plagued her sleep for the past week.

The dream's setting remained unchanged: A hospital reception area, its classic architecture and graphic posters identifying it as Henry Ford's main campus in Detroit, Michigan; the large, digital clock hanging behind the service desk marking the time at twelve-twenty p.m.

Several staff members were huddled in terror by the vending machines while Nina's dream-self tried to reason with the haggard Caucasian male dressed in tan fatigues waving around a large gun. The reasons behind his rampage remained unknown for his voice was consistently drowned out by the gun's thunderous rapport, though tonight was the first time she actually saw herself being shot.

11

A spiritual person might take the dream as some sort of omen. Such notions had never played much of a part in Nina's life, despite the best efforts of a parochial minded mother. A more logical assumption would be that the nightmares were a by-product of stress brought about by her latest business venture; the transformation of one of Downtown Detroit's numerous abandoned buildings into a Youth Recreational Center.

An innate understanding of the stock market, coupled with several lucrative investments had netted the young woman a considerable fortune, and allowed her an early exit from the corporate sector. Unlike so many of her wealthy contemporaries, Nina was a firm believer in the concept of "giving back to the community", and a good portion of her wealth funded various philanthropic efforts in and around the Metro Detroit area.

The alarm clock released its six-a.m. chime, and Nina promptly hit the off switch to silence its thunderous clang while shielding her eyes from the digital display's green glow which seemed unusually bright. In fact, all of her senses seemed...off. The pungent smell from the garbage she'd neglected to take out the previous night assailed her nostrils and her silk sheets felt course against her skin. Could she be coming down with something?

She felt her forehead but detected no sign of fever, nor did she feel ill. Actually, it was just the opposite. She felt completely recharged despite having slept only four hours instead of her customary nine. Maybe it was the new vitamins she'd recently started taking. The advertisement for them had promised "miraculous improvements to your overall health."

Nina chuckled. Whatever it was that had her feeling like Wonder Woman this morning she was thankful for it. She gave her body a brief stretch then hopped out of bed to prepare herself for what promised to be another busy day.

An hour later she was giving her appearance a final check in the free-standing oak mirror positioned by the apartment's front door. Nina felt that her new black linen pantsuit tastefully accentuated her tall, athletic figure, striking the perfect balance of authority and sensuality.

Nina never considered herself a raving beauty. Prominent cheekbones set in an oval face, coupled with a slightly offset nose and wide lips, were far off the mark of what she considered "pretty" features. Though she had to admit the hazel color of her eyes, a gift from the father she had never met, combined with her mocha skin, a product of her Latino heritage, did give her face an exotic quality that most men found appealing. There was certainly no shortage of potential suitors jockeying for position. It was just a shame that quantity didn't always signify quality when it came to finding a good man.

"Alright, girl, enough preening," she chided herself after giving her backside a final glimpse. "Let's go bully some contractors."

Nina left her apartment and made her way to the elevator frowning at the pungent smell of the cleaning chemicals that assailed her nose. The Jeffersonian Apartments located on Detroit's East Jefferson Avenue was considered one of the city's historical landmarks. The building's maintenance staff was committed to keeping the aging high-rise in pristine order but today they seemed to have gone a bit overboard.

The elevator arrived and she hopped aboard, grateful that she didn't have to share the ride with Misses Watson, her elderly neighbor from the floor above who felt it her duty to attach the single Nina to one of the numerous bachelors that lived in the building.

The elevator came to a gentle stop on the first floor and the doors slid open bringing Nina face to face with the matchmaker herself, accompanied as always by her Chihuahua, Angel.

Not wanting the woman to engage her in a lengthy discussion, Nina put a note of urgency into her voice as she quickly stepped forward into the Jeffersonian's elegantly furnished lobby. "Good morning, Misses Watson, Angel."

"Hello, Nina dear. You're off to an early start."

"Yes, well you know what they say about the early bird and the worms."

Misses Watson's smile was so wide that her eyes turned into narrow slits on her lined face. "Indeed, I do! In fact, I was just having a similar conversation with that handsome young man who lives in apartment 12 C: Jeremy's his name. You really should meet him, dear. He's a doctor you know, and he was telling me..."

"I'm sorry Misses Watson, but I really must be going," Nina interrupted giving the other's bowed shoulder a gentle squeeze. "Perhaps you and I can finish this conversation over tea one morning."

"Oh, that would be great, dear." The elderly woman gave Nina's hand a parting grip then stepped into the waiting elevator. "Just let me know when. You know I'm always available."

The elevator doors slid shut and Nina exhaled sharply. "Indeed, I do."

"I see old Madame Cupid's trying to hook you up again, Miss D," Carl the gray-haired security guard chuckled as Nina made her way past the lobby's front desk. His stocky body was framed by the row of monitors showing various views of the apartment's four entrances and adjoining lot. "That woman needs to seriously get a life."

"Be nice, Carl. We have to respect our senior citizens."

Carl made a rude noise with his lips. "Hell, *I'm* a senior too, but that don't give me the right to butt into everybody's private life the way she does."

Nina chuckled. "Yeah, she can be overbearing at times. I think it's because she's lonely. The old girl's been by herself since her husband died and could probably use a little company." Nina gave Carl a saucy wink. "Some male company, if you catch my drift."

Carl balked at the idea. "I'm not *that* dedicated to my job!"

Nina laughed at the look of dismay on his weathered face. "I don't know Carl; a handsome, debonair fellow like yourself? A little romance might bring the old bird new life."

Carl released a disgusted snort. "I'd rather cozy up to Angel."

Nina burst out laughing. "And on that note, I'd better get going. I'll see you later Carl." She waved as she made her way toward the lobby's rear entrance.

"Take care, Miss D," Carl hollered back then sighed. *Man, if I were thirty years younger.* His eyes followed her out the door then picked up her image on the monitor overlooking the back parking lot where he watched her get into her custom, black Jeep Grand Cherokee and drive off the lot.

*

Nina merged onto the Lodge freeway, weaving in and out of the morning traffic with the precision of a NASCAR driver. She reached her first destination, Traci's Cookie Emporium, at the same time as the shop's vivacious owner. Nina had quickly learned that fresh pastries tended to motivate construction workers, and Traci's was a local favorite.

The two ladies chatted amiably while Traci prepared the order, and Nina found herself in good spirits when she pulled into the Center's parking lot fifteen minutes later.

Her contractor's daily list of problems was shorter than she'd expected, and Nina was able to get the majority of the issues resolved by one p.m. Rather than go home and cook she decided to stop by Tony's Pizza and Sandwich Shop for a quick bite. It was there that her day took a turn for the worse.

She had just stepped through the shop's leaded-glass doors when the nightmarish vision flashed before her eyes. Its searing clarity caused her to cry out in alarm, and she staggered against the door jamb. Luckily Tony, the Shop's owner, was standing by the front counter.

Moving with a speed and grace that belied considerable bulk, he snaked an arm around Nina's waist to steady her.

"You okay, Nina?"

The shaken woman blinked hard several times trying to clear the image from her mind. "Yeah, Tony, I'm alright. That trick ankle of mine gave out and it caught me off guard," she lied, not wanting to alarm Tony or the numerous patrons scattered about the dining area.

Tony's wide lips curved into a smile. "Yeah, that happens a lot with my shoulder." He flexed his muscular right arm for emphasis as he led her to the table closest to the counter. "Here, have a seat and give the thing a rest while I get you a bowl of Maria's Minestrone soup. That way we can talk over some lunch."

Nina's spirits lifted instantly. Minestrone was her favorite, and Tony's wife Maria made the best.

The Savellis were good people, and the food at the Sandwich Shop was top notch. Nina made it a point to stop by whenever she could, but not just for the cuisine. She had met the winsome couple during a luncheon celebrating the reopening of Detroit's famed Fox Theatre after a lengthy renovation. The Sandwich Shop had catered the event, and Nina spent the majority of her time there chatting with the shop's jovial owners. The three had shared a close bond ever since. That same year their support had also sustained Nina following the tragic death of her mother in an auto accident.

Tony returned to the table with two steaming bowls and a small basket of warm French bread, and Nina's mouth watered. "You must've read my mind."

Tony flashed a toothy grin. "What, you think I don't know your appetite; oatmeal before nine, soup and bread before two, and the Shop's Deep Dish Delight any day after six."

Nina burst out laughing. "You've got me pegged to a tee!" She reached for the breadbasket and noticed the peculiar way Tony was looking at her. "Is something wrong?"

A slight frown furrowed Tony's wide brow. "You seem a bit on edge today; any particular reason?"

Nina's reply was cut off by the sudden expletive uttered by one of the patrons sitting at the counter, his outburst drawing everyone's attention to the shop's television. A special news report was being broadcast about a shooting incident that had just taken place at Henry Ford Hospital.

A recently discharged employee had attacked the hospital's central reception area. Details were sketchy but so far there were two confirmed deaths: one of the residents and the gunman.

Nina's spoon fell from her fingers, its contents spilling, but the horrified woman barely noticed the mess or Tony's concerned plea. Her eyes were riveted to the television as the gunman's picture appeared on the screen.

It was the same gunman from her dream.

Chapter 2

The sun's rays glistened brightly over the vast Mourning Ocean, one of the planet Nirvana's principal bodies of water. On the southern tip of the Cairn Peninsula, where the ocean split into the Trinity Rivers, lay the island city of Heaven; its intricate web of crystal spires and marble structures rising majestically into the blue cloudless sky.

A mile or so off the island's coast a school of dolphins broke through the water's glassy surface, their raucous voices calling out an invitation to the winged male hovering in the air above. The man seemed oblivious to the dolphins and the heavy droplets of water produced by their antics that were rolling down his bare muscular chest soaking into the loose silken trousers tied innocuously around his chiseled waist with a length of braided cord; it's flaxen color matching that of his closely cropped hair.

The dolphins squealed again, but this time the playful racket brought a brief smile to the Archangel Michael's angular face. Nirvana's dolphins were notorious gossips, and he often enjoyed listening to the wondrous adventures they sometimes shared with their aquatic cousins throughout the Realms. Today however the Archangel declined their offer for there was a far more pressing matter occupying his mind.

A sudden change in the air pressure drew his attention upward where the Archangel Gabriel was gliding steadily toward him, the wind created by the mighty down strokes of his elegant wings churning up the water in a way that added even more excitement to the dolphin's game.

Michael smiled again at the dolphins' whistled greetings to the newcomer. They were one of the few species in the Creation that did not find Gabriel's malevolent demeanor disconcerting.

"Good morning, brother," Gabriel's deep voice rang out as he came to a deft stop in the air besides Michael. "Your chatty friends appear to be in good spirits today."

"They always are." Michael's tenor was a sharp contrast to Gabriel's baritone.

"However, you seem somewhat troubled," Gabriel noted as he hooked his thumbs in the braided cord about his waist. Unlike Michael's, his lariat was black, its texture and shine echoing that of the Archangel's hair trimmed in the militaristic style often copied by Mortal soldiers.

Michael released a weary sigh. "The Almighty ordered me to initiate the Emergence of a new Harbinger. It would seem that another Reclamation is upon us."

Gabriel released a snort, the pronounced muscles of his broad back and shoulders rippling as he fanned his wings outward to their full length so they could catch the ocean's spray. "You knew this day was coming given the appalling state of Mortalia's moral and spiritual fronts. The current wave of unrest could prove disastrous if the Balance is not restored."

Michael's lips turned downward. "On that we both agree, but I had hoped that, given the strides many of the Races have made in those areas, the current Rising would ebb on its own, thus negating the need for such drastic measures."

Gabriel snorted again, his ebony eyes flashing with vexation as he retracted his wings to a position suitable for hovering. "Hope is a word I no longer equate with the Mortal condition. True, some of the Races have matured, but the majority have once again grown fractured and vile, their connection to the Almighty tenuous at best. They must be called to heel, or the entire Creation will suffer."

"I don't argue the facts, brother, but like you said; not all of them have strayed from Father's bosom," Michael noted with conviction.

"It is those righteous souls I wish to spare from a Reclamation's harsh effects."

"Harsh?" Gabriel jumped on the word, his left eyebrow arching upward. "Is that criticism of the Almighty's law I hear in your voice, Michael Keeper of Benevolence?"

Michael's wings rustled slightly, his hazel eyes flashing with aggravation. He had never liked the nickname ascribed to him by the members of the Hierarchy. "You know that I would never criticize Him or His ways, Gabriel Bringer of Death," he replied in kind. "It's just that something about this new effort feels...different."

Gabriel regarded Michael through narrowed eyes. "In what way?"

"For starters, The Almighty's imposed new limits on The Watch's involvement. Our not being able to properly steer the course of this Divine endeavor make me doubt its success."

"The addition of said limits will *ensure* its success," Gabriel countered. "The Mortal mindset has changed considerably since the Starting Time. Their beliefs are no longer easily captured through Divine works which has made them less malleable to our influence."

Michael smiled at his brother's disdainful remarks. "They have evolved."

Gabriel frowned. "Yes, into a gaggle of cynical liberalists, especially the rabble that populate Earth; a fact that I find particularly offensive. Father has poured a considerable amount of His Grace into that lot but what good has it done? Their minds have become so preoccupied with games of mental intrigue and physical gratification that they've all but lost their Divine distinction amongst the Realms which is why their salvation above all the others *must* be earned. Only by tempering their souls in the fires of hardship can they prove themselves worthy of the Vanguard position they were meant to assume within the Realms."

"You've always frowned on Mankind's evolutionary advances."

Gabriel pinned Michael with an uncompromising look. "And you've not frowned enough," he cried, his voice laced with scorn. "Your affection for The Almighty's Creational favorites, though laudable, is often misplaced and rarely is it reciprocated."

Michael considered the point for a moment then a slight smile crept its way onto his face. "Perhaps," the Archangel speculated as he shifted his gaze away from Gabriel's disapproving scowl to focus on the lone dolphin rapidly approaching the pod still splashing in the waters below them from Trinity's inlet. "But it's a fault I'm willing to accept. Guiding them is my job."

A predatory gleam appeared in Gabriel's eyes as he too focused on the newcomer now happily frolicking with its fellows. "And disciplining them is mine."

Michael sighed. "Of this I am also well aware."

Gabriel regarded Michael through narrowed eyes. He sensed that there was more on his mind than the Realms' current crisis. "What else about this Reclamation is troubling you?"

Michael's jaw tightened briefly as he met the other's unflinching gaze. "Nina is the one Father has chosen to usher in this new effort," he finally said.

Gabriel's face registered his surprise. "A rather mundane Task considering her attributes..." the Bringer of Death paused when he noticed the sudden twitch of Michael's wings. "Ah," he uttered as the source of the other's anxiety became apparent. "She is still ignorant of her heritage and abilities."

Michael's expression hardened. "It was the only way to ensure her a normal life."

"Perhaps," Gabriel begrudgingly allowed. "But your coddling has also left her woefully unprepared for the role she must now play."

"You think I don't know that?" Michael snapped with more heat than he intended. His wings fluttered rapidly as he struggled to reign in his conflicting emotions. "My apologies, brother," he began once he had regained his composure, but Gabriel's raised hand cut him off.

"None needed; I know the affection you hold for Nina and understand your angst."

Michael uttered words of gratitude for his brother's unexpected compassion to which Gabriel responded with a sharp nod.

"However," the raven-haired Celestial continued sternly. "Given the situation at hand, Nina must be...brought up to speed as the Humans say. Have you any ideas on how to accomplish this?"

A look of uncertainty crossed Michael's face. "I do not. At the moment I've allowed her Transition to mirror that of an ordinary Harbinger."

"Then I suggest you continue in that vein," Gabriel said after a thoughtful pause. "I will also have Omen assign one of the Celemors the Task of Protection while she adjusts to her new stature."

Some of the tension left Michael's face. "Knowing she was in the care of a Celestial Mortal would ease my mind considerably. Have you an idea as to which one would be best suited for this?"

"I do..." Gabriel said but stopped as he noticed how intently the dolphin that had recently joined the pod still happily swimming below was observing their discourse. "Perhaps we should continue this conversation away from the prying ears of The Creation's biggest eavesdroppers," he said with a nod toward the dolphins.

"Agreed," Michael assented having also taken notice of the aquatic denizen's scrutiny.

With a mighty flap of their wings, the two Archangels quickly soared off toward Heaven's glistening skyline, all but one of the dolphins saddened by their abrupt departure.

Chapter 3

The mid-day sun blazed prominently in the Arizona sky, raising the temperature of the stony landscape to a dangerously hot degree. The tall, shirtless man hefting a large slab of granite from an angled wooden stand seemed completely unaffected by the harsh rays beating down onto his muscular back.

Gabriel Leyr's dark complexion gave him the appearance of a Negro, but the silky texture of his long black hair currently tucked under a safari style hat, and the thin lines of his handsome face hinted at a Middle Eastern, possibly Arabic influence.

He carefully laid the slab in the newly trenched pathway, the latest in a series of decorative renovations being done to the old Clawson ranch.

In the early eighteen hundreds, Clawson had been one of the Southwest's premier vacation spots. Situated in the desert roughly seventy miles north of Flagstaff, its natural springs and abundant mountain vistas had attracted families from all over the country. Sadly, mounting hostility between the Spanish and Apache tribes that once occupied the region began to dissuade people from visiting the isolated ranch. This eventually led to its closure.

Clawson remained vacant for several years until it was purchased by Gabriel and his wife Clarissa. The couple bought the sprawling, seventy-acre ranch with the intentions of one day returning it to its former glory; a dream that sadly never came to fruition.

Gabriel gave the top right corner of the slab a deft slap to reposition it then swore softly. The muttered curse was not from an injury received while striking the granite, but for the fluttering impingement upon his awareness. A Celestial's calling card.

"Hello, Gabriel."

"Omen," Gabriel stiffly greeted the Celestial Overseer appearing beside him. "Have you ever considered ringing my doorbell to see if I want company as opposed to just popping in my yard whenever you want?"

"I find the direct approach more efficient when dealing with you Celestial Mortals," Omen told the disgruntled man. "A trait you would do well to immolate."

Gabriel snorted. "Yeah, well life would get pretty dull if we all subscribed to your level of efficiency." He effortlessly lifted the slab from the trench and balanced it atop one hand. With his other hand he adjusted the level of the layer of sand on the trench's bottom then gently repositioned the stone. "I mean what's the point of having all this Celestial energy if you can't occasionally stop and smell the roses; or create them depending on your place on the power scale." A slight glow emanated from his body as he exerted more pressure on the granite to seat it permanently.

"Your levity is misplaced, Gabriel and your efforts wasteful. As a Celemor you should be using your *enhancements* for something nobler than...landscaping."

"Such as?" Gabriel asked as he made his way back to the stand where he retrieved the second half of the slab from its padded timbers.

"A Divine Task set by the Archangels requiring your immediate attention."

"Do tell?" Gabriel positioned the second slab beside the first. "Well at the moment this pathway requires my 'immediate attention'. So, unless you plan on helping me." He indicated a large pile of unshaped granite pieces stacked beside the stand. "You and the winged duo are going to have to wait."

Omen's stance didn't change, but Gabriel could sense his irritation. "Your ego can be very exasperating at times." He waved his robe-covered hand over the path. A flash of white light discharged from his slender fingers, and Gabriel instinctively shielded his eyes with his forearm.

"There," Omen's voice sounded when the light had faded. "Consider yourself helped."

Gabriel gaped in wonder at the pathway, the remaining slabs of granite now shaped and fitted with perfect precision against one another. There was even a row of neatly potted rose bushes ringing the path that led from the main house out to the ranch's central courtyard. "You know those potted roses will never survive in this climate."

Omen gave the plants a brief glance. "Then I trust you'll discover a way to ensure that they do. But given the fact that your path is complete, may I now have your undivided attention?"

"Yeah, okay." Gabriel removed his cap, allowing his hair to fall to its full-length midway down his back. "What be thy bidding, great-layer-of-stone?"

Omen ignored his sarcasm. Long association with the reticent Mortal had allowed the Overseer to build a partial tolerance to Gabriel's customary jibes. "A Harbinger has Emerged in the city of Detroit, Michigan. Her name is Nina Delcielo. You must ensure that no harm befalls her."

"Ni-na Del-ci-e-lo," Gabriel rolled the name over his tongue as he stepped gingerly on the newly laid stones. "Well, it's obvious *she's* destined to do great things. Any idea as to what they might be?"

"Her purpose is not your concern. Protecting her is."

Gabriel regarded the Overseer through speculative eyes. "What's the matter, O? The dynamic duo didn't take you into their confidence?"

Again, Gabriel sensed the Overseer's irritation. "It's not my place to question the Archangels," Omen snapped, his eyes glowing softly under his hood. "Nor is it yours. Just ensure her safety."

A mischievous smile tugged at the Celemor's thin lips. An inner perversity prompted him to continually test the limits of the stoic

Overseer's patience. "Alright, alright; I'll play the role of Celestial babysitter if it'll make the boys upstairs happy."

"Your levity is misplaced Gabriel. You know how important a Celemor's position is within the Divine Infrastructure."

Gabriel's expression hardened. "I know the consequences should I choose to relinquish my position."

Omen made no response to the charged statement, but Gabriel could sense compassion radiating from beneath his hood. Despite the perverse pleasure he took in antagonizing the Overseer, Gabriel still held a fondness for his Celestial handler.

"Is the woman to be aware of my presence?"

Omen inclined his head toward the Celemor, managing to also convey in the simple gesture his sympathy for the Mortal's plight. "I leave that entirely up to you."

Gabriel studied the Overseer's hovering form for a moment but as usual, Omen's face was concealed behind the shadowy folds of his hooded shroud. The Celemor often wondered if the Celestial even had one.

Gabriel let his eyes range over the ranch allowing the image of what could've been to superimpose itself over the barren portrait of what was. His mind drifted back to a particular day shortly after he and his wife had taken possession.

We'll plant a hedge row here, Clarissa declared, her voice laced with the slight accent many Native Americans inherited upon learning English. *It will help soften the look of the livestock pens. The barn can stay as is, after you paint it a different color.* She flashed him a teasing smile, her gray eyes sparkling. *Something warm that will blend better with the land. And we can set up an outdoor dining area there.* She indicated the large clearing twenty yards from the decaying hulk of the main house. *The mountains will frame the sun when it sets and provide an excellent backdrop for guests enjoying the evening meals.*

And what about that? Gabriel indicated the large boulder resting midway between the existing barn and the spattering of tall cacti on the ranch's eastern border.

Clarissa studied the area for a moment while shifting their wiggling three-year-old daughter, Gabriella, to a more comfortable position on her left hip. *That would make a good spot for nightly campfires.* Gabriel gave the weedy gravel strewn area a quick look then turned dubious eyes on his wife. *Don't give me that look!* Clarissa waggled the forefinger of her right hand under his nose. *With a little effort we can make this place beautiful again...*

"Gabriel?"

Omen's voice snatched Gabriel from the past and projected him painfully back to the present where the mental image of Clawson evaporated into the ranch's current view.

The barn *had* been repainted a soft tan. A large circular area ringed with wooden banquet tables and a large roasting spit now rested exactly where Clarissa had specified, though no meals had ever been served there. Nor had any campfires burned in the neatly raked, sandy area under the large boulder.

"Are you alright?"

Gabriel turned clouded eyes to the Overseer. "Never better."

"So will you take on this Task?"

Gabriel sighed heavily. "Tell the Great Ones not to fret. I'll keep their Harbinger safe."

"The Archangels never doubt your abilities," Omen said as his body began to fade. "But they sometimes question your methods."

Gabriel released an amused snort. "What a coincidence," he whispered after Omen had vanished. He focused once again on the boulder; specifically on the small cairn marking Clarissa's and Gabrielle's grave nestled quietly in its shadow. "Cause I sure as hell question theirs."

Chapter 4

On the northern ridge of Nirvana's arctic shelf lay the city of Hell. From his vantage point atop the massive, alabaster edifice known as the Tower of Self, Iblis gazed out over the sprawling metropolis, and a pleased smile creased his lips.

Most Mortals thought of Hell as a land of fire and brimstone, where the souls of the damned spent eternity roasting in agony for the sins committed during their brief, troublesome lives.

Such gruesome imagery was a useful form of propaganda to keep the Mortal's corrupt religious infrastructure in power, but the real Hell bore no resemblance to the demonic stereotype shamelessly perpetuated by the so-called righteous. In fact, it was very similar in form and fashion to the crystal spires of Heaven.

Minus the Divine pomp-and-circumstance, Iblis mused, a mischievous glint lighting his vibrant blue eyes.

Of course, given the Mortal's lack of spiritual cohesiveness, this misconception was understandable. Few of the so called "True followers of God" even knew Iblis's real name. *Yet they consistently single* me *out as the enemy of the Creation.*

"My lord?"

Iblis shifted his gaze to the Morphling materializing beside him. "Yes, Silas."

"Forgive this intrusion, but I've just learned from my sources that your brothers have initiated another Reclamation within Mortalia."

Iblis took note of Silas's damp, flowing black hair, and the soaked coverlet clinging to his emaciated body. "Been swimming with the dolphins again?"

A wicked grin parted the Morphling's thin, colorless lips. "Their chatter is often useful."

"As is your ability to assume any form," Iblis chuckled. The motion caused the large wings folded across his muscular back to twitch while their feathers brushed lightly against the silken texture of his suit. Unlike the majority of his Celestial brethren, Iblis was fascinated by the varied styles of Mortal fashion, with a particular fondness for garments manufactured on Earth.

His current attire, a black single breasted Armani suit suitably altered to accommodate his wings, was one of his favorites. It gave him the appearance and bearing of what the Earth Mortal's termed a corporate CEO, which in a sense he was considering Nirvana's complex Celestial infrastructure, and Hell's position within it. "Have the Seers confirmed this?"

"They have, my lord."

Iblis's wings gave another twitch. "And have my brothers selected the hapless puppet that will usher in their latest scheme of Divine meddling?"

Silas made a circular motion with his hands, and a shimmering image of an attractive, caramel-skinned Mortal woman appeared in the air before them. "Her name is Nina Delcielo."

Iblis studied the image with a growing sense of consternation. There was something peculiar about this Mortal; a familiarity tugging at the edge of his senses. "There's something...different about this one."

"Apparently your brothers feel the same way," Silas noted as he too studied the image floating in the air before them. "They've placed her under the watch of the Overseers and their Celemors."

Iblis' wings gave another twitch at the news. "That is unusual. Were you able to ascertain the reason behind their peculiar consideration?"

A look of chagrin appeared on the Morphling's face. "I'm afraid my Veil of Deception was not woven nearly as tight as I had hoped. The Archangels sensed my presence and decided to continue their conversation elsewhere."

Iblis laughed. "Try not to overly concern yourself, Silas. "We members of the Archian Caste are a particularly suspicious lot."

"Perhaps," Silas drawled. "But we still need to ascertain why the woman is being guarded. Such information will give us insight as to her purpose, and whether or not her abilities can be of benefit to you."

Iblis's wings twitched again as he considered the Morphling's statement. "Your point is valid, Silas. Send a few Disciples to plague Miss Delcielo. Such an occurrence should quickly draw out whichever of their Mortal pets my misguided brothers have called forth, a revelation that might also prove informative."

Silas accorded him a respectful bow. "It shall be done at once."

Chapter 5

Sublimia's unstable molecular structure produced a constant fluctuation of the Realm's physical properties. This instability was painfully disconcerting to most beings within the Creation, save for the spattering of Celestial entities that chose to dwell within the shifting miasma.

For Dichotomy, a creature whose physical form continually fluctuated between the male and female halves of his dual personality, Sublimia's erratic environment was both sanctuary and tool while its sparse population afforded him the privacy he craved.

"The woman's Emergence progresses well," a feminine voice rang out as the blended being listened to the Chatter of the Realms created by Sublimia's nebulous composition, the communing of which allowed Dichotomy to monitor significant events throughout The Creation. Currently his attention was focused on the Archangel's latest attempt to restore the Balance between the eternal forces of Order and Chaos.

Dichotomy's features blurred as the male persona became dominant. "Yes, it does," the now masculine voice announced. "Hmm, it appears Iblis as taken an interest in her as well. The Disciples have been unleashed. Shall we intervene?"

"No," the re-emerging female answered after listening intently to the Chatter for a moment. "Potential threats to the Harbinger were anticipated which is why the Overseers gave Gabriel the Task of protection."

Dichotomy's features blurred once again as the two personas reconfigured their body into a grotesque apparition that bore little resemblance to any creature brought forth during the Starting Time. "A wise choice on their part," Dichotomy's blended voice decreed once his form had solidified. "Let us continue to monitor the

Harbinger, as well as our friend's progress, so that we may render aid if necessary."

Chapter 6

Nina stared apprehensively at the massive oak doors comprising the front entrance of Saint Christopher's Catholic Church. She often wondered why most spiritually motivated structures invariably resembled medieval fortresses.

A place of worship should convey feelings of warmth and comfort, but the stark gray slabs and marble blocks that made up Saint Christopher's hulking exterior did nothing of the sort. Not even the bright-colored flora permeating the church's manicured lawn could rid the place of its gothic overtones.

Perhaps that was why she had never felt connected to Saint Christopher's. Even though she had spent the majority of her childhood Sundays seated beside her mother on one of the massive oak pews, or with a group of fellow sufferers around the circular tables in the church's Sunday School classes.

"Morning, Nina!"

The loud cry startled Nina out of her reverie. She turned and smiled at the tall slim man jogging up the church stairs.

"Good morning, Ty!"

Tyree Griffin was Nina's closest friend and another former inmate of the Saint Christopher Youth Program. Unlike Nina, the lessons learned seemed to have taken root. He was now Saint Christopher's head minister. He was also well-versed in supernatural phenomena.

At one time he was the man Nina thought she would spend the rest of her life with, but those days were long gone. Now he was the person that could hopefully help her make sense of the crazy visions continuously plaguing her mind.

"This is a surprise." Tyree huffed, coming to a breathless stop beside her. He used the front of his t-shirt to wipe the dampness from his face and neck. "Excuse the sweat. I was out getting in my morning run."

Nina gave his lean chiseled frame a speculative look. "Staying in shape for those Sunday school teachers?"

"Hah!" Tyree cried as he unlocked the church doors. "You know running helps me maintain my sanity so I can deal with these wicked folks. Besides, have you've seen the ladies that run our Sunday school program?" A shiver went through his body. "Frightening creatures!"

Nina chuckled. Tyree's sense of humor and keen eye for the ridiculous were two of the main reasons the young Minister was so popular with the members of Saint Christopher's congregation. His boundless compassion was another.

He finished toweling off then gave the heavy door a yank to free its aging latches. "So, what brings you by, bud? Have you finally come to your senses and decided to join my flock?"

Nina balked at the suggestion. "Hardly! The truth is, I'm in a bit of a situation and could really use some...spiritual advice."

A pleased grin appeared on the Minister's face. "Is that right?" He opened the door wider. "Well come on in so you can bask in the light of my wisdom."

Nina shook her head from side to side as she stepped into the church's foyer. "You're such a goofball."

The foyer's lights were off, and it took a few moments for her eyes to adjust to the dimness. She immediately took note of the multi-colored decorations hanging from the vaulted rafters. All the light fixtures were festooned with gold ribbon. "You guys planning a party?"

"The church is celebrating its fiftieth anniversary," Tyree told her after exchanging pleasantries with the small group of parishioners meticulously decorating the archway with strands of red and gold garland. Another group was fastidiously cleaning the pews and balustrades, and the sweet smell of Murphy's Oil Soap filled the sanctuary. "The celebration starts Friday and runs through the weekend. We're doing a carnival theme so it should be very exciting. If you're not busy, stop on by."

"Maybe I will. I could use some fun in my life right about now."

Tyree took note of the sadness in Nina's voice but made no comment as he ushered her down the hall and into his small office, where he gently closed the door behind them.

He motioned for Nina to take a seat in one of the leather-covered armchairs positioned in front of his desk while he slipped into the office's private bathroom. The sound of running water echoed from behind the lavatory's partially closed door for several minutes then ceased. A few minutes later, Tyree emerged wearing a loose-fitting navy sweat suit emblazoned with Saint Christopher's name across the chest and down the right pant leg.

"*Tre' chic*, Ty."

"Hey, don't knock it," Tyree admonished with mock severity. "As the head honcho around here, I've gotta represent!" He raised both hands into the air, fingers curled into an intricate imitation of the territorial signs often touted by the progenitors of hip-hop. Nina couldn't help but laugh at his antics, and some of the weight lifted from her shoulders.

Tyree flashed a roguish grin then settled his lean frame comfortably into the high-backed chair behind his desk. "So, what's been going on, bud?"

Nina hesitated for the barest moment then told him of the bizarre visions plaguing her for the past few weeks.

By the time she finished, all traces of Tyree's former levity had vanished from his face. "And you're saying this all started with your dream about that unfortunate incident at Ford Hospital?"

"Yeah." Nina was relieved at having finally been able to confide in someone.

"That's pretty intense," Tyree commented after a thoughtful silence. "And have any of these other premonitions come true?"

A look of chagrin appeared on Nina's face. "To be perfectly honest I haven't read a paper or turned on a television since that day for fear of what I might see."

Tyree favored her with sympathetic eyes. "Yeah, I'll bet. Look Nina, I can certainly understand your fear, but this isn't something you should run away from."

"Then what would you suggest I do, Poppa Griff?"

Tyree smiled at the nickname she had saddled him with after his ordainment, stating that "Father Griffin" made him sound too old. "Well for starters we can call up the local news on the web and see if any recent events correspond with your dreams." He activated the Dell laptop resting on top of his desk. "Maybe the Ford vision was a fluke. Okay, here we go, the Detroit Free Press. Now then," he turned expectant eyes on her. "Give me some specifics from some of your other visions."

Nina pursed her lips. "There was a particularly vivid one the other night. A tanker was overturned on the Lodge freeway, and one of those new Dodge Chargers was pinned underneath it. There were two people trapped in the car, but only one of them was killed. A woman: a celebrity, I think. She seemed familiar, but I couldn't place her."

A look of apprehension appeared on Tyree's narrow face. "Could it have been Pamela Ayers?"

"That's her! She plays Doctor Lavenly on that comedy show they film here at Detroit Receiving."

"Emergency Room Angels," Tyree quietly supplied the show's name.

"That's the one." Nina's expression turned serious. "Is there something about her on the web?"

"She was killed in a car accident on her way to the show's set yesterday evening."

Nina stiffened in her seat. "Did they give any details?"

Tyree turned troubled eyes on her. "It happened just like you saw it."

Nina began to tremble. "I knew it; I'm turning into one of those people you see on the psychic-network!"

"Now hold on a moment." Tyree tried to forestall her panic. "Let's check out a few more of these visions before we go jumping to any conclusions."

She agreed and the two of them spent the next half hour doing just that only to discover that all her visions matched perfectly with recent events reported in the news.

Tyree turned off the laptop, and Nina regarded him through miserable eyes. "Are you convinced now?"

"Completely," he said reclining thoughtfully into his chair. "This truly is an amazing ability you seemed to have developed."

Nina gaped at him in disbelief. "I'm turning into a freak! What so amazing about that."

"You're not turning into a freak, Nina..."

"Yes, I am! I've seen this kind of thing on the cable channels. I'm gonna end up locked away in a padded room 'cause people will think I'm crazy, or they'll hunt me down 'cause they think I've been possessed by some kind of demon; like in that movie, the Exorcist!"

"Oh, stop it, Nina!" Tyree's sharp tone cut through her hysteria. "Have you ever witnessed a real exorcism?"

Nina gave a negative shake of her head.

"Well, I have!" A slight shiver ran down his spine at the memories of those harrowing experiences; particularly the one involving a sixteen-year-old girl named Katey...and the fifteen members of her dance class that she butchered one Tuesday afternoon. Expelling the demonic spirit that had taken up residence within the child's body nearly cost Tyree his life.

He was still haunted by the image of a possessed and blood-soaked Katey hovering in the air over her victims, and even more so by the one of her sitting cross-legged on the floor of a padded cell in the psyche ward of Dawson's Juvenile Detention Center, completely consumed by guilt.

"Trust me, Nina. You are not possessed. And you're not going crazy, either," he added before she could say it, prompting the distraught woman to throw her hands up in resignation.

"Alright then, genius, what *is* happening to me?"

Tyree regarded her through speculative eyes. "Are you familiar with any of those stories in the bible?"

"I haven't touched a Bible since grade-school," Nina confessed unashamedly. "Why do you ask?"

"Because what you're going through sounds a lot like the trials experienced by some of the biblical Prophets I studied at the seminary."

She stared at him for a moment then released a bark of laughter. "Please!"

"I'm serious, Nina. Your situation has all the earmarks of what the church calls, a Divine Manifestation."

"And just what the hell is that?"

"It's the sudden appearance of talents beyond the normal capabilities of men and women." He smiled at her look of skepticism. "I'm not kidding. These unusual abilities are generally thought to be Divine in origin."

Nina arched a cynical eyebrow. "So, what are you saying; God's giving me these crazy visions?"

Tyree shrugged. "The Bible is full of stories about ordinary people, like yourself, given extraordinary abilities for one reason or another. Maybe you've been chosen to become a modern-day Prophet."

"Now why would God choose someone like me for something like that? You know how I feel about churches and organized religion."

"All too well," Tyree chuckled. "But there's a lot more to serving God than going to church. It's also about the way you live your life. Misses Jenkins hasn't missed a service since you and I were here as kids, yet she still continues her extra-marital endeavors with that young pup that lives across the street from her."

"Tyree Griffin! You're not supposed to divulge confessional secrets."

A mischievous grin appeared on his face. "I'm not. She brags about it at bingo every Thursday to Miss Hawkins when she thinks no one's listening."

"You shouldn't be eavesdropping either."

"Then she shouldn't sit so close to the podium when I'm calling out numbers. At any rate, the point I'm trying to make is that a lot of people sit their phony, smiling faces in service every Sunday, knowing full well they'll be doing the devil's work come Monday. How do you think God responds to that type of hypocrisy?"

"To be honest with you, I've never given it much consideration."

Tyree released a disgusted snort. "Most people don't. They treat salvation like it's one of those free-music websites where you can download everything you want without contributing to the source, and that's not how it works at all. You've got to prove yourself worthy by living the life." He slapped the top of his desk for emphasis then relaxed back into his chair. "I tell you, Nina; when judgment day comes, a lot of these so-called believers are in for a rude awakening."

Nina leveled disdainful eyes on him. "Considering my own spiritual track record, that's not exactly filling me with the warm and fuzzies, Poppa Griff."

"I don't lump you in with those pseudo-Christians, Nina. Despite your cynical views on religion, you do live your life in accordance with the Christian system of values."

Nina's left eyebrow arched upward. "How in the world did you arrive at *that* conclusion?"

"It wasn't that hard." He began counting off points with his fingers. "You're hard working, kind-hearted, humble, and you adhere to a positive, moralistic code."

A slight flush colored Nina's face. "Jeez, Ty, you're making me sound like a choir girl."

"No, you're definitely not that," the Minister laughed. "But you're no wild-child either. Most of the time you conduct yourself like a proper *Christian* lady. "He gave her a teasing wink. "Which is commendable considering your steadfast separation from all things Holy.

A shadow of uncertainty darkened Nina's hazel eyes. "It's not that I don't believe in God...I just find it hard to accept that he wants us to praise him through the use of arcane rituals and spiritual bullying which seems to be the basis for a lot of modern-day religions; that and rending money out of people," she added with a snort.

Tyree sighed. "Yeah, there are some pretty esoteric faiths out there. Even the Catholic Diocese, though I love it dearly, has done some things that I find questionable."

"There," she exclaimed waving a hand in his direction. "You're one of the most devout Catholics I know, and even you have doubts about your chosen faith."

Tyree flashed another smile. "There's nothing wrong with having doubts, Nina. It's in our nature, and that's why the church's role is so important. It provides the rules and standards that allow us to structure our lives in accordance with God's Divine Plan."

Nina glared at him through skeptical eyes. "That's what *you* believe. Personally, I think religion is just another way for the government to control the masses."

Tyree's smile deepened. "That's the beauty of living in a free society. Everyone's entitled to their own opinion. Even someone as spiritually jaded as you."

"I guess," she muttered.

Tyree relaxed into his chair. "Well, whether you believe in religion or not, you're still a righteous person."

"I'm a cautious person," she corrected him. "The world's a weird place these days, and I'm not trying to get caught up in any craziness."

Tyree acknowledged the difference with a nod. "Fair enough, but your overall character is still laudable; particularly that philanthropic streak running through your body. A lot of native Detroiters who become financially successful tend to turn their backs on our city, but not you. You make it a point to conduct most of your business here, you're involved in several vital city organizations, and you're a staunch financial supporter of Detroit's youth programs." The tone of his voice indicated how important Nina's dedication to the city's children was. "I'm always telling my congregation that if we don't take care of our kids today, we run the risk of losing our tomorrow."

"You and I have always agreed on that, but I don't do what I do in order to buy my way into some utopian Heaven. Inner-city kids *deserve* the same opportunities as the suburbanites, and it's up to us to make sure they get them."

Once again Tyree slapped his hand against the top of his desk. "And that mentality is what sets you apart from a lot of these other so-called philanthropists! You don't do something because you think you're gonna receive some type of reward or official acknowledgment. You do it because it's the right thing to do. In God's eyes that makes all the difference."

"Well, if that's the case, and I am living the way He wants me to." Nina made a mocking gesture with her hands. "Why is He punishing me?"

Tyree's eyes widened with surprise. "Punishing you? Don't look on this as a punishment, Nina. Think of it as a Divine gift!"

Nina balked at his absurd suggestion. "I've become death's preview channel, Ty. What the *hell* kind of gift is that?"

"One that's needed," he responded quietly, his gray eyes troubled.

Nina gave him a questioning look, and Tyree released a weary sigh. "It's like you said, the world is getting crazier by the minute, and people are starting to lose hope. What if you've been given this ability to help alleviate the situation; to let people know that miracles do still happen?"

Nina considered his position for a moment. "Well, if God wants to give the world a cosmic sign, why doesn't He just pop on down here himself, or send one of those angels you holy guys are forever going on about?"

Tyree gave her a knowing look and shifted his voice into a tone of reverence. "Maybe he has...*Nina Delcielo*."

"Let's not have *that* discussion again, Poppa Griff!" Nina wondered for the millionth time why her mother chose to straddle her with such a pretentious name. "I got enough of that during my two years of Spanish. Besides..." She opened her arms wide. "I hardly fit the profile."

Tyree shrugged. "The Lord does work in mysterious ways. Maybe this is the reason you've always been such a whiz at the stock market."

Nina glared at him through narrowed eyes. "Making profitable investments based on the study of accurate data is a far cry from seeing the future, Poppa Griff."

Tyree aimed a shrewd look at her. "Maybe, maybe not; if it was that easy *every* informed broker would know what stocks to buy or avoid."

Nina was still unconvinced that her sharp business acumen was the result of some latent heavenly power. "If that's the case; how come this...gift is only just now manifesting itself? And why me? Like I said, I hardly fit the Prophet profile."

"No, you don't but your situation is not without precedence. The apostle Paul was a *persecutor* of Christians before he got straightened out."

It was clear from her expression that Nina remained skeptical, but she made no comment.

"In all honesty, Nina, I can't say why God's bestowed this gift upon you." Tyree rolled his chair from behind the desk then positioned it in front of hers, taking her hands in his. "But if I'm right, and you are being called to a higher purpose, it's something you're just going to have to accept."

Nina's expression hardened and she pulled her hands free. "Yeah, you told me the same bullshit when you walked out on me and took this job."

A pained look consumed the Minister's features, and she instantly regretted her harsh words. "I'm sorry, Ty. You didn't deserve that."

"I suppose to some extent I did," he whispered giving her cheek a gentle stroke with his fingers. "Look Nina, what we had was special, but..."

She held up a finger. "I know. God called and you had to answer." Tyree offered her an apologetic grin as he once again took hold of her hands, and Nina managed a weak smile. "You know for a benevolent being, God's got lousy timing."

Tyree gave her nose a playful tweak. "Yeah, He does." His expression turned serious. "All kidding aside Nina; I respect your beliefs, but I still want you to consider the possibility of this whole thing being Divine in nature."

"It's not like I have a choice with all these crazy episodes running through my mind." She pulled her hands free and pushed herself up in one fluid motion.

Tyree rose to his feet as well. "Where are you going?"

Nina stretched her arms above her head. "I think I've given this subject enough consideration for one day. I've got a meeting in an hour with the state's funding board, and I need to get some air; try to digest some of these spiritual notions before I deal with those penny-pinching bastards."

Tyree laughed then escorted her back to the main entrance. "You call me if you need anything," he said when they reached the door. "And don't forget about the gala next week."

"I won't, and thanks."

"For what?"

Nina shot a surreptitious look down the hall to make sure they were alone then gave his lips a gentle kiss. "For always being my voice of reason."

Tyree touched his forehead lightly to hers while calming the surge of desire shooting through his body. Her kiss had brought back memories of their previous relationship. "Somebody has to keep you out of trouble." He gently pushed her away so as not to offend. "Do try to take care of yourself."

"I will," Nina promised, also aware of the lingering heat between them.

She released a wistful sigh for what could've been and quickly made her way to her Cherokee parked on the street in front of the church. She gave him a final wave then hopped inside, completely oblivious to the silent figure perched atop the church's towering steeple, his presence celestially masked as he observed her every move.

Nina started her Jeep, and Gabriel rose gracefully into the air hovering patiently until she pulled away. The Celemor spared Tyree a brief glance then quickly soared off after his charge.

*

Tyree stared after Nina's jeep for a moment then retraced his steps to his office, once again shutting the door behind him. He quickly settled into his chair then picked up the phone.

The young minister had witnessed several strange and unexplainable events during his twelve years of service to the Lord, but all those other experiences paled in comparison to this. *Almost all of them,* he thought with a shiver as an image of Katey flashed before his eyes. He sharply steered his mind from that direction and back to the topic at hand.

Tyree had always felt that Nina was special, but even his expectations fell short of this. Her abilities were nothing short of miraculous. This matter would require further investigation, but whatever his friend was going through was totally beyond the scope of his experience. Fortunately, there was a faction already in place within the Catholic Diocese to handle this sort of thing.

He punched in the numbers on the keypad then held the receiver to his ear, trying hard to ignore the lingering taste of her lipstick.

Chapter 7

Cardinal Calvin Tullis stared impassively through the stained-glass window overlooking the Vatican courtyard. His corner-office was small when compared to those of some of his contemporaries also housed in the Civil Administration Building, but the view it afforded him of the Papal Gardens more than compensated. One look at the elegant landscape was enough to soothe away the stresses his job as head of the Vatican's public relations department sometimes entailed.

The current Pope's conservative stance on several controversial issues, most notably his steadfast denouncement of homosexuals and women clergy, had brought much criticism from the liberal front. The situation was also compounded by persistent rumors of scandal and misconduct within the Vatican. As a result, approval ratings for the Holy See were rapidly declining. Tullis and his staff were hard-pressed to stem the flow of negative publicity and reverse the steady migration from the church.

Many saw the Vatican's struggle as testimony to the erosion of Christian values around the world. Tullis felt the problem was more complex. To him it seemed as if society's incessant push toward technological thrills had all but erased its spiritual consciousness.

The shrill ringing of the telephone drew his attention away from the window. He made his way to his desk to retrieve the annoying contraption. "Cardinal Tullis," he spoke gruffly into the handset. "Ah, Father Griffin!" The Cardinal's mood brightened instantly.

In a world of decaying morals and religious abandonment, Tyree was a rare gem. A young man completely in tune with modern society yet totally devoted to his faith. More such leaders would be needed for the church to reverse its apathetic position.

"It's been far too long since we last spoke. How fares Saint Christopher's parish on the eve of its fiftieth anniversary?"

"Better than expected," Tyree's excited voice boomed from the handset. "Especially considering the visit I just had from an old friend."

Tullis had to steady himself against his desk after listening to the young minister's incredible tale. "And has this woman ever shown any signs of Divine favor before this?"

"None whatsoever; her faith in our Lord's way is sorely lacking."

"Then hers truly is a unique situation. Have you spoken to anyone else about this?"

"Yours was the first and only number I called. I felt it best to let you and the other Elders determine how we should precede."

A pleased smile appeared on Tullis' face. "A wise decision my son. You can be sure that this matter will be addressed with all haste. In the meantime, keep a discreet vigil over Miss Delcielo, and inform me immediately of any changes in the situation."

Tyree assured the Cardinal that he would and disconnected. Tullis kept the receiver to his ear for a moment then depressed the intercom button at the phone's base.

"Yes, Your Grace?" the deep voice of Tullis' personal assistant responded.

"Summon the *Presbyterii*, Donald. A matter of great urgency is upon us."

There was a brief pause then Donald's voice echoed from the intercom. "The message has been sent, Your Grace. All three are in route and should be here within the hour."

"Excellent. Send them to my office the moment they arrive."

"Of course, Your Grace." The intercom went silent.

Tullis resumed his former position at the window, pondering the significance of this woman's appearance. Could this be the sign that he had prayed for? An indication from God that all hope was not lost.

A discreet knock signaled the arrival of his guest.

"Enter," Tullis called, and the door swung open to reveal a short portly man, a look of tense anticipation etched across his aged face, waiting in the hall. "Ah, Cardinal Gionni," Tullis greeted the newcomer. "Thank you for responding so promptly. I trust I didn't pull you away from any pressing matters?"

"Nothing that can't be handled at a later time," Gionni quickly reassured him, firmly gripping the other's outstretched hand. "I saw Cardinal Milan's van coming through the gate as I was making my way to the door. Cardinal Dresden rode with him so they should be here directly."

"We're here now," Dresden's stern voice announced as he strode purposefully into the office, a grim-faced Cardinal Milan right behind him. "Good to see you both." Dresden accorded Tullis and Gianni a respectful nod. "Now what's all this about?"

Tullis motioned for the others to have a seat then recounted the information he had received from Tyree.

"I am unfamiliar with this Father Griffin," Cardinal Milan's voice penetrated the shocked silence that followed the Cardinal's report. He was a dark-skinned man of slight build, his soft tenor a perfect complement to his quiet demeanor. "Is he a reliable source?"

Tullis favored him with a pleased smile. "Completely. Tyree is a former student of mine, and one of the brightest of the new ministerial generation."

"He's also been directly involved with several viable Manifestations over the years," Dresden spoke up, a look of concern carved into his wizened face. "Of more importance is what impact this woman's abilities will have on the spiritual front." The Cardinal's lean frame and sure movements were mute testament to the older man's excellent physical condition. His voice resonated with the authoritative timbre of one used to giving orders.

"If they truly exist," Gianni cautioned, his hands resting atop his protruding belly. He pinned each of his fellow Elders with a hard stare. "The world is full of so-called Prophets proclaiming their ability to do this or that, when in actuality they're petty charlatans using the people's faith to turn an ill-gotten profit. That is why this brotherhood was formed; to separate fact from fiction."

"Father Griffin feels strongly that the woman's talents are genuine," Tullis pointed out.

A look of skepticism appeared on Gianni's round face. "I know of Griffin's talents and would normally agree that his judgment was to be trusted, but this case is anything but normal."

Dresden nodded in agreement. "Gianni is right. This woman appears to be the recipient of Heavenly favor, yet she lives a life without religious structure. Such a combination could be dangerous."

"Then perhaps the verification of Miss Delcielo's claim should be our first priority," Milan suggested, turning resolute eyes to Tullis. "Have we any operatives in that area of the United States?"

"No, but Quinlan and Sanders are due back from France next week. As soon as they've closed out their current assignment, I'll apprise them of this new situation and have them on a plane to Detroit as quickly as possible."

"Good," Dresden approved the Cardinal's choice. "Both are experienced Seekers and should quickly be able to ascertain just what it is we're dealing with. Only then will we know how best to proceed."

The remaining *Presbyterii* agreed, and the meeting was adjourned.

Chapter 8

A slight breeze swept through the air, rustling the few wisps of hair that had escaped the pleated strand running down Gabriel's back. He'd toyed with the idea of cutting it all off, but the bald look that seemed to be so popular these days just didn't suit him. Plus, Clarissa had always preferred his hair long.

She would've really liked it now. The wistful thought flashed through his mind as he recalled the last time his wife had braided it.

You really should spend less time rolling around in the hay, Clarissa teased as she picked the numerous straw particles from the tangled mass. *You're worse than Gaby!*

Gabriel sharply steered his mind away from the past. He let his gaze range over the bustling pedestrian traffic moving along Detroit's East Jefferson Avenue. With his presence Celestially masked, his vantage point atop one of the numerous light posts dotting the Avenue afforded him the perfect view of the areas many shops and eateries. He focused his attention on Tony's Gourmet Sandwich and Pizza Shop.

Tony's was reputed to be one of Detroit's finest restaurants. Judging from the steady flow of customers making their way through the shop's leaded-glass doors, Gabriel assumed it to be true.

His new charge certainly enjoyed their entrees. The sausage and mushroom deep-dish pizza appeared to be her favorite. Considering the pizza's high caloric count, and Nina's frequent consumption, it was amazing she was able to maintain her lithe figure. Then again, given the woman's hectic schedule and manic workout sessions, gorging herself on Tony's gastric delights was probably the only reason she hadn't wasted away.

A slight smile creased Gabriel's lips for the woman's peculiar idiosyncrasies. Over the years the Celemor had protected numerous Harbingers. As a rule, most Mortals chosen for the burdensome role were somewhat removed from the accepted parameters of human reality, however they generally shared a few common threads; most notably their unswerving faith to the Almighty and what they perceived to be His way.

Nina Delcielo was their antithesis if ever one existed. She completely despised Mortalia's religious organizations, the number of which seemed to multiply on an hourly basis as more and more self-proclaimed preachers put forth their own twisted version of the Divine Way to the multitudes of fools who willingly followed them.

Given the sad state of Earth's religious infrastructure, Nina's reluctance to participate was certainly understandable, but her steadfast resistance to all things "Holy" was also hindering her Divine progress. Such resistance could delay the deliverance of her message and prolong the Celemor's Task; not that he minded.

Over the past several weeks, Gabriel had developed a genuine interest in this peculiar *Child of Heaven* who, ironically, was anything but. He had even considered informing her of his presence. It was all just conjecture of course. The performance of a Task such as this was easier when the subject remained unaware of their Celestial steward, but the notion did add a touch of intrigue to the situation. How would the religiously apathetic woman respond to such a revelation?

The Celemor's gaze fell on a pair of Catholic nuns leaving the coffee shop two doors down from Tony's place, and he couldn't help the wicked smile rising to his lips. What would happen if the stately duo where to learn the truth of their existence as well; that their reality was only a third of the overall Creation, and hardly the most important.

They would probably drop dead on the spot.

The nuns continued up the street and were treated to a barrage of whistles and lewd comments from the trio of young toughs coming from the opposite direction. The nuns ignored their raucous behavior, but there was an eerie familiarity about one of the three that made Gabriel pay closer attention. He tried to focus on their faces, but they were partially hidden by the caps all three were wearing. The angle of the Celemor's position didn't allow for a clear view.

The rag-tag group came to a halt near Tony's place and took a seat at one of the numerous picnic tables set up in front of the shop. Their conversation appeared casual, but Gabriel quickly noticed their furtive glances toward the Pizza Shop, indicating an interest in something inside. Whether or not it was Nina or Tony's cash register remained to be seen.

He got his answer when one of the three shifted in his chair, revealing the square-jawed squinty-eyed features of Azreal; one of Iblis's Disciples.

. *I guess Miss Delcielo will be making my acquaintance after all,* the Celemor mused as he shifted his position to the light post directly in front of Tony's

*

"Is this gonna be all for you, Nina?" Tony carefully closed the lid on the box of the steaming pizza.

"Yeah, that'll do it, Tony; although the garlic sticks you just took out of the oven do look rather tempting."

The tall, barrel-chested shop owner chuckled at the woman's wistful tone. He grabbed one of the sticks, wrapped it in a napkin, and handed it to her. "Here, take one for the road."

She graciously accepted the tasty package then took a quick bite. "Oh, this is heavenly! If I keep eating like this, I won't be able to fit through the door!"

Tony gave her lean frame a speculative look. "I seriously doubt that. The way you rip and run all over the place like that battery bunny, I'm surprised you're able to keep any meat on your bones."

"I'm not that bad, Tony!"

"Oh yes you are. You really do need to slow up a bit, Nina. Maybe settle down with a nice man and have a few kids."

"You're starting to sound like your wife," Nina chuckled then took another bite of her bread stick.

Tony's eyes widened with mock terror. "God forbid! Seriously, though, you do need to schedule some fun time for yourself."

"I did go to Saint Christopher's anniversary bash a few weeks ago," Nina responded defensively. Her inability to maintain a lasting relationship was often the topic of discussion with the Scavelli's. It was their life's mission to get Nina, whom they jokingly called "the Lone Ranger", married off.

"I guess that's a start," Tony said brightly. "Meet any prospects?"

"Not a one! I swear, Tony, there's a shortage of eligible men in this city."

"Well don't give up just yet. Maybe you'll meet Mister Right at the rally."

Nina laughed. "We can only hope. And speaking of which; I want to thank you and the Misses again for donating most of the food. Are you sure you don't want anything in return? I can easily factor your expenses into our budget."

Tony waved her offer aside. "Nah, you keep your money, Nina. It's a good thing you're doing for those kids, and we're just happy to be a part of it. Now go home and eat before that pie gets cold."

Nina's stomach growled a reply. "You don't have to tell me twice." She made sure the pizza's lid was secure then made her way to the door. "Give Maria my love and I'll see you both Friday evening."

Nina left the shop feeling surprisingly upbeat. A welcome change from the stress she had endured while planning the upcoming rally for the Recreation Center. The process was tedious, but Nina felt it necessary to start things off with a bang. A festive gala to celebrate the Center's official opening fit the bill perfectly. She just wished the *other* preoccupation in her life could be handled as easily.

The past couple of weeks had seen a decrease in the frequency of her premonitions, but what they lacked in quantity was more than made up for in clarity. A couple of them were so vivid they prompted Nina to make a few anonymous calls to the Detroit Police Department's fledgling psychic hotline. Whether or not her tips were acted upon she didn't know, but the fact that there was no mention of the forecasted events on the news or in the paper led the budding Prophet to believe the police had taken her warnings to heart.

Perhaps Tyree was right about her abilities being Divine in nature. She had to admit the prospect of becoming a heavenly fortune-teller, though still ludicrous to her, was a lot more palatable than the fear that she was degenerating into a delusional nutcase; particularly if it saved lives.

"Hello," Nina spoke to the three young men seated at one of the courtyard tables.

The burliest of the three got up from his seat. "Hello, yourself!" He gave the pizza box and Nina's figure, nicely displayed in her beige cotton pantsuit, an appraising look. "That's a lot of pizza for a fine little honey like you. You sure you can handle all of it?"

The predatory gleam in the big man's black eyes filled her with apprehension. "Oh, I think I can manage," Nina told him politely, tightening her grip on the box.

"I'm sure you can," another of the three said as he and the third punk joined their companion. "But why bother? My buds and I would be glad to take some of that pie off your hands."

Nina did not like the direction this conversation was taking. "I appreciate the offer, fellas, but really I'm fine." Her heart rate increased when she noticed there were no other pedestrians around, and she was an unhandy distance from Tony's entrance.

An angry look crossed number one's face. "What, you too good to share?" He snatched the pizza from Nina's startled grasp, and her fear gave way to indignation.

"Hey, give that back!" She grabbed for the box, but found herself restrained by punks two and three, the latter placing a meaty hand over the struggling woman's mouth to prevent any screams.

Nina was just starting to panic when the sound of a ball hitting a bat sounded in her ear. The hand covering her mouth fell away, and its owner dropped heavily to the ground.

The smack was repeated, and Nina's second captor joined his partner on the sidewalk's unyielding concrete.

The startled woman blinked several times, uncertain what to make of the bizarre turn of events. A shadow fell across her vision, and she gasped at the sudden appearance of the stranger now standing beside her.

He was tall, dark-skinned, and dressed in a pair of gray khakis with a black polo-style t-shirt fitted tightly against an extremely muscular physique. Long black hair, braided in a thick strand, ran down his back. His eyes, a shade of brown so dark they almost seemed black, were fastened with disconcerting intensity on Nina's remaining aggressor whose own eyes widened with recognition.

"Gabriel."

The Celemor acknowledged the Disciple's muttered comment with a barely perceptible nod. "I believe you're holding something that doesn't belong to you."

Azreal's hands tightened on the pizza box. He spared his cohorts a brief glance. Both had regained consciousness and were now rising shakily to their feet. Azreal's baleful gaze shifted back to Gabriel's expectant glare, and a smug look settled on the Disciple's face.

His Master's question had been answered which meant that this little show was over. The Disciple was tempted to bring his own power to bear for the indignities suffered by his friends, but his instructions on the matter were clear. Azreal knew better than to risk Iblis' censure. Vengeance against the upstart Celemor would have to wait.

He casually handed the shaken woman back her pizza. "Sorry for scaring you, lady." A hint of contrition colored his voice. "We were just having a little fun." His comment was directed at Nina, but his eyes never left Gabriel's face."

Nina released an indignant snort. "You guys need to reevaluate your idea of fun!"

Azreal's gaze briefly settled on the woman's trembling form then met the expectant stares of his companions, neither showing signs of their earlier discomfort. "Let's get out of here." He shot Gabriel a final scowl then followed his friends as they hustled up the street.

The Celemor watched their progression for a moment then turned to Nina.

"Are you alright?"

Nina turned grateful eyes to her rescuer, and breathed a sigh of relief, most of the tension from her ordeal draining away. "Yeah, thanks to you! I'm not sure what would've happened if you hadn't popped up when you did."

Gabriel smiled at the compliment. "I was on my way to grab a cup of coffee next door when I noticed what was going on. The situation looked a little tense, so I decided to step in."

"Well, I'm sure as hell glad you did. I'm Nina, by the way." She extended her right hand, and Gabriel gave it a firm shake.

"It's a pleasure to meet you, Nina. I'm Gabriel."

∎"It's certainly a pleasure to meet *you*, Gabriel." She craned her neck upward so she could get a better look at his face.

At first glance he appeared to be African American, but there was a sharp element to his features that put her in mind of the Saeed brothers who owned and operated the small, middle-eastern restaurant down the street from her apartment.

Nina risked a glance at her attackers and breathed another sigh of relief when she saw that they were already a good distance away. "Boy, you sure put the fear of God into those three."

Gabriel couldn't help but smile at the irony of her statement. He was also glad she hadn't heard the Disciple identify him by name. That could have made things awkward. "Bullies like that always talk tough, but they're usually cowards. That's why they travel in packs and pick on people they consider weaker than them. I'm just glad they didn't hurt you while they were trying to prove they're manhood."

A chill ran through Nina's body. "So am I. I'm surprised this happened. This part of Jefferson's usually very safe."

Gabriel shrugged. "There are always a few bad apples in every barrel. Not to be forward or anything, but I think it might be best if I escorted you to wherever it is you're going; just in case those creeps are still in the area."

She searched his face for any signs of duplicity but found only genuine concern mirrored in his eyes; that and a curious sadness. "That's fine by me. My apartment's only a few blocks away, but I'd sure appreciate the company. This whole incident's left me a bit jumpy."

The Celemor offered his arm to her. "I'd say that's all the more reason to get you someplace where you'll feel safe."

Nina gave his face another scrutiny then casually linked her free arm through his. It was like wrapping her arm around a piece of iron.

"So, what is it that you do, Gabriel," she asked as they headed down Jefferson in the direction she indicated.

"I run a small security firm in the area."

Nina's eyes widened with surprise. "Really; you mean like alarms and stuff?"

"Occasionally I consult in those areas, but the majority of the time my contracts are more along the lines of personal protection and secure transportation."

"Sounds like a pretty dangerous line of work."

Gabriel's expression hardened. "Only when my clients fail to adhere to the precautions I set in place." Many were the times that subjects aware of his presence had taken advantage of their protected status, engaging in foolish activities knowing no harm would come to them. That, above all else, was the main reason the Celemor preferred to keep his presence concealed.

"I can see how that could be a problem." Nina wondered how anyone under this man's care could work up the nerve to defy him. "I can assure you that I'll be maintaining my position at your side until you've delivered me safely to my door." Her facetious statement produced a smile on his face. "What's the name of your company?"

A mischievous glint lit Gabriel's eyes. "Heaven Sent Security."

Nina's left eyebrow arched upward. She hadn't pictured him as the religious type. "That's an Interesting name. How did you come up with it?"

Gabriel's smile deepened; to Nina it seemed to take on a secretive edge. "It's a long story."

"I'd like to hear it if you'd like to share it."

For a moment, the Celemor considered doing just that, but decided against it. "Maybe someday I will." He tried to imagine what her reaction would be when she did learn the truth. "And what about you; what do you do when you're not picking up pizzas?"

Nina laughed. "I'm a stock and real estate broker by trade, but lately I've been spending most of my time trying to get a new Recreation Center going for this area."

"That's a noble cause," Gabriel complimented her.

"And a demanding one! Had I known all the trouble opening a center would be, I might've taken the easy road and simply donated to Detroit's Youth League."

Gabriel gave her face a sidelong glance. "Somehow I don't picture you as the 'simply-make-a-donation' type."

Nina released a tired sigh. "I guess you're right. And to tell you the truth I really don't mind all the headaches. Detroit's a great city, but she's got a lot of problems. It's up to those of us who are a little more fortunate than others to do something about it."

Gabriel chuckled. "Spoken like a true Samaritan."

"Oh hush." She gave his arm a playful pinch, and nearly broke a fingernail against his bicep. *This guy must live in the gym.* "You're not much better."

He turned questioning eyes on her. "How so?"

"As a bodyguard I'm sure you spend the majority of your time putting yourself in harm's way for the sake of others. If that's not a conspicuous display of selflessness, I don't know what is."

Gabriel's respect for his charge went up another notch. Weeks of observation had already shown her to be a woman of strength and character; he could now add compassion to that list. "I suppose. But I'm not as passionate about my job as you seem to be."

Nina grimaced. "Sorry. I tend to get a carried away when it comes to helping others."

"Don't apologize. It's nice to meet a genuinely good person."

Nina turned tender eyes on him, this time giving his arm a gentle squeeze. "Same here." A stab of regret pierced her heart when the Jeffersonian's front sign came into view. "I'm afraid this is my stop."

"Then I guess my job is done." Gabriel reluctantly relinquished her arm.

Nina was heartened by the fact that he too appeared disappointed that their impromptu date was coming to an end. "Thank you for walking me home and listening to me ramble on."

Gabriel laughed. "It was my pleasure, madam, and I enjoyed our conversation."

"Ah, so you're a gentleman and a good liar," she teased, drawing another smile from her new friend.

"No seriously, I did. I'm sorry we had to meet under such poor circumstances but I'm glad we did."

Sensing his attraction to her, Nina decided to throw all caution to the winds. "Maybe we can see each other again sometime,"

If Gabriel was surprised by her forwardness, he didn't show it. "When did you have in mind?"

Nina couldn't suppress the girlish grin that rose to her face. "How about this Friday? You can be my guest at the rally I'm holding at the Recreation Center." She reached into her purse and fished out one of the event flyers. "Here's the address. We've got lots of activities planned, plus Tony's is providing most of the food."

"In that case, I'll definitely be there," he beamed, graciously accepting the flyer. "Until then you take care of yourself."

"And you as well." *Not bad, Nina-girl,* she mused as she watched him go. *A cutey-pie with manners and a job!*

She couldn't wait to see the expressions on Tony and Maria's faces when she told them the good news. Boy would they be surprised!

Nina had surprised herself. She didn't normally warm up to strangers this quickly, but there was something about Gabriel that just felt...right. Judging by his eager acceptance of her invitation, he must have felt it too. This could turn out to be a good week after all.

Easy, Nina; you should probably wait a date or two before you start calling him your knight in shining armor.

She watched until he had completely faded from view then made her way inside.

"Good evening, Miss Delcielo," Carl greeted her as she sauntered through the apartment's reception area.

"Hello, Carl."

Carl took note of the gleam in her eyes. "You're looking pretty chipper this evening. It wouldn't have anything to do with that handsome chap that walked you home, would it? Misses Watson's going to be pleased."

Nina shot the guard an unscrupulous look. "You, my friend, spend entirely too much time in front of those monitors."

Carl flashed an ingenuous smile. "That's my job, Ma'am."

"That and keeping up with the latest gossip," Nina told him, smiling to take the sting out her words.

Carl gave her a lascivious wink. "Only the juicy stuff."

Nina burst out laughing. "Yeah, I'll bet! Well at the moment, I've got nothing...juicy to share. But if something develops, I'll be sure to let you know."

Carl tipped his hat in appreciation. "I can always count on you, Miss Delcielo. Have a good night."

"You too, Carl." She gave him a cheery wave then boarded the elevator.

*

Perched atop a nearby broadcast antenna, Gabriel's enhanced vision easily discerned Nina in her apartment going about her bedtime rituals. The Celemor didn't know if the Avon products she was lathering on her face really did all the miraculous things for skin that they claimed to, but he had to admit they added a pleasant fragrance to her natural scent.

"I see you've made plans for Friday evening," Omen's deep voice sounded in Gabriel's ears as the Overseer materialized in the air beside him. "Does this mean that our burgeoning Harbinger has managed to unlock the iron-gate around your heart?"

Gabriel sighed. "Give me a break, O. You of all people should know that I never allow my Tasks to get personal."

"So that curious smile on your face was brought about my arrival."

Gabriel gave the Overseer a trenchant look. "Is there a reason for this visit, or do you just enjoy annoying me?"

"Causing you grief is entertaining, but in this case, I am here to discuss the attack on the Harbinger." Omen shifted his hooded gaze toward Nina's now darkened apartment. "It would appear that Iblis has taken an interest in her."

"Yes, it does, and given that the Disciples are involved I've decided to assume a more visible position in her protection."

A wave of surprise emanated from Omen. "That's a different approach for you."

"I know, but Azreal's restraint told me that our little sortie was just a test to see if Nina was being protected."

"Possibly," said Omen. "And depending on what Iblis's intentions are, your next encounter with that brutish simian and his cronies may not be so benign."

"I was thinking along those same lines, which is why I need to be ready."

Omen took a moment to consider the Celemor's point. "Your reasoning is sound. I will, of course, be monitoring your progress." The Overseer accorded Gabriel a slight nod then vanished.

"Nothing like babysitting the babysitter," Gabriel muttered as he resumed his vigilance of Nina's apartment.

Chapter 9

Iblis's wings fanned slightly outward as he listened to Silas's account of his Disciple's first confrontation with Nina.

"Gabriel." He let the name roll slowly off his tongue. "The new Harbinger must be of significant importance if my brothers have assigned that dullard the Task of protection."

Silas pursed his thin lips. "Dullard or not, he is lethally efficient."

Iblis smiled, his blue eyes sparkling. "That goes without saying. The question now is how can I take advantage of the situation."

"I'm afraid we won't know that until we ascertain how the Delcielo woman figures into the Almighty's overall plan. Given the Archangel's coddling of her, I've a feeling she's more than just a simple Harbinger."

Iblis regarded the Morphling in thoughtful silence for a moment then folded his wings tightly against his back so he could relax into his chair. "You're right, of course, but with Gabriel alerted to my interest we'll have to use a more subtle form of scrutiny."

"Shall I assign one of the Desomors?"

A tender smile played on Iblis's lips "No, I'll handle it." He mentally projected the name *Mayhem* into the Celestial ether.

Within moments, an attractive woman materialized before his desk. She was dressed in tight black leggings and a low-cut lavender blouse that amply displayed her heavy bosom. "You summoned me, my lord?" Her voice was a sensual purr, and Iblis's smile deepened.

"Yes, Mayhem; I have need of your talents to handle a new Harbinger."

A predatory gleam appeared in Mayhem's brown eyes. "And where would you like the body displayed when I'm done?"

Iblis chuckled at the Desomor's destructive eagerness. "Nowhere. The Harbinger's name is Nina Delcielo. I need you to discover the reason behind her sudden Emergence, and the extent of her abilities."

Mayhem cocked a questioning eyebrow. "Is that it? I was hoping for something a bit more challenging."

Iblis regarded the disappointed woman through calculating eyes. "Your wish might come true. Gabriel has been given the Task of Protection."

An excited flush darkened the Desomor's Caucasian features. "Now that's more like it. I've been waiting for another chance to lock heads with that noble simpleton."

Silas released a contemptuous snort. "I think we can all agree that 'locking heads' isn't the only thing you want to do with him."

Mayhem turned cold eyes on the Morphling. "Meaning?"

"Meaning that your peculiar obsession with that Celemor has been an issue on more than one occasion," Silas bit out. "I would expect someone of your pedigree to show a bit more professionalism."

Mayhem's eyes narrowed dangerously. "Listen, you shape-stealing maggot..."

"Silas does have a point," Iblis interrupted what promised to be a potent verbal blast. "Gabriel does have a way of driving you to distraction. For the moment, I need your surveillance to be discreet. Do you think you can manage that?"

Mayhem turned smoldering eyes on Iblis. "You needn't worry yourself, my Lord." She leaned forward and brushed an imaginary speck of lint from his immaculately pressed, white oxford." I'll shadow her every move, and neither Gabriel nor the bitch will know I'm there."

She gave Silas a final scowl then vanished.

"I will never understand why you put up with that woman's irreverence."

"The same reason I put up with your egocentricities," Iblis told the disgruntled Morphling. "You're both so entertaining."

Silas cleared his throat. "Yes well, entertainment notwithstanding, I'm still not sure assigning that volatile nymph to monitor the Harbinger was the sensible thing to do."

Iblis gave his minion a reassuring smile. "Worry not, my friend. Volatile or not, Mayhem is well versed in the art of discretion."

Silas strongly disagreed but made no further comment. The Desolate One's peculiar fondness for Mayhem was nearly as great as hers was for Gabriel. The Morphling just hoped that it would not prove as equally distracting.

Chapter 10

Dichotomy's eyes widened with alarm at the latest whisperings gleaned from the Chatter.

The peculiar being had kept a close watch on Gabriel and was thus far pleased by the way things were developing. Gabriel was not one to allow others to get close to him. Dichotomy hoped the grim Celemor's uncharacteristic attraction to the Harbinger was a sign that the emotional wounds left by the passing of his wife and daughter were finally healing. If that were the case, now was not the time for the beleaguered Celemor to contend with any undue stress from Hell's minions.

"Iblis's interest in the Harbinger must be great indeed if he's called upon Mayhem to discover her purpose," Dichotomy's male persona reasoned. "For both their sakes, I feel we should become a more active participant in this Reclamation."

"Agreed," a light alto responded as the feminine half assumed dominance. "The Desomor's penchant for living up to her namesake, as well as her twisted infatuation for Gabriel, could quickly complicate the matter. If that happens, our friend will have need of our strength."

"In that case let us prepare ourselves for the transition to Mortalia," the male decreed.

A nimbus of pure energy surrounded Dichotomy's amalgamated body, restructuring it into that of a young, Mortal male of middle eastern Earth descent.

"Many centuries have passed since we last wore this form," the blended being said, flexing muscular arms when the transformation was complete. "Let us hope it is up to the Task!"

Chapter 11

A current-model, black Dodge Ram pickup truck rolled to a stop in front of Saint Christopher's Church. The two, smartly dressed men riding in the front seat quietly got out. They did a quick survey of the surrounding area then made their way to the sanctuary's main entrance, where the taller of the two rang the doorbell.

Several moments passed then the door swung partially open revealing a smiling Tyree. "Good morning, Gentleman," he greeted pleasantly while giving his visitors the once over. One was tall and lean, his sandy brown hair cropped short against his head. Large brown eyes set in an oval face were tinged with an affable curiosity. The other was a few inches shorter, his powerful frame and thick neck putting the Minister in mind of a wrestler. Unlike his companion his eyes were dark and brooding, his blunt features drawn into a pensive frown. "May I help you?"

"Father Griffin?" the taller man asked. Tyree responded with an affirmative nod. "I'm Brother Quinlan and this is Brother Sanders," he indicated his stocky companion. "We've been sent by Cardinal Dresden to investigate the Prophetic Manifestation you recently reported."

Tyree's face brightened at the news. "Yes, of course." He opened the door wider. "The Cardinal told me that a Seeker team would be arriving soon. Please come in."

The Seekers stepped into the foyer. "You have a lovely parish, Father," Sanders' noted in a heavy voice that matched his dark demeanor.

"Thank you, Brother Sanders." Tyree secured the door then led them down the main hallway to his office. "I'll pass your compliment on to our preservation committee. They take great pride in Saint Christopher's classic architectural style and work hard to maintain it; here we are."

He ushered the Seekers inside then gently closed the door, directing them to have a seat in one of the chairs sitting in front of his desk. "Would either of you care for some coffee?" He pointed to the small pot resting on a service cart under the office's one window. "It's some of Trader Joe's finest?"

Both men accepted, and Tyree poured them each a cup. He replaced the pot on the cart then settled his lean frame into his chair after straitening the folds of his sweatshirt. Unlike so many of his contemporaries, Tyree rarely dressed in the traditional suits and collar often associated with his profession. He felt such attire erected unnecessary walls of formality between himself and the members of the church and surrounding community that often called upon him for advice and guidance. "Now then, where would you like to begin?"

"Cardinal Tullis already briefed us on the nature of the Manifestation," Quinlan said, after taking a cautious sip of his coffee. "What we need from you is some personal information on Miss Delcielo so we can have a better understanding of the type of person we're dealing with."

Tyree chuckled. "Not a problem." He then gave the Seekers a brief but concise description of Nina, both on a personal and professional level.

"Miss Delcielo appears to be an extremely motivated woman," Quinlan remarked when Tyree had finished, taking another sip of his coffee.

"Yes, she does," Sanders agreed, enjoying a more generous swallow of his. "And you say she's steadfast in her rejection of the spiritual world?"

"Of the religious world," Tyree corrected. "Nina believes in God, but not in established religions. She feels they're just a subtle form of governmental control."

A regretful sigh escaped Quinlan's lips. "To some degree she's right. In many cultures the religious infrastructure is the driving force of oppression. That type of exploitation is one of the main reasons the world is in such spiritual disrepair."

Tyree responded with a snort. "It's definitely the cause of Nina's disillusionment. I've been trying for years to convince her that the Catholic Diocese isn't the oppressive regime she's making it out to be. So far, I've had no luck. That woman can be downright stubborn when she wants to be."

Sanders focused sharply on the minister's face. "The two of you are close?"

"Very. We grew up together."

Sanders' eyes narrowed slightly. "I see." He set his cup down on one of the coasters Tyree had laid out on the front of his desk then focused on the Minister's face. "And has there ever been a time when the two of you were, how shall we say; more than friends?"

"What type of question is that?" Tyree demanded rising angrily from his seat, the Seeker's query having caught him off guard.

"Please do not take offense, Father," Quinlan calmly interjected. "When proving the legitimacy of a suspected Manifestation, we also have to determine the reliability of the source. In order to do that, we must account for any personal bias that could possibly cloud the claimant's judgment, such as an emotional or sexual bond with the subject."

Tyree's aggravation abated. "I guess I can understand that." He eased back into his chair then leveled cool eyes on Sanders. "And in answer to your question: Yes. Nina and I were romantically involved for a number of years, however that aspect of our relationship ended once I received the Lord's calling."

Sanders nodded, unperturbed by the minister's lingering hostility. "Based on your continued friendship I take it the dissolution of your romance was an amicable one."

Tyree held the man's eyes for another moment, taking note of the thin scar bisecting his left eyebrow which gave the Seeker a menacing countenance. "To be honest with you, things between us were a bit...tense for a while, but once Nina understood where my heart truly lay, she supported my decision to join the priesthood."

"Then you're very fortunate to have such an understanding friend. Too often people of faith are ridiculed for their decision to lead a life of purity while the morally corrupt are glorified for living a life of sinful excess."

Tyree wondered at the curious undertone in the Seeker's voice. "I totally agree. I also feel that Nina was given her abilities to counter that imbalance."

The eyes of both Seekers widened with surprise. "What made you come to that conclusion?" Quinlan asked.

Tyree favored them with a solemn expression while opening his arms wide. "Take a good look around gentleman. Our worlds in chaos, and not just spiritually. A good portion of society has fallen out of touch with God's grace, and as a result lost its way. I believe the Lord has chosen Nina to be a living example of His Divine might; to show everyone, through her abilities, that He still exists."

Sanders considered the Minister's statement. "Your theory does have merit, Father. The world needs a spiritual jump-start, but do you truly believe the Lord would choose a woman such as Miss Delcielo to be his messenger? By your own admission, she's not exactly a poster-child for Christianity."

"No but she is one for moral responsibility. Someone like Nina would be more apt to make an impact on today's jaded society."

Sanders cocked a skeptical eyebrow. "And why would that be?"

"Because she's *not* a religious person," Tyree answered smugly.

The Seekers regarded him in silence for a moment then a slight smile creased Quinlan's full lips. "The words of a Prophet not laced with traditional, religious rhetoric would hold more weight in today's liberal society."

Tyree returned his smile. "Exactly; add to that the coincidence of her name, and I'd say Nina fits the bill perfectly."

Quinlan threw him a puzzled look. "What's her name got to do with anything?"

A mischievous smile tugged at Tyree's lips. "What, you guys didn't learn Spanish in Seeker school?"

"Of course, we did, but I still don't see what...Oh..." Quinlan jerked in surprise. "My God!" He turned excited to Sanders. "The spelling and pronunciation threw me off but he's right. *Nina del Cielo*..."

"Or 'Child of Heaven,'" Sanders finished his partner's sentence. "I'll admit it does lend credence to your theory, but before Miss Delcielo can truly live up to such a mantle, she needs to be convinced of her dubious position herself. And based on your description of her religious antipathy," he pointed an accusing finger at Tyree. "That may prove difficult."

Tyree regarded the Seekers through cunning eyes. "That depends on who's doing the proving. Can you think of a better way for the Lord to convince someone of his power than by making that person a living conduit for it?"

Quinlan looked at Sanders. "He does have a point."

"Perhaps," Sanders allowed. "But I think I'll reserve judgment until after we've met Miss Delcielo."

"I can take you to her right now, if you like," Tyree offered. "There's a big rally this Friday at the new Recreation Center she's opening on East Lafayette. If I know Nina, she's there badgering the workers to make sure everything's ready."

"Thank you, Father, but I think it would be best if we made the initial contact on our own," Sanders politely told the Minister. "That way we can observe Miss Delcielo in a more natural state."

"Suit yourself, but I have to warn you: Nina can be a bit brusque with strangers; especially when she's preoccupied."

"I think we can come up with something that'll secure both her attention and cooperation."

Tyree gave Quinlan's smiling face a questioning look. "And what might that be?"

Quinlan's smiled deepened. "A grant from the Helping Hands Organization."

Tyree jerked in surprise then burst out laughing. "Yeah, that would do it! And if I'm not mistaking, she really did apply for one of their grants."

"You're not," said Quinlan. "We have her application with us."

The smile on Tyree's face disappeared. "You do? How did you manage that; some kind of Vatican leverage with Double H's funding board?"

"Not exactly," Quinlan chuckled. "We actually are the Funding Board; or rather the Elders are."

The look of confusion on Tyree's face intensified. "What?"

"The Double H was founded by the original Elders to provide a plausible front for the *Presbyterii's* investigative efforts," Quinlan explained.

Tyree was stunned. "But...I don't understand. Helping Hands is a driving force in the philanthropic community. In fact, they've been a staunch supporter to dozens of Metro Detroit charities. If the organization is just a front, where does all that money come from?"

"I'm afraid we're not at liberty to say," Sanders cut in, glaring coldly at his partner. "But I can assure you the funds are allocated from a legitimate source."

"Amazing," Tyree whispered in awe. "I never would've dreamed the Double H was anything but what it seemed."

"Which is why we normally do not divulge its secrets," Sanders growled, shooting Quinlan another reproving look. "To often the Vatican is criticized for its financial assets."

"Oh, your secret's safe with me," Tyree assured the aggravated Seeker. "In fact, your revelation is quite a relief."

Quinlan's left eyebrow arched with interest. "And why is that?"

Tyree grimaced. "Now I don't feel so bad about ratting Nina out to you guys."

"You did nothing wrong by contacting us," Sanders firmly told the Minister. "If Miss Delcielo truly is the recipient of our Lord's favor, she will have need of the Presbyterii's guidance; and possibly its protection."

Tyree's eyes widened with concern. "Protection from whom?"

"No one, at the moment, but that could change if word of her talents leaked out."

"He's right," Quinlan chimed in. "Knowledge of the future is considered by many to be the ultimate power, and there are countless factions that would stop at nothing to possess it."

A guilty look appeared on Tyree's face. "Nina expressed similar concerns when she first told me of her abilities, and I told her she was just being paranoid. I guess I was so caught up in the miracle of the Manifestation that I never stopped to consider the possible dangers."

"Not to worry, Father," Quinlan reassured the troubled priest. "Should Miss Delcielo's abilities turn out to be all that you say, the *Presbyterii* will ensure that she has the support she needs. Now if you will excuse us." He and Sanders rose from their seats. "Miss Delcielo has an unscheduled appointment with the Double H."

A pleased grin erased the Minister's worried frown as he got to his feet as well then escorted them back to the main entrance.

"You'll keep me posted on your progress?" he called to the departing duo.

"We most certainly will," Quinlan assured him as he and Sanders climbed into the truck. "Take care, Father."

Tyree waved as they drove off then went back inside the church, the door closing behind him with a gentle thud.

*

"GPS puts the center close to downtown Detroit," Quinlan announced as he wove his way through the city's morning traffic. "This freeway should take us right there."

"Sounds good," Sanders replied, settling himself as comfortably as he could into his seat. "So, what did you think of the good reverend?"

Quinlan smiled. "He's definitely a likable chap and seems very dedicated to his calling as well."

Sanders regarded his friend through disapproving eyes. "Is that why you were so candid with *Presbyterii* business,"

"I guess you could say that. There's something very trustworthy about him; an almost child-like exuberance."

"Yes, he does appear to be a very earnest person," Sanders grudgingly admitted. "He's also still very much in love with our subject."

Quinlan chuckled. "Oh, without a doubt. I thought he was going to hit you with his crucifix when you questioned him about their relationship."

"Yeah, the lad did get a might defensive. And that makes me question his objectivity toward our budding psychic. It'll be interesting to see if her abilities really are as impressive as our smitten friend claims."

"We're about to find out." Quinlan nodded toward the street markers mounted on an approaching overpass. "Lafayette's coming up."

Sanders braced himself as his partner abruptly switched lanes then exited the freeway. Having grown up in a rural town in Arkansas, the Seeker found the heavy traffic common to metropolises like Detroit unnerving and Quinlan's aggressive driving made the situation even worse.

"I guess we're not in Kansas anymore, Toto," Quinlan muttered at the numerous dilapidated store fronts and vandalized structures that greeted them as they cruised slowly down the street.

"Apparently not," Sanders agreed, also shocked at the radical difference between the idyllic neighborhood surrounding Saint Christopher's and this socially depressed area. "There's the Center coming up on the left." He pointed to a large, industrial building.

"Nice place." Quinlan was immediately impressed by the Center's brightly refurbished exterior and gated parking lot. "It definitely brings a ray of light to this gloomy neighborhood."

"It does," Sanders agreed as Quinlan pulled the Ram into one of the angled parking spaces at the front entrance. "I think my opinion of Miss Delcielo just increased a notch."

Quinlan shot his habitually cynical partner a surprised look. "Why is that?"

Sanders nodded in the direction of the Center. "Anyone willing to invest that type of money and effort in an area like this can't be all bad."

The two men left the truck and made their way toward the main entrance; their movements observed by the Celestially masked figure squatting atop the ornate canopy mounted above the double glass-doors.

Quinlan and Sanders. Gabriel frowned. He had encountered the stalwart duo on more than one occasion. Their presence meant Nina's priest friend had alerted the *Presbyterii* of her abilities.

The Seekers entered the center, and Gabriel released an amused snort. *First the Disciples make a play for Nina. Now these two religious zealots show up at her door. I wonder who's gonna pop up next.*

He shifted his body through the Center's tiled roof so he could track their movements.

*

"It's looking good, guys," Nina shouted to the group of workmen meticulously rigging decorations from the gymnasium's steel rafters. "This place is starting to feel very festive!"

"Yeah, it's coming together," one of the riggers yelled back. "Another hour or so and we'll be done up here!"

Nina flashed him an approving grin. "That's great news, Mike. What's the speaker setup looking like? You know we gotta have the place jumping tomorrow night."

Mike flashed a toothy grin. "Arts already got you tight on that with those new sub-woofers. Trust me; you're gonna be rockin' half of downtown!"

"Miss Delcielo?" a deep voice sounded, and Nina focused on the two men making their way toward her.

"That's me," she said, studying the tailored suit wearing duo through suspicious eyes. "And you are?"

Quinlan offered her a polite smile. "My name is Thomas Quinlan, and this is William Sanders." Sanders dipped his head in silent greeting. "We represent the Helping Hands Organization and are here to discuss your recent application for financial support."

Both men presented their credentials, and Nina's face brightened instantly. "It's certainly a pleasure to meet you!" She eagerly took hold of Quinlan's outstretched hand. "I hope you're here with good news."

Quinlan smiled. "As a matter of fact, we are. Your application for funding has been approved."

Nina stiffened as the man's words washed over her. "Did you say we were approved?" For a moment she was afraid that this was a dream she was about to wake up from.

"That's correct," Quinlan said then steadied himself as the excited woman threw her arms around him in a joyous hug.

"Oh, thank you, thank you, thank you," Nina chanted until she remembered she was accosting a total stranger. "I'm sorry!" She smoothed the wrinkles from the front of his jacket then wiped away the tears welling up in her eyes. "It's just this whole thing's been nothing but an uphill battle from the start."

"That's quite alright," Quinlan assured her. "And considering the Center's limited budget your reaction is perfectly understandable."

"Quite frankly, were amazed at what you've been able to accomplish with this place considering the scraps the state awarded you," Sanders spoke up, casting appraising eyes around the gym's decorated interior.

Nina released a frustrated sigh. "Yeah, they've been pretty tight on project funding this year. The Chrysler Corporation's been very helpful, but their support is contingent on a monthly review of their revenue. And with the big hit the auto-industry's taking these days their continued support may not be forthcoming."

"Well, the Center looks great, so you've definitely made good use of your resources," Sanders noted. "I'm particularly impressed with the computer lab." He nodded in the direction of the small room off to the side of the gym's main entrance where some of the workers were setting up several computer terminals. "Those machines alone must've severely cut into your budget."

"They really did! It's ridiculous what those hunks of plastic and wires cost. Fortunately, I was able to liquidate a few personal assets to get what we needed." Nina gazed fondly at the lab's modest equipment. "I think it's important for kids to have access to the latest technology; particularly in low-income areas such as this one where their families may not be able to provide it at home."

"We at the Double H feel the same way. The youth are our future and it's up to us provide them with the tools needed to...to..." Sanders paused when he noticed the stricken look on Nina's face. "Are you alright, Miss Delcielo?"

Nina did not respond. She was totally focused on the vision burning itself into her mind.

"Mike......NO!" She turned from the concerned Seeker and bolted toward the gym's rear wall. With desperate haste, she yanked open the steel door of the building's electrical closet and studied the panel. She then shut off one of the circuit breakers, and half the gym lost power.

"Hey Nina, what gives?" Mike yelled down waving his now dead saw in the air.

Nina turned frightened eyes to him. "Check your blade, Mike! Just do it," she snapped when the puzzled foreman hesitated.

Mike complied, and the color drained from his face. "The damn lock-bolt's broke!"

"Damn, Mike," another workman spat. "That blade could've popped loose and cut your head off!"

"Yeah, no kidding!" Mike looked at Nina in amazement. "How did you know?"

Nina became acutely aware that all eyes were upon her. "It was rattling when you started it," she lied. Now was not the time for awkward questions. "I've heard you crank that thing up so many times over the last few weeks that I knew something wasn't right."

"Yeah, well thank God for your sonic ears," another worker called out. "With all the echoes up here, we didn't hear a thing."

"Alright people take five and check your tools!" Mike instructed his crew, a slight tremor in his voice. "Let's not look a gift-horse in the mouth on this." He refocused on Nina. "Thanks, Nina. You're my new guardian angel!"

Nina released a nervous laugh but made no further comment.

She waited until Mike gave her the thumbs-up sign then restored the power, after which she made her way back to Quinlan and Sanders.

"Sorry about that, gentlemen. This place has been crazy the last few weeks with the rally and all."

"I'm sure it has been." Quinlan was stunned by what he had just witnessed.

"I'll tell you what," Nina motioned toward the gym's entrance. "Let's head to my office so we may continue our conversation in a more peaceful setting."

Quinlan moved jerkily in the direction indicated, Sanders quickly falling into step beside him. The two Seekers exchanged looks, and Quinlan easily interpreted the excited gleam in his partner's eyes: Father Griffin had not been exaggerating!

With Nina in the lead, they quietly left the gym.

*

Sweeping up debris by the gym's entrance, her features partially concealed by a dusk mask, Mayhem studied the departing trio for a moment. A pleased smile parted her sensual lips. Her ruse as a maintenance worker at the Hell-forsaken place had finally paid off.

For the past few days, the Desomor had maintained a discreet presence at the Center, carefully masking her Celestial aura so as not to alert the senses of the ever-present Gabriel. She had yet to observe anything phenomenal about Nina and had begun to think that Iblis's interest in her was unwarranted.

Nina's recent display of power had quickly cast all of the Desomor's doubts aside.

During her Prophetic moment, the woman's body had become a beacon of Celestial energy, nearly overwhelming Mayhem's heightened senses. Even now, tendrils of energy were still swirling in the air around her. Clearly, she was more than a simple Mortal Touched by the Archangels. This woman had *power*.

The Desomor was tempted to confront Nina on the spot, but Iblis's instructions on that matter where clear. She shot a quick glance at the gym's ceiling, and another smile parted her lips as her enhanced vision caught a glimpse of Gabriel's translucent form passing through the gym's walls.

*

Gabriel watched the Seeker's truck pull away, and a wistful sigh escaped his lips. Their involvement would definitely complicate things.

He contemplated taking them out of the picture, but they're pledge of financial assistant to Nina's center was a blessing for the beleaguered woman. He didn't want to risk her losing it.

"You seem troubled my friend," Omen's voice sounded softly in his ears. "Has the appearance of those two *Presbyterii* puppets put a snag in your plans?"

"They always do," Gabriel answered the Overseer materializing beside him. "I tell you, O; I get so sick and tired of all these wannabe God-servers getting in my way. Maybe it's time I had an enlightening chat with that pair of idiots. Perhaps if they understood the full scope of my Celestial position, they would let me do my job."

"I doubt it," Omen told his irritated colleague. "Despite their good intentions, Quinlan's and Sanders' minds are totally immured in the lie of their reality. Their misplaced faith would not allow them to accept the truth."

A wicked smile parted Gabriel's lips. "They would if I put a lightning bolt up their sanctimonious butts."

The glow around Omen's eyes intensified. "You know an abuse of power such as that is forbidden!"

"I was joking," the Celemor grumbled. "I guess I'm just tired of being treated like one of those troublemaking Demonstratives by a bunch of idiots who have no idea how the universe really works."

Omen floated closer, his eyes glowing softly under his hood. "I know the Tasks you're given can often be untenable Gabriel, but you must not despair. What you do is necessary in order to preserve the Divine Balance."

Gabriel's expression turned sour. "Yeah, old Death Boy explained the whole Order and Chaos thing to me when I took this job."

Omen's form wavered slightly. "And I laud your decision to serve. Most Mortals would've found the mantle of Celemor to daunting of a challenge."

Gabriel released a disgusted snort. "It's not like I had a choice, given the fact that my refusal would've led to the dispersal of Clarissa's soul."

Omen placed a bony hand on the Celemor's shoulder. "You are still to be commended. Mortals are quick to pledge their lives for this cause or that, yet when the time comes, few make good on that promise. Your sacrifice to the Almighty on your wife's behalf goes far to dispel the belief held by the majority of my brethren that Mortals are nothing but bestial aberrations; undeserving of our Creator's favor."

Gabriel cocked a cynical eyebrow. "So, being the shining example of my race is supposed to make me feel better about all of this?"

"It should," Omen said as his body began to fade. "Or at the very least proud," he added before disappearing completely.

Chapter 12

"Hey Nina, you got a visitor!" Tony fought to make his voice heard above the hard-driving music blaring from the Center's speakers.

True to his word, Mike's audio tech had done an excellent job installing the new sound system. The multi-watt subwoofers, coupled with the strobe lights and festive decorations, had the Center's rally in full swing.

"Here I come, Tony!" Nina burst through the Center's kitchen doors carrying a tray laden with sandwiches. Her face split into a huge grin when she saw who was waiting for her. "Gabriel! You made it!"

The Celemor returned her smile with one of his own. "Are you kidding? I've been looking forward to this all week. Here, let me help you with that." He lifted the tray out of her hands. "Where do you want it?"

Nina pointed to a set of black skirted tables situated toward the front of the crowded gymnasium. "Serving station number six."

Gabriel nodded. "I'll be right back."

"The man has got some moves," Tony commented as he watched Gabriel deftly weave his way through the frolicking partygoers. "Who is he?"

Nina's eyes were also on the Celemor's muscular physique. "Someone I met after I left your shop the other day."

"Is that so?" charged the husky voice of Tony's wife, Maria, making her way from the kitchen with another tray of sandwiches. "And when were you gonna share the good news with us?"

A smiling Nina opened her mouth to respond but Gabriel returned.

"Delivery made, ma'am." He accorded Nina a slight nod then lifted the tray from Maria's pudgy hands. "I take it these are going to the same place?"

"If you wouldn't mind," Maria said, batting a flirtatious eye at him.

"Not at all," he chuckled then immediately set off with the tray.

"My God, Nina, wherever did you find him?"

Nina laughed at Maria's dreamy expression then quickly related the tale of her and Gabriel's introduction.

"I like him already," Tony declared.

"Me too," another voice sounded as Tyree, having caught most of Nina's tale, stepped from the kitchen, wiping his hands on the apron tied about his waist. "Strong, protective, and good manners to boot."

"Not to mention gorgeous!" Maria's gush drew an indignant snort from her husband and a laugh from Tyree. "He definitely seems like a keeper, Nina. I just hope he's not gay."

"Oh, stop it!" Nina scolded the older woman as Gabriel made his way back to them. "Gabriel, I'd like to introduce you to my good friends, Tony and Maria Scavelli, and Father Tyree Griffin."

"It's a pleasure to meet you all." He gave Tyree's and Tony's hand a firm shake, and Maria's a gentle kiss. "I understand you're the caterers of this affair," he directed at the Scavellis

Tony wrapped a possessive arm around his wife's shoulder. "That's us: Tony's Gourmet Pizza and Sandwich Shop; best eating in the tri-state area!"

"Well from the comments I overheard at the serving stations, you're definitely living up to that reputation," Gabriel told the shop owner. "In fact, I'm about to find out for myself." He unwrapped the sandwich he had grabbed from the tray, took a generous bite then sighed in appreciation. "Oh, this is delicious! I haven't tasted corned-beef this lean in years."

"Glad you like it," Tony beamed proudly. "I buy only the finest cuts from the butchers. It's a little pricier, but it makes all the difference."

"It most certainly does." Gabriel raised the sandwich to his mouth for another bite. "Uh oh." He nodded toward the beverage bar set up by the gym's rear entrance. "Looks like someone's not happy with their drink."

Nina glanced at the bar and sighed as she observed what appeared to be a disagreement between her staff and a group of patrons. "There's always something." She wiped her hands with a towel. "If you all will excuse me; I'd better go see what the ruckus is about."

"Wait." Gabriel finished his sandwich in two, quick bites. "I'll join you."

"Me too," Tyree chimed in, hastily removing his apron.

"That's okay, guys, I can handle it. Besides, Ty, I need you to keep the Carlson twins out of trouble." Nina nodded toward the two teenage girls arguing furiously with one another in the kitchen.

Tyree took one look at the squabbling pair and groaned. "Not again. I wonder what it is *this* time."

"They probably can't agree on how to place the sandwiches on the tray," Maria chuckled as the Minister made his way back into the kitchen.

Gabriel turned to Nina. "I guess that just leaves me."

"No Gabriel. You're supposed to be my guest, not one of my staff!"

The Celemor gave his mouth a perfunctory wipe with his napkin. "I'm happy to help. Plus, I need something to drink."

The Scavellis grinned at his statement, and he and Nina headed toward the bar.

By the time they arrived the situation had escalated into a full-blown argument, and Nina was glad Gabriel had accompanied her. Several of the young men involved were sporting leather jackets embroidered with the logo of the Crimson Tigers; one of the more prolific gangs in the area.

"Hi guys," she spoke pleasantly, placing herself between the angry gang members and the nervous bartenders. "I'm Miss Delcielo, the head facilitator here. What seems to be the problem?"

"The problem is your girl back there asking me for my I.D.," one of the Tigers snapped. "All I want is a stinkin' beer!"

Nina offered the man a polite smile. "I do apologize for the inconvenience, but we have to adhere to the state's guidelines in terms of alcoholic beverages. I'm afraid if you can't verify your age, we can't serve you."

The glowering Tiger took a step toward her but found his way instantly blocked by Gabriel.

"That's enough, bud," he firmly told the disgruntled youth. "If you and your sect don't agree with the Center's drinking policy then perhaps you should leave."

One of the other Tigers, a comely female, laid a hand atop the angry youth's shoulder. "C'mon Tip, let's bounce. This party's lame anyway." Her comment broke the tense silence between her fellow and Gabriel.

"Yeah, alright, Ray," Tip growled. He gave Gabriel a final scowl then turned menacing eyes on Nina. "You watch yourself, lady. I'm the big dog in this hood."

He turned away, and Gabriel leaned closer to Nina. "And all this time I thought Tigers were cats."

He meant his comment for her ears alone, but an unexpected pause in the music allowed Tip to hear it also.

The angry youth swung back around to face Gabriel. "Bad move dissin' the Tigers, bitch. Now I gotta teach you some manners!"

Tip lunged forward crashing headlong into the bar's mahogany counter after Gabriel angled out of the way. The dazed youth slid quietly to the ground, and the remaining Tigers surged to his defense.

Gabriel spared Nina, who was yelling for security, a quick glance to be sure she was safely out of the way then turned his full attention on the attacking youths.

Tip's female companion reached him first. The Celemor easily blocked her wild punch, countering with a quick back-fist to her temple, effectively rendering her unconscious. She slumped against him, and he lowered her to the floor rolling sideways to avoid the kick of another Tiger trying to take advantage of his awkward position. Gabriel's low sweeping kick knocked the youth's legs from under him, and he crashed to the floor, air whooshing from his body.

The remaining two Tigers trying to trap Gabriel between them in a pincer move fared no better. The Celemor responded to the coordinated attack with a flurry of fist and elbow strikes to various parts of their bodies, the ferocity of his defense astounding the crowd of people that had gathered around at the onset of the fight.

By the time the Center's security team, led by Tyree, managed to press their way through the throng of onlookers, the five gang members were all sprawled on the floor in various states of consciousness.

Nina hurried to Gabriel's side, searching his face for any signs of injury. "Are you alright?"

"Oh, yeah," he quickly assured her. "It turns out the Tigers' roar was nothing more than a 'meow.'" His statement drew a chuckle from Nina. "Sorry about the mess though." He nodded in the direction of the gang; the ones still unconscious being carried away by the burly security guards while Tyree set about settling the crowd. "But I couldn't let them spoil our evening."

Nina chuckled. "Yeah, I guess not." She favored him with an approving grin. "You know you're pretty good with your hands and feet, bud. I may have to put Heaven Sent Security on the Center's payroll."

Gabriel smiled. "I'll make sure you get a discounted rate." The smile vanished when he noticed the sultry, platinum-haired woman staring at him from the opposite side of the room. "Mayhem," he growled, a slight glow emanating from his eyes as he watched her saunter toward one of the gym's rear exits. The Desomor blew him a kiss then slipped out the door.

Nina noticed the sudden tension in his face. "Is something wrong?"

Gabriel's eyes were still focused on the exit. "I'm not sure. Stay close to your friends and security, Nina." He gave her shoulder a brief squeeze. "There's something I need to check out."

He dashed off through the crowd, leaving a stunned Nina to wonder what was going on.

"You do throw one heck of a shindig, Miss Delcielo," a familiar voice sounded in her ear.

Nina whirled around and smiled at the unexpected sight of Quinlan and Sanders.

"Ah, you made it!" She placed a gentle hand atop Quinlan's forearm. "Thank you so much for coming. I'm just sorry you showed up when things got ugly."

"That little melee doesn't appear to have dampened any one's spirits." Quinlan waved his free hand at the people dancing around them. "But tell me; who's your athletic friend?" The seeker kept his voice neutral as his eyes swept over the crowd. "And where did he go? I'd like to shake his hand for standing up to those punks."

Nina cast worried eyes toward the rear exit. "I'm not sure."

Quinlan followed the direction of her gaze then looked pointedly at Sanders.

The Seekers knew full well who her benefactor was, having encountered the enigmatic being known as Gabriel on other occasions.

"Well maybe he'll come back," Quinlan said, turning his attention to one of the serving stations. "In the meantime, I think I'll help myself to some of those tasty looking sandwiches."

"That sounds good to me." Nina's polite smile didn't mask the concern in her eyes. "Would you care for something Mister Sanders?"

"No, you two go on ahead." Sanders nodded toward the carnival booths set up along the back wall. "I think I'll try my luck at some of those games; see if I can win myself one of those vintage lava-lamps." He accorded them a brief nod then set off to start a discreet search.

*

"I was wondering if you had the nerve to come after me," a feminine voice rang out from above.

Gabriel shifted his gaze up to the glowing figure crouched atop a nearby streetlight. The Celemor checked to make sure no one else was around then propelled himself upward, coming to a hovering stop in front of his adversary. "Now you know I'd never pass up a chance to dance with you, May."

"You always were such the gentlemen, Gabriel."

He shrugged. "One tries. I take it you're the precipitator of that little incident back at the rally?"

A wicked smile parted Mayhem's sensuous lips. "I just wanted to see if you were keeping yourself in shape, lover."

"Always." He opened his hand to her. "Care to test the waters yourself?"

"I thought you'd never ask!" She flashed him a girlish grin then launched herself from the pole.

Gabriel met her charge head on, their bodies colliding amidst a blinding flash of energy that briefly turned night into day as they battled midair.

"You're getting slow, old girl," Gabriel teased as he slipped through her defenses, slamming an uppercut into her chin. "Maybe you need to get out of the kennel a little more often!"

The Celemor's taunts spurred Mayhem to greater efforts, but she was still no match for his superior speed and technique. Frustrated by her own failings, the Desomor released a staggering blast of Celestial energy. Gabriel, twisted out of the way, but his awkward position left him unprepared for the elbow smashing into his jaw.

Seizing the advantage, Mayhem wrapped her arms tightly about his waist, and flew them higher into the air. "My turn to lead, lover," she crowed then plummeted straight down, reversing positions at the last moment so that Gabriel hit the ground first, plowing a deep furrow in the street's pitted asphalt. The impact was more than Mayhem anticipated, and she staggered backward, trying to regain her equilibrium.

It was Gabriel's turn to unleash his Celestial power. The blast fired from his trembling hand caught the Desomor full on, its concussive force pushing her through the plate glass windows of the boutique on the opposite side of the street.

All was quiet for a moment then a bloodied Gabriel rose unsteadily to his feet. He stumbled across the street to where an equally battered Mayhem lay unconscious amidst the rubble her passage had produced. "I guess this dance is over, May."

"Don't bet on it, Celemor," a cold voice declared as Azreal stepped from the shadows of a neighboring store, the two Disciples from the altercation at Tony's flanking him. The trio swiftly took positions in front of the boutique's demolished window, forming a protective wedge around the injured Mayhem.

Gabriel squared his shoulders, wincing at the pain the motion caused him, his eyes glowing with Celestial fire. "Okay, Azreal. Let's see if you and your dogs can do better than your girl."

"You got balls, Gabe, I'll give you that," Azreal chortled, a crackle of energy forming around his clenched fists. "It's too bad I gotta rip 'em off!"

The Disciple and his minions attacked in unison, raining blows upon the beleaguered Celemor at superhuman speed.

Though Celestially Touched by their Master, Disciples were not nearly as powerful as a Celestial Mortal of Gabriel's caliber. Normally he would have had little trouble repelling their onslaught, but the injuries sustained in his battle with Mayhem were beginning to take their toll. Within moments, the Disciples had the Celemor on the verge of collapse. A final kick by a zealous Azreal knocked him to the ground.

"You're good Gabe, I'll give you that. But today we're just a little bit better!"

He took a menacing step toward the downed Celemor then screamed as a nimbus of white light suddenly engulfed his body, searing the flesh from his bones. The remaining Disciples met with similar fates, and a startled Gabriel watched as their writhing bodies were quickly reduced to piles of smoldering ash.

"It appears we have arrived just in time," Dichotomy proclaimed, his glowing form solidifying on the scene. He spared the charred remains of the Disciples a brief glance then kneeled beside the injured Celemor. "Still getting yourself into trouble, Gabriel?"

Gabriel managed a weak smile. "You know me." He regarded the Celestial's illuminated form through half-lidded eyes. "I see you're wearing the Caleb suit."

A ghost of a smile appeared on Dichotomy's lips. "We felt it best to assume our pre-Celestial form while we aid you in this Task."

Mention of the word "Task" brought a flash of fear to Gabriel's eyes. "Nina...!" He tried to raise himself up, but Dichotomy placed a restraining hand atop the Celemor's chest

"Fear not, Gabriel. She is currently in the company of her friends and subordinates. When she leaves their protection, we shall continue to watch over her until you've recovered."

Gabriel breathed a sigh of relief. "Thanks, Caleb. I owe you one; both of you," he added with a smile before slipping into unconsciousness.

"Anytime, old friend," the Celestial whispered. A bemused smile parted his glowing lips as he studied the Celemor's bruised face. "We were right about Gabriel's feelings toward this woman." Dichotomy gently lifted the Celemor's prone body off the ground. "Perhaps it is time for us to meet her as well."

A low moan signaled Mayhem's return to consciousness, and Dichotomy shifted his glowing gaze in her direction. The Desomor looked around uncertainly then stiffened when she met Dichotomy's sullen frown.

The Celestial regarded the haggard Desomor through contemptuous eyes for a moment then disappeared amidst a flash of blinding light. His departure produced a flood of relief within Mayhem, until her eyes fell on the three charred piles in the street before her.

"Azreal," she groaned in agony when the residual essence of the Disciple's spirit brushed against her awareness. A hard knot formed in the pit of her stomach. Iblis was going to be furious once he learned of this debacle brought about by her flagrant disregard of his orders.

With her mind preoccupied on the dire fate that awaited her, Mayhem failed to notice the excited presence of the man crouched behind the hulking frame of a delivery truck parked up the street.

Sanders had arrived on the scene just as the fight between Gabriel and the mysterious woman had reached its climax. The Seeker had quickly found what he hoped was a secure spot then focused amazed eyes on the heavenly spectacle.

He now watched in rapt fascination as the woman placed a gentle kiss on her fingertips and waved them over the piles of ash that had once been her comrades. Within moments a strong breeze rose up around her, scattering the ashes through the air. After all their remains were dispersed, the woman breathed a heavy sigh then quietly faded away.

Sanders held his position for a moment to make sure no other glowing creatures were going to appear then carefully abandoned his hiding place. He surveyed the damaged area, and an awed whistle escaped his lips.

First Miss Delcielo's clairvoyant moment at the Center, now a battle between Divine beings! This was turning out to be one prolific Manifestation.

The Seeker retrieved his smart phone from his jacket's inner pocket, and took a few shots of the battle ravaged area, all the while berating himself for not thinking of it earlier. A recording of tonight's events would have been an invaluable addition to the *Presbyterii* archives. He gave the area a final glimpse, released another awed whistle then hustled back to the Center.

Chapter 13

"....and I just wanted to thank you and Maria again for all your help," Nina spoke into the phone pressed painfully against her ear as she prepared herself a cup of tea. "No, I haven't heard from Gabriel yet, but I'll let you guys know as soon as I do. Yes, Tyree followed me home...Okay; take care, Tony." She let the phone drop to her hand and breathed a sigh of relief. "Whew, what a night."

Despite the altercation with the Tigers the rally had been a huge success. She even managed to secure some additional funding for the Center from the Detroit chapter of the Junior League. By all rights this should be a time of celebration, but the fact that Gabriel had not returned from his abrupt departure had Nina in a state of worry. Where could he have run off to?

The answer to her question came sooner than expected as a flash of blinding light and a rush of cool air signaled the arrival of Dichotomy with the subject of Nina's anxiety cradled in his arms.

Nina dove for cover behind the kitchen counter, her hand grabbing the knife she had used to cut the lemon slices for her tea.

"Fear not, Nina Delcielo," the Celestial soothed the terrified woman. "We are Dichotomy, and we mean you no harm."

The intense light radiating from his body, coupled with the curious resonance of his voice had a calming effect on Nina. She lowered the knife, and slowly stood up. She still had no idea what was happening but sensed that she was in no danger.

Dichotomy gently laid Gabriel on the sofa then stood back as Nina knelt beside him.

She gasped at the sight of the numerous lacerations on the exposed parts of his body. "Oh my God." Nina wiped the streaks of blood from Gabriel's face with the sleeve of her shirt. "What happened?"

A hard look appeared on Dichotomy's face. "He was injured during a confrontation with the Desolate Mortal known as Mayhem." His expression softened at the concerned mirrored in Nina's eyes. "Do not worry. Despite the severity of his wounds, Gabriel will recover shortly."

Nina studied Gabriel's face for a moment then turned incredulous eyes to the glowing being beside her. "Who, or...what are you?"

A slight smile crept into place on the Celestial's face. "As we said, our name is Dichotomy. We are friend to the Celestial Mortal, Gabriel, who has been given the Task of protecting you during your time of Emergence."

Nina stared at him through dumbfounded eyes. "My time of what?"

"Emergence," Dichotomy repeated. "As you might have already surmised, you have been chosen by the Almighty to become the latest in a long line of Harbingers charged with the task of ushering in significant changes to the Tenets here in the Realm of Mortalia." Dichotomy took note of the deepening confusion on the woman's face, and a regretful sigh escaped his lips. "It is obvious through your reaction that much has yet to be revealed to you, including the true nature of the universe."

The air around Dichotomy's hand shimmered for a moment then a large, leather-bound book appeared before him. "This volume was taken from the Journals of the Archangel Michael," he explained as the book settled gently into Nina's open hands. "Perhaps it will help lessen your confusion and indoctrinate you into the workings of the Hierarchy."

Nina stared at the unearthly tome for a moment, a knot of apprehension settling in her stomach. "And just what exactly is this...Hierarchy?"

Dichotomy favored her with a solemn look. "The Creation's ruling tier, which you are now a part of."

Nina gaped in astonishment. "Me?"

Dichotomy inclined his head respectfully toward her. "As a Harbinger you are now a living conduit of the Almighty's will, hence your inclusion."

Nina swallowed hard several times, trying to digest all that was happening. She glanced uncertainly at the heavy Journal still clutched in her hands. "But...why did God pick *me*?"

"The reasons behind your selection are unknown to us, but we are certain that all will be made clear to you in due time. For now, we shall take our leave."

"Now?" Nina turned worried eyes to Gabriel's battered figure. "What about him?"

Dichotomy's solemn expression shifted into one of affection. "As we said before, Gabriel will recover soon. Farewell Harbinger. We've no doubt that our paths shall cross again."

The Celestial disappeared amidst another blinding flash, leaving a dazed Nina sitting numbly on the floor, trying valiantly to make sense of all he had told her.

She spared Gabriel a concerned look and stiffened at what she saw. A soft glow was emanating from his body, and his injuries were healing at an incredibly accelerated rate. Within seconds, all traces of them were gone.

Nina blinked several times then lifted troubled eyes to the ceiling. "Why on Earth did you choose me?"

She got no reply.

Not really knowing why, she placed the journal gently on the table and opened it. Sparing the still glowing Gabriel a final glance, she focused wary eyes on its iridescent pages and began to read: "In the Beginning of all Beginnings there was the Event, a molecular cataclysm that spawned all that exists including the infinite expanse of Celestial Energy known as The Void.

It was from The Void that The Almighty drew forth the raw matter to fashion The Creation; a system of three intertwining dimensional Realms to contain and nurture the myriad forms of sentient life developing around Him..."

Acceptance

Chapter 14

Tullis stared hard at the small speaker resting on the table's tiled surface; the look of incredulity on his face matching those of his fellow Elders. "And you're sure this being was Divine in nature?"

"Without a doubt," Sander's disembodied voice echoed throughout the closed-in patio of Dresden's Roman country villa where the four Cardinals were gathered. "After he incinerated the three late-comers, the creature lifted Gabriel off the ground and literally disappeared."

"Amazing," Tullis whispered. "And the woman?"

"She recovered a short time later," Sander's replied. "She used the wind to scatter her companions' remains then vanished herself."

An uneasy silence settled over the room as the Elders exchanged nervous looks with one another.

"And you say Miss Delcielo's abilities are also viable?" asked Dresden, his mind still reeling from the Seeker's incredible tale.

"Extremely," Quinlan's voice joined the conversation. "She had a vision which probably saved one of her worker's lives while we were standing there. We haven't had time to ascertain her religious standings, but on the surface, she appears to be a decent woman."

"Then let us hope that in this case, appearances are not deceiving," Tullis called out. "I must say this is exciting news, gentlemen. We will confer on this matter at once and contact you when we determine a course of action. In the meantime, I want you to drop the Double H facade and reveal yourselves to Miss Delcielo."

"Are you sure that's wise, Your Grace?" A note of concern colored Quinlan's voice.

"Yes, I am. Considering Miss Delcielo's antipathy for the Catholic church, our first step toward swaying her to our cause must be the establishment of her trust in the *Presbyterii*. The two of you must now begin that process."

"We understand, Your Grace, and we'll take care of it," Quinlan assured the Cardinal then disconnected.

"What do you think, brothers?" Milan's tenor broke the poignant silence surrounding the table.

"That we're dealing with something profound," Dresden observed, his pensive features drawn into an even tighter frown.

"I'll say," Gianni cried. "Not only is this woman a confirmed recipient of Divine power, but she also appears to be in direct contact with Heavenly beings."

"Or demonic," Tullis cautioned. "We've never determined the true nature of this Gabriel character, nor what his purpose is. All we know for certain is that whenever we've investigated a suspected Manifestation, he's there."

"No, he only appears at the confirmed ones," Gionni contradicted the Cardinal. "And it must be noted that in every instance he's gone through great lengths to avoid confrontation with our people. Considering his apparent abilities, this leads me to believe that his intentions are not evil."

Dresden regarded Gionni through skeptical eyes. "Are you saying you think he's some type of angel?"

"I won't go that far, but he could be some type of...guardian sent to look after the Divine recipient."

"If that's the case then why run from us?" Dresden pressed. "If he is one of God's agents then he obviously knows who we are. Why not introduce himself so that we might coordinate our efforts?"

Gionni threw his hands up in the air. "Who knows? Maybe he doesn't need our involvement."

"Or maybe he doesn't want it," Milan interjected. "You're assuming his intentions are the same as ours. He could just as easily be one of Hell's agents trying to sway the subject to the side of the unrighteous."

"I suppose anything's possible," Gionni allowed.

"Well whatever side this Gabriel and the beings associated with him are on, one thing *is* certain," Tullis declared, pinning each of his fellow *Presbyterii* with a troubled stare. "Nina Delcielo has the power to see the future. Of more immediate concern is what she plans on doing with it."

A deathly calm descended over the patio as the four men considered the ramifications of Nina's abilities.

Gionni broke the silence first. "Let's just hope we can shake her out of her religious apathy and instill a bit of Catholicism in her before she makes that decision." The others solemnly agreed.

A slight frown appeared on Milan's face. "Perhaps the time has come to inform His Imminence of this development."

Dresden gave a negative shake of his head. "Not just yet. I'd rather wait and see how Miss Delcielo responds to Quinlan's and Sander's revelation of this Order and its purpose. Her subsequent actions following their disclosure will give us insight as to how cooperative she will be."

Tullis regarded him through hard eyes. "And should she prove unwilling to aid our cause?"

"Then we will take the proper steps to ensure that she does not become a threat to His Imminence, whether *he's* aware of her or not." Dresden looked pointedly at Milan. The younger Elder's unswerving loyalty to the Holy Father sometimes interfered with his sense of discretion in matters such as these.

"I will remain silent," Milan vowed, calmly returning the other's regard. "Let's just pray that such action does not become necessary."

"Amen to that," Tullis put in quietly, and the meeting was adjourned.

Chapter 15

Omen glided purposefully through the central courtyard of the Apex; an immense marble pyramid, several times larger than its similar counterpart on Earth's Giza plateau, resting at the northern edge of Heaven's borders. He nodded pleasantly to the small group of beings seated at one of the numerous white-granite tables situated throughout the courtyard. The looks of wonder and awe on their faces marked them as New Arrivals to the crystalline city, still adjusting to the Ways of Divinity.

The Overseer often wondered what the various Mortal races of Mortalia felt upon their transition to the Afterlife. The true Heaven contrasted sharply to the images put forth by many of the Realm's fragmented religious infrastructures.

Omen had never understood why The Almighty allowed such varied levels of understanding to continue. Why were the amphibian race on the watery world, Cayem, allowed a true disclosure of the nature of the universe while the Humans of Earth, supposedly the race valued most by The Almighty, were left to plod along a spiritual path riddled with half-truths and gross misrepresentations of The Creation.

The pyramid's entryway cycled open at Omen's approach, and the Overseer pulled his thoughts away from the intriguing riddle to focus on the reason for this visit to the Seat of Authority.

No member of the Hierarchy, with the notable exception of the Horsemen and the Archangels, had the right to interfere in the execution of a Divine Task. That was why Omen had not come to Gabriel's aid during the fight with Mayhem and the Disciples. As a former Celemor, Caleb, or Dichotomy as he now preferred to be called was well aware of this fact. He also knew the possible consequences for such an infraction, yet he chose to intercede. In

Omen's eyes, such blatant disregard for the Tenets could not go unpunished.

The Overseer moved quickly along the pyramid's vast granite-lined corridors, coming to a stop at the entryway to an immense, spherical chamber. Inside the chamber floated the fluctuating expanse known simply as The Window; a nexus of time and space created by The Almighty. Through it, the entire Creation could be easily accessed and monitored by the Divine Watch. As usual, the Archangel Michael stood before the Window's rectangular dimensions, observing a confrontation between two opposing Mortal armies on the planet Earth.

"Hello Omen," Michael acknowledged the Overseer.

"Michael," Omen responded, inclining his head respectfully toward the Archangel. "I trust I'm not interrupting you?"

A slight smile creased Michael's lips. "Not at all; I was merely monitoring this latest conflagration within the Land of Abraham."

Omen's gaze shifted to the Window's contents, and a wave of aggravation emanated from him. "The Mortals of Earth's Middle Eastern region are forever battling one another; usually over the most ridiculous things."

A regretful sigh escaped Michael's lips. "Such is their nature." He turned away from the Window, and focused hazel eyes on Omen's hooded features. "I take it you're here to discuss the actions of your former protégé?"

A ripple of surprise flowed through the Overseer. "Then...you're aware of Caleb's transgression?"

"You of all beings should know that there is little that transpires in Mortalia that I am not aware of; especially on Earth." Michael nodded toward the Window. "Their pronounced curiosity makes them a difficult species to guide."

"That and their boundless arrogance," Omen noted.

Michael smiled. "You're starting to sound like Gabriel. The Bringer of Death also finds Humanity's increasing temerity somewhat distasteful."

"Then his feelings mirror my own. My Task would be so much easier if Mortal minds were structured more along the lines of a Celestial's ordered mentality."

Michael's wings gave a slight flutter. "They are as the Almighty intended them to be. We all are."

The Overseer cocked his head slightly to the left. "Including Caleb?"

A look of uncertainty flickered across Michael's face. "I have to admit Caleb's bizarre reasoning places him in a category of his own."

A wave of irritation emanated from Omen. "That goes without saying. Still his current behavior is odd even for him. Since his rejection of the Tenets, Caleb rarely concerns himself with Mortalia. His timely appearance suggests that he's been monitoring Nina's Emergence, though for what reason I cannot fathom."

"Caleb's interest lies not with the woman but rather her guardian," the Archangel Gabriel announced as he soared unceremoniously through the Window. "That hapless tangle of Celestial confusion seems to have developed an uncharacteristic fondness for my namesake; prompting him to stick his dual-gendered nose into places it doesn't belong." The Bringer of Death favored Michael with a reproving look. "But such is often the case when a Celestial allows his objectivity to become compromised by personal considerations." His malevolent gaze shifted to Omen. "Or attachments."

The Overseer bristled at the Archangel's insinuation. "My rapport with Gabriel has in *no* way interfered with my duties. Nor will I allow it to."

"So, you say," Gabriel drawled. "But I wonder; are you angry with Caleb because he rendered aid to the Celemor or because he did so before *you*?"

Omen's hooded form trembled with indignation. "Had Caleb not arrived Gabriel would have received no help from me."

"But your champion was on the verge of defeat," the Bringer of Death cried dramatically. "If not for Caleb's actions he would have surely perished. Are you telling me that you would have calmly stood by and let that happen?"

"Unlike some Celestials, I strenuously adhere to the Divine Mandates of non-interference in matters of this nature."

Gabriel's sensitive ears detected the slight inflection in Omen's tone. His ebony eyes narrowed. "Are you implying something, Overseer?"

"I'm merely reiterating my commitment to Celestial law. Had the situation been one in which the *Harbinger* were directly in danger then yes, I would have intervened, but in this instance, no." The Overseer's glowing gaze bored hard into Gabriel's. "Even if it meant watching my friend end his Mortal existence."

Gabriel regarded Omen's hovering form through skeptical eyes then a slight smile creased his lips. "Bold words, Overseer; for your sake I hope you mean them."

"I can assure you I do," Omen ground out. He turned pointedly away from the Archangel's condescending glare and focused his attention on Michael. "What are your orders in regard to disciplining Caleb?"

"For the moment you will do nothing."

The glow around Omen's eyes intensified. "Nothing...? But he is setting a dangerous precedent here."

"Of that we are well aware, Omen; just as we are of the fact that his intervention could influence the future actions of other members of the Watch."

Omen's eyes flared again. "I was unaware of Caleb's continued inclusion on that roster."

Gabriel's voice became surly. "Despite his current...disillusion with Heaven's politics, your former charge is still held in high regards by The Almighty. As such he enjoys a degree of latitude for his behavior."

Omen couldn't believe what he was hearing. "And because of that, I'm to ignore his disregard for Celestial law?"

"For the moment: yes."

The tone of Gabriel's voice prevented Omen from questioning him further. However, it did not quell the Overseer's rising concern.

Why *was* Caleb being shown such leniency? What role did the former Celemor have to play in this unfolding mystery, and more importantly, how would his meddling affect Gabriel and the Harbinger?

Clearly this matter needed investigating, but Omen sensed he would learn no more from the Archangels. Fortunately, they were not the only sources of pertinent information within The Creation.

Omen drew his hooded shroud tighter around his bony shoulders. "My original purpose for coming here was to inform you of Caleb's transgression. Since the situation seems to have already been dealt with, I'll take my leave." He inclined his head respectfully and withdrew from the chamber.

"I think Omen disapproves of Caleb's current Celestial stature," Michael noted, resuming his observation of the battle taking place on Earth.

"He is not the only one," Gabriel snapped then launched himself back through the Window, leaving the Keeper of Benevolence alone to contemplate the day's events.

You seem troubled, my child, The Almighty's heavy voice echoed through the Archangel's mind. *Do you also disapprove of my consideration for Caleb?*

"It is not my place to question your judgment, my Lord. But I must confess that I am surprised at your tolerance for his erratic behavior, considering the limits you've imposed on the Watch's involvement during this Reclamation."

Worry not, Michael. The Archangel was surprised by the sadness in The Almighty's tone. *All matters are progressing as I intended; particularly where Caleb is concerned.*

Chapter 16

A black Dodge Ram pickup sped down Detroit's Lodge freeway. Inside, two grim Seekers contemplated their current assignment.

"I'm still not sure if Cardinal Tullis is right about this," Quinlan remarked as he eased his way around the slower moving station wagon in front of them.

"Nor am I," Sanders replied. "But he does have a valid point. Miss Delcielo might be more receptive to our cause if we simply tell her the truth about our purpose here."

Quinlan gave his partners face a quick glance. "I suppose. It just feels strange breaking from normal procedures."

"Trust me," Sanders muttered, a slight shiver running through his body as the events of the previous evening flashed through his mind. "Normal is not a word we'll be associating with this assignment!"

*

"Daddy, are you coming home, now?"

Gabriel gently stroked his daughter's cheek with the back of his hand. "Not yet Gaby; I've still got some work to do."

"But you've been work a long time already," the three-year-old protested, her lower lip drooping sadly. "And we really miss you!"

Gabriel winced as her anguished cry pierced him to the soul. "I'm sorry baby." He took hold of her tiny hands and drew them to his cheek. "I'm so sorry."

"We know you are," a new voice answered, and Gaby's little body morphed into that of an adult woman, her cinnamon skin glistening, her brown eyes boring into his. "But it doesn't make it any easier."

"Clarissa!" Gabriel clutched desperately at her hand. "No," he screamed as she began to fade. "Don't go! Please...!"

"Don't leave me alone..." The dream ended, and he was thrust back into consciousness. He lay still for a moment, taking a series of deep breaths to reverse the metabolic reaction dreams of his wife and daughter invariably induced within him. His pulse and heartbeat quickly returned to their normal, easy rhythm, and Gabriel breathed a relieved sigh.

"Feeling better?"

His eyes snapped open at the sound of that unexpected voice. "Much," he said to Nina sitting on the low table in front of the sofa he was laying on. The Celemor gave his surroundings a quick glance. "I take it Dichotomy delivered me to your door?"

Nina's left eyebrow arched upward. "Are you talking about that glowing thing that just...appeared in my dining room last night?"

"Yeah, that's them."

Nina's eyebrow arched upward again. "Them?"

"Dichotomy has two distinct, fluctuating personalities; one male and one female, hence the name."

Nina studied his face for a moment then released an amused snort. "You know, there was a time when hearing something like that would have totally freaked me out."

Gabriel's lips twitched with amusement. "And now?"

Nina shrugged. "The way my life's been going lately I'm learning to take such things in stride."

"I'll just bet you are," Gabriel muttered. "So..." he spoke up in the awkward silence that followed. "Did the glowing thing, as you put it fill you in on what's going on?" In answer to his question, Nina pointed to the Journal sitting conspicuously to one side of the table. "Ah. Have you read any of it?"

"Only the first few chapters." Nina's mind was still ablaze from what she had learned about the world around her. "I suppose it's too much for me to hope that this is all just some sort of crazy dream?"

Gabriel gave her a sympathetic smile. "I'm afraid not."

"Wonderful." Nina's shoulders sagged with disappointment. A part of her mind still held on to the hope that she was locked in the grip of some overwhelming delusion and would snap out of it at any second. His somber announcement quickly erased all such notions. "Dichotomy said that you were a Celestial something or other, sent here to protect me."

"Celestial Mortal," Gabriel corrected. "Celemor for short; it's the name given to Mortals chosen by the Archangels to carry out specific Tasks throughout the Realms."

"Ah. He, or they," she restated with a sardonic grin, "also said that you got hurt fighting someone named Mayhem." Gabriel gave an affirmative nod. "Who is he and why were you fighting?"

"*She* is one of Iblis's people, no doubt assigned by him to monitor you, and fighting is usually the outcome of our meetings."

"And just who, or what, is Iblis?"

"The Celestial being most Mortals refer to as the 'Enemy' or 'Devil.'"

Nina jerked in surprise. "I guess I should've kept reading that journal. I thought his name was Satan, or Lucifer?"

Gabriel frowned. "Most people do, thanks to a misinterpretation of the original scriptures that's been propagated throughout history. The real 'Lucifer' was a Babylonian king, mentioned briefly in the biblical book Isaiah, whose arrogance cost him God's favor. The name 'Satan', roughly translated from ancient Hebrew and Aramaic, means 'rebel' or 'outcast.'"

Nina massaged her temples with the tips of her fingers. "This just keeps getting better and better. First that Dicho-thing gives me a holy book that basically tells me everything I thought I knew about the universe is wrong; now this. Is any of that Bible-crap the nuns used to cram down our throat during Sunday-school true?"

"The passages of the original Bible were taken from the First Journal that Michael gave to Moses following the Exodus. But with so many different authors putting their own spin on the copies handed down over the millennia, the true contents have been lost."

"What do you mean?"

Gabriel adjusted his muscular frame to a more comfortable position on the sofa. "Take Iblis, for example. Most mortals who subscribe to the Judeo-Christian belief system are taught that he was an angel who was thrown out of Heaven after staging a revolt against God."

"Are you're telling me that's not what happened?"

"Not exactly. The angel part is true. Actually, he was an Archangel, but it wasn't a lust for power that got Iblis in trouble. It was his refusal to accept the Divine Tenets God set in place to guide the Realms, particularly the ones pertaining to Mortalia. Iblis believed that the limited understanding of the Creation, as well as the system of Celestial subservience being subtly instilled in our collective subconscious, was wrong."

Nina stared at him in disbelief. "Wait a minute. Are you telling me that the devil was actually *our* advocate?"

"For all intents and purposes, yes. Iblis felt that all beings within the Creation, including Mortals, should be allowed to live their lives based on their own designs instead of being led by the nose down a preordained path."

"I definitely agree with that." Nina declared.

Gabriel flashed a wicked grin. "So do I. Unfortunately, God felt otherwise, but that didn't stop Iblis from pleading his case. Eventually his negative position drew support from other residents of Nirvana, sparking what many Celestials have come to call, Iblis's Idealistic Revolt."

"Amazing," Nina whispered. "How did the whole thing end?"

"God told His detractors that this was the direction he had chosen for Mortalia, and that was that. Once Iblis and his followers realized that their protests were basically falling on deaf ears, they disassociated themselves from God's mandates and took up residence elsewhere; living what most Celestials considered a desolate existence, earning Iblis the nickname, The Desolate One."

"Whew," Nina exhaled loudly. "Heaven's politics sound even more screwed up than ours."

Gabriel chuckled. "They are. In ways you can't even begin to imagine."

"I don't doubt it," Nina muttered under her breath. "And you're saying that everything you just told me is in there?" She pointed to the Journal, and Gabriel nodded. "Then I'm glad I put it down." Her comment drew a smile from the Celemor. "But if this Iblis is such an opponent of God's plans, why the heck is he keeping tabs on me, since I seemed to have been chosen for some holy purpose?"

"Because as a Harbinger whatever message you've been picked to deliver could potentially affect the lives of millions of people, possibly creating an opportunity for Iblis to reveal the truth of his being and lay down his infamous reputation as a two-horned, pitchfork-wielding monster; a description that's totally off the mark."

Nina glanced sharply at him. "You've met him?"

"A few times; when you have a job like mine, it pays to have an unbiased impression of your potential opponents."

"I guess that makes sense. But explain to me this: if Iblis really *isn't* evil, why do all religions portray him that way?"

"Because every soul-saving organization needs a villain to stand against," Gabriel said with a wink.

"Hmm," Nina uttered as she considered his point.

"Add to that the fact that most modern religious leaders aren't aware of the ancient truths laid down in the Journal, nor of the true nature of the Creation, and you start to see how such a negative image can be consistently perpetuated."

"So basically, what you're saying is that the Christians, Jews, Muslims, and so forth have got it all wrong"

"In terms of their belief in God, no," Gabriel pointed out. "Most modern religions are unanimous in their acknowledgement of a singular, Supreme Being who oversees all, which is surprising considering the general misunderstanding of the Hierarchy. The problem starts with the various ideas on how we should interact with that being."

"Back up a second. What do you mean by, 'misunderstanding of the Hierarchy'? Most religions have always claimed that God has all sorts of angels and spirits working for him."

"*Now* they do," Gabriel stressed. "During the early days of Creation, it wasn't like that. Members of the Hierarchy used to move freely between the Realms; some even establishing rapports with Earth's fledging Human race. That's where the problem started. The primitives mistook the various Celestial's for gods themselves and started worshiping them."

"I've never heard *that* before," Nina cried.

Gabriel flashed an ingenuous grin. "What; you're not a fan of ancient, Greek and Egyptian mythology?"

Nina's eyes went wide with amazement. "Are you telling me...that all those stories and legends..."

"Refer to actual members of the Hierarchy who once roamed the Earth," Gabriel finished her sentence. "This...confusion is why travel between the Realms is mostly forbidden now. There are some Celestials who, for whatever reasons choose to ignore these mandates and involve themselves with Mortals. They're known as The Demonstratives, or 'Demons' if you will, and generally like to stir up trouble in the Realms just to piss off God and the Hierarchy; usually at the bidding of Lie."

Nina's eyebrows arched upward. "And Lie would be...?"

Gabriel's expression hardened. "A particularly troubled Celestial who feeds on the suffering of others; many of history's atrocities can be attributed to her manipulations. In Celestia she's known as the 'Child of Chaos.'"

"But why does God allow such a creature to get away with such behavior? Why doesn't he just clear up all these misconceptions about the universe? If he is The Almighty, it should be easy."

"It would be, but for Him to do so would disturb the Balance between Order and Chaos."

"I take it that's a bad thing," Nina said after pausing a moment to ponder his statement.

A pensive frown appeared on Gabriel's face. "Order and Chaos are the two prevailing Forces that sustain all reality. According to the Archangel's, if left unchecked an imbalance between the two would lead to the destabilization and eventual destruction of the entire Creation, which is why God generally tries to use more subtle ways to help the Realms maintain the Divine status quo."

"Such as?" Nina prompted after considering the concept for a moment.

Gabriel shrugged. "He'll have The Watch initiate Proclamations, Reclamations, and Decimations such as the Great Flood if the situation warrants it. His biggest attempt at a Reclamation was the inception of Christianity after the elevation of the Prophet, Christ."

Nina focused sharply on the Celemor's face. "The *Prophet* Christ?"

"Originally Jesus Christ Emerged as a Prophet, charged with the Task of clearing up the growing amount of incorrect religious rhetoric. But his popularity at the time was such that God thought elevating him to a more prominent position within the Hierarchy would turn him into a beacon to which all wayward Mortals would be drawn; an effort that ultimately failed."

Nina gave him a startled look. "What are you talking about? Half the people in the world look to Christ as their savior!"

A wicked gleam lit Gabriel's eyes. "Yeah, but God wanted *all* the people in the world. With everyone on the same Divine page, the truth of Reality could've been reintroduced, and humanity steered back on the course he set for us. But human nature once again came into play and Christianity ended up being divided into countless splinter groups."

"That's another thing I don't get," Nina jumped on his statement. "How can one religion have so many variations?"

"It goes back to mankind's misinterpretation of the original Journal," said Gabriel. "Add to that the countless number of tyrants and egomaniacs that have put their own spin on the tenets to suit personal agendas, especially the ones governing Christianity and you end up with one big mess."

"If that's the case, and a lot of the rhetoric floating around is a result of our corruption of the Archangel's holy tell-all, why doesn't God just republish the thing and straighten it all out?"

Gabriel regarded her through speculative eyes. "I've often wondered that myself. Maybe that's why *you're* here." He pointed a finger at her. "To usher in a new Reclamation that will allow for a greater understanding of the Tenets and a final Revelation of The Creation's true history."

"Give me a break," Nina said with a snort. "The only things I've ushered in are a bunch of crazy visions."

"Visions that have saved the lives of several people," Gabriel quietly put in, drawing a surprised gasp from her.

"They have?"

"Yes, they have. Every one of the premonitions you reported to the police and were acted upon resulted in the prevention of several deaths."

A pleased look appeared on Nina's face but was quickly replaced by one of concern. "What about the warnings the police ignored?"

Gabriel's grim expression answered her question, and a chill shot through Nina's body.

"I'm sorry," the Celemor offered sympathetically.

"Yeah, me too," she muttered, surprised at the keen sense of remorse she felt over people that she had never even met. "Wait a minute." She turned startled eyes on him. "How did *you* know I've been telling the police?"

"I've been looking after you since your initial emergence." Gabriel smiled at the stricken look on her face. "Don't worry; I don't watch *everything* you do; although I must admit I do find your nightly aerobic routines very entertaining." His smile deepened at the embarrassed flush that rose to her cheeks.

"That's just great. My guardian angel is also a voyeur."

Gabriel laughed and she punched him on the arm. "Ouch!" She had forgotten how solid he was. "At least now I know where you got the name of your company, Mister, 'Heaven Sent Security."

"You have to admit it is a clever play on the truth. Well, it is," he added when she shot him a trenchant look.

"Yeah, I guess," she grudgingly admitted. "I take it you're walking me home and pretending to be interested in me was just a way to maintain your cover?"

Gabriel heard the disappointment in her voice, and gently took hold of her hands. "Seeing you safely home was part of my Task," he admitted, catching, and holding her eyes. "But getting to know you was an unexpected bonus."

"Oh, you're a smooth one, aren't you?" She gave him a fierce scowl, though she did squeeze his hand in return. "So how come you didn't just tell me who you were from the start?"

Gabriel shrugged. "Most people, particularly the ones I deal with, tend to be very self-conscious when they learn they're under surveillance, or they try to exploit their protected status for personal gain. I find it's easier to do my job when I maintain a *discreet* vigil over my clients."

"What made you change your routine for me?"

"Remember the three punks that accosted you at Tony's place?"

Nina shivered. "How can I forget?"

"The big one's name was Azreal. He and the punks that were with him were Iblis's Disciples."

Another shiver went through Nina at the memory of that day. "I definitely don't want to run into those goons again."

"You won't," Gabriel said quietly, and she turned questioning eyes on him.

"How do you know that?"

"They're all dead."

Nina stared at the Celemor in shock. "When did that happen?"

"Last night. They showed up right after my battle with Mayhem, looking for some payback while I was too weak to fend them off. Fortunately, Caleb popped in and incinerated them."

"Who's Caleb?"

"That's Dichotomy's real name," Gabriel said. "Or at least it was before the...incident."

"What incident?" Nina asked when he failed to clarify his statement.

Gabriel stared uncomfortably at his hands. "The one that turned 'him' into 'them.'"

He made no further comment and Nina didn't press. She had enough of her own mysteries to deal without adding the origins of a gender-mixed creature to the pot.

"So, what's your story," she switched to what she hoped was a safer topic. "How did you become a Cellular?"

"'Celemor,'" he corrected her with a smile. "And let's just say that at the time, becoming a Celestial errand boy was the lesser of two evils."

Nina regarded him in mild surprise. "Evil isn't a word I'd normally associate with Heaven and angels."

Gabriel's jaw tightened briefly. "Give it time. You will."

Nina was struck by the bitterness in his voice. She began pondering the significance of that statement when the apartment's intercom sounded.

"Now I wonder who that could be." She rose from the table and made her way to the front wall where the system was mounted. The flashing sequence on the panel indicated that it was the front desk calling her. "Yes Carl?" she said after pressing the receive button.

"Good morning, Miss Delcielo," the watchmen's voice boomed through the small speaker. "I've got a Mister Sanders and a Mister Quinlan down here asking to see you."

Nina blinked in surprise. "Sanders and Quinlan?"

"Yes ma'am. Shall I tell them you're unavailable?"

"No that's alright Carl. You can send them on up. Thanks." She let go of the button, turned to the sofa, and blinked again: Gabriel was gone!

Now where the hell did he disappear to? A light nock on the door announced the arrival of her guests. She shot a quick glance toward the bath and bedroom as she made her way to open it, but there was no sign of him. *Maybe I really did dream the whole thing.* Nina knew she wasn't that lucky.

"Good morning, gentlemen," she greeted the two men through the limited opening allowed by the door's security chain. "I must say this is a surprise."

"We know it is Miss Delcielo, and we're sorry to disturb you at home," Quinlan offered. "But there are several matters that we really need to discuss with you."

Nina took note of the urgency in their faces then, sensing no malice from them, removed the chain and opened the door all the way. "Well since you put it that way, please come in." Both men nodded their thanks and stepped quickly into the apartment. "Would either of you care for some coffee or tea," she asked after directing them to have a seat at the small dining table. Both declined and she settled herself into the chair at the table's head. "Now what can I do for you. There hasn't been a change in our grant status, has it?"

"Not at all," Quinlan hastily assured the worried woman. "In fact, the funds have already been allocated and should show up in the Center's account by noon today."

"Then what's this all about?"

The two Seekers exchanged uncertain glances then Quinlan spoke up. "The recent...abilities you seem to have developed."

Nina gave him a puzzled look. "And just what abilities are you talking about?"

"Your recent *psychic* abilities," the Seeker clarified.

Nina went rigid. "How could you possibly know about that?"

"Don't worry Miss Delcielo, we're not here to hurt you," Quinlan quickly reassured her. "In fact, we may be able to help."

Nina gave the Seeker a measuring look. "In what way?"

Quinlan hesitated for the barest second then released a heavy sigh. "I'm afraid we haven't been entirely honest with you about our true identities, Miss Delcielo. Helping Hands is actually a cover organization for a secret Vatican Order known as the *Presbyterii*, established in the late eighteen hundreds for the sole purpose of investigating matters of the supernatural."

A jolt of surprise shot through Nina's body. "But...how did you find out about me?"

"Our Elders were contacted by Father Griffin of Saint Christopher's parish," Sanders quietly informed her.

Nina's jaw dropped open. "*Tyree* called you?"

"He did," Quinlan confirmed. "After you told him of your visions, he reasoned that you were experiencing what we of the

Presbyterii call a supernatural Manifestation. He communicated his suspicions to our Elders who then dispatched us to see if your abilities were valid."

Nina's expression became guarded. "And what have you concluded?"

"That you truly have been blessed by the Lord with some form of premonitory sight."

Nina issued a derisive snort. "You guys kill me with this 'blessings' crap."

"But what else could you call the ability to see the future?" Quinlan didn't bother to hide his awe at the sheer notion of such a thing.

"A pain in the ass," she curtly informed him. "And something I would gladly give back to whoever it was that gave it to me!"

It suddenly occurred to Nina that, given her newfound knowledge of the *real* spiritual world, God and his people might take offense to her statement, but at this point she didn't care. It's not like they *asked* her if she wanted to be a walking preview channel.

"Under the circumstances I can understand your reluctance in this matter," Quinlan said. "But eventually you're going to have to lay down your reservations and accept the role that God's chosen for you."

The Seeker's statement mirrored Tyree's pious drivel and she shot him an irritated look. "Is that some kind of standard line they teach you guys in preacher school?"

Quinlan cocked his head slightly to the left. "I beg your pardon?"

"Bad joke," she mumbled, her mind concentrated on the ass-kicking she was going to give Tyree for not keeping his big-mouth shut. "So..." she refocused her attention on Sanders. "What exactly is it that you and your...Elders want from me?"

"It's what we may be able to do *for* you," Sanders spoke up.

"And what might that be?"

"Provide you with the support and guidance a person in your position often requires."

Nina favored the stocky man with an unscrupulous look. "Like the unsolicited guidance of the Catholic Church?"

"He was referring to the knowledge and resources of the *Presbyterii*," Quinlan smoothly interjected before the aggravated Sanders could respond. "But a dose of Catholicism thrown in for good measure could be beneficial; particularly considering your religious antipathy."

Nina gave him another startled look.

"Father Griffin was very forthright in his description of you," Quinlan quietly explained.

"I can see that," she bit out. Oh, yeah; Tyree was definitely catching a beat-down!

"There's also your personal safety to consider," Sanders intoned, having regained his composure. "If word of your talents got out you could be in danger from every megalomaniacal organization seeking to use your abilities for their own ends."

Nina looked him squarely in the eye. "Like what the *Presbyterii* are trying to do now?"

Sanders' ire for this upstart woman flared again. "The *Presbyterii* are not trying to exploit you, Miss Delcielo. We're simply offering you a path. The power to see the future can be an extreme boon for humanity, and a spiritually grounded foundation will help you to use that ability to its fullest potential."

"I suppose," Nina admitted with some reluctance. "But being spiritually grounded as you put it is not something I've ever aspired to, and this situation hasn't changed my standing on the subject."

"Fair enough," Sanders said after a brief silence. "But there's still the matter of your potential need for protection."

A wry smile tugged at Nina's lips. "I've already got that covered. As it so happens, I contracted the services of a private security firm this morning." Her revelation drew surprised looks from the Seekers, and Nina chuckled inwardly at the ironic truth of that statement. "After my run-in with those Tigers I figured I'd better get a little protection in place for myself and the Center."

Quinlan nodded. "These street gangs can be pretty brutal when you make them loose face on their own turf."

"My thoughts exactly," Nina solemnly agreed. "And the next time I run into them there might not be a Samaritan around to save the day."

Quinlan shifted uncomfortably in his seat. "And speaking of which, did you ever hear from the man who intervened last night?"

Nina wondered at the sudden change in the Seeker's demeanor. Sanders seemed to be affected as well. Their peculiar behavior prompted her to prevaricate. "He never came back to the rally after his abrupt departure, and I really hoped he would. I never got the chance to properly thank him. I just hope he didn't run into any of those Tigers."

The two Seekers exchanged nervous looks then Sanders turned grim eyes on her. "He did run into something, but it wasn't the Tiger Gang." He then related to her what he had witnessed the previous night. He also told her of her rescuer's numerous encounters with various *Presbyterii* agents over the years.

"And you think this Gabriel character is some type of angel or something?" Nina made sure to exude the proper amount of disbelief that such news would draw.

"We're not sure *what* he is," Quinlan candidly admitted. "We were hoping you could fill in some the blanks."

"I'm sorry guys but that was my first time meeting him." Nina was glad she hadn't revealed anything to them. Not that she had any great loyalty to Gabriel, but she had to admit that the Celemor had already acted on her behalf; twice. "And to be honest with you," she allowed a touch of fear to creep into her voice. "Considering what you just told me, I'm not really sure I want to meet him again."

The memory of Gabriel's actions sent a fresh wave of shivers down Sanders' spine. "I can definitely relate to you on that one, Miss Delcielo, but if he should happen to contact you again would you please give us a call? We would very much like to speak with him." He handed her a card with two phone numbers printed on one side and the image of a cross, a calligraphic "P" embedded in its center, on the other. "You can reach us at either of those numbers, twenty-four-seven."

"You can also contact us if you change your mind about accepting the *Presbyterii's* offer," Quinlan added.

Nina studied the card for a moment then placed it on the table before her. "I'll definitely keep that in mind." She rose gracefully from her seat. "I must say, gentlemen, this has been a very...enlightening morning for me."

"I'm sure it has been," Quinlan said, he and Sanders picking up on her less than subtle hint getting to their feet as well. "And we do apologize for our original deception."

Nina waved his apology aside. "Considering the circumstances, I completely understand."

She led them back to the door, Quinlan reiterating once more that she should not hesitate to call upon them should the need arise.

Nina assured them she would and closed the door, relaxing against it with a relieved sigh.

"Oh, come on Nina," Gabriel's amused voice startled her as he materialized on the sofa. "Their little interrogation wasn't *that* bad."

Nina plopped down on the sofa next to him. "That's easy for you to say; and where the hell did you disappear too anyway?"

"I was right here all along." He allowed his body to fade partially away.

"That's a neat trick," she cried, impressed by his vanishing act.

Gabriel became fully visible again. "It comes in handy for evading *Presbyterii* puppets."

"I take it you don't much care for them."

"Oh, they're a decent enough group of fellows. At the least the ones that I've run to have been, but they're dedication to their sad little crusade makes my job harder than it needs to be."

"Then why don't you drop the facade and tell them who you are?"

"It's up to God to make that kind of disclosure."

"What the hell is He waiting for?"

Gabriel shrugged. "I have no clue. The higher-ups never include me in the Heavenly board meetings."

Again, she heard the bitterness in his voice. "If you dislike being a Celemor so much, why do you continue to do it?"

A myriad of emotions flickered across his face, and a wistful sigh escaped his lips. "You give up a few things...when you're taking care of your family."

His whispered response asked more questions than it answered but Nina didn't press the matter. "So...what happens now?"

"You go on with your normal life," Gabriel replied, his moment of introspection passed. "Now that you know the truth of who you are, and how the universe works, you may start to discover the reason for your Emergence."

A hopeful look appeared on Nina's face. "That would be nice; and what about you?"

The Celemor flashed the Harbinger a reassuring smile. "I'll always be close by; though not *too* close," he added with a wink.

Nina opened her mouth to respond, but he disappeared before she could utter a word, leaving her feeling surprisingly alone.

Chapter 17

The agonized scream echoing through the halls of the Tower of Self gave credence to the horrific stories of torture and suffering usually associated with Iblis and his minions. Ironically enough, the Lord of Hell rarely meted out severe forms of punishment to his erring servants, but for the current transgressor, he decided to make an exception. Her disobedience deserved *special* attention.

"I distinctly remember telling you to keep a *low* profile," Iblis drawled running a delicate finger across the seared flesh of Mayhem's cheek. "What part of that request didn't you understand?"

The Desomor made no attempt to respond for she knew that offering petty excuses would only draw out this torturous process. Her safest recourse was to remain silent and endure; a resolution being soundly put to the test as a renewed surge of Celestial Fire engulfed her hovering form, drawing another painful cry from her charred lips.

To Silas, hovering silently by his master's side, Mayhem's agony was a joy to behold. He had suffered numerous indignities from the upstart Desomor. Perhaps this ordeal would instill a bit more respect in her platinum-haired skull.

"What you can't appreciate, Mayhem is that my taking full advantage of the Harbinger's talents requires her willing cooperation," Iblis patiently explained. "I planned to accomplish that through a few simple manipulations and given the woman's tenuous hold of Mortalia's accepted religious parameters, that Task might've been easily accomplished."

Iblis's eyes emitted a soft glow, and Mayhem's suspended form floated closer to him. "But now that you've alerted that pompous ingrate, Gabriel, whose affection you so desperately crave," he added icily. "Garnering her trust will require considerably more effort."

"I'm...sorry...my...lord..." Mayhem croaked. "Please...for...forgive...me..."

Iblis coldly regarded the Desomor. "Given the additional losses I have suffered as a result of your impetuousness, do you truly feel forgiveness is what you deserve?"

Mayhem knew he was referring to Azreal's death, and she lowered her head in despair, unable to meet the censure in his eyes. "No, my lord," she uttered in a small voice, preparing herself for what was sure to be her final moments.

Iblis gave her face a searching look then laid his hand against her cheek. Mayhem flinched then relaxed as a nimbus of energy flowed from his fingers, instantly regenerating her burned flesh. "Be thankful that you are one of my favorites," he whispered, his lips brushing lightly against her ear. "But disobey me again and you'll spend eternity as a rotting corpse. Have I made myself clear?" He released his hold over her body.

"Abundantly so," she whispered after gracing his lips with a gentle kiss. "And I swear I will never fail you like that again."

"You'd better not." Iblis's whispered warning reverberated coldly in her ear.

"I told you that woman could not be trusted to act accordingly in matters concerning Gabriel," Silas ground out after Mayhem had left.

Iblis dismissed the Morphling's censure with an amused snort. "Yes, you did. It's not the first time your instincts have proven accurate, and I'm sure it will not be the last."

"Then why do you continue to suffer that arrogant wench?"

Iblis rubbed thoughtfully at his lips, the taste of Mayhem's kiss still upon them. He had long ago chosen to avoid dalliances with those beholden to him, but the Desomor's pronounced sexuality tempted him none the less. "I often wonder that myself. At any rate her disobedience proved to be quite fortuitous."

Silas arched a questioning eyebrow. "In what way?"

The Lord of Hell's lip's parted in a devious smile. "When have you ever known Caleb to involve himself in anyone's crusade other than his own?"

A look of disbelief crossed the Morphling's face. "Are you saying that the Archangels have relaxed their censure of him and enlisted his aid as well?"

"I'm saying that his presence indicates that something major is in the works."

"Perhaps the Almighty has decided to end the charade of the Human belief system," Silas speculated. "They are the so-called chosen race. Maybe He feels that the time has finally come for them to grow up and assume that responsibility. And if that is the case, perhaps it would be best if you removed yourself from the equation and allow matters to proceed accordingly."

Iblis's eyes bulged slightly. "And why would I want to do that?"

"Your negative position within the majority of Mortalia's spiritual infrastructures are due mostly in part to their misinformed belief systems. If the Almighty *is* prepared to re-educate the Realm, the truth of your being will be revealed as well. When that happens, the Mortals will not look upon the choice to follow you and your Doctrines of Self as the damnable course such a decision has always been portrayed."

The office was silent for several minutes as Iblis pondered Silas's theory. What the Morphling was saying did have merit. In the beginning, all Iblis had wanted to do was prove to his father that omnipotence didn't necessarily translate into infallibility of judgment in what was 'right' and what was 'wrong' where Mortalia was concerned. Somehow the message had gotten twisted, resulting in him bearing the brunt of the Realm's antipathy as well as the censure of his Celestial peers.

Perhaps that's the reason The Almighty has allowed the lie to continue for as long as it has. To engineer my defeat through circumstance as opposed to a direct confrontation.

"You're point is valid Silas," he said to the Morphling waiting quietly beside him. "But it still begs the question of 'why' is he doing it, which is what I need to determine."

"And you have a plan for doing that?"

A curious gleam lit the Lord of Hell's blue eyes, and he favored the Morphling with a devious grin. "As a matter of fact, I do; one that even *your* cynical mind will appreciate."

A subtle realignment of the Morphling's sallow features effectively conveyed his skepticism. "That would be a first."

Iblis's smile deepened. "Summon the Desomor, Darius to me at once," he ordered, his folded wings giving a slight flutter as he altered his position in front of the office's large windows so he could gaze out over his domain. "His particular talents are aptly suited for what I have in mind."

Silas's hovering form grew still for a moment, his eyes unfocused. Within moments, there came a discreet knocking against the office's closed door.

"Enter," Iblis called, and a tall smartly dressed Mortal strode purposefully into the office.

He gave Iblis a respectful bow. "You summoned me, my lord?"

"I have a new Task for you Darius. A Harbinger has recently Emerged on Earth; one who's ability could serve me well. I want you to acquaint yourself with her in a manner that will show her the value of my Doctrines. Feel free to use whatever means necessary to sway her to our cause, but under no circumstances are you to manipulate her sensibilities."

The Desomor's thick eyebrows arched upward. "You want her conversion to be of her own free will?"

"It's imperative that it is," Iblis stressed. "I've a feeling that this woman will eventually hold a significant amount of influence within Mortalia's spiritual infrastructure. If I can garner her honest support, I may be able to erase the wretched stigmatism currently associated with my existence."

An excited gleam lit Darius' brown eyes. "I understand; and the Harbinger's name?"

Silas made a gesture with his hand, and Nina's image materialized in the air before them. "Nina Delcielo."

Darius studied the image closely. "Do we have any specifics on the type of woman she is?"

"Extremely intelligent and very dedicated to her philanthropic pursuits, most of which centers around helping underprivileged children," Silas replied.

A pleased smile lit the Desomor's handsome features. "That's definitely something I'll be able to use to our advantage. Are there any other pertinent details I should know about?"

A look of displeasure appeared on the Morphling's face. "The Celemor Gabriel has been dispatched as her guardian."

The Desomor's smile deepened. "Ah, the ever-reliable Gabriel; his presence will make this assignment all the more interesting."

Iblis's eyes narrowed slightly. "I trust interesting will not become distracting."

"You have nothing to fear on that account," Darius confidently assured his master. "Unlike Mayhem, I harbor no attraction for Omen's pet guardian."

Iblis studied the Desomor for a moment, and a slight smile curved his lips. "Good. See that it stays that way."

"Of course, my lord." Darius inclined his head respectfully toward his master, gave the Morphling a parting nod then quietly exited.

*

Darius carefully wove his way through the mist-shrouded region of Sublimia known as the Wastelands, wondering as always why the Almighty would craft such a dismal abyss considering the glorious splendor he poured into the other Realms. But then little of God's logic made sense to the Desomor, particularly the callous indifference he often showed the inhabitants of Mortalia.

Memories of his mother's final agonizing days as the cancer finished ravishing what was left of her frail body flitted through Darius's mind, rekindling the Desomor's bitterness for the Almighty's so-called mercy.

Darius did not blame God for his mother's illness. Such were the banes of being Mortal, but a woman as devout in her Christian faith as she was should not have been made to suffer as she had.

"Benevolent and loving god, indeed," he spat.

"Your tone bears the sting of anger, Darius," a raspy voice sounded in the Desomor's ear, pulling his attention sharply away from his reflections. "What troubles you this day?"

"Just a few...Divine reflections, Shift," Darius responded to the Morphling materializing in the murky air before him. "Nothing you need concern yourself with.

The Morphling's form solidified into that of a comely female. "Concerning myself with your needs is a habit I find most enjoyable, my love, that one in particular." She looked suggestively at his groin.

Darius took hold of Shift's hand and drew her close so he could place a kiss against her soft lips. "You, my shape-changing nymph, are deliciously wicked. But I have another use for that delightfully formless body of yours; one that involves the swaying of a recently Emerged Harbinger to my master's side."

"Sounds interesting," Shift purred, letting her hands follow the trail blazed by her eyes. "And just what might this new Task be?"

Darius groaned, his body responding to the Morphling's skillful touch. "I'll tell you after you've tended my...'needs'!"

Chapter 18

The fire burned with a white-hot intensity, searing Nina's eyes as she desperately tried to claw her way through the wreckage. If she could just make it to the theatre's flaming entryway, she knew she would be safe.

All around her the screams and whimpers of several other patrons assailed her ears but there was nothing she could do. The wall of fire was coming closer. Already she could feel its deadly touch as flecks of charred debris began raining down from the massive screen in front of her. If she could just make it to that door...!

The screech of tearing metal sounded loudly over the roar of the flames. She risked a glance upward and her eyes widened with horror. A massive speaker tore free of its heat-damaged clamps and crashed down in front of her, blocking her escape.

"No," she screamed as the flames licked at her skin. "NO!"

"Easy, Nina," a soothing voice penetrated the haze of smoke and confusion. "You're safe."

"Safe?" Nina blinked several times, her head swiveling around while she tried to discern her surroundings. "Gabriel," she cried in relief when she realized that it was him sitting beside her on the bed.

"In the flesh," he whispered. He took gentle hold of her trembling hand. "Was it another vision?"

"It was more like a nightmare." She moved his hand to the back of her neck.

The Celemor took the hint and began a gentle massage, infusing his touch with a small amount of the Celestial energy coursing through his body.

Nina reveled in the unusual sensation. "That feels *wonderful*. Is this something you learned in Celemor School?"

Gabriel smiled. "More or less." He readjusted his position on the bed so he could bring his other hand to bear on her knotted muscles. "Tell me about your nightmare."

Nina stared at the Canadian skyline visible through her bedroom window. When she finally spoke, her tone was subdued. "I was at the IMAX Theater, the one at the Henry Ford Museum I think, and the place was packed..." Her voice faltered as the image of burning bodies loomed before her. Gabriel gave her shoulders a reassuring squeeze, and she continued. "From what I could tell, something exploded behind the screen catching the front seats on fire. After that everything seemed to be burning."

"Sounds pretty intense. Perhaps you should put in a call to that Thomlin fellow; tell him to pass the word on to the theater so they can check their equipment."

A touch of reluctance stirred in Nina's chest. "I don't know, Gabe. Maybe this really *was* just a bad dream."

"No, it was definitely a premonition."

She turned to him with questioning eyes. "How do you know that?"

He removed his hands from her shoulders and nodded toward her dresser's mirror on the opposite wall. "Take a look for yourself."

Nina turned her head and stiffened. A yellow aura was emanating from her body. "I'm...glowing!"

"It's the after-effects of the Celestial energy you expended during your vision," the Celemor explained.

Nina brought her hands and arms to her face for a closer examination. "But I've been having these crazy scenes for close to four months, now. I've never turned into a light bulb before."

"Actually, you have."

Nina blinked in surprise. "When?"

"The day Quinlan and Sanders first came to see you at the Center. You had a vision about one of the construction workers."

"Mike's saw blade," she muttered. She gave him an odd look. "You were there?"

"I was watching you from the rafters. The moment the vision hit, your body was wreathed in Celestial light."

Nina gave a slight shudder. "How come nobody said anything?"

"The effect is only visible to beings with Celestially enhanced vision."

"Then how come *I'm* able to see it?"

Gabriel gave her a knowing look. "You're a Harbinger."

An excited gleam appeared in Nina's eyes. "Does this mean I'll be able to do all sorts of cool, superman stuff too?"

"It's difficult to say. The Emergence process is different for each individual subjected to it. Like the Harbingers and Prophets before you, I'm afraid you're just going to have to wait and see."

Nina shot him a trenchant look. "You're not the most reassuring kid on the block, are you?"

Gabriel smiled. "Gradually discovering your abilities is part of the process."

Nina gave him a final scowl then turned once again to her iridescent reflection. "So...what do I do now?"

Gabriel gave her hands a brief squeeze. "Figuring that out for your-self is also part of this process. But in this case, I think the answer is clear." He nodded toward the cordless phone resting in its cradle on her nightstand then vanished.

"A lot of help you are," Nina muttered. She gave her reflection a final glance then snatched up the phone. Heaving a heavy sigh, she began punching in the number that had become all too familiar over the past several weeks.

*

Officer Jake Thomlin stared impassively out the window of his minuscule office on the third floor of Detroit's central Police Station located at Six Hundred Beaubien. The office's corner position afforded him a decent view of the city's bustling downtown, a distraction that kept him from going mad with boredom.

A car accident during the high-speed chase of a suspect had left Thomlin partially disabled. Too young to retire yet unfit for active patrol, the displaced officer had been reassigned to the Department's fledgling Psychic Unit or PU, an acronym which had earned the group the less than glorious nickname: The Stink Squad.

Thomlin had been less than thrilled with his new assignment, but thankful there was still a place in the Department for someone in his position.

One of the numerous phones situated on his desk began to ring, and Thomlin swiveled his chair around to answer it. "Psychic Unit; Officer Thomlin here," he spoke into the handset. "How may I help you?"

"Hello Officer."

Thomlin stiffened in his seat.

Most of the calls he fielded from the numerous weirdos claiming to have had this or that vision were never substantiated, but occasionally a legitimate tip came through. One such case was the caller currently on the line. Over the past two months, information from the mysterious woman who called herself Del had led to the prevention of several heinous crimes, including a recent assassination attempt against Detroit's scandal-ridden Mayor.

"'Morning Del; you got something for me?"

"Possibly; I saw an explosion at the Henry Ford Imax due to a malfunction with the equipment behind the main screen."

Thomlin's hand tightened on the receiver. "Any idea when?"

"Definitely today; and judging by the number of people trapped in the theater I'd say it was during one of the evening shows. I hope that's enough for you. Goodbye Officer Thomlin."

"Del, wait," Thomlin called out.

"Yes?"

"The mayor called yesterday."

"And..." Del prompted after a brief pause.

"He wanted me to convey his thanks to you the next time you made contact. Swat found the bomb. It was attached to the port side motor of his yacht just like you saw it. From what I hear it was a real amateur setup. The folks in forensic were able to trace it back to the source."

"Let me guess. That nutcase from Flint he's dating?"

"*Was* dating," Thomlin replied with a nasty laugh. "Apparently home girl didn't appreciate being dumped by our illustrious leader and decided to exact a little vengeance. From what the shrinks told me; she got the idea to blow him up from a movie and found a make-it-yourself bomb site on the web. It's scary what a person can Google these days."

"Yes, it is," Del agreed with a soft chuckle. "I'm just glad everything turned out for the best. Maybe this little incident will teach His Honor to choose his mates more carefully."

"I doubt it. The man's a decent politician, but his taste in women leaves a lot to be desired."

Del chuckled again. "Well maybe someday he'll meet the right one."

"Yeah maybe; and speaking of meeting, why don't you come down to the station yourself. A lot of the higher ups feel you deserve some serious recognition. Your visions have saved quite a few lives."

Several seconds passed before Del responded. "I appreciate the offer, but I think it best if I remain anonymous. Too much recognition tends to have a negative impact. Have a good day Officer Thomlin. Hopefully you won't be hearing from me for a while."

The line went dead and Thomlin gently placed the receiver back into its cradle. "Yeah," he whispered as he pulled up the number for the IMAX on his computer's directory. "Hopefully."

*

Nina stared hard at the phone, replaying the conversation with Thomlin over in her mind. She was actually being credited with saving the mayor's life. How wild was that? Maybe she should take Thomlin up on his offer of a little public appreciation.

Several vivid fantasies flashed before her eyes: The Mayor giving her the key to the city; subsequent interviews on The Talk and The View. Hell, it could happen. Plus, the notoriety could generate a whirlwind of support that would really benefit the Center.

Or destroy it, she reasoned as reality settled back in. Yeah, a few big wigs were singing her praises now. Who's to say she wouldn't be labeled as some kind of freak, or phony. Such negative publicity would ruin her reputation in the philanthropic circles, not to mention the community at large.

No, it was best to maintain her distance, and content herself with the knowledge that her peculiar talents had brought about some positive changes in the world.

"Now that you know what you are, you may discover the reason for your Emergence," Gabriel's words echoed through her mind. For the first time she began to take heart in her newfound position as a Harbinger. Maybe God hadn't dealt her such a bad hand after all.

She also recognized that her feelings for her stalwart guardian had begun to change. Over the weeks her initial attraction to him had grown into a genuine interest. There was something oddly compelling about his brooding nature, and for the life of her she couldn't figure out what it was.

But then maybe that was it.

The majority of the men she encountered, both professionally and privately, generally fell into two categories: arrogant wannabe world-conquerors or needy immature jerks. Gabriel's calm, almost stoic demeanor was a refreshing change; particularly in someone so young. Nina had never asked him his age but judging by his appearance she assumed him to be right around her own thirty-three, give or take a year or two. Maybe he had what Maria termed an "old soul".

Whatever it was she liked it. She had also come to enjoy the numerous chats the two of them shared throughout each passing day, and the emotional rapport slowly developing between them.

Gabriel had easily identified Nina's resentment toward Miguel Delcielo, the father that had abandoned her, as the motivating force behind her philanthropic pursuits. Several in-depth discussions on the subject with the Celemor had purged Nina of most of her anger but had done little to alleviate her regret at having never met him.

The Celemor's compassion *had* helped Nina come to terms with the lingering grief from her mother's sudden passing, allowing her a welcome sense of closure. He had even taken to accompanying the Harbinger on the bi-monthly visits she made to her mother's grave, a gesture that only served to further endear him to her.

Nina was less than pleased with the limited amount of information she'd managed to pry from him. She knew that he once had a wife and daughter, and that both were now deceased, but not the circumstances surrounding their deaths. Nor had he been forthcoming with any details concerning his life prior to becoming a Celemor. At times, his reluctance to confide in her was frustrating, but Nina never pushed him to share more than he was willing to.

Building a good relationship took time, and she had already decided that forging one with her solemn guardian was worth the effort.

Occasionally the circumstances of their situation would impinge upon her sensibilities. When that happened, she would content herself the knowledge that her bizarre twist of fate was indeed allowing her to positively affect the lives of others. In the greater scheme of things, that's what truly mattered.

The excitement generated from her new perspective stayed with her throughout the day as she carried out her normal routine of meetings, meetings, and more meetings. It wasn't until later that evening, as she sat at the desk in her office which overlooked the Center's gymnasium that things took a turn for the worse.

Several youths were engaged in a game of basketball, the noise from their efforts echoing through the gym's walls to her office providing a spirited backdrop as Nina worked diligently trying to balance the Center's budget. For the most part, everything seemed in order, but after a solid hour of number crunching, the beleaguered woman decided to take a break. She rose from her chair to give her stiff muscles a much-needed stretch, and a wall of fire engulfed her.

Nina cringed as the sounds of terrified people thundered in her ears. All around her, bodies lay burned and mangled, some of them partially buried under the chunks of molten plastic raining down from the smoldering ceiling...trapping her...killing her...!

"Easy, Nina," Gabriel's calm voice penetrated the flaming chaos, pulling her mind sharply away from the horrid scene. "It's just another vision."

"Gabriel!" She fell gratefully into his iron embrace. The afterimage of the apocalyptic sight remained in her eyes for another few seconds then vanished with the same abruptness that it had come.

Nina sighed in relief then stiffened as the vision's significance became apparent. "Oh my, God," she cried, raising horrified eyes to his face. "That was the Imax again. But...I don't understand." She gave the phone a puzzled look. "I called the police..."

"And the Officer you spoke with forwarded the warning to the theater's management. I told you I've been keeping tabs on that," he responded to the questioning look she aimed at him.

"Well, what happened? Didn't they believe him?"

A look of regret flitted across the Celemor's face. "I'm afraid not. The manager on duty at the Theater told the officer that their equipment was serviced regularly, and he wasn't about to 'suffer the outlandish claims of some crackpot fortune-teller.'"

A wave of nausea swept through Nina. "Then...what I saw just now..."

"Was the vision coming to fruition," he somberly informed her.

Nina pressed her head harder against his muscular chest, sudden tears welling up in her eyes. "No. All those people...I failed them."

"What happened wasn't your fault," Gabriel said, trying to forestall the tide of grief and self-loathing he sensed rising within her. "You did everything you could."

"Apparently not enough," she choked out with a sob.

The Celemor brushed gentle fingers across her tear-streaked face. "Some tragedies aren't meant to be prevented."

Nina sniffed. "Not by me, anyway." Her voice was laced with bitterness. "I'll bet if you had of been there, things would've turned out different."

"I was there," he quietly told her.

Nina turned startled eyes on him. "Then why didn't you stop it?"

Gabriel calmly brought his gaze down to meet hers. "It wasn't part of my Task."

A surprised jolt shot through Nina's body. Clearly, she hadn't heard him right. "What did you just say?"

"Saving the people in that theater was not part of my Task."

This time there was no mistaking his callous response.

Nina abruptly pushed herself away from him, her body trembling with anger. "What the hell kind of answer is that? What type of heartless monster are you that you can let so many people die?"

Gabriel's voice hardened. "I can assure you I'm neither heartless nor a monster."

"Then just what the hell *are* you, Gabriel Leyr," the infuriated Harbinger bit out, glaring at him through smoldering eyes.

Gabriel met her censure with an icy reserve. "I'm a Celemor, and as such am not permitted to interfere with the natural course of Mortal history."

Nina's widened in amazement. "You consider letting a bunch of people get roasted natural?"

"In this case, yes." He winced from the sting of the hard slap she dealt his face.

"That's bullshit!" She slapped him again for good measure. "You're practically a damned superhero. You're telling me that you're not supposed to use that power to save lives?"

"Not when it doesn't pertain to my assigned Task," he ground out through tightly clenched teeth. "The rules set down by the Archangels are *very* specific on that topic."

"Hell, break the damn rules!"

A humorless smiled tugged at his lips. "There are some things you just don't do."

"And just why the hell not?"

Gabriel stared hard at her for several seconds. "For me, the cost of disobedience would be high; *very* high."

Nina sensed the emotional maelstrom barely contained beneath his calm facade, but it did nothing to abate her anger. "And you think that cost outweighs the lives of innocent people?"

Gabriel's eyes blazed with Celestial energy. "In the first place, there are no 'innocent people' in the world. The sooner you understand that the better off you'll be."

Nina was stunned by his palpable hostility.

"And as far as the cost is concerned," Gabriel continued, his voice calmer, the glow fading from his eyes. "It was."

A toxic silence permeated the office as Celemor, and Harbinger regarded one another across the resentful void that now lay between them.

Several minutes passed then Nina released a tired sigh. She dropped wearily into her chair. "You know, for a while I thought I was finally getting a handle on things; really starting to understand my purpose in all of this craziness." Their eyes met briefly, but the contact was broken when she abruptly turned her chair away from him.

She let her gaze fall on the youths still playing on the court, completely oblivious to the harsh realities being revealed around them. "Now I don't know what to believe."

"Welcome to my world," Gabriel grunted then vanished in a flash of light; leaving the disillusioned Harbinger alone with her troubled thoughts.

Chapter 19

Hovering silently before the Window, Omen observed the discord between the Harbinger and Celemor with a growing sense of apprehension.

Many were the discussions he had shared with Gabriel in which the Celemor voiced his steadfast disagreement with the limitations put on his actions. The Overseer knew that the incident at the theater would only serve to deepen Gabriel's growing resentment for his Celestial post.

"You're turning into Michael, my friend," a silvery voice rang out as the Overseer Intuition strode gracefully into the room, her thick plait of red hair billowing in the slight breeze created by her passage. "What fascinating events within the Realms have garnered your attention this day?"

"Nothing of any great significance," Omen replied, touching his slender hand gently against hers in the traditional Celestial Greeting of Equals. "I was merely observing the progress of our fledgling Harbinger."

Intuition's eyes flicked briefly to the shimmering image in the Window. "It looks to me as if you're more concerned with her guardian."

"He has been charged with the Harbinger's safety," Omen replied stiffly. "It is a matter of prudence to maintain a vigil over them both."

"Prudence can also be served by maintaining your objectivity."

Omen's eyes flared briefly. "Meaning what?"

Intuition leveled a stern look on her fellow Overseer. "Gabriel Leyr holds a place of unusual importance within your heart. Such affection can have disastrous consequences if you allow it to compromise your judgment."

"Distancing ourselves from the Celemors can be equally damaging. Or have you forgotten the circumstances that led to Caleb's current condition."

"Caleb's situation was entirely different," Intuition fired back, her gray eyes flashing. "That Mortal was unstable even before he was subjected to Iblis's bilge. No telling what state that hapless fool's mind was in by the time Michael recruited him."

"My point exactly," Omen cried. "Caleb agreed to leave Hell's ranks and take on the mantle of Celemor out of some skewered sense of betrayal he felt he had suffered at Iblis's hand. If we Overseers had maintained a more proactive rapport with him, his development of similar feelings toward the Archangels, and subsequent rejection of the Divine Tenets, might have been avoided."

The chamber was silent as Intuition considered Omen's position. "Perhaps; I still say Caleb's and Gabriel's situations are entirely different."

"And in my opinion Gabriel's is far more volatile," Omen countered. "You forget; Caleb willingly accepted the Archangel's invitation. Gabriel was coerced."

A distasteful frown appeared on Intuition's face. "That Mortal was not coerced."

"Oh, come on, Intuition," Omen snapped, his hovering form trembling with aggravation. "You know just as well as I that the Bringer of Death's use of the Mortal's wife as a bargaining chip was totally unscrupulous."

Intuition regarded him through haughty eyes. "Such Mortal concepts do not hold sway for Members of the Watch. We are not their companions, Omen. We are their shepherds, honor bound to herd them in the manner the Almighty sees fit in order to preserve the Balance." Her eyes bored into the dark recess of his hood. "And that means using whatever measures necessary to do so."

"That still doesn't' make it right," Omen muttered, turning once again to the Window.

"Take caution old friend; your rhetoric mirrors that of Iblis."

Omen's eyes flared briefly. "And is that really such a bad thing?"

Intuition studied his back for a moment. "It can be," she warned as she made her way back to the chamber's archway. "Hopefully you will remember that before it is too late. Losing your companionship would grieve me deeply."

Omen cocked his head in her direction. "I thought such Mortal notions did not apply to Celestials."

Intuition's full lips parted in a devious smile. "There are, of course, exceptions to *every* rule," she drawled then left.

Omen studied the empty archway, his eyes flaring again when he realized the subtle message she had just conveyed.

"Thank you for understanding," he whispered.

A gentle, *you're quite welcome,* echoed promptly through his mind.

*

Standing before a similar "Window" situated somewhere within the hazy Realm of Sublimia, a concerned Dichotomy also took note of the sudden tension between the Celemor and the Harbinger.

The blended being knew the reason behind Gabriel's steadfast obedience to the Divine Tenets that governed all Tasks, yet something needed to be done to prevent Nina's current disillusion from festering into full-blown resentment. *If it hasn't already,* the Celestial thought grimly.

Convergence

Chapter 20

Gabriel's gaze swept across the large crowd moving through the open expanse of Detroit's famed Heart Plaza. His Celestially masked position atop the large, circular fountain located in the Plaza's center gave him a perfect view of the numerous festivities taking place in both, the main courtyard and lower-level retail center.

Today was the start of River Days, Detroit's annual summer-opening festival. The two-mile stretch of the waterfront known as the River Walk was lined with kiosks as numerous vendors presented their various wares to the throngs of people taking advantage of the carnival-themed event.

Though cognizant of the activities going on around him, the Celemor's main focus was on the large group of teens and pre-teens moving in a loose cluster throughout the gaming area. With the help of the city's Neighborhood Services Department, Nina had arranged a fieldtrip for the Center's ever-expanding clients, and the kids were having a ball.

Over the past few months, the Center had become a beacon of neighborhood reform throughout Detroit's lower east side, garnering the support of local merchants and private sectors alike. In fact, so great was the Center's popularity, plans for opening another branch in Detroit's lower-income Brightmoore district were already underway.

For Nina, the Center's success was a tremendous personal achievement and an affirmation of her belief in Detroit's potential to become one of the country's leading cities. Her new stature in the philanthropic community had also helped her attain additional State funding, allowing her to hire a full-time administration staff in addition to the several education specialists the Center now employed.

Freed of the arduous task of running the Center's day-to-day finances, she was able to concentrate more on improving the overall curriculum. Nina's selfless dedication to the community had also caught the eye of the media, and the subsequent interviews and feature stories had turned her into quite the local celebrity.

The added attention occasionally made Gabriel's Task a bit more tedious than he would have liked, but overall things were running very smoothly. He just wished the same could be said about their relationship, still somewhat strained after the IMAX incident.

"You seemed troubled Gabriel," Dichotomy's deep voice sounded as the Celestial materialized atop the fountain beside the Celemor. "Is there anything we can do?"

"Yeah, you can tell me how to get my point across to my charge," Gabriel grunted, his eyes focused on Nina moving amongst her group, taking pictures for the Center's weekly newsletter. "That woman's frenetic hold on her moralistic beliefs leaves a lot to be desired."

Dichotomy's left eyebrow arched upward. "And why is that, because she doesn't subscribe to a Celestial's casual acceptance of mass slaughter for the perceived Greater Good? Perhaps instead of criticizing her beliefs you should immolate them."

Gabriel turned startled eyes to the Celestial. "Are you saying I should've violated my restrictions and saved those people?"

"What we're *saying* is that we can relate to the Harbinger's sentiments on this matter. Most Celestials have become so immured in their Divine indifference that they've all but lost sight of their moral responsibility."

"Don't aim your righteous arrows at me," Gabriel angrily fired back. "I'm always conscious of the moral implications of my actions as well as the consequences of my inactions."

"Yet you chose to stand by and let those people burn."

"I had no choice! You know what will happen if I go against the Archangel's on this."

Dichotomy's expression softened. The Celestial laid a comforting hand atop the Celemor's trembling shoulder. "Indeed, we do, but before you fall too far into the abyss of self-sacrifice, ask yourself this: Considering the situation at the theatre, and your proximity at the time, would it really have been a violation to save those patrons?"

A look of uncertainty flickered across the Celemor's face, and a sigh escaped Dichotomy's lips. "It's obvious by your silence that such a consideration never crossed your mind."

"No, it didn't," the Celemor confessed, his pensive expression turning into one of regret.

"Believe us when we say that we understand your reasons for remaining obedient to the Archangels, Gabriel, yet we can't help but wonder: Had yours and Clarissa's positions been reversed, would she have succumbed so easily to the lure of Divine complacency?"

"I honestly never gave it much thought," Gabriel admitted in a quiet voice.

Dichotomy studied the Celemor's face for a moment then gave his shoulder another squeeze. "Perhaps you should," he said, his body starting to fade. "The answer to that question might give you the insight you need to deal with our burgeoning Harbinger."

The Celestial's words echoed through Gabriel's mind for a long time. Dichotomy's perspective was often skewered, but in this instance the blended being was right. Clarissa would've never let the threat of Divine reprisals keep her from doing what she knew was right. The ability to follow her convictions had been one of his wife's greatest attributes. In that respect, he had to admit she and Nina were a lot alike.

Gabriel returned his attention to the plaza only to find Nina staring up at him.

Their eyes locked and the barest hint of a smile appeared on the Harbinger's face; the first one she had given him in the month sense the IMAX incident.

Nina's attention was drawn away by the smartly dressed, man and woman approaching the group.

Gabriel also focused on the peculiar pair as they exchanged pleasantries with Nina, particularly the male. The stranger's angular features seemed vaguely familiar, yet the Celemor couldn't place him.

Their conversation with Nina lasted for several minutes. Afterwards, the Harbinger shook each of their hands, and the couple left. Gabriel tracked their departure through the crowd and realized that he wasn't the only one interested in them.

Standing on the upper level of the Plaza, the positioning of the kiosks blocking them from Nina's view, were Quinlan and Sanders.

Gabriel was not surprised to see them. Over the past several weeks the Seekers had made frequent stops at the Center, reiterating to Nina their offer of *Presbyterii* aid. Despite her polite but steadfast refusal, the two continued to maintain a discreet presence. At the moment, their eyes were on Nina's mysterious visitors who were now headed toward the vendor area.

Gabriel watched as the Seekers exchanged, what appeared to be, terse words. After sparing Nina a brief glance, they made off in the couple's direction.

He toyed with the idea of joining the chase but decided against it. He would find out the identity of the mysterious duo soon enough. For now, he resumed his vigilance over Nina as the Center's group made their way toward the food-court.

*

"You do realize we're being followed," Shift said to Darius as she perused the selection of hats at one of the many kiosks lining the crowded marketplace.

"Of course," Darius responded, catching sight of the Seekers' positions through the large mirror hanging from the kiosks' metal frame. "I had a feeling the *Presbyterii* would be lurking about, though it wasn't *their* interest I expected to draw."

Shift also focused on the conspicuous duo as she tried on a garish pink cap. "No, it wasn't. But given the fact that it's *not* Gabriel behind us, I would have to say my Veil of Deception has sufficiently blocked his Celestial senses."

Darius smiled. "Apparently so. Let's consider this little test a success and get on with the business of recruiting this woman."

Shift's return smile faltered when she caught another glimpse of the Seekers, now standing two kiosks over. The bothersome oafs were feigning interest in the vendor's impressive collection of hand-crafted jewelry, but to the Morphling's acute senses, their surveillance efforts were pitifully obvious. "And what of our pursuers?"

A soft glow briefly eliminated the Desomor's eyes. "They obviously think there's something different about us; something...supernatural perhaps." He casually linked his arm through hers. "Let's not disappoint them."

Shift smiled in delighted anticipation of the mischief to come as she and the Desomor strode casually away from the market area.

*

"Looks like they're leaving," Sanders informed Quinlan who immediately handed the stone necklace he was studying back to the vendor. He gave the woman a polite nod then quickly fell into step with his partner.

"Tell me again why we're following this pair," he muttered as they discreetly tracked their quarry through the milling crowds.

"Call it a gut feeling, but something about those two just seems...off. Given the strange company our reluctant psychic tends to keep, I'm curious to know who they are and what their interest is with Miss Delcielo."

"Maybe it's not her they're interested in per-se," Quinlan suggested as they excused themselves around a slower moving group of elderly ladies. "That Center of hers has garnered quite a following in the metro area. Maybe those two were potential sponsors."

"Perhaps," Sanders allowed. "But I still want to get a closer look at them; just to quell my own suspicions." Quinlan gave his partner a skeptical look and Sanders released an exasperated sigh. "Just trust me on this," he said then took off after their departing quarry.

That's becoming increasingly difficult, Quinlan mused as he reluctantly followed, thinking of the drastic change Sanders' personality had undergone over the past several weeks.

The man's suspicion had increased to the point that he now looked upon *anyone* that came into contact with Nina as a possible, heavenly creature in disguise. Quinlan could understand the man's increased anxiety considering the battle the Seeker had witnessed on that fateful night after the Center's rally, but this borderline paranoia was becoming bothersome.

Especially went it sends us on wild goose chases through crowded fairs, the Seeker thought as he tried valiantly to keep up with his determined partner's rapid pace.

"Where the blazes are they going?" he heard Sanders growl just as he was beginning to wonder the same thing himself.

"Looks like they're headed toward the main stage," Quinlan noted as the couple darted around the massive, skirted platform that was set up in the tiered expanse directly in front of the Renaissance Center. "They just ducked in behind those bins." He directed Sanders's attention to the large storage pods lined in neat rows to the side of the stage. "I wonder what they're looking for in there."

"Let's go find out," Sanders urged, quickening his pace so as not to lose their subjects, Quinlan following suit.

The two Seekers rounded the first pod, coming face to face with their quarry calmly waiting for them in the clearing between the first and second pod.

"We do appreciate the exercise gentlemen, but I'm afraid this is as far as our little race goes," the man said in a pleasant voice. He gave his companion an affectionate look. "Say goodbye, love."

"Goodbye," the woman smiled, blowing the Seekers a playful kiss before disappearing with her partner in a flash of light.

Both men stared at the now empty space in silence for a moment then Sanders looked pointedly at Quinlan. "I trust this validates my concern?"

Quinlan made no comment.

Chapter 21

"First the joy, now the pain," Nina muttered while going over the itemized list of the Center's expenses from the day's field trip. The Center's accounting needs were now serviced by one of Detroit's prominent firms, but Nina still preferred to personally author the initial spreadsheets before turning them over to those she jokingly called, the suit-wearing-bean-counters.

A slight flutter impinged upon her awareness, and a wry smile tugged at her lips. As the weeks progressed so had Nina's adaptation to the Celestial energy coursing through her body. While she had yet to display any superhuman augmentation in terms of strength, her senses had taken on a keen sharpness. "I take it you're chat with the glowing two-some went well?" she asked, her eyes still focused on her laptop's humming screen as Gabriel materialized beside her.

"It was fairly productive," the Celemor acknowledged with mild surprise. "I see your eyesight's improving."

A look of annoyance flashed across Nina's face. "That and my hearing; I never realized how *loud* this city was."

Gabriel's nose and lips twisted with distaste. "Detroit is nothing compared to New York. That place is a twenty-four-hour circus."

"So, I've been told." Nina closed out the spreadsheet so she could give the Celemor her full attention. "How do you deal with it?"

"Eventually your body will adapt." Gabriel wasn't sure what to make of their casual discourse, but definitely preferred it over their recent terse exchanges. "Until then you'll just have to ride it out."

Nina issued a disgusted snort. "A lot of help you are." She rotated her head in a circle, trying to relieve stiff neck muscles. "And speaking of rides; how long will I have you as my seatbelt?"

"Until the Archangels say otherwise," the Celemor replied. "Why do you ask? Has my presence become overly intrusive?"

"Not at all," Nina quickly reassured him. "To tell you the truth, I *like* having you around; it makes the world feel a lot less...lonely, if you know what I mean."

A slight smile appeared on the Celemor's face. "As a matter of fact, I do."

He moved closer to her, raising a tentative hand. Nina obligingly shifted positions in her chair so that he could message her neck.

"Ah," she sighed at the soothing warmth flowing through her body. "Now this is one trick I'm looking forward to learning."

Gabriel chuckled at the look of unabashed pleasure on her face. He hoped that her surrender to his ministrations meant the rift between them was on the mend.

While Gabriel pondered the state of their relationship, Nina took a moment to reflect on the drastic turn her life had taken. *I've gone from dutiful philanthropist to glow-in-the-dark fortune-teller in eleven months.* She wondered if there was some type of holy standard by which to compare her progress.

"Who were the two fashion-plates that approached you in the plaza?"

Nina blinked at the Celemor's unexpected question. "The two, what?"

"The couple that came over and talked with you at the Plaza," Gabriel clarified working at a particularly tense spot in her left shoulder blade.

"Oh, them; they were from the Spiritway Foundation. They're interested in funding some of the Center's out-reach programs."

Gabriel arched a skeptical eyebrow. "And they chose to ask you about that at a crowded fair?"

"They tried the Center first. When the receptionist told them about our field-trip they decided to come on down and see us in action."

"Ah," Gabriel said. "And were they impressed?"

"They seemed to be. They've invited me to lunch down at the MGM Casino next week so we can further discuss it. From what I hear, the place has got an amazing food-court. Why don't you join us?"

Gabriel laughed. "As what, your personal secretary?"

"Or you can be my date."

The humor on the Celemor's face disappeared. "I'm not so sure that's a good idea."

Nina pulled away from his massaging fingers so she could face him. "Why not? I've been playing the dutiful Harbinger for almost a year, and you've been right there with me. An afternoon lunch at the MGM will do us both a world of good."

"Maybe," Gabriel reluctantly admitted. "I'm just surprised you want me along as your companion?"

"And why wouldn't I?"

Gabriel regarded her through speculative eyes. "I haven't exactly been at the top of your preferred-visitors list."

Nina dismissed this consideration with an airy wave. "That was last month. This month I've decided to acknowledge the fact that I've got a good-looking man in my life and take advantage of it."

Gabriel cocked a skeptical eyebrow. "Even though said man is a...'heartless monster?'"

His comment elicited a quick chuckle from the Harbinger, and she gave his chin a playful jab. "I think there may still be a spark of humanity left in you," she drawled. "And if so, I'd like to be the one to reignite it."

Gabriel squatted on his haunches in front of her. "So, this gesture is tied in with your philanthropic work?"

"That and the fact that I would *love* to see that chiseled bod of yours in a tailored suit," Nina gushed with girlish enthusiasm, to which Gabriel burst out laughing.

"And what brought about this sudden change of heart?"

Nina's lips curved into a devious smile. "You're not the only member of the Hierarchy the glowing two-some chat up."

Gabriel stiffened. "What do you mean? Did Dichotomy...?"

"Divulge all of your secrets?" she finished his statement. "No but the dynamic duo did stress the fact that the terms of your service left little room for deviation. Hey, that's the way they put it," Nina responded to his cynical look.

Gabriel was unsure what to make of Dichotomy's curious initiative on his behalf. "And based on this...disclosure, you've come to the conclusion that my actions at the IMAX were justified?"

Nina glared at him. "I wouldn't go *that* far. But it did make me realize that until I learn your reasons for serving, I have no right to judge you."

Gabriel gave her face a searching look. "I guess that's my cue to divulge more of my own secrets."

Nina placed a gentle hand against his cheek. "Not at all. That's just my way of telling you that, although I don't like what happened, I accept the fact that you had your reasons."

Gabriel placed his hand atop hers. "Thank you."

She favored him with a tender smile. "Don't mention it." Her expression turned mischievous. "However, if you still feel the need to let me into the closet where you hide all your skeletons, please do so."

Gabriel shook his head from side to side. "You truly are a unlike any one I've ever protected. But you've also made your point," he added, thinking of the countless details of her life that she had shared with him over the months. He took gentle hold of her hand still against his face and straightened up from his squatting position. "Will you come with me?"

Nina gave him a wary look then used the proffered limb to pull herself up. "And where are we going?"

A wry grin tugged at his lips. "The closet where I keep my skeletons."

A nimbus of bright light engulfed their bodies, whisking them through time and space away from the office. The unnatural mode of transportation made Nina a bit queasy, but they arrived at their destination before the effect became overwhelming.

The glow faded and she gaped in wonder at the breath-taking beauty of the desert landscape around them. "Where are we?"

"Arizona," Gabriel said, directing her attention to the sprawling ranch set against a mountainous backdrop. "Welcome to Clawson, Miss Delcielo."

Nina's eyes bulged outward at the ranch's main house and accompanying structures. "Is this your home?"

"Yes, it is," he said proudly.

Nina used her hand to shield herself from the sun's harsh glare as she gave the ranch the once over. "This is definitely not what I was expecting. You really are a man of mystery, Mister Leyr."

"So, I've been told. C'mon, let's get you out of this sun." He motioned for her to precede him up the winding stone pathway that led to the main house. "You can catch a nasty burn out here if you're not careful."

Nina started walking in the direction indicated; deeply enjoying the balmy weather that was a far cry from the chilly Detroit spring they had just come from. She took note of the potted plants ringing the path and stopped dead in her tracks. "Those are rose bushes," she exclaimed, turning incredulous eyes to him. "How the blazes did you manage that?"

A mischievous glint appeared in Gabriel's eyes. "Celestial energy has its benefits."

"Obviously." Nina wondered if her guardian realized the curious irony the potted roses represented. The Archangels didn't mind their agents using their powers for the creation of a whimsical desert garden yet forbade its use for saving innocent people in a burning theatre.

They continued on to the porch, and Nina quickly ascended the cedar-plank steps, grateful for the shade provided by the porch's ceramic tiled canopy.

"Thank you, sir," she acknowledged as he held the front door open so she could enter. "Oh, my," she uttered at the elegantly furnished parlor that greeted her. "This is lovely!"

She let her gaze drift around the room, marveling at the oversized sofa and chairs. The rich, caramel color of the leather cushions provided a stylish contrast to the dark mahogany wood used in the furniture's construction. Muted light from the numerous brass sconces lining the walls gave the entire room a cozy yet rustic feel.

"This place makes my apartment look shabby." Nina ran her hand along the intricately carved arms of one of the chairs sat in a loose semi-circle in front of a large, stone hearth. "The patterns on these chairs are amazing. Wherever did you find them?"

"I made them."

Gabriel's admission drew a surprised look from Nina. "*You* made all these pieces?"

"It's what I do to pass the time between Tasks. That and tend the rose bushes," he added with a wink.

"You must have a lot of time between Tasks," Nina muttered as she continued her inspection of the parlor's contents.

She took particular interest of the large painting hanging on the wall above the hearth. In it, a beautiful woman, dressed in what appeared to be some form of Native-American ceremonial garb was sitting pristinely on a fallen log amidst a lovely forest background.

Perched on the woman's lap, also dressed in ceremonial clothing, was a young girl. She looked to be about three or four years old, and though her skin was noticeably darker, she bore a striking resemblance to the woman; and to Gabriel, Nina noted upon studying the girl's eyes.

"Is that your family?"

A pained expression crossed Gabriel's face. "That's my wife, Clarissa, and our daughter Gabriella."

"They're both beautiful."

"Yes, they were."

Nina studied Clarissa's image a little closer. Though dressed in the proper attire, her tanned skin bore few traces of the physical characteristics associated with America's first inhabitants. "Was your wife a true Native-American?"

Gabriel gave a negative shake of his head. "Clarissa's mother was a member of the Sioux Nation and raised her in accordance with their traditions. Clarissa's father was reportedly a Caucasian, but she had no memory of him."

Nina favored Clarissa's image with a compassionate smile. "It sounds like she and I were kindred spirits. How did the two of you meet?"

Some of the angst lifted from Gabriel's expression. "During a family vacation to the Grand Canyon; the Leyrs hired her as one of our native guides."

Nina gave him an odd look. "Aren't you a Leyr?"

Gabriel hesitated. He always knew the time would come for him to reveal his troubled past. He had wanted to confide in her during their heated discussion over his actions at the IMAX, but uncertainty as to how she would react had stayed his voice. Their current situation was in no way the emotional maelstrom that day had been, yet he was still concerned as to how she would react to what he was about to tell her.

So far Nina had masterfully adapted to the bizarre twists her life had taken, but the human psyche could only endure so many shocks. Hopefully the story he was about to relate wouldn't push hers over the edge.

Steadying his resolve, he took a deep breath, and answered her question. "The Leyrs are my adopted parents. My birth parents were killed during an excavation in the Valley of the Kings when I was two. They were exploring a newly opened tomb when the internal structure collapsed."

Nina's hand tightened briefly on his forearm. "Oh, Gabriel, I'm so sorry."

Gabriel frowned. "It's okay. I was so young when it happened that I really don't remember them."

Nina favored him with a tender look. "I could see how that could happen. Were your birth-parents archaeologists?"

"My father was. My mother was a preservationist at the Cairo Museum."

Nina blinked. "Cairo...in Egypt?"

Gabriel studied her expression closely. "That's where I was born."

Nina blinked again. "That's amazing. I've always been fascinated by Egyptian culture. How did you end up with the Leyrs?"

"Nathaniel Leyr and my father met during an earlier excavation and remained close friends thereafter. When he learned of my parents' death, he and his wife, Catherine, came to the Cairo orphanage where I had been placed, and adopted me."

"You had no other family in Egypt?"

Gabriel's voice turned bitter. "None that wanted me; my father was Egyptian, but my mother was British. Their respective families wouldn't accept their marriage, let alone me."

Nina shook her head from side to side. "I will never understand the ignorance of racism."

Gabriel released an indifferent snort. "The world is what it is."

Nina jumped on his statement, her hazel eyes flashing with anger. "That's why folks like us have to put in the effort to change it!"

Gabriel gave her hand a soothing pat. "As I've heard you say on numerous occasions."

His teasing comment brought an embarrassed flush to Nina's face. "Sorry. It's easy for me to fall into lecture mode."

"Don't apologize. The world needs people like you who are willing to care for those that can't take care of themselves."

Nina smiled. "I guess that's something you and I have in common.

Gabriel's eyes flared briefly. "No. It's not."

Nina gave him a puzzled look. "What do you mean?"

Gabriel's eyes shifted back to his family's painting. "You do what you do because you *want* to. My cooperation was forced."

Nina lightly touched his face drawing his attention back to her. "Tell me. Please," she added when she sensed his hesitation.

"I'm afraid this is the part where the story gets...interesting."

A look of worry briefly touched Nina's face. "Interesting as in bad?"

The Celemor shrugged. "Interesting as in...*Interesting.*"

Nina searched his face for a moment then gave him a shrewd look. "I'm a heavenly Harbinger who consorts with glowing Celestial beings. I think I can handle it."

Gabriel hoped she was right. "Suit yourself," he said then continued his tale. "

"As I said earlier, I met Clarissa while in the States on vacation with the Leyrs. Nathaniel had always been fascinated by America's southwest region and decided that the time had finally come to satisfy his curiosity.

Clarissa and I became very close during our six-week expedition. When it finally came time for the Leyrs to return to England, I chose to stay behind in the hopes that she and I could one day have a future together. The elders of her tribe accepted me, and we were married two months later."

"It sounds like you made the right call. How did the Leyrs take you not returning home with them?"

Gabriel smiled at the memory of his adopted parents' reaction. "It was a mixed blessing. They were saddened by my decision to make a permanent home in America, but happy that I had found love."

A dreamy sigh escaped Nina's lips. "That's nice. I take it they approved of Clarissa as a mate for you?"

"Absolutely," Gabriel declared. "When I wrote to them about our plans to marry, they wired me a substantial dowry for us to get started in our new life. Clarissa and I used most of it to purchase this place." He waved his hands around the parlor. "Back in its heyday Clawson had been a popular resort. We had this grand idea to bring it back to its former glory." The Celemor gazed fondly at his wife's portrait. "I think she would've like what I've done with the place."

Nina nodded her head in stout agreement. "I think she would've been *very* pleased. Hell, I've only seen this one room and I'm blown away."

Gabriel grimaced at the compliment. "Thanks." He returned his gaze to his family's portrait.

Nina easily read the look of yearning on his face. She gently took hold of his hand. "How long have they been gone?"

Gabriel tensed. This was it. The moment he had been dreading. Hopefully his answer wouldn't push her away as it had done with the scant few he had shared his history with in the past.

Without taking his eyes from the portrait, he answered her question. "I lost them 111 years ago."

Nina stiffened, her eyes growing wide. "What?"

Gabriel sighed and brought his eyes down to meet hers. "My wife and daughter were killed in the Great Quake that destroyed most of San Francisco in 1906."

It took the Harbinger several seconds to digest this startling revelation, and several more to regain the use of her voice. "How is that possible?"

A humorless smile curved Gabriel's lips. "One of the by-products of being a Celemor; when you join the Hierarchy, you're in it for the long haul."

Nina's left eyebrow arched upward. "Are you saying your immortal?"

"I'm afraid so."

Again, Nina paused as she tried to wrap her mind around such an amazing concept. "Now *that's* deep," she finally uttered as she eased her body into the closest chair retreating gratefully into its oversized embrace. "So...when exactly were you born?"

"Eighteen-eighty-three; on August ninth, to be exact."

Nina did the math. "You're a hundred and thirty-eight years old?" He nodded, and Nina let out an appreciative whistle. "You must be doing something right because you don't look a day over one-thirty."

Gabriel released the breath he'd been unconsciously holding. Once again, his charge had proven her self-resilient to a disturbing revelation. Smiling at her quip, he sat down in the chair beside hers. "Why thank you ma'am. I'll take that as a compliment."

Nina noticed that the humor on his face didn't erase the sadness in his eyes. She leaned forward and laid a gentle hand atop his shoulder. "All jokes aside, Gabe, if this is something you'd rather not talk about I completely understand."

He covered her hand with his and brought it to his lips where he gave her knuckles a light kiss. "I appreciate your concern but no. You've come to mean a lot to me these past several months. I would rather there not be any more secrets between us."

A pleased smile appeared on Nina's face. "I'd like that, too."

"I'm just glad the revelation of my age didn't spook you."

Nina released an amused snort. "Like I said before; I'm a heavenly Harbinger who regularly consorts with glowing beings.

Finding out that you're a walking talking relic just isn't that big of a deal."

Her comment elicited another quick smile from the Celemor. "I suppose I should continue the story."

Nina gave his hand another squeeze. "Only if you're ready."

Gabriel met the compassion in her eyes, and some of the heaviness lifted from his heart. He took a deep breath, exhaled sharply then continued his tale.

"On our fourth wedding anniversary, Clarissa and I decided to take a family trip. She had never been away from her tribal lands and wanted to know what a big city was like. I chose San Francisco because I had visited there many times with the Leyrs."

A shadow fell over the Celemor's face, and his voice became robotic. "The morning of the quake, I woke before dawn. For some reason I couldn't fall back to sleep. I decided to go for a walk so I wouldn't wake Clarissa and Gaby. I'd gotten about two blocks away from the hotel when the tremors started." His words faltered, and Nina tightened her grip on his hand.

"When it was over half the city was in ruins, the other half on fire. I was pretty much unscathed, but the hotel..." He paused again, swallowing hard several times. "The hotel's ceiling had collapsed under the stress of the quake...while they were still in there..." A haunted look consumed his features. "Then the whole place caught fire."

Gabriel abruptly shut his eyes trying to block the horrid memory that a century of living had done nothing to erode. "I heard Gaby crying out for me, but I couldn't...I couldn't reach them...couldn't save them..."

Tears formed in Nina's eyes at the pain in his voice. Not knowing what else to do she drew him closer, hugging him as tight as she could. "I'm sorry Gabe," she whispered in his ear. "I'm so sorry."

"Thank you," he said, drawing comfort from their embrace. He remained in her arms until he regained his composure, at which point he sat up and resumed his tale. "Once the fire subsided, I was able to dig through the rubble. I recovered their remains and brought them back to Arizona. Clarissa's family performed their customary rituals and wanted to bury them in their sacred ground, but I had them laid to rest here at the ranch."

He gestured to his left, and Nina caught a glimpse of the stone memorial through one of the parlor's windows. "It was probably selfish of me to deprive Clarissa's family of their traditional rites, but I didn't want to have to share them with anyone else."

"I don't think it was selfish at all. I felt the same way when I lost my mother. I still get peeved when there are other people at the cemetery when I visit her grave. Present company excluded, of course," she said with a quick grin. "So how is it that you became a Celemor?"

Gabriel's face turned somber. "About a week after they were buried, the Archangel Gabriel appeared during one of my daily vigils at their grave."

Nina's eyebrows arched upward. "I'll bet that was a shocker."

"It was. An extreme one. He was quite a site, too; all bathed in light with these enormous wings sticking out of his back. I asked him if he was there to take my family to Heaven. He promptly told me 'No' then revealed the truth about The Creation...and the spiritual *requirements* for entering the afterlife."

"Which are?" Nina prompted when he said nothing else.

A weary sigh escaped Gabriel's lips. "Contrary to what they teach you in church, the Mortal soul is not some ethereal apparition contained within our bodies. It's a collection of Celestial particles assigned to a specific consciousness. These particles disperse upon our deaths unless the deceased has a foundation of faith in The Almighty hard wired into their subconscious mind. This allows the particles to maintain their cohesive structure during the transition to the afterlife. The process begins at the time of baptism and is reinforced through the practice of mono-deity, religious systems, such as Christianity, Judaism, or the Muslim faith."

"Weren't you and your family Christians?"

Gabriel's expression turned bleak. "The Leyrs indoctrinated me into the Lutheran faith when they first adopted me, and insisted that Gabrielle be baptized as well, but Clarissa was a Sioux Indian. Clarissa respected their wishes where our daughter was concerned out of gratitude for their support. But she didn't believe in the concept of a singular god, nor did she have any interest in becoming a Christian."

"Which meant there would be no afterlife for her," Nina said as the pieces fell into place. "You became a Celemor so they would grant her a pass into Heaven."

"It was more like an exchange of services."

Nina focused sharply on his face. "What do you mean?"

"I'm a direct descendant of Abraham, the original father of the Israelite nation, though don't ask me how considering that my father was Egyptian, and my mother British. Something in my blood connects me to Sublimia, allowing me to naturally draw forth and manipulate Celestial energy. It makes people like me a valuable commodity in the Hierarchy."

"So, people like you, with this...special blood, are kind of an elite strain of humanity," Nina surmised.

Gabriel shrugged. "Or a cursed one depending on how you look at it."

"Hey, don't knock it, mister," Nina snapped. "Whatever's floating around in your blood let you secure your wife's soul."

"Oh, I know. It's just that sometimes following the Hierarchy's Tenets can be a bit...difficult."

A look of compassion appeared on Nina's face. "Like what happened at the IMAX?"

Gabriel released a disgusted snort. "The IMAX was minor compared to some of the other atrocities I, and others like me, have been forced to endure. I could've kept the Towers from collapsing during the Nine-Eleven tragedy, saved hundreds of lives, yet was forbidden by the Archangels to act. And don't even get me started on the positive role I could've played during the Jewish Holocaust and the American Civil Rights movement. So much death," he ground out through clenched teeth. "So much...waste!"

The anguish in his voice pierced Nina's heart. She laid a gentle hand against his cheek. "I'm sorry for calling you a monster."

The Celemor heaved a massive sigh. "That's okay. Considering the circumstances your reaction was completely understandable."

Nina flashed him a shrewd look. "Magnanimous type, aren't you?"

Gabriel shrugged. "It comes with age, I guess."

Nina flashed him a teasing grin. "Yeah, you are getting up there, old timer."

Gabriel gave her a roguish look. "I'm still young enough to attract *your* attention."

Nina burst out laughing. "That's only because I felt sorry for your old carcass!"

"Well in that case I I'd better accept your invitation," Gabriel replied with feigned indignation. "I'd hate for all that pity to go to waste."

"If you're so inclined," Nina said in haughty voice. "But do me a favor and keep the Icy-Hot to a minimum. The smell of that stuff is wicked."

"I'll do my best, honey," Gabriel croaked, affecting the posture of an extremely old man.

His antics drew more laughter from Nina who leaned forward and gave his trembling lips a kiss.

She meant it as a teasing gesture, but neither Harbinger nor Celemor were prepared for the spark of energy that occurred the moment their lips made contact.

"Wow," Nina gasped. "That was different. What's the Celestial dictionary say about that?"

"That's a new one for me, too." Gabriel was baffled not only by the incident but by the sudden tingling in his groin during the brief moment of contact. Not wanting to draw Nina's attention to his confusion, he quickly dissembled. "Maybe it's a sign that you're a bad influence, and I should keep my distance."

"On no, you're not getting out of our date that easy," Nina exclaimed, completely oblivious to the subtle change in him. Still smiling, she grabbed him by the hand and pulled him up from the chair. "C'mon old man; I've got a staff meeting in a couple of hours, and I want to see the rest of this western paradise before we go."

"It would be my pleasure." He gestured for her to precede him, and Nina strolled eagerly from the parlor.

Gabriel moved to follow but paused at the doorway, his eyes locking briefly with those of Clarissa's image. He experienced a sudden stab of guilt but managed to suppress it as he rushed to catch up with Nina.

*

"Our fledgling Harbinger appears to be interacting well with her guardian," the Archangel Michael remarked to Omen as he made his way through the Chamber's vaulted entrance. He took up a position beside the Overseer at the Window.

"Indeed, she does," Omen replied after according the Keeper of Benevolence a respectful bow. He then turned back to his observation of the casual discourse being shared between Nina and Gabriel as they strolled about the ranch.

"I suppose the same can be said of the Celemor," Michael commented on the smile on Gabriel's face.

Omen had also noticed the Celemor's happy expression. "He does seem to have taken an uncharacteristic liking to Nina. In fact, this is the most content I've seen him since his entrapment into Celestial service."

Michael regarded the Overseer through disapproving eyes. "I have always been tolerant of your involvement with him, Omen. But in the future, I would advise you to exercise a bit more discretion when commenting on the Celemor's recruitment. To the wrong ears, your words might ring of sedition."

Omen knew full well whose ears Michael was referring to. "I meant no disrespect to you *or* the Bringer of Death. I was merely pointing out that Gabriel's service has been begrudging at best, due mostly to his initial...*indoctrination,*" Omen temporized at the look of warning the Archangel directed at him; "to the Hierarchy. Perhaps his interaction with the Harbinger is an indication that he has finally come to terms with his Celestial post."

Michael gave Gabriel's image a speculative look. "Perhaps," he drawled. "But it could also stem from the pleasure he seems to derive from her company; in which case it might be prudent for you to impart to him the importance of maintaining his objectivity. Particularly in this instance," he added when he noticed the curious flaring of Celestial energy that took place whenever the two mortals touched. "I would hate for him to become *too* attached to Nina."

Omen's hooded features swiveled in the Archangel's direction. "Considering Gabriel's tragic history," the Window shimmered as the Overseer used it to focus in on the small cairn marking Clarissa and Gabrielle's graves. "Would the formation of a deeper relationship between the two truly be such a negative thing?"

"The Celemor's history is the reason I brought it up," said Michael.

Omen's glowing eyes flared brighter with concern. "Why is that?"

A pained looked flitted across Michael's face. "The Almighty has yet to reveal Nina's eventual position in the Reclamation. I would hate it if her destined role proved...difficult for Gabriel to accept." Michael gave the image of the Celemor and Harbinger a final glance then strode quietly from the Chamber.

Omen sensed an unusual amount of anxiety in the Archangel and pondered its significance. Perhaps Gabriel wasn't the only Member of The Watch that would have a difficult time if Nina's fate turned out to be a dire one.

*

In a secluded anteroom at the rear of the main sanctuary of the Sistine Chapel, the state of Nina and Gabriel's relationship was the topic of another conversation.

"It's obvious through these photographs that Miss Delcielo has been totally dishonest with us from day one about her relationship with this Gabriel character," Dresden's stern voice rang out. He dropped a heavy manila envelope onto the small table before him. "In fact, judging from the majority of these shots Quinlan and Sanders have managed to capture, the two appear to be inseparable!"

Cardinal Tullis quietly retrieved the envelope, and deftly undid the metal clips. He carefully pulled out the stack of high-resolution photographs then spread them on the table for a closer inspection. "The periphery position depicted in every shot suggests he's taken on the role of bodyguard as opposed to a consort."

Dresden released an irritated snort. "I don't care what position he's assumed; the fact of the matter is that we *know* he's not of this earth."

"Yes, but that doesn't necessarily mean his intentions are evil," Tullis reasoned.

"If that's the case then why has the Delcielo woman repeatedly denied any association to him?"

"You forget Miss Delcielo's general mistrust of religious organizations," Tullis pointed out. "Which I'm also sure is the cause of her continued refusal of the *Presbyterii's* guidance that Quinlan and Sanders have repeatedly offered these past several months."

Dresden issued a disgusted snort. "Given the preponderance of supernatural entities in her life, I'm beginning to wonder if that truly is the case."

"I'm afraid I've had similar thoughts," Tullis confessed. "Although I have to admit, in spite of her religious antipathy, Miss Delcielo has become a driving force in the philanthropic world. Her tireless efforts lead me to believe in the sincerity of her heart."

Dresden eyed his fellow Elder through impatient eyes but refrained from refuting the other's altruistic conclusion. It would be a wasted effort. Tullis was a strong leader and a devout believer in the *Presbyterii's* sacred mission, but his eternal optimism could sometimes be quite pernicious.

Dresden knew that it wasn't because his esteemed colleague didn't recognize the inherent danger of the modern world. Tullis was fully cognizant of the ever-rising taint of the unrighteous, and the Church's inability to route it. Unfortunately, when it came to assigning blame, he was prone to giving a suspected infidel the benefit of the doubt; regardless of the evidence stacked against them.

Dresden did not share this trait. To him, Nina Delcielo's obvious disdain for religion clearly showed her for what she was: a powerful protagonist for the agnostic cause and a potential threat to proper Christian values, such as those laid down by the Catholic Church.

"As always I respect your opinion, old friend," Dresden said after Tullis had returned the photos to the envelope. "And I laud the mercy that often tempers your justice. I just pray that it has not blinded you to the reality of our current crises."

"It hasn't," Tullis quickly reassured his peer. "I'm just not ready to advance to the next Protocol. Despite her antipathy for religion, and her association with Celestial entities, Miss Delcielo has done nothing untoward to warrant disciplinary action from this body."

Dresden eyed Tullis through beetled brows. "And what happens if the faith you have in Miss Delcielo's moral character turns out to be misplaced?"

A look of apprehension crossed the Cardinal's face. "Then God help us all."

Chapter 22

"I still don't see what the problem is." Exasperation colored Nina's voice.

"The problem," Gabriel stressed, "is that it's not appropriate. A man and woman shouldn't live together unless they're married."

"Maybe that's how it was in *your* day, but this is the twenty first century. Folks now are a bit more liberal."

Gabriel released a disgusted snort. "That's one of the reasons the world is so screwed up." He turned away from her disapproving scowl and focused on the thunderstorm raging on the other side of the apartment's sliding glass doors.

Nina bit back her sarcastic response. The Celemor's pious position was beginning to grate on her nerves. All she had suggested was that he move into the apartment with her during his continued vigilance as opposed to hanging around outside perched on light posts and antennas, which to her made perfect sense. Unfortunately, Gabriel's ethics were still mired back in the eighteen hundreds.

Gritting her teeth, she placed herself between him and the door-wall. He tried to not meet her eyes, but she stood on her tiptoes, forcing him to look at her.

"Look Gabe; I'm not trying to ignore or trivialize your values, but this whole situation is ridiculous. It would be different if I weren't *aware* of your presence. Then I could understand you skulking about in the shadows, but let's face it; you and I have become pretty close these past few months, and I don't like to see people I care about in uncomfortable situations. Case in point." She pointed toward the heavy drops of rain pelting the door-wall and terrace.

Gabriel spared the downpour a brief glance then shrugged. "My Celestial aura protects me against inclement weather."

The Harbinger resisted the urge to slap the obstinate look off his face. "Then do it for me. So that *I'll* feel more comfortable."

Gabriel maintained his sullen position for a moment then his expression softened. "Very well," he said in a resigned tone. "But I'm *only* doing this for you. I was perfectly content where I was."

"Well thank you sir." Nina gave him a flourished bow. She turned her back to him and hunched her shoulders. "Now that that's settled, tell me what you thought of the Spirit Way Foundation."

Taking the hint, Gabriel began a gentle kneading of her neck and shoulders. "I respect their philanthropic mission, and I checked the organization's credentials. On paper everything appears legitimate."

"Then why do I hear suspicion in your voice?"

"It's your two new friends."

Nina's eyes arched upward. "I thought Darius and Sheila were pleasant enough."

Gabriel frowned. "Yes, they were, almost overly so."

"And that's a problem?"

"It could be. I'm not sure yet."

Nina thought about it for a moment then her lips curved into a smile. "Maybe you're feeling a bit nervous because Darius is a good-looking guy, and you're sensing a bit of competition."

Her teasing comment turned into a hiss for the slight but painful discharge of energy from the Celemor's fingertips.

"I'm sorry, Nina!" Gabriel immediately released another jolt of energy to soothe the affected area. "That was completely unintentional."

Nina shot him a wary look over her shoulder. "Are you sure?"

"Yes," he muttered continuing his massage. "I've been feeling a bit out of sync lately. I guess it's affecting my control."

"How long have you been this way?"

"Ever since..." he began to say then immediately clamped his mouth shut. "It's not important. I'm sure it'll pass."

Sensing an unusual amount of tension in his touch, Nina pulled away and faced him. "Ever since when?"

Gabriel refused to make eye contact. "I told you it's not important." He started to turn away, but the strong grip she placed on his forearm prevented him from doing so.

"Tell me." Her voice carried a note of steel, and a resigned sigh escaped Gabriel's lips.

"Ever since the day you...kissed me at the Ranch."

"Oh," Nina said in a quiet voice, releasing his arm. "Look Gabe, I'm sorry if..."

"On no, it's nothing like that," Gabriel hastily assured her. "It's just that," he paused for a moment, shifting uncomfortably on his feet. "You're the first woman I've kissed since Clarissa," he confessed, looking everywhere but at her. "And I know you only meant it as a joke," he continued briskly before she could respond. "But...I really liked it, and that's the problem."

Nina gave him an unscrupulous look. "And just why is that a problem?"

"Because now I can't help but wonder what it would be like to *really* kiss you."

He tried again to turn away, but Nina's hand on his wrist stopped him once more. She had to admit that her attraction to her stalwart guardian had grown considerably over the past few months, but she hadn't realized that he shared similar feelings. And if that were the case, his reluctance to move into the apartment made more sense.

Her lips curved into a sensuous smile as she drew him closer. "Again, I ask: why is that a problem?"

Gabriel looked totally flustered. "Because my Task is to *protect* you; not romance you."

Nina's voice grew husky. "Learn how to multi-task." Before he could respond she pressed her lips hungrily against his, the flash of energy brought about by their contact rivaling the thunderstorm's periodic lightning strikes.

At first the Celemor tried to pull away, but the Harbinger held on tightly, doubling her efforts. The feel of her lithe body pressing into his while her tongue continued its eager exploration of his mouth quickly drove all thoughts of resistance from his mind.

"So how was it?" Nina whispered when their lips finally parted.

Gabriel rubbed his nose against hers. "I'm not quite sure yet. I think we should do it again so I can draw a more accurate conclusion."

Nina smiled and locked her lips against his once more. Their combined passion created a wave of pure emotional energy that reverberated across the Celestial ether drawing the attention of several members of the Hierarchy, including a solemn Michael observing through the Window's shimmering dimensions.

"This situation is becoming dangerously precarious," the Archangel Gabriel's deep voice reverberated in Michael's ears as he stormed into the Chamber, having also felt the psychic backlash.

"Why is that?" Michael questioned, sparring his brother a curt nod.

A look of mild disgust appeared on The Bringer of Death's face as he observed the two Mortals. "An emotional attachment to his charge could hinder Gabriel's objectivity in regard to fulfilling his Task."

Michael shifted his gaze back to the duo now standing quietly before the apartment's door-wall, Nina's head resting against Gabriel's broad chest as they silently watched the falling rain. "Perhaps," the Keeper of Benevolence drawled. "It could also prove fortuitous. His taking an active interest in her may compel our brooding Celemor to greater diligence in his Task."

"Or it could prompt him to chafe even more at the restrictions inherit in his position," the Bringer of Death speculated.

A thoughtful frown consumed Michael's features. "I guess only time will tell."

Gabriel leveled stern eyes on him. "Take caution, brother. Your attitude in this matter is starting to mirror Omen's. Don't let your...affection for the woman taint *your* objectivity."

A slight smile creased Michael's lips, but he made no response, prompting an irritated snort from Gabriel.

The Bringer of Death accorded the scene in the Window a final scowl then stormed out of the Chamber.

Chapter 23

An unabashed smile covered Iblis's face as he soared across the barren plains of Nirvana's artic shelf.

As his mighty wings beat effortlessly against the frigid crosswinds, the Desolate One's mind wandered back to happier times. Before his separation from Heaven, he and his brothers would race the Northern Planes in their never-ending quest to determine which of them was the fastest. Most of the time it was Gabriel who immerged victorious, but occasionally Iblis, Michael, and even the solemn Raphael would give their arrogant sibling a run for his trumpet.

My Lord?

"Yes Silas," Iblis responded to the Morphling's voice echoing through his mind.

Darius has arrived as you requested.

"Have him wait in my office," Iblis instructed as he banked sharply to his right. "I'll be there directly."

As you wish.

Iblis's altered flight plan put him in direct line with the Tower of Self which, from this height, was a grayish speck against the region's pervasive white. The Lord of Hell folded his wings and plummeted straight down; setting what appeared to be a collision course with the tower's eastern face. At the crucial moment he snapped them open. The drag created by the wings' huge expanse brought him to an abrupt halt before the open doors of the Tower's aerie, and he lightly touched down on the landing deck's smooth pavers.

I would've definitely put your speed to the test today, Gabriel, Iblis mused as he made his way to his office; the air around him shimmering as the molecules of his traditional angelic garb, which was more suitable for flying, reconfigured themselves into a pair of sharply creased black slacks and a white oxford. "Ah, Darius," he greeted the Desomor standing behind his desk. "I trust you're enjoying the view?"

Darius turned away from the sight of Hell's teeming streets and accorded Iblis a respectful bow. "As always, my lord. It's a shame my people have such a horrid perception of this city."

Iblis sighed. "It is indeed. But perhaps the situation can be rectified. Tell me; what progress have you made with the Harbinger."

Darius' expression brightened. "Much, my lord. Shift and I have established Spirit Way's philanthropic credentials, and Miss Delcielo is very enthusiastic about working with our organization, though her companion seemed a bit hesitant."

Iblis's folded wings gave a slight flutter. "What companion?"

Darius looked pointedly at his master. "Gabriel."

Iblis's eyes widened with surprise. "Do tell! He's finally tired of his customary background-skulking."

"I'd say the motivation behind Gabriel's actions were more...visceral."

"Visceral...wait...are you saying our pensive Celemor is *attracted* to this woman?"

"I believe so."

Iblis's wings twitched again. "And you're sure his behavior is genuine and not just a facade to hide his awareness of you?"

"Positive. The Veil of Deception has totally blinded him to our true natures. This surprised me at first considering that buffoon's keen senses. But having observed their interaction, I'd say his curious lack of focus is due in part to his preoccupation with the Harbinger.

Iblis considered this bit of news for a moment. "Gabriel always maintains a high degree of emotional detachment during a Task. If what you suspect is true, this woman's charms must be considerable."

"They are."

Iblis focused sharply on the Desomor. "What do you mean?"

A bemused look appeared on Darius's face. "I'm not sure how to explain it. Miss Delcielo exudes an aura that's all most...magnetic. It's easy to see why that Center of hers has become such a success."

"She definitely seems to have captured *your* favor," Iblis noted through narrowed eyes.

The Desomor flashed his master a cunning smile. "Only in the sense that I recognize her potential; people like Nina tend to attract followers."

"Which is why I need her to embrace my Doctrines of her own free will," Iblis reiterated.

"I doubt if that's going to be a problem," Darius confidently assured his agitated master. "Nina's apathy toward religious structure is quite pronounced, yet I sense in her a curious yearning. She *wants* to believe in *something*. She's just not sure what that 'something' is."

Iblis' wings gave a slight flutter. "Then perhaps you and Shift should discover a way to fill that void."

A devious grin creased the Desomor's lips. "I was thinking the same thing, my lord."

Chapter 24

Cardinal Tullis stared impassively at the television as he listened to the casual discourse being shared by the man and woman on the screen.

The show was called Motown's Up and Comers. It was a Detroit based program that highlighted citizens who were making a name for themselves on the national front. Quinlan and Sanders had taped the previous week's episode and forwarded a copy to the Elders.

Tullis normally did not subscribe to such exploitive fair, but the spotlight of this particular episode was focused on Nina Delcielo, and the recent opening of five additional Youth Centers in the Metro Detroit area. There were also plans to take the Center's concept nationwide thanks to Miss Delcielo's successful collaboration with the nationally renowned, Spirit Way Foundation; an organization whose credentials Tullis had always questioned.

The conversation turned to matters of the spiritual, and a frown furrowed the Cardinal's brow. Over the past year and a half, Nina's rising popularity had provided her with a casual pulpit from which to espouse her skewered notions on organized religion and its place in modern society. She readily acknowledged God's existence but felt that service to him would be better achieved through the realization of the inherent spirituality within oneself, and using that knowledge to affect positive changes as opposed to becoming subservient to esoteric doctrines established by men.

Such radical heresy was frightening to the devout Catholic sentinel, but even more disturbing were the number of people who were beginning to ascribe to her beliefs thanks to the unlimited reach of cable television and the Internet. In fact, in addition to the DVD containing the episode Tullis was watching and other similar shows of interest, the Seekers had included a list of newly formed websites whose forums were dedicated to the woman's venomous rhetoric. These sites, and their steadily rising number of subscribers, were an indication that Nina had indeed found her audience amongst the spiritually disenfranchised masses.

The frown on the Cardinal's face deepened as he continued to watch the show. Any hopes that Tullis might have entertained about bringing Miss Delcielo into the *Presbyterii's* fold where gone. She and the diatribe she was spewing was fast becoming a threat.

After the show ended, Tullis put in a call to Cardinal Dresden.

"Hello Calvin," Dresden's stern voice sounded through the receiver. "I trust you're calling to discuss the disturbing media the Seekers sent us."

"I am," Tullis replied. "Did you get a chance to look at the DVD?"

Dresden issued a disgusted snort. "I finished it this morning. It's obvious that Miss Delcielo has no intention of aiding our cause."

Tullis released a weary sigh. "I've come to that conclusion as well."

"I've already spoken with some of my associates within the Episcopalian and Lutheran societies, as well the Rabbinical Assembly and the Nation of Islam," Dresden announced.

Tullis' eyes widened at the news. "What prompted that?"

Dresden's voice took on a hard edge. "Apparently Miss Delcielo has found a far broader audience than we anticipated. Her naive proclamations are drawing attention and a steady stream of acolytes across the spiritual front."

Another sigh escaped Tullis's lips, this time one of regret. "Then perhaps we need to take steps to...silence her rhetoric."

"I've a team of Neutralizers already in position," Dresden promptly announced. "I'll have them start the negative propaganda immediately. They've been fed all of Quinlan and Sanders reports on this matter and will know how best to proceed."

"Will the Seekers be aiding the Neutralizers in this endeavor?"

"Absolutely not," Dresden declared in a firm voice. "Nina Delcielo is no longer Quinlan's and Sanders' concern."

Tullis's hand tightened on the receiver. "You've taken them off the case?"

"As of this morning," Dresden confirmed. "The two are exemplary operatives but, like most Seekers I've encountered, lack the mental fortitude to accept the less savory aspects the *Presbyterii's* policies concerning problems of this nature."

"A fallacy that I too, share," Tullis remarked.

"Strengthen your resolve, brother," Dresden snapped. "The hand that serves the Lord is often dipped in blood."

Resignation settled heavily onto Tullis' shoulders. "Of that I'm well aware of. I just pray that we'll be able to discredit Miss Delcielo and short circuit her rising popularity *before* the Final Option becomes necessary."

"As do I," Dresden said and the line went dead.

*

"So that's it then?"

"I guess so," Quinlan grimly answered his partner's anxious query. "Our investigation of Miss Delcielo is officially closed.

Long association with Quinlan allowed Sanders to detect the hint of apprehension in his normally stoic partner's voice; the same feeling that settled in his own stomach after their receipt of the telegram containing Cardinal Dresden's terse dismissal.

Sensing that something was not right, Quinlan had immediately put in a call to Tullis's office. The Cardinal was marginally more polite, but the message was still the same: Nina Delcielo was no longer a Seeker priority.

"You do realize what this means?" Sanders asked.

Quinlan sighed heavily. "Yes."

Despite the Elders' attempt at discretion, few Seekers were ignorant of the darker aspects of the *Presbyterii*. For them to have been taken off of a viable Manifestation such as Nina's, without securing her within the Vatican's structure, meant that her particular talent had been deemed a potential threat. Given the broadening scope of Nina's popularity, coupled with her vociferous opposition against organized religions, it was easy to see why that determination had been made.

Quinlan's eyes bored into those of his partner. "What's our next move?"

The small apartment where the two Seekers had taken up residence during their lengthy assignment was quiet as Sanders pondered his partner's question.

Technically Dresden's order meant their affiliation with Nina was ended, but the two men had grown attached to their intrepid subject. And even though they were wary of her connection to the obviously supernatural Gabriel and the couple from the Spirit Way Foundation, the Seekers were quite impressed with her tireless efforts on behalf of, as she termed it: "Those exceptional individuals who lack only the necessary resources to achieve their full potential."

"Despite what the Elders think, I'm not ready to give up on Nina just yet," Sander's declared in a firm voice.

Quinlan's left eyebrow arched upward. "Then I take it our return to Rome will be delayed?"

A devious smile tugged at Sanders's lips. "Considering the amount of time and effort we've put into this Manifestation I would say that a little r and r is long overdue. And since the lease on this apartment *is* paid up through the end of this year..."

"We might as well stay here and recover our energies while awaiting our next assignment," Quinlan finished his partner's sentence. "And what if during our sabbatical it becomes apparent the Elders have decided to...permanently deal with Nina?"

Sanders did not respond to the ominous question, but the squaring of his broad shoulders and tightening of his jaw gave Quinlan his answer.

Chapter 25

"Are you sure you're not overreaching yourself, Nina?"

Nina took note of the concerned mirrored in Maria's eyes and gave her head a vigorous shake. "Not at all," she said after swallowing down another spoonful of the woman's famous Minestrone soup. "Now that Spirit Way's backing us, I've got a whole battalion of workers and resources at my disposal, and Darius is connected with all the right people, both here and abroad. He's very good at getting done what needs to be done."

"Ah." Maria eyed Nina through the steam rising from her mug as she took a sip of her coffee.

Nina could sense the other woman's suspicion. "Don't tell me you still have reservations about him? He, Sheila, and Spirit Way's executive board have been nothing but accommodating. Thanks to them we've been able to expand in a way that I never dreamed possible."

"Oh, I no," Maria said after taking another sip of her coffee. "It's just that there's something...odd about that guy. I can't put my finger on it, but I get a weird feeling whenever you talk about him."

"You and Gabriel both," Nina admitted. "He thinks the Center's expansion is progressing *too* smoothly."

Maria's plump features twisted into a frown. "Then he's keying into the same weirdness that I am. Add to that the slew of negative publicity you and the Center have been subjected to these past couple of months..."

"Let's not make a mountain out of a molehill," Nina exclaimed. "I'll admit I was taken aback by all the flack I've been getting over my religious views, but hey: that's what freedom of speech is all about. I'd say that the positive changes the Centers have affected in every area we occupy speak for themselves. The ever-increasing list of applicants for our services supports my belief."

Maria placed a hand atop the agitated woman's forearm. "Oh, I totally agree with you. I just don't want you to lose sight of the potential danger someone in your position could be placed in. There are a lot of rotten bastards out there who don't *want* to see a woman raise to such prominence the way you have; especially one that's calling for an end to organized religion."

"I'm not calling for an end to *anything*," Nina proclaimed. "I'm just saying people should take a long, hard look at themselves and determine on their own what's right, instead of blindly giving their time and money to some robe-wearing, incense-burning charlatan spouting misinformation!"

"You and I have always agreed on that point, Nina. I'm just worried about the lunatics and nut-bags out there who feel your words are an insult and may try to...you know...do something about it."

Nina was touched by the older woman's concern. For a brief moment she contemplated telling Maria the truth of The Creation and her new role in it but realized that now was not the time. Instead, she placed a gentle hand atop hers, and allowed a mischievous grin to tug at her lips. "That's why I keep Gabriel by my side at all times. He's my lunatic deterrent."

Maria hastily cleared her throat, her dark eyes twinkling. "And speaking of Gabriel: How are you guys doing as a couple?"

Nina couldn't help the flush that colored her cheeks. "We're doing just fine, thank you very much."

A wicked smile creased Maria's wide lips. "Is that so? Am I right in assuming that cutie's every bit the stud he appears to be?"

Nina's flush deepened. "You are so bad, Maria Scavelli!"

Maria's smile turned into a confident smirk. "I'll take that as a yes,"

"Let's just say he's accommodating in that area; *very* accommodating," Nina said, her lips curving into a sensuous smile at the memory of she and the Celemor's first sexual encounter.

It had happened exactly three months ago to the day. That morning, Nina had experienced a rather horrific vision involving an accident between a semi-truck and a school bus full of children. She immediately put in a call to the Psychic Unit and was assured that her warning would be forwarded to the proper channels. After two years of accurate predictions, Thomlin, and his partners in the P.U., knew better than to question the validity of warnings from the mysterious woman still known only as Del.

Secure in the knowledge that everything was being handled, Nina continued on with her day, but the vision returned during a meeting she was having with the executive staff of the newly opened Center in west Detroit.

Nina knew that the vision's return meant that the events she foresaw had come to fruition, but she managed to control her reaction to the point where none of the other people seated around the conference table had an inkling of what was going on.

As soon as the meeting ended, Nina immediately raced to one of the wall-mounted flat-screens in the Center's media room. She began searching the channels for any news of the accident. Within thirty seconds she found it.

The Harbinger braced for the worse as she listened to the details then gasped in shock when footage of the accident, captured by a witness using his cell-phone's camera, rolled across the screen.

The clip was accompanied by the voice of the astonished anchorman: "And here we see the unidentified man seemingly unfazed by the flames bringing out more of the children...Ladies and gentlemen, I have to say that I've never seen anything like this," the man's voice intoned as a lone figure waded through the wall of fire created by the burning fuel leaking from the semi, his arms and shoulders laden with the inert bodies of several children.

He quickly released his burden to the anxiously waiting rescue workers then dashed back through the flames to the overturned bus.

"Gabriel," Nina whispered, a rush of excitement surging through her limbs.

"That's one brave dude, Miss Delcielo?"

Nina looked away from the television to acknowledge the teen girl who had addressed her and was stunned by the multitude of people that had gathered in the room to watch the event.

"Yes, he is, Carly." The Harbinger returned her attention to the television, and a proud smile lit her face. "He's a real-life, guardian angel."

The footage came to an end with the anchorman reiterating his praise for the unknown Samaritan, followed by an expression of disappointment that he could not be located for question or comment afterwards. "...And authorities still have no clue as to the identity of this incredibly brave individual who seems to have vanished into thin air."

Nina chuckled softly. If the anchorman only knew how true that statement was.

The report of the incident droned on, and Nina excused herself from her position in front of the television. She quietly left the media room then retraced her steps to her office. Easing her lithe figure into her chair, she pondered the significance of Gabriel's unexpected intervention, wondering what could have prompted it. A question she immediately put to him when he materialized in her apartment later that evening.

"You did," he answered after placing a gentle kiss on her forehead. "I guess watching you run yourself ragged for the sake of others all these months is starting to have an effect on me. When it became obvious that neither the trucking company nor the school of that bus were going to heed your warning, I decided to act."

Nina chuckled at his candid admission. "And how did it feel being a superhero?"

Gabriel's face brightened at the memory. "It was totally bazaar. One of the kids even asked me if I was an angel."

"And what did you say?"

The Celemor shrugged. "I told her that I just worked for them, which for all intents and purposes, is true."

His humility in the face of such heroism sparked a surge of desire within Nina. Putting thought to action she reached up, drew his head down, and kissed him hungrily.

At first Gabriel tried to pull away, but Nina's arms, wrapped tightly around his waist, kept him in place. "Please, Gabriel," she whispered huskily into his ear.

The poignant look in her eyes intensified Gabriel's yearning to finally end his century-long abstinence. The urgency in her voice and touch swept away the last vestiges of guilt sparked by thoughts of Clarissa flitting through his mind.

He effortlessly lifted her trembling body into his arms and carried her into her bedroom where he gently laid her down atop the bed's embroidered duvet. Their clothes were quickly shed, and they began an urgent exploration of one another's bodies that culminated quickly in a wave of mutual pleasure that left them both breathless. With their initial hunger for one another sated, they began again at a more leisurely pace, savoring the pain and pleasures of the moment until they collapsed together into a deep and restful slumber.

"You still with me, Nina?"

Nina blinked. The memory of that incredible moment, and the numerous others of similar intensity they had shared since, fading as Maria's call thrust her back into the present. "I'm sorry, what?"

A knowing smile tugged at Maria's lips. "Boy, that young man's got your head in the clouds!"

Another flush darkened Nina's cheeks. "Yeah, he does; in and out of the bedroom." She felt no shame imparting such details to Maria who had graciously assumed the role of nurturer, friend, and confidant in the wake of Nina's mother's accident.

"You think he could be the one?"

Nina chuckled at the hopeful tone of Maria's voice and the exaggerated fluttering of her heavy lashes. "He could be." Nina let it go at that. Though hopeful, she was hesitant to commit more to her and Gabriel's relationship due to its peculiar dynamics.

During the hours following their lovemaking, the Harbinger and Celemor had discussed the topic at length. To Nina's surprise Gabriel had expressed a sincere desire to remain in her life even after his Task was completed. The Harbinger had readily agreed. Now if they could just figure out what it was that God, and whoever else, wanted her to do so she could get it over with, life could be a whole lot sweeter.

She had finally concluded that having life-saving visions wasn't the damnable curse she'd first made it out to be. She just wished she knew what the endgame was in all of this.

"And just what are you two hens clucking about," Tony's deep voice rang out as he and Gabriel entered the shop's leaded-glass front door, both men stomping and shaking the snow from their boots and coats.

Nina was secretly amused by Gabriel's efforts. The Celemor's Celestial aura made him impervious to Nature's follies, prompting Nina to suggest he tone it down a bit whenever he revealed his presence in public. People might think it a bit strange seeing a man walking around in ten-degree weather with no coat; particularly when they noticed the unnatural deflection of snow or rain from his body. Gabriel had taken her advice to heart and made sure to draw his energies inward on such occasions.

Nina favored the two men with a playful smile. "We were just having a little girl-time."

"Did you guys have any luck getting Miss Goldstein's car started?" Maria asked, tilting her head slightly to the left to accept the kiss her husband aimed at her cheek.

"He did." Tony jerked his head in Gabriel's direction as he slid into the booth beside Maria. "I tell you Nina; your guy here's a jack-of-all-trades. I might have to steal him away and put him to work here in the shop."

Nina chuckled as she rose from her seat. "I'll keep that in mind." She slipped her arms into the heavy jacket Gabriel was holding for her. "He might look kind of cute serving up sandwiches in one of those little white aprons."

A look of disdain crossed the Celemor's face. "Not with the steady flow of oddballs and attitudes you guys get in this place. I swear I don't know how you two do it," he directed toward the Scavelli's.

Tony shrugged. "I find that a big smile and a kind word works with most people; along with the occasional swing of my meat cleaver."

Nina laughed while buttoning up her coat. "That would definitely work for me. You guys take care. Your future employee and I have a date with about thirty kids back at the main Center. Tonight is taco night."

"Enjoy," Tony called out as Nina and Gabriel left the shop. He waited until their reflections faded from the shop's windows then turned serious eyes to his wife. "There's something very peculiar about that boy."

"How so?"

"Well for one thing the way we got that car started," Tony grunted, helping himself to one of the scones on the plate sitting in the middle of the table.

Maria leveled impatient eyes on her noisily chewing husband. "Would you care to elaborate?"

"I can't for the life of me figure out how he did it," Tony mumbled through a mouthful of scone. "When we got to where the car was parked, old lady Goldstein already had the hood popped. I tried to crank it, but the battery was dead. I was about to call Triple A on my cell when Gabriel stopped me. He gave the car an odd look, placed his hand against the battery cables for a moment then told me to try it again."

"And?"

"The damn thing kicked right over." Tony was still awed by the incident.

Maria was unconvinced. "Maybe the cable was just a little loose and he wiggled it into the right position."

"Nah, that was the first thing I checked. I'm telling you that battery was dead."

Maria's left eyebrow arched upward. "Are you saying that Gabriel jumped started her car?" Her amusement faded at the look in her husband's eyes. "You are saying that, aren't you?"

Tony shifted uncomfortably in his seat. "I don't know what I'm saying. All I know is that the boy is...different."

"Define different." Maria was warming up to the subject.

"Well for starters, he never gets tired."

"What do you mean?"

"I mean I've been watching him play ball and such with some of the teenagers at the Center. The man runs circles around those kids and never even breaks a sweat."

"Well, he is a professional bodyguard," Maria stated. "For that kind of job, you need to be in top shape."

"He's also strong; *unnaturally* strong. I happened to catch sight of him cleaning up the weight room at the Greenfield Center the other day when I was dropping off those sandwiches for Parent

Feedback Night. He put all the plates onto the barbell, lifted it off the bench with one hand, walked across the room with it, and set it down on the pads."

"What's so unnatural about that?"

Tony's expression turned bleak. "I counted the plates; there was easily four hundred fifty pounds on that bar!"

Maria blinked. "Well...like I said, he is in extremely good shape," she reasoned, though a note of uncertainty now colored her tone.

"I've been in good shape all my life too, but I was never like that," Tony said with a snort. "But it's more than just the physical stuff. The guy's also got a *phenomenal* understanding of history and current events. He looks to be about Nina's age yet every time we have a conversation, I get the feeling that I'm talking to someone my own age or older."

"And probably wiser," Maria teased, smiling at the evil glare her husband directed at her. "Maybe Gabriel spends a lot of time Googling historical events. On the other hand, I've never asked Nina his age. Maybe he's older than he looks. At any rate, he really is a nice guy and Nina adores him."

"And the feeling is definitely mutual on Hercules's end," Tony grunted. "He hovers over her like a mother hawk, and his eyes light up every time her name is mentioned."

Maria pinned her husband with a hard stare "Then for Nina's sake, let's keep these wild notions to ourselves. It's about time she had a little romance in her life, and I don't want you adding any unnecessary stress to the mix."

Tony wrapped his arm around his wife's plump shoulders and gave her a squeeze. "Alright, I'll keep the interrogations to a minimum." He gave her lips a quick peck to seal the deal. "But however good of shape he's in, if he breaks Nina's heart, he'll have me to deal with."

"And your meat cleaver," Maria added with stout nod of her head.

She pushed away from him and rose from her seat to greet the brace of customers making their way into the shop, signaling the start of the evening rush.

*

"So how have you and Tony been getting along," Nina asked Gabriel when they reached her Grand Cherokee parked several spaces down the street from the shop.

Gabriel opened up the driver side door and helped her in. "Okay, I guess. He's been playing the new-girlfriend's-threatening-uncle/father role with me."

Nina smiled at the news. "Do tell; and how have you been making out?"

"The fact that he hasn't introduced me to his prized cleaver seems to indicate that I've passed the initial inspection."

Nina laughed. "I'd say that was an accurate assumption. Tony's always had a paternal leaning toward me, which is nice since I never knew my own father."

Gabriel's sensitive hearing picked up the wistful undertone that was always present in Nina's voice whenever she spoke of the man she knew so little about.

While Nina was growing up, her mother rarely spoke of him, and any questions on the subject put to her by her daughter were always met with vague answers or stern admonishments for her to just let it go.

Earlier that year at Gabriel's urging, Nina had initiated an exhaustive search through city and state records in an attempt to locate her father but had met with no success. It was as if Miguel Delcielo had never existed. Despite the failure of her quest, Nina still held on to the hope that she would find him, and that they would one day be reunited.

She strapped herself into the Jeep's seatbelt, and Gabriel gave the shoulder harness a quick tug to make sure it was secure.

"Thank you, sir." Her expression became tender. "And thanks for being so patient with Tony and Maria. I know they can be a bit overwhelming at times, but they mean well."

Gabriel gave her shoulder an affectionate squeeze. "I know they do." He leaned his head into the Jeep and stole a quick kiss. "To be perfectly honest, it feels good to interact with regular people; makes me feel normal."

Nina smiled. "If that's the case, why don't you jump in?" Her right hand patted the Jeep's empty passenger seat. "I guarantee serving up tacos to a bunch of hungry teenagers will get you all the interaction you need."

Gabriel abruptly released her shoulder and stood up. "No thanks. Feeding the masses is not my idea of interaction." He quickly shut the Jeep's door, gave the street and surrounding area a surreptitious glance then vanished.

"Coward," Nina muttered. She started the Jeep then headed off toward the Center, comforted by the fact that although Gabriel wasn't physically sitting next to her, he was still there.

*

Perched atop the central tower of Detroit's famed Renaissance Center, Dichotomy watched as Nina's vehicle merged smoothly into the throng of oncoming traffic. His keen eyesight also detected Gabriel's translucent form soaring after her, and a slight smile spilt the Celestial's lips.

"I see your interest in this particular Emergence has not abated old friend," Omen's deep voice echoed through the air as he materialized beside his former protégé.

"Nor has yours toward Gabriel," Dichotomy said, a pleased smile on his face as he inclined his head toward the hovering Overseer.

"I've learned that vigilance is often the best policy when dealing with you Celemors."

Dichotomy gave Omen a bland look. "That title no longer holds meaning for us, Omen."

"Of that I'm well aware, Caleb. Though you have to say your recent activities, and current location, tends to lend evidence to the contrary."

Dichotomy's left eyebrow arched upward. "You've been keeping an eye on us?"

"I'm curious as to your continued interest in the Harbinger. Nor am I the only Member of the Watch that has taken notice of it."

Dichotomy's expression turned severe. "We take it you're referring to the Archangels. Have you been dispatched by them to chastise us?"

"Actually, my orders from The Seat are to leave you alone."

Dichotomy's form wavered slightly. "If that's the case then why are you here?"

"As I said before, I find your interest in Nina most curious. Would the two of you care to explain it?"

Dichotomy studied the Overseer's hooded features for a moment, trying to get a sense of his mood.

Despite his abandonment of his Celestial post, the former Celemor had never harbored any animosity toward his former handler. In fact, it was just the opposite. Toward the end of his service to the Watch, Dichotomy, or Caleb as he was still known at the time, often took solace in the Overseer's encouraging words.

In the end, not even Omen's sage advice could prevent Caleb's subsequent split from The Watch, but the dual being he had become still held a note of gratitude for the Overseer's efforts.

"In truth, we have no singular reason for maintaining our vigil, other than the persistence of a feeling of...unease in regard to the Harbinger."

Omen's eyes flared briefly. Caleb's senses had always been heightened to a degree that far exceeded the Celestial norm, and his concern also echoed that of the Overseer. "I must admit that I too have experienced a touch of trepidation toward Nina. Yet I cannot fathom the reason why. So far her Emergence is proceeding well."

"Yes, it is," Dichotomy agreed. "You might say it's going *too* well. She accepted her role far quicker than we would've thought possible, given her negative spiritual stance and lack of any Celestial buffering. Plus, her focus is much more pronounced at this stage of her development than any of the other Harbingers we've encountered throughout the centuries; with the exception of one," the Celestial added glaring at the Overseer through beetled brows.

"Yes, she does seem to have adapted rather well to the Celestial energy coursing through her body," Omen blatantly ignored Dichotomy's bait. Now was not the time to engage in *that* particular discussion. "I'm also surprised at how taken Gabriel is by her."

"Considering how long he remained in mourning over his wife and daughter, we thought you would be pleased."

"I am," Omen quickly assured the Celestial. "But the Archangels have indicated to me on several occasions that such ties may not be in his best interest; particularly when it prompts him to push the boundaries of his restrictions, like when he rescued those children."

Dichotomy's eyes narrowed suspiciously. "And why is that?"

"Both Michael and the Bringer of Death have been vague as to their reasons." Omen's voice was laced with aggravation for his inability to illicit more pertinent details from the Archangels. "I've consulted other Members of the Watch, and none of them have a clue as to why those two are devoting so much time to Nina, nor the reasons behind her Emergence."

Dichotomy's form wavered again. "We assumed that she was the initiate of a new Reclamation."

"As did I, but given the length of time that has passed, and the Archangel's peculiar interest, I'm beginning to wonder."

"Perhaps you should consult with other Celestials removed from The Watch for the answers you seek."

"You know discussing matters of this nature with non-Members of The Watch is prohibited," Omen bit out sharply. "I'm taking a chance as it is talking to you." His glowing eyes focused intently on Dichotomy's face. "Despite my curiosity, as an Overseer, *I* am unable to pursue this matter."

A slight smile tugged at Dichotomy's lips. "Then maybe a Celestial *not* bound by the Tenets of the Watch should investigate further," the blended being suggested mildly.

Omen's features remained hidden under his cloak, but the slight shift in his hovering form seemed to convey satisfaction. "What the two of you do on your own time is no longer my concern," he replied stiffly then promptly vanished, leaving Dichotomy to ponder the course of action he should take.

"Omen's concern must truly be great for him to have approached us about it," a male voice rang out as Dichotomy's dual personalities briefly separated themselves. "Such duplicity on his part is an indication that there is more to Nina's Emergence than the simple imparting of some new addition to the Tenets."

"Then let us return home and seek counsel from one also removed from Nirvana's political infrastructure," The female responded, and a nimbus of light engulfed the Celestial's body. "What we discover may aid the Harbinger and Gabriel in the fulfillment of their respective Tasks."

The view of Detroit's skyline dissipated as Dichotomy shifted through the dimensional Crossroads that surrounded and bound the three Realms together, appearing moments later within the shifting miasma of Sublimia.

As the carrier nimbus faded from the Celestial's body, the air before him coalesced into a glowing, feminine shape.

"Greetings Caleb," a sultry voice rang out from within the form's midst. "Or do you prefer your new title?"

Dichotomy accorded the form a respectful nod. "Caleb will do, Twilight, but we do appreciate your courtesy on the matter."

"Of course," Twilight responded in kind. "So; what new riddle have you brought for me to solve this day?"

"One concerning the Emergence of the Harbinger, Nina Delcielo; as the embodiment of Celestial Energy, we were hoping you might lend insight as to the extent of her abilities."

Twilight's form shimmered slightly. "You wish to discover the reasons behind her Emergence?"

"Yes."

"And for what reason do you seek this information?"

"The satisfaction of our own curiosity as to the woman's place within the Creation."

"Yours and Omen's I presume," Twilight said with a chuckle for Dichotomy's startled reaction. "Come now, Caleb; you of all beings should know little that transpires throughout the Creation escapes my notice."

A look of chagrin appeared on Dichotomy's face. "A trait you share with the Keeper of Benevolence."

Twilight chuckled again. "One of many, but in answer to your query: The Mortal's destiny is being shrouded, though by whom I cannot tell. I *do* know she possesses a link to Sublimia's reserves that surpasses that of most Celestials including He Who Became The Son."

Dichotomy shuddered, thinking back to the tumultuous events Twilight was referring to; the results of which forever altered the course of his existence as well as that of Mortalia itself. "Do *you* think she's the initiation of another Reclamation?"

"Considering the fragmented state of Mortalia, that would be my first guess. Of course, that's only speculation on my part. For a more concise view on the matter, you need to consult with the Keeper of Benevolence...or his brother."

Feelings of regret coursed through Dichotomy's blended psyches for the enmity that lay between themselves and the Archangels. "We seriously doubt that either Michael or Gabriel will answer any of *our* questions."

"Michael has more than one brother, Caleb."

"True, but the Lord of Hell will be even less accommodating than the Bringer of Death."

A wave of mischief emanated from Twilight's glowing form. "Neither of them are the brother I was referring to."

Dichotomy's jaw tightened painfully when he realized what Twilight was suggesting. "You think *Raphael* would confer with us on this?"

"Why wouldn't he? He is, after all an Archangel."

"Yes, but he lay down that title ages ago."

"As did you the mantle of Celemor," Twilight pointed out. "Yet here you are still involving yourself with matters of the Watch."

"We already told you our reasons were the satisfaction of our curiosity."

"Then perhaps his for talking with you will be the same."

"We seriously doubt that," Dichotomy muttered. "But there appears to be no choice on the matter if we're to discover the answers we seek."

"We always have a choice, Caleb," Twilight said, her form beginning to disperse. "You just have to be able to accept the ones you make; a Task that most beings within the Creation have never excelled at."

"That's true," Dichotomy whispered to the now empty air.

The blended being took a deep breath and exhaled sharply, the two personalities residing within in him preparing as best they could for what would surely be a memorable meeting with the Celestial whose antipathy toward the Hierarchy was even more pronounced than theirs.

*

"And you're sure of this?" Iblis questioned Silas as he gazed out over the streets of Hell.

"Absolutely," the Morphling assured his master. "Caleb's unique aura generates a considerable amount of static within the Celestial ether. His presence was detected by several of my brethren beholden to Twilight."

"Now why would that witless fool seek consultation from her?" Iblis wondered.

"Perhaps he seeks the same information that you do; the woman's true purpose."

Iblis turned away from the window, a look of concern reflecting from his blue eyes. "It is a mystery," he said, the slight twitching of his wings indicating his agitation. "It has been a little over two Mortal years since her Emergence, yet the Almighty has yet to make known his intentions for her."

A look of consternation consumed Silas' sallow features. "That's not entirely accurate, my Lord. The woman's voice has steadily gained volume within the Mortal's spiritual infrastructure. Her rising popularity, along with her message of personal realization as opposed to the adherence of religious dogma, has made her a target of their reigning spiritual institutions." Silas gave the Lord of Hell a pointed look. "Do you sense the parallel that seems to be taking form?"

The office was silent as Iblis considered the Morphling's suggestion. "Perhaps you're right, though I think it a peculiar path for The Almighty to revisit."

"Your inability to understand His mindset is the very reason the city of Hell was built," Silas pointed out.

Iblis sighed. "That it is old friend, and if what you surmise is true, I'd best move forward with my own agenda. A miscalculation of The Almighty's resolve led to me missing the opportunity the first time He tried this. I will not ere twice in the same fashion. Have Darius reveal himself to the Harbinger and relate my desire to collaborate with her."

"And what of the Celemor?"

Iblis took a moment to consider the Morphling's question. "According to Darius, Gabriel is very much taken with this Child of Heaven. That could work to our advantage. See if he would also be amenable to an accord between us."

Silas gave Iblis a respectful bow. "It shall be done at once, my Lord."

Chapter 26

"I still don't see why I have to wear this thing," Gabriel grumbled as Nina carefully adjusted the black, silken bowtie around his neck then smoothed the front of his tuxedo jacket.

"Because this is a black-tie affair and proper attire is mandatory," she said, stepping back so she could give his outfit a final appraisal. "Besides, you look yummy!"

Gabriel couldn't help but chuckle. "And you look, radiant."

The Harbinger's long black, silken gown hung elegantly about the lean, chiseled figure she had acquired thanks to numerous resistance and cardio sessions under Gabriel's expert tutelage.

"Maria did an amazing job with your hair, too," he added with a complimentary nod toward Nina's intricately braided coif.

"Yeah, she's a whiz with a styling comb." Nina checked her reflection in her prized, free-standing mirror, its aging wood gleaming brightly thanks to Gabriel's refinishing efforts. "Before she and Tony got married, she was a stylist at the hair salon in the old J. L. Hudson store that used to be downtown. Okay," Nina said with a final smooth of her gown. "Let's get going."

A slight frown appeared on Gabriel's face. "Are you sure going to this event is the right thing to do; considering everything that's been going on of late?" He was referring to the continuous stream of media attacks against Nina and the Spirit Way Foundation from an ever-widening list of detractors, the most outspoken of them being a radical group calling themselves The True Christian's Society.

Their blasts centered mostly on Nina's liberal views on religion, with some of the more outspoken members of the TCS accusing her of outright heresy.

Darius had immediately launched an extensive P.R. campaign to stem the flow of negative publicity, but the stress of the ordeal was starting to get to Nina; particularly the rash of vandalism perpetrated on several of the Centers, and the never-ending stream of threatening mail and phone calls.

Gabriel's constant presence had thus far spared the Harbinger from any violent overtures, but the sheer viciousness of the verbal and media assaults had the beleaguered woman wondering what in the world she had done to garner such hostility?

"The recent drama we've been going through is the *main* reason I think tonight's a good idea," Nina told her pensive guardian as she draped her lace shawl around her exposed shoulders. "We could use a little fun in our lives right now. Besides," she continued as they left the apartment and made their way toward the elevator. "Darius and Sheila were kind enough to invite us, and I don't feel we should be rude."

Gabriel released a soft grunt but, catching the look in Nina's eyes, made no comment. Over the months, his initial unease over the winsome couple had abated somewhat, but he still didn't completely trust them. The odd thing was that he couldn't figure out why. Neither Darius, nor his dutiful companion Sheila, had done anything to garner such suspicion. They had actually gone out of their way to ensure Nina's success, yet the Celemor couldn't shake the feeling that something wasn't quite right with them.

The elevator reached their floor, and the doors opened revealing a garment-bag laden Misses Watson and her ever-present canine companion, Angel. "Good evening, ladies," Gabriel brightly greeted the duo as he and Nina boarded the elevator.

"And a good evening to you," Misses Watson beamed. "My, my, don't you two look glamorous this evening. Are you going someplace special?"

"We've been invited to the premier of the new play, Enemy at the Door, down at the Fox Theatre," Nina answered while Gabriel playfully rubbed at the soft fur under Angel's chin.

Misses Watson's smile deepened. "How lovely! I hear it's a great play. You should really enjoy it."

"And what about you?" Gabriel nodded toward her packages. "You seem to have an interesting evening planned as well."

A wistful sigh escaped the old woman's lips. "These are some of Mister Watson's clothes. Gerald always was a slave to fashion."

Nina placed a tender hand against the woman's arm. "He most certainly was, and fearless when it came to trying new styles."

Misses Watson's face brightened at the memory. "That was my Gerald. Keeping his things in our closet made it seem as if he were still with me. But it's been nearly five years now since his passing, and I feel its time I started moving on. I'm taking these items to the Jefferson Shelter. Hopefully someone will benefit from them."

"That's very thoughtful of you." Gabriel favored the older woman with a tender smile. "I'll tell you what; Nina and I have to pass the Shelter to get to the Fox. Why don't you let us drop these off for you?"

"Are you sure you don't mind? I would hate to interrupt you're plans."

"It's no trouble at all," Nina said, graciously relieving the elderly woman of her burden.

Misses Watson thanked them both. She bid the young couple a pleasant evening when they disembarked at the lobby while she and Angel remained on the elevator.

"I'm glad you're not upset with me for volunteering our services," Gabriel said to Nina as he ushered her toward the apartment's rear entrance after exchanging pleasantries with the night watchmen.

Nina smiled. "How could I be; Lady Watson can be a bit of pest sometimes but she's a sweet old girl." The Harbinger ran appraising eyes over the numerous garments. "She appears to be a giving one too."

"Actually, she's quite the philanthropist; particularly where you're concerned."

They had reached to rear door, and Nina paused before exiting, giving Gabriel's face a sharp look. "What do you mean?"

A mischievous smile tugged at the Celemor's lips. "Do you still personally write the letters of appreciation the Centers send out to their contributors?"

"As often as I can. I think it's important to maintain a personal connection with our supporters. Why do you ask?"

Gabriel's smile deepened. "I take it you've never bothered to look up the executors of the Little Angel Foundation."

Nina's eyes widened with surprise. "No!"

"I'm afraid so."

"But that can't be right," Nina protested. "The executor of the Little Angel Foundation is a guy named Willi Kerner."

"Kerner is Misses Watson's maiden name, and Willi is short for Willimena."

"Wow," Nina uttered, still in a state of shock. "Little Angel has been on board since the Center's beginning."

"I know," Gabriel smiled as he pushed the door open so they could exit.

"Come to think of it," Nina said as they crossed the lot to her Jeep. "Little Angel has been a contributor to *all* of my philanthropic projects; even the causes I championed while I was in college." A feeling of unease settled in the pit of Nina's stomach. "How did you find out she was behind it?"

"I spotted her at the open-house at the Lafayette Center a few months ago. I thought it odd for her to be there and not tell you, so I decided to do a little Celestial investigation. Apparently, she's more a fan of your work than I realized if what you say is true."

"I guess so," Nina uttered as Gabriel held the driver's side door of Cherokee open for her. She took a seat then waited for him to get in on the passenger side before starting the engine. "Maybe she and I should have a little chat on the matter."

"Maybe you should," Gabriel said, tensing up as Nina moved the Cherokee off the lot an into Jefferson's oncoming traffic.

Nina hid her amusement for the Celemor's reaction. It always astounded her that the man who could lift cars over his head, had never ridden in one.

They quickly made it to the Shelter where they were greeted with the excessive fanfare that had become commonplace for Nina whenever she went out in public.

After chatting with the administrators and posing for a few photos with some of the staff and clients, Nina waved a cheery goodbye and she and Gabriel continued on to the Fox. A crowd for the evening's performance had begun to gather, and they took their place in the long line of vehicles waiting to park.

When it was their turn, Nina surrendered her keys to the suspiciously young-looking attendant at the valet booth then she and Gabriel made their way into the theatre's elegantly furnished lobby. Darius, Sheila, and several other members of the Spirit Way administration were waiting for them at the bar.

Nina eyed the various beverages lining the bar's refrigerated cabinet with keen interest. "I think an ice-cold green tea would do me a world of good right now."

Gabriel chuckled then stepped up to the bar to put in her request. A few moments later, one of the bar tenders placed a frosted bottle of Lipton Green Tea on the counter in front of them.

"I'm afraid I'll have to see some ID before I can allow you to drink that," the young man announced in a somber voice.

Nina turned startled eyes on him. "For a bottle of tea...?" She stopped when she got a look at the bartender's face. "You!"

Alerted by the tone of her voice, Gabriel also focused on the young man, his eyes widening with surprised recognition. "If I'm not mistaken, your name is Tip; member of the Crimson Tigers."

A slight flush darkened the man's Caucasian features. "*Former* member. After you whipped our tails that night at the Center, I thought it might be a good idea for me to find a new outlet for my energies."

"Do tell," Gabriel cried. "And what prompted such a change?"

"She did," Tip nodded at Nina. "The judge slapped me with six weeks of community service in lieu of jail time for that mess, and I got a chance to see all the cool things you've been doing for the hood. It made me wanna get my act together too, so I quit the Tigers, enrolled in some culinary classes at Baker Community College, and here I am. Tip Jefferson, mix-ologist-in-training; got my girl Raymonda to go clean too." Tip jerked his head toward the attractive young lady serving drinks at the other end of the bar.

Nina barely recognized the ruffian who had been the first to jump to Tip's defense during the altercation at the Center. Raymonda waved them all a cheery hello then turned her attention back to her customers.

"That's wonderful!" Nina clapped her hands at their accomplishments.

"What's wonderful," Darius asked, and Nina quickly filled him and the Spirit Way execs in on Tip's story. "That *is* an accomplishment, young man." Darius gave Tip's hand a congratulatory shake. "I'll tell you what." He fished a business card out of his jacket's inner pocket. "We're having a big banquet at the Westin next month, and my catering guy is always looking for some good people. His operation is very extensive, and he pays *very* well. Give me a call, and I'll set you up with an interview."

A shocked Tip stared at the card for a moment then turned grateful eyes on Darius. "Are you serious? Yo, dude, thanks; thanks to all of you!"

Nina gave his forearm a gentle squeeze. "No; thank you, Tip. Stories like yours are the reason we do what we do. You take care now."

"You too, Miss Delcielo, and thanks again!"

After giving Tip a final wave, Nina turned to Darius who then led the group to their seats in Spirit Way's reserved box situated in the center of the auditorium.

"When this is over would you and Gabriel join Sheila and me for a cup of coffee at our apartment?" Darius whispered in Nina's ear as they were settling into their individual chairs.

"We'd love to," Nina whispered back, noting the curious intensity of his eyes.

The blaring sound of the orchestra's opening notes drew her attention back to the stage as the play got under way.

The music and actors were top-notch, and Nina found herself totally rapt in the intricate plot revolving around a mysterious stranger's arrival and subsequent corruption of a small, Michigan town.

The play concluded to a round of thunderous applause from the appreciative audience followed by several curtain calls for the cast. When at last it was over, and the majority of the patrons were filing out of the auditorium, Darius reached out and lightly tapped Nina's hand.

"Did you valet?"

"Yes, we did."

"Oh, great; we can have the attendants pull our cars around so you guys can follow us back to our place.

"Sounds good," Nina said as she rose from her seat. "We're going to join Darius and Sheila for refreshments," she told Gabriel who had assumed his customary position at her left side.

A slight frown appeared on the Celemor's face, but whatever comment he was going to make was cut off by the rising sound of angry voices coming from the main lobby. At the same moment, Darius's cell phone began to ring."

"Now who could this be," he wondered as he studied the unfamiliar number. "This is Darius," he spoke into the handset. "Oh, hello Tip. This is a surprise. What can I..." Darius's voice trailed off and his chiseled features took on a grim note. "I see." He looked toward the auditorium's northwest exit. "Are the main doors compromised? Okay, we'll try to get out through exit H. Thanks for the warning." He disconnected and turned troubled eyes to Nina and Gabriel. "That was our young friend from the bar," he spoke in urgent tones. "There's some type of protest going on in the lobby. Perhaps it would be better if we exited out the back of the theatre."

Before any of them could move, the doors to the box were flung violently open, and a group of angry men and women poured through.

"Here she is," the burly woman leading the group shouted. "Little miss don't-believe-in-the-church herself!"

The woman stepped forward then crumpled to the ground as a wave of Celestial energy engulfed her and her companions, pushing them roughly back through the box's entrance toward the stairs, where several of them tumbled backwards.

Nina looked to her side expecting to see Gabriel, and was shocked to discover Darius, the fading white glow emanating from his outstretched hand identifying him as the source of the Celestial barrier.

"Who are you, Darius?" Gabriel grated out, grabbing hold of the Desomor's arm and spinning him about to face him.

"Please, Gabriel," Darius soothed as the repelled attackers began regrouping for another surge. "Now is not the time to..."

"I asked you a question," the Celemor growled, his eyes glowing with Celestial fire as he tightened his grip on Darius's arm.

Darius deftly freed himself from the Celemor's grip just in time to release another wave of force against the throng of protesters trying once again to enter the box. He turned fierce eyes back to Gabriel. "I'll gladly confess all to you once the Harbinger his safe. Now GO!"

The Celemor spared the Desomor a final scowl then moved to comply only to find that Nina was no longer at his side.

The Harbinger had moved forward and was kneeling beside one of the protesters writhing on the carpeted floor in agony; her left leg broken at the spot where it had impacted against the door jamb during Darius's second thrust.

As if in a trance, Nina reached forward, a golden aura encircling her body as she laid a gentle hand against the woman's mangled leg.

"What...what are you doing to me?" The woman's choked question became a startled cry as the glow about Nina's body enveloped her own, and the broken bones of her leg began knitting themselves back together. "My God," the woman whispered. The fear and hostility in her eyes disappeared, replaced by a wondrous gleam. She reached a trembling hand toward Nina. "Who...who *are* you?"

Nina gave no answer, amazed herself over what had just occurred. She tensed as she felt her body being lifted from the ground, but relaxed when she saw that it was Gabriel's strong arm encircling her waist.

The healed woman continued to gape in wonder then gasped as her glowing healer, and the tall muscular man holding her, disappeared amidst a flash of blinding light.

*

The entire incident, as well as the couple's precipitous exit, was also noted by the lone, winged figure observing quietly from the Window housed within the Apex.

The glow of Gabriel's carrier nimbus faded, and the Archangel Michael allowed the view of the theatre to dissipate from the Window.

"You're Emergence is now complete, my child," he whispered to the now opaque expanse. Nina's instinctive act of healing would unlock the final gates to her considerable abilities.

Michael's wings twitched with the Archangel's sudden anxiety. Her Celestial awakening would also allow her to uncover the truth of her heritage. He prayed that she wouldn't despise him when she did."

Worry not, Michael, the Almighty's voice sounded softly in the Archangel's mind. *All matters are proceeding accordingly.*

For the first time in his eons of existence, the Keeper of Benevolence found no comfort in his lord's assurance, and with good reason. Nina's life was about to be irrevocably changed.

Already the Archangel could feel the subtle shift in the Celestial ether as the various entities throughout The Creation became aware of their new Celestial Kinsmen sparking a feeling of foreboding within the Archangel unlike any he had ever felt before.

Something momentous was on The Creation's eternal horizon. He just wished he knew what it was.

*

Cardinal Dresden's wrinkled hand tightened around the phone's receiver as he listened to the Neutralizer's excited chatter coming through the speaker.

"I understand," Dresden barked roughly when the man had finished his report. "I'll confer with the Elders on this so we can determine the proper course of action. After that I will apprise you of your next assignment. Tell me; what effect has this had on Cara?" Dresden's pensive features turned even grimmer when he received the answer to his query. "That's unfortunate, though after an experience like that I'm not surprised at her wanting some time away to reflect on what happened. No, go ahead and grant her request. Do keep an eye on her and inform me immediately if she begins to exhibit any...peculiar behavior."

Dresden laid the receiver back in its cradle, his hand trembling with suppressed emotion. The heretic's powers were growing! Healing with a touch?

Nina's ability to see the future was frightening enough; Lord only knew what other surprises this woman had yet to unleash. Fortunately, the only apparent witnesses to this feat were the Neutralizers that had perpetrated the Fox assault. The Cardinal shuddered to think what would happen if word of this incident leaked out to the masses.

If an operative as dedicated as Cara could be led astray by such devilry, then those poor sods with little or no affiliation to the Catholic Church, or any church for that matter, would be easily consumed by the offerings of this silver-tongued temptress.

Dresden stared at the magnificent view of Saint Peter's Basilica through the leaded glass windows of his office, marveling as always at the steady flow of souls seeking spiritual solace and refuge within the great church's hallowed walls. Those sublime pilgrimages were now being threatened by Nina Delcielo's very existence.

Over the past several months, her naive message of 'self-actualization' had caused quite a stir along the spiritual front. Several churches, or "Fellowships" espousing her doctrines, were materializing all over the globe; particularly in areas besieged by political oppression and economic hardships. Even Rome was becoming affected, with scores of devout Catholics turning their backs on the Diocese in favor of this sport religion and the simplistic concepts of salvation it offered.

Dresden gritted his teeth in anger over such blasphemy. Only through rigid adherence to the time-honored doctrines of the church could one come to know the true might, glory, and salvation of the Lord. Without such structure, there could only be chaos.

Even the haughty Jews and those insufferable followers of the Muslim faith maintained strict discipline in the observance of their skewered beliefs. Nina Delcielo's agnostic proclamations were wishful thinking at its best!

Dresden just prayed that the *Presbyterii* would be able to extinguish this troublesome flame before it blossomed into a full-blown inferno.

Chapter 27

"Authorities are still unclear as to what sparked the violent confrontation at the Fox last night, between members of the True Christian Society and theatre security, that left two people dead and several more injured. Among those in attendance were Detroit's Mayor, several members of the Spirit Way Foundation's executive board, and philanthropist Nina Delcielo who, according to sources, appears to have been the target of the group's protest."

"They were after *me*," a somber Nina spoke to Gabriel who was materializing beside her. "I knew that a lot of folks were beginning to take stock in my opinions on organized religions and such, but I never dreamed I was being taken so seriously." She turned haunted eyes to the Celemor. "According to CNN, I've amassed quiet an audience, and not just locally."

Gabriel gathered the disturbed woman into his arms. "Yours is a message of Self-actualization, Nina. Considering the world's current spiritual state, such a concept is bound to have a universal appeal. But such views also tend to draw an equal amount of animosity from those whose beliefs you challenge."

Nina rested her head against his broad chest. "That's the part I don't get. I can read the futures of people I've never even seen, but I can't do the same for myself?"

"I'm afraid that's usually how it works. The theory being, that if a Harbinger knew of the tribulations that lay ahead, they might become prejudiced in the use of their abilities."

Nina released a derisive snort. "So, what are you saying; after God crams our bodies with all these holy powers, he throws us out to the wolves to fend for ourselves?"

Gabriel chuckled. "No, He assigns people like me to fend off the wolves while you go about His business."

Nina released another disgusted snort. "That's just stupid," she muttered, and turned her attention back to the television.

Gabriel grunted in agreement as he, too, focused on the news cast. "Given the fact that your stance on religion *has* drawn such a considerable amount of attention, last night's attack was probably the first of many to come."

Nina abruptly pushed away from the Celemor. "How can you be so damn calm about this? This is my life we're talking about!"

"I'm sorry if I sounded callous, Nina," Gabriel quickly offered. He placed a gentle hand on her shoulder, infusing his touch with a soothing flow of Celestial energy. "I'm afraid my Celestial internment has left me somewhat desensitized."

"And I'm sorry for biting your head off," Nina sighed. She reclaimed her spot against his chest. "This whole thing's got me rattled in a way that I can't even begin to describe."

"I'm sure it has." Gabriel hugged her trembling body closer. "For what it's worth, you're handling this far better than the majority of your predecessors."

Nina chuckled weakly. "Gee thanks,"

The Celemor gave the top of her head a light kiss, savoring, as always, the tropical scent of her shampoo. "There were some positive outcomes to last night's debacle."

Nina tilted her head up and regarded him through skeptical eyes. "Oh really; and just what were they?"

"One was our discovery of the changes our friend Tip, who did make it safely away from last night's drama, has made to better his life."

A pleased smile appeared on Nina's face. "That's a *very* positive outcome. What else?"

"Your instinctive use of your Celestial abilities when you healed that woman."

"Don't even get me started on that one," Nina cried, her voice muffled as she buried her face back into his chest. "I'm still trying to get used to being death's preview channel, not to mention the 'voice of religious anarchy,'" she quoted one of the more memorable labels currently ascribed to her. "I don't think I'm ready to start being Heaven's Urgent Care."

Gabriel smiled. "Fair enough."

Nina snuggled closer. "What's the other bright spot in this mess?"

A smug look appeared on the Celemor's face. "The vindication of my ambivalence toward Darius and Sheila."

Nina let out a startled cry and pushed away from him again. "My God you're right! I've been so wrapped up in the news that I completely forgot about that."

"Don't worry; I've already dealt with it."

Nina's eyes clouded with concern. "Is that where you vanished off to this morning?"

"It was. I thought it best to confront them without you being present, in case things got out of hand."

"And did they?"

"It was just the opposite, which surprised me considering who they serve."

A knot of apprehension formed in Nina's stomach. "You mean they're not Celemors added to the mix as your support staff?"

Gabriel frowned. "Not exactly. Sheila's true name is Shift. She's a member of a shape-changing race of Celestials known as Morphlings."

"I read about them in the Journal. They're sort of the free-lancers of the Creation, doing this and that with no particular loyalty to any faction."

Gabriel smiled. "That's as good a description as any. It also explains my ambivalence toward them. Morphlings are able to generate a field of energy that allows them to partially mask their Celestial auras. The Overseers call it the 'Veil of Deception'. It can be highly effective depending on the degree of proficiency of the initiating Morph."

"I take it Sheila, or Shift," Nina corrected herself with a shake of her head, "is pretty high up in the Morph proficiency ranks."

"She's one of the most adept shape-changers in the Creation."

"It figures," Nina said with a snort. "And what about Darius?"

The smile on the Celemor's face disappeared. "He's one of Iblis's Desomors."

Nina cringed. "*What?*"

"It seems the Lord of Hell feels that your Emergence signals the coming of some major changes in the Creation's spiritual infrastructure, particularly where Mortalia is concerned. He hopes that these events will allow him to shake the horrific negativity associated with his existence."

It took several minutes for Nina's shock to abate enough to allow her the use of her voice. "And you believe that?"

Gabriel met her skeptical gaze evenly. "To be perfectly honest with you I do. But I've known the true history of the Creation, as well as Iblis' position within the Hierarchy for some time. What matters now is how *you* feel."

Nina frowned. "I don't really know what to feel. I've learned so much about how things really are it's hard for me to gain a proper prospective on what's right and what's wrong. I mean, my heart tells me that anyone or thing associated with Iblis is evil, but that's based on my previous understanding. Now that I have the contents of that blasted Journal rolling around in my head, I'm inclined to give him the benefit of the doubt."

"I think that is a good way to start," a deep voice rang out from the nimbus of white light appearing in the air before them.

"Iblis!" Gabriel hissed as the light coalesced into the Lord of Hell's impeccably dressed form. "I thought we agreed to let me fully explain the situation to her first."

"I apologize for my impatience, Gabriel, but upon hearing the Harbinger's statement I truly felt it the most opportune moment to make an appearance."

Gabriel studied the former Archangel's face for a moment then released a heavy sigh. "Fair enough."

Iblis accorded him a slight nod then focused his gaze on an awe-struck Nina.

"Wow," she breathed. "The Journal didn't say you were gorgeous."

Gabriel hastily cleared his throat, and Nina cringed in embarrassment when she realized she had spoken out loud.

Iblis' lips curved into a smile. "I am what the Almighty made me, but the compliment is well received, and returned."

He gave the Harbinger's features a closer scrutiny and a soft chuckle escaped his lips. "I now understand the feeling of recognition I experienced when your image was first shown to me, as well as the reasons behind the considerable amount of Celestial energy I sense in you. You've inherited much from your father, including several of his physical characteristics. They add a pleasingly unique distinction to your Mortal form."

Nina stiffened at his words, her eyes blinking rapidly. Her voice became the barest whisper. "You know my father?"

"Of course," Iblis replied then gave her a speculative look. "But apparently you do not." The Lord of Hell's gaze fell on Gabriel. "And judging from the confusion mirrored in your guardian's face it would seem that he is also ignorant of your true lineage; most curious."

"Wait...STOP!" Nina's body began to tremble violently. "Tell me about my father! Where is he? Why did he abandon..."

"Be at peace, Nina," Iblis gently but firmly interrupted her tirade. "I know you have many questions, but I think, in this instance, I will heed your guardian's advice, and allow you to receive your answers from the party best suited to give them."

Nina's shoulders sagged with disappointment. "But I don't understand."

Iblis gently took hold of her hands, his blue eyes full of compassion as they locked onto hers. "I know you don't, but I suspect all will soon be made clear to you."

Nina wasn't sure if it was the intensity of his compelling gaze or the warmth flowing through his fingers, but something inside her sensed the truth of his words. She found herself strangely comforted.

"Now then," Iblis continued brightly, allowing her hands to slip from his. "Getting back to *our* situation; I would like to thank you for altering your negative attitude towards me."

Nina released an amused snort. "Yes, well it's not like I had much choice in the matter." She was still in a mild state of shock over that fact that she was actually having a *conversation* with the Devil! "Your story is documented quite thoroughly in the Journal."

"You could've chosen to disbelieve it," Iblis pointed out, flattening his wings tightly against his back so as not to disrupt the apartment's furnishings.

Nina regarded him through narrowed eyes for a moment than shrugged. "I suppose, but considering the company I've been keeping," she spared Gabriel a brief glance, "and the things I've done and witnessed these past two years, it would be pretty hard to see the Journal as anything other than the truth. But there is *one* question I would like you to answer."

"And that is?"

A flash of anger reflected from her hazel eyes. "Why go through all the drama and deception with Darius and Spirit Way? If you truly wanted my help, why didn't you just approach me from the start?"

A wistful sigh escaped Iblis's lips. "In hindsight I have to say that my actions were needlessly wasteful, but at the time I was basing my decisions on the typical Mortal reaction to my presence. To most of your kind I am, after all, the Enemy of God."

"Yeah, well you keep hiring people like that Mayhem chick and those goons that accosted me, and they're going to keep on seeing you in that light."

A look of contrition appeared on Iblis's face. "I do apologize for any and all indignities you suffered at the hands of my minions. I only wanted them to draw out your protector so I could determine your importance. They were given implicit instructions as to how invasive their actions were to be." Iblis's gaze shifted once again to Gabriel. "Mayhem was as well, and I have already disciplined her for her callous behavior."

"Not that it'll do any good," Gabriel chortled. "That woman is volatile."

A look of chagrin appeared on Iblis's face. "I've been told that repeatedly by my assistant. I do hope that her rash actions haven't prejudiced you against working with me," he directed at Nina.

Nina gave him a puzzled look. "I'm still not sure what it is you want from me. I mean I'm grateful for Spirit Way's aide and all, but what's the end game? What is it that you hope to accomplish through aiding me?"

Iblis's expression turned solemn. "You were chosen by The Almighty to deliver His decrees. The fact that your message, so far, has been one of *free* will in terms of worshiping him leads me to believe that He has initiated another Reclamation. Your voice may be the instrument he's chosen to announce the *truth* of the Realms, and that includes an accurate accounting of my existence as well."

Nina's eyes widened with surprise. "Surely you don't expect me to start preaching *your* doctrines?"

"Absolutely not," Iblis hastily assured the Harbinger. "Though if time permits, I would like to discuss the philosophy behind my Doctrines of Self. Perhaps they could be of use to you."

Nina studied his face through speculative eyes. "We'll see."

Iblis accorded her a respectful nod then resumed his oration. "At the moment, my main purpose is to ensure that you're able to continue your effort to encourage the masses to seek the *truth* of their God, and rid themselves of the blind adherence to oppressive, spiritual doctrines."

Nina cocked her left eyebrow. "And the Truth shall set them free?"

"Exactly; free to choose which spiritual path is best suited for them. Free to acknowledge their Creator's true masterpiece instead frolicking about within this distorted aberration you Mortal's call reality."

"And free to serve *your* interests if they so choose."

Iblis chuckled. "Again, you misinterpret my intentions, Harbinger. Whether or not I gain prominence during this Reclamation is irrelevant."

"Then why are you so determined for me to succeed in doing whatever it is I'm supposed to be doing?"

"Because first and foremost I believe in the power of *choice*," Iblis stated firmly. "My Father bestowed Mortals with Divine Intellect yet hampers you in its use by demanding adherence to His Tenets. In my opinion, that has to change."

Nina considered this for a moment. "And what would *you* have us do?"

Once again Iblis took hold of her hands. "I would have you be free. As you said, Truth is the pathway to freedom." He released her hands, and a nimbus of light engulfed his body. "You, Child of Heaven, now possess the Truth of your existence and I, as well as those who serve under me, will help you use that Truth to free the minds of your brethren."

The light intensified for a moment then faded as the Lord of Hell vanished from sight.

An exhausted Nina collapsed onto the sofa. "Now there's a guy who really knows how to make an exit."

"Most Celestials do," Gabriel remarked dryly as he sat down beside her. "I think it's some kind of holy requisite."

Nina snorted then gave his shoulders a gentle nudge, indicating that he should change his position. Gabriel obliged, shifting his torso so that his back was now to her. Nina ran her fingers through his hair, marveling as always at its soft, silky texture while her deft fingers began braiding the mass into one thick strand. It was an exercise she had come to find enjoyable and therapeutic.

"I feel like I'm at a crossroad," she said, her hands moving at a slow but steady pace. "People are after me because they think I'm some kind of heretic. I can see the future and mend broken bones with a touch. Now the Devil has just pledged his support of a cause that I'm not even aware of; not to mention his spiel about knowing my father!" She regarded the back of the Celemor's head through troubled eyes. "What do *you* think I should do?"

"I'm afraid this is new territory for me also. Although I think I know someone who may be able to offer you some insight."

Nina's left eyebrow arched upward. "Who?"

"Tyree; he's been a part of this since the beginning."

"Only on the periphery," Nina pointed out. "He knows about my visions, but I've never explained to him the full extent of my abilities or the truth about the Creation; not to mention the *real* reason you've become such an integral part of my life," she added, giving the top of his head a playful pat.

"Then perhaps it's time you did; even if it's just to ease the poor lad's mind over your well-being."

Nina's hands faltered for a moment. "What do you mean?"

"Tyree loves you very much Nina, and still feels guilty over the pain you suffered after the dissolution of your previous relationship. Perhaps if he knew that you've indeed found someone who truly cares about you, and who has no intentions of abandoning you for some higher purpose," the Celemor added in a pious tone. "He will be able to lay that burden to rest."

A slight smile creased Nina's lips. "Is that your roundabout way of telling me how *you* really feel?"

"I would've thought my affections for you would've been obvious by now, you incorrigible psychic vamp."

Gabriel hissed as she tugged painfully on his hair.

"Sometimes a girl just wants to hear the words," Nina whispered sweetly in his ear.

"Point taken," the Celemor replied, altering his body's density just enough for his hair to pass through her fingers so he could turn and face her. His body solidified, and he gently cradled her face with his hands. "I still have no idea what God's plan is or what your purpose is in it. But I'm very grateful that the Archangels deemed me worthy enough for the Task of protecting you.

Tears of joy sprang to Nina's eyes as he leaned forward and pressed her lips firmly against his. There were still a thousand questions that needed answering, and even more decisions that needed to be made regarding her dubious role in this heavenly madness. But for the moment, all was right in the universe.

Chapter 28

In the region of Sublimia known as the Heights, a tall muscular woman sat cross-legged in the solitary patch of black grass sprouting from the top of a stony ridge. Her position gave her an unimpeded view of the Infinity Basin, one of the Realm's more turbulent bodies of water

Celestial society was divided into two primary categories; those that subscribed to the Almighty's Tenets and those that, for whatever reason, did not. Celestial's that chose to live apart from The Almighty, while not living in accordance with His doctrines, still acknowledged His authority and accepted the limitations on Celestial interaction with Mortalia.

The woman on the ridge was not in that category.

Piercing green eyes set in an attractive angular face gazed out over the Basin's raging waters while long, slender fingers gracefully braided a heavy plait of platinum waist-length hair. Had she been raised in the Realm of her birth, her peculiar beauty and natural charisma would have easily propelled her to a life of stardom and admiration. But such notions were anathema to the woman. For her, the shadows were a source of comfort, and Sublimia's dismal planes suited her just fine.

Lillian was the name given to her by her Mother, but to the majority of The Creation's inhabitants aware of her existence she was known as Lie; a self-proclaimed label chosen for its fitting description of her reality.

The Members of the Hierarchy had ascribed another name to her. One that was aptly suited to her temperament: The Child of Chaos.

Mistress?

"Yes, Kaela," Lie answered the disembodied voice of her Morphling handmaiden echoing softly in her mind.

Your Seers have just become aware of another female Halfling living on Earth in Mortalia.

Lie's hands faltered for a moment. "Which of my uncles is she the progeny of?"

The Halfling's origins are unknown, but her abilities and potential appear to rival yours; they may even surpass them.

A thoughtful frowned appeared on Lie's face as she considered the information. "Has my father reacted to her presence?"

No, but that is not unexpected. He rarely concerns himself with matters outside of Sublimia.

Lie's lips twisted in disgust. "No, he doesn't." Her hands resumed the braiding of her hair. "Keep me apprised of the woman's actions and have one of the Seers initiate a discreet Watch over my father. Any signs of involvement from him could indicate the importance of my new Celestial cousin..."

And allow you to determine whether or not you should involve yourself in her endeavors; Kaela finished her Mistress's thought.

Lie's sensual lips curved into a devious smile. "You know me so well."

Mine was *the hand the cleaned and clothed your Mortal backside.*

Lie chuckled. "Those days are millennia past, Kaela. Now attend to your duties and leave me in peace."

As you wish, Mistress.

The Morphling severed the mental connection, leaving Lie alone to ponder the ramifications of this woman's arrival.

Chapter 29

Father Tyree Griffin stared at the television screen mounted on the rear wall of his office at St. Christopher's Catholic Church, a knot of apprehension forming in his stomach.

The news broadcast he was watching was a recap and update of the attack perpetrated by the True Christians Society against philanthropist Nina Delcielo; the latest in a series of disturbing incidents sparked by the outspoken woman's liberal religious views.

For Tyree the matter was of particular concern. Nina was a dear and treasured friend. *And now she's the center of an ever-widening religious controversy*, he mused as he flicked off the television, and relaxed into his chair.

A soft chime, announcing a visitor, echoed through the church halls.

"I'll get it Misses Pearson!" Tyree called to the elderly woman that manned the receptionist station during the weekday morning hours. The Minister knew that the recent spate of cold weather was having an adverse effect on the woman's arthritic joints.

He rose nimbly from his chair; gave his tall frame a brief stretch then made his way to the church's main entrance. He gave the metal handle a sharp yank to free the aging lock then pulled the heavy wooden door open.

"May I help you," he asked the burly, haggard woman waiting anxiously on the other side.

"Are you Father Griffin?" she asked in a hushed voice, shooting furtive glances around the church's manicured lawn.

Tyree took note of the woman's anxiety and opened the door a little wider. "I am."

The woman's shoulders sagged with relief. "Thank God. I never saw the surveillance photos, so I wasn't sure it was you. Please, Father, you've got to help me!"

"Alright, ma'am; just try to calm down," Tyree soothed as he took gentle hold of the woman's trembling arm and led her into the foyer. "Now what kind of trouble are you in, and what's all this about surveillance?"

The woman exhaled loudly. "I'm sorry, Father. I know I'm not making much sense..." she halted mid-sentence when she noticed Miss Pearson eyeing them from her perch at the reception desk. "Uh...can we talk someplace private?"

"Of course." Tyree gave Miss Pearson a polite nod then led the woman down the hall to his office. Once inside, he quietly closed the door and motioned for her to have a seat in one of the chairs arranged in a loose semicircle in front of his desk, after which he settled into his own chair.

"Now what seems to be the problem?"

"My name is Cara Simmons," the woman introduced herself then proceeded to tell the Minister of the Elders' decision on the Delcielo Manifestation, her own position within the *Presbyterii's* Neutralizer divisions, and her miraculous encounter with Nina following the Fox attack where the woman had mended Cara's broken leg with nothing but the touch of her glowing hand. "And I figured that since you were the one that initially reported Miss Delcielo to the Elders, I could come to you."

"I'm certainly glad you did," Tyree managed to respond, his mind working furiously trying to digest the woman's startling revelations: Nina healing by touch, and the Elders actively seeking her demise?

Tyree was stunned. This couldn't be right. The Elders couldn't be that ruthless. Or could they?

His mind drifted back to the news broadcast of the Fox incident. Many were the stories about the unsavory practices both condoned and perpetuated by other sects of the Vatican. The majority of the rumors the Minister chalked up to paranoia and conjecture on the part of the less informed but now, sitting across from one of the very agents of said groups, he wasn't so sure.

He focused troubled grey eyes on Cara. "Exactly what is it you want from me?"

A look of uncertainty flickered across Cara's face. "I guess advice. As I said earlier, I know you're the one who initially identified Miss Delcielo, and the original Seekers have consistently spoken very highly of you throughout their reports on this Manifestation."

Tyree's eyebrows arched upward. "Quinlan and Sanders?"

"Yes. They were the ones that suggested I come here after I met with them and told them what happened."

"I appreciate the confidence you've all placed in me, but I still don't see how I can help."

Cara stared at him for a moment then leaned forward and placed folded hands atop his desk. "You can start by telling me what to do," she bluntly informed him. "I've always done what was asked of me by the Elders and I've never questioned it but now..." Her voice trailed off and she swallowed hard several times. "They said Nina Delcielo was a heretic; that her...abilities were evil and posed a grave threat to our Lord's way. Since what happened at the Fox, I've been doing my own research, and I can't find a single thing she's done to warrant such censure. Not only that, but she also healed *me*; the woman who had just attacked her! If she was evil, why would she do that?"

Tyree placed a comforting hand on top of hers. "I've known Nina since we were kids, and I can assure you she is definitely not evil," he stoutly declared. "Nor is she some heretic out to lead us down some wicked path," he added with a snort. "I'm not sure why the Elders have decided upon this course of action, but I intend to find out. And as for what *you* should do." He gave her hands a reassuring squeeze. "Weigh what you've been told against the evidence you've gathered then trust in what your heart tells you."

Cara cocked a skeptical eyebrow. "Are you telling me to step out on Faith?"

Tyree smiled. "Faith in our beliefs is what led both of us to our current stations in life. In the face of all that's happened I see no reason to change that now."

"Nor do I," Cara agreed after a reflective pause.

The two chatted for another few minutes then Tyree escorted her back to the door. He bid her a cheery goodbye after telling her to feel free to contact him whenever she wanted to.

Cara thanked the Minister then left the church feeling markedly better than when she had first arrived, but her mood changed when her eyes fell on the two men sitting in the black Dodge Durango that was parked directly behind her beige Stratus.

"'Morning Car," the man on the Durango's passenger side greeted her as he slid smoothly out of the vehicle. He was tall and muscular with auburn hair slightly graying at the temples, and dark piercing eyes that were fastened intently on hers.

"Hello Malakai," Cara responded coolly.

Malakai's eyes flicked briefly to the church. "Been confessing your sins to the good Father?"

"Spending some time in prayer seemed like the thing to do considering what I've been through," Cara replied. "You guys here for some spiritual guidance too?"

Malakai frowned. "Not exactly; Cardinal Dresden is a bit...concerned about your well-being, and asked Joey and me to check on you."

Cara's gaze shifted to the burly bald-headed man sitting behind the steering wheel, his eyes hidden behind a pair of black utilitarian shades then back to Malakai who was now standing in front of her, his arms folded lazily across his broad chest. "The Cardinal is most kind."

"Yes, he is." The Neutralizer gave the front of the church another speculative look then turned his attention back to Cara. "What advice did the intrepid Father Griffin have to offer?"

Cara shrugged. "He basically told me that all things happen for a reason and that I should have faith in God's way."

Malakai smiled. "Sage advice," he drawled. "What about your faith in our way?"

A feeling of unease slithered down Cara's back. She didn't like the direction the conversation was starting to take. She pinned the Neutralizer with a hard stare, making sure to keep the uncertainty from her voice as she answered. "I'll admit it has been tested. But my obedience to the Elders is still absolute."

Malakai studied Cara's face for a moment then flashed an amiable smile. "Very good." His smile then vanished. "Hopefully it'll remain that way."

Cara's pulse quickened when she noticed his right hand drifting casually toward his jacket pocket, and the 9mm Beretta she knew was nestled there. Her tension doubled when she belatedly remembered that hers was tucked in the glove compartment of her Stratus. "Only time will tell," she replied evenly, determined not to let him intimidate her.

Malakai regarded her through narrowed eyes for a moment then relaxed, the smile returning to his face. "Enjoy your vacation, Cara." He accorded her a slight nod then headed back to the Durango and nimbly climbed in.

Joey cranked the engine and pulled away from the curb. He drove to the end of the block, whipped a U-turn, and accelerated slowly toward Cara.

"Be seeing you, Car," he spoke as they drove by, his raspy voice sending additional chills down Cara's spine.

She watched the Durango turn onto the busy through-street that bisected the church's quiet block then jumped in her car, quickly closing and locking the door. Next, she retrieved her Beretta from the glove compartment, the familiar feel of the gun's custom poly-carbonate grip providing an instant tonic for her frazzled nerves.

Malakai's and Joey's presence meant that she was under surveillance. Such an occurrence wasn't surprising considering her leave request, but the fact that Dresden had dispatched those two was an issue of no small concern. The loathsome duo had a penchant for brutality. She would have to watch her step while continuing her investigation of Miss Delcielo.

Father Griffin had suggested she step out on faith. Well, that faith told her that something momentous was underway, and she was determined to find what it was.

*

Tyree replayed the conversation with Cara over again in his mind as he stared out his office window at the neatly manicured shrubs ringing Saint Christopher's back lot; Nina healing with a touch, and the Elders pursuing a course of hostility against her?

Was this why all of his inquiries to Cardinal Tullis on the matter were consistently met with vague answers? True, his friend's current stand against organized religion could be seen as blasphemous, but that was no reason for the Elders to have taken such a hostile stance.

Considering her amazing abilities, Nina's rhetoric could be the precursor for the revelation of a greater truth. Was that not the church's main purpose; to provide society the most accurate interpretation of God's plan?

Tyree's eyes shifted to the phone resting on his desk, and a tired sigh escaped his lips. Stilling his resolve, he picked up the receiver and began punching in Nina's number.

Out of respect for her privacy, and the desire not to receive another tongue lashing, he hadn't pressed Nina for information on her situation. Nor had he inquired as to the true nature of her and Gabriel's intense relationship, but it looked as if the time had come for him to do so. If what Cara said was true, the aggression against Nina would only escalate. She needed to be prepared.

*

Sitting in her high-back leather chair, her faithful canine companion Angel curled in her lap, Willimena Watson's normally sanguine features took on a worried look as she watched the news on the television. The topic of discussion: the growing controversy concerning the religious views of Nina Delcielo.

"I fear Nina's life is about to become hectic, dear one," she whispered to Angel as she gently patted the Chihuahua's furry head.

As always, your insight serves you well, Willimena, a deep voice echoed softly through the old woman's mind.

A slight smile tugged at her thin lips. "Hello father. It's been a while."

Yes, it has been, and for that I apologize. I trust your time away from the Hierarchy has been...constructive.

Willimena chuckled. "You know perfectly well how I've been spending the past several years."

Yes, and I must admit that your quiet support of Nina during that time has been most admirable.

"Well, you told me to be discreet, though maintaining my distance hasn't always been easy; particularly in the wake of her mother's death."

I, too, was troubled by that incident, the voice responded.

"Apparently not enough to protest it," Willimena snapped.

It was the will of The Almighty that said Task be carried out. You of all beings should know that I am honor bound to obey.

Willimena's ire dissolved at the regret she sensed in her father through their mental rapport. "Unfortunately, I do, which is why I've tried to support Nina and her endeavors as best I could from the outer periphery; so as not to draw attention to my, as the Bringer of Death put it, 'blatant disobedience of The Almighty's will.'"

And I laud your efforts; however, I fear such...blatancy may soon be needed.

A look of surprise appeared on Willimena's face. "And why would my direct involvement in Nina's life be necessary now? Is she not under the protection of the very capable Gabriel?"

She is but she will need guidance in the ways of her heritage if she is to achieve her true potential. There are few beings, besides yourself, who are qualified for such a Task.

"Then assign it to one of those 'few' and leave me be."

You already know the reason I want you to attend to her tutelage.

A weary sigh escaped Willimena's lips. "Indeed, I do, father," she whispered. She could already feel the weight of Duty pressing down upon her shoulders.

For nearly three millennia, Willimena had walked among her mortal brethren, but the gradual decline of Earth's moral consciousness over the last few centuries had made her begin to question the effectiveness of the Tenets as well as her place in the Creation's ever-changing infrastructure. Her spiritual malaise had been lifted somewhat upon discovering the existence of Nina, and she had tried in her own way to offer what quiet support she could to the Child's unusual plight. With the limitations put on her actions by the Seat, most notably the direct order forbidding her prevention of Nina's mother's death, she had assumed that any future contact would be minimal at best. She should have known better.

"Worry not, father," Willimena finally spoke when she sensed his impatience. "When the time comes, and should she need it, I will offer Nina what aid I can."

I feel the heaviness in your heart, my child but do not let it linger. This time I will ensure that you receive no censure for whatever action you choose to take on Nina's behalf.

"You'd better," Willimena replied, her tone sharp.

Her eyes begin to glow as Angel transformed into a swirling mass of Celestial energy that was then absorbed into Willimena's body. "For there is only so much hardship I will allow my youngest sibling to endure," she stated firmly when her absorption, and subsequent transformation into her true form, was complete.

Chapter 30

The light shone with an intensity that blinded Nina as she valiantly tried to shield her eyes with her hand. Several seconds passed then the light coalesced into the form of a man, though unlike any she had ever seen.

He was extremely tall, his tanned shirtless torso rippling with muscles that would put the current Mister Universe and all of his predecessors to shame. Closely cropped blonde hair framed his beautiful face, while hazel eyes much like her own, were focused intently on her. An immense pair of wings protruded prominently from his wide back, and Nina found herself mesmerized by the alternating shades of white and silver running throughout their feathery expanse.

"Who...who are you?"

A wave of compassion enveloped her, and a deep voice resonated through her mind.

"Look into your own heart, my child, and you shall find the answers you seek."

Nina frowned. "I...don't understand."

"I know, but soon you will."

"Wait!" Nina called as the man's image began to fade. "Please..."

"Don't go," she whispered as her eyes opened.

She lay still for a moment, trying to collect her jumbled thoughts. This was the third time the bizarre dream had imbedded itself in her head, but she had yet to make any sense of it. Was it a warning? Was it some type of revelation?

Her thoughts were interrupted by the ringing of her cell phone, and she quickly grabbed it from her nightstand. She checked the caller ID, and her mood brightened. "Hi, Tyree; what's up?"

"I was wondering if you would like to have to lunch with me this afternoon," Tyree's disembodied voice echoed from the handset. "I could really use your insight on a matter that's come up here at the church."

"Uh...sure," Nina replied. She could tell by his tone that something was wrong. "How about we meet at Tony's at noon?"

"Noon is good but I would prefer someplace more private."

His unusual intensity piqued Nina's curiosity. "In that case we can have lunch right here at the apartment."

"Sounds like a plan. I'll grab the food myself. See you soon."

"I can't wait." Nina disconnected then smiled at the slight impingement on her awareness. Gabriel would be arriving soon.

Nina's smile deepened at the memory of the first time she'd met the enigmatic man who would eventually become such an integral part of her life, and a warm feeling suffused her body. A heavenly Harbinger and a Celestial Mortal: Theirs truly was a unique relationship.

"The good reverend sounds a bit stressed," Gabriel observed as he materialized on the bed beside her.

"I see you've been ear-hustling again," Nina teased, leaning forward to accept the kiss the Celemor planted on her cheek. She tried to intercept him with her lips, but Gabriel gently turned her head in the opposite direction.

"Not until you've brushed. The sweet and sour chicken you ate last night left a lasting impression on your breath."

"Hah-h-h," Nina breathed in his face before making her way to the bathroom.

After seeing to her hygienic needs she headed to the kitchen where Gabriel was leaning casually against the counter, his attention focused on the wall-mounted television. "It's amazing how far off the mark some of these so-called historians are," he said as he passed the steaming mug of green tea he had prepared for her.

Nina took a cautious sip of the hot liquid. "What show is this?"

"Secrets of Stonehenge," Gabriel quoted the info guide. "They're talking about the structure's religious significance."

"When in actuality it's a giant target for God when he wants to practice hurtling lightning bolts," Nina put in, her eyes sparkling with mischief.

Gabriel chuckled. "Not exactly." His amusement faded as he took note of the tension in her face. "Is something wrong?"

"I had that dream again," she said after taking another sip of her tea. "Same as before, only this time I was able to sense...feelings."

A thoughtful look appeared on Gabriel's face. "It sounds like you experienced some type of psychic transference."

"But from whom and for what purpose?"

"I don't know," Gabriel answered. "Maybe another Celestial is trying to communicate with you, or maybe this is another facet of your adaptation to the increased levels of Celestial energy I sense in you."

"I don't understand that one either," Nina sighed. "I've been feeling like an energizer battery ever since that night at the Fox, and my senses are off the chart!"

Gabriel favored her with an apologetic grin. "I'm afraid I can't give you any answers. None of the other Harbingers I've protected have ever gone through such a metamorphosis. Perhaps Shift can offer you some insight?"

Nina's eyes widened. "Shift?"

"She is a being composed entirely of Celestial energy," Gabriel noted. "I'm sure her perspective on the matter will be entirely different than ours."

"Perhaps you're right," Nina said, marveling at how easy it was becoming for her to accept the unearthly origins of the people around her. "Hell, at this point what have I got to lose?"

Gabriel smiled and they both turned their attention back to the television. "So, what's the real story behind those rocks?" Nina nodded toward the screen.

"It's a Celestial gate that connects Earth to the other inhabited planets of Mortalia."

"So that's the Gateway the glowing book's always going on about." Nina couldn't help the awe that filtered through her voice.

Gabriel favored her with an approving look. "I see someone's been doing some reading."

Nina grimaced. "I have to admit Michael's Journal is hard to put down once you get into it. And the fact that it's all true makes reading it a surreal kind of thing."

Gabriel smiled. Nina's easy acceptance of the bizarre twist her life had taken over the past two years never ceased to amaze him. "I'm glad *you* think so. I've always felt it was a bit...condescending."

Nina flashed him a wicked grin. "Well, the author is an Archangel!" Her expression turned serious. "Though I have to admit the book does tend to portray Mortals as a bunch of immature brats; especially us humans." Nina shuddered at the numerous accounts of Mankind's folly chronicled throughout the Journal's iridescent pages. "Is that really how the Celestials see us?"

"Unfortunately, yes," Gabriel soberly informed her. "Our lack of spiritual cohesiveness and propensity toward violence is the main reason the Mortal races remain separated, despite the best efforts of some of the more enterprising extraterrestrial species."

Nina's expression turned into one of regret. "That's too bad."

"Yes, it is," Gabriel agreed.

"Do you think any of us will ever be deemed...mature enough to put the gates into use?"

"I'd like to think so. Though considering what I've seen over the past century, I'd say we Mortals have a l-o-o-o-n-g way to go."

"Yeah, we do," Nina said with a snort. "What this Realm needs is a Celestial drill sergeant to whip us into shape."

"Or an overachieving Harbinger to teach us the error of our ways," Gabriel said, nodding at her.

Nina laughed at the reverent look aimed at her. "Yeah right; I seriously doubt that I've been granted these Celestial quirks to be this Realms guiding light!"

Gabriel made no response to her quip. Even after two years and her steadily progressing Celestial talents she still chose to downplay her significance in the greater scheme of things. "So, what's on Father Griffin's mind?"

Nina shrugged; her eyes now focused on the television. "I have no idea, but I'm sure he'll explain everything when he gets here. So how did that thing really get built?" She nodded toward the series of computer-generated simulations on the screen portraying the various theories on how Stonehenge's massive lintels were set in place. "The Journal never mentions that."

"It was designed and assembled by the Archangel Raphael."

Nina's left eyebrow arched upward. "I've been wondering about that guy. There are a couple of references to him in the first two chapters, but after that he's never mentioned again. What's his story?"

A loud buzz sounded from the apartment's intercom before the Celemor could answer.

"That must be Tyree," Nina announced sparing the kitchen clock a brief glance. "Yep: twelve o'clock on the dot. That man's punctual to a fault."

"Like you're any different," Gabriel shot back.

"And just where are you disappearing to?" Nina questioned his fading form as she made her way to the intercom.

Just giving you guys some privacy, the Celemor's disembodied voice floated through her mind. *Do try to behave yourself while I'm gone.*

The Celemor's parting comment brought a slight flush to Nina's face. Gabriel had never begrudged her and Tyree's previous romantic relationship, but she considered the hint of jealousy she sensed in her earnest guardian's mental voice both compliment and mute testament to his own feelings toward her.

"Yes Carl," Nina spoke after pressing the receive button on the intercom.

"Father Griffin's on his way up with some bags of food that sure smell good!"

Nina laughed. "Thanks Carl. When he leaves, I'll have him bring you a plate."

"If there's any left," Carl speculated.

"Knowing Tony there'll be enough for you and half the first floor!"

Carl's chuckle echoed through the speaker. "You're probably right. Thanks Miss D."

Nina disconnected then reached over to the door and flipped the deadbolt to open. She made her way back to the kitchen where she grabbed a couple of plates and some glasses from the cabinet and sat them on the counter. Within minutes the door's chime sounded.

"Come on in, Ty!"

"Hey, Nina," Tyree greeted her as he made his way into the apartment.

Nina balked at the number of bags he was carrying. "When we're done, I'm gonna fix a plate for you to take down to Carl. There's no way you and I are going to eat all that!"

Tyree smiled. "You know, Tony. He's convinced that none of us 'young-up-and-comers' as he puts it ever eat enough."

Nina gave her friend's lean frame a speculative look. "Well, you are looking a bit thin."

"You're one to talk," Tyree cried running approving eyes over Nina's chiseled figure. "You get any more ripped, I'm gonna enter you in a body-building contest!"

Nina released an indignant snort. "Then go yell at Gabriel. He's the one that's been keeping me on my toes."

"Don't even get me started on him. Down at Main Center the kids call him the Gabe-inator."

Nina burst out laughing. "I'd say the name suits him."

"Where is the poster boy for physical fitness anyway?" Tyree asked after sitting the bags down on the kitchen counter.

"He popped out for a while." Nina couldn't help but smile at the literal truth of her statement. "You sounded kind of tense on the phone, and he didn't want to intrude on our personal time."

"I appreciate the courtesy but that wasn't necessary. I actually need to talk with both of you; about what happened the other night at the Fox."

"Haven't you been watching the news?"

Tyree gave her a pointed look. "The incident I'm referring to didn't make the evening broadcast. It was brought to my attention this morning by a young woman named Cara Simmons."

A puzzled frown appeared on Nina face. "Is that name supposed to many anything to me?"

Tyree's left eyebrow arched upward. "It should. She's the woman whose leg you miraculously mended after she and her colleagues assaulted you at the Fox."

Nina jerked in surprise then favored the Minister with a slight smile. "In that case I'd better fetch Gabriel back. The three of us need to have a long overdue chat."

Tyree flashed a humorless smile. "I think that would be best."

Nina held his gaze for another moment then turned her eyes upward. "Oh, Gabe, darling; come out come out, wherever you are!"

The look of confusion on the Minister's face quickly morphed into one of astonishment as Gabriel appeared beside Nina amidst a flash of light.

"My God," he gasped, leaning heavily against the counter to steady himself. "Would somebody please tell me what in the name of Saint Christopher is going on!"

The Harbinger and Celemor exchanged amused looks with one another then, after leading a trembling Tyree to the living room where he collapsed wordlessly onto the sofa, began their tale.

An hour later, the dazed Minister was sitting in the driver's seat of the church's battered Dodge Caravan, his hands tightly clutching the steering wheel while his mind tried to grasp all that he had just learned. He shot a quick glance at the worn, leather-bound journal sitting on the seat beside him and a chill went through his body. Everything he thought he knew about God and the world around him was wrong. *Everything!*

The minister took several deep breaths to calm his racing heart, his jaw working silently in an effort to return moisture to his dry mouth. A part of his mind held on to the hope that this was all some sort of silly prank or delusion. The soft unearthly glow emanating from the book completely dispelled it. He'd come here seeking answers and had gotten way more than he bargained for! The question now was: what to do with this startling revelation?

Focused as he was on his thoughts when he drove off the lot, Tyree paid no attention to the black Durango sliding smoothly into place behind him as he puttered down Jefferson.

*

Cardinal Charles Dresden's wrinkled hand tightened on the phone's receiver as he listened intently to Malakai's report. "And what was Griffin's response?" he asked when the Neutralizer had finished.

"After Cara's visit he left his office," Malakai's controlled voice sounded from the receiver. "Joey and I tailed him to the Jeffersonian Apartments."

"Straight to the serpent's lair," Dresden mused. "How long was he there?"

"I'd say roughly an hour, but it must have been a productive hour."

Dresden's eyes narrowed. "What do you mean?"

"We took up position across from the apartment's front lot where Griffin parked. I'm not sure what the Delcielo woman said to him, but he appeared to be a haunted man when he left. He was also carrying a large book."

"Could you tell what it was?"

"We were too far away to get a good look but the way he had it wrapped up in his arms makes me think that it was something important."

All was silent for a moment as Dresden pondered the Neutralizer's report. "I'm curious as to what he was given by that witch."

"We could...retrieve it for you," Malachi suggested.

"Please do so. Quietly, if possible, Malakai; I'd rather not invoke a scandal."

"We'll do our best, Your Grace."

Chapter 31

Lie stood quietly before the shimmering Window hovering in the center of her circular meditation chamber. Her piercing green eyes gazed intently at the scene displayed through the Window's space displacing expanse while a smile of amusement curved her full lips.

And what mystery within Mortalia fascinates you today, Mistress?

The Halfling's smile deepened at Kaela's question echoing through her mind. "I was merely enjoying the results of my little...addition to the skirmish between the two Jihad factions currently battling in the Land of Abraham. The heart attack I induced in the master strategist of the more dominant of the two should add a little excitement to the ongoing melee."

Do you ever tire of toying with your Earthly brethren?

A touch of contempt flashed through Lie's eyes. "Take caution with your words, Kaela. Though a drop of Mortal blood runs through my veins, I do not claim the vermin as my kin, nor will I accept that designation from you."

Whether you accept them or not is irrelevant, Kaela sharply informed her agitated charge. *You are a child of both the Celestial and Mortal worlds, and if you ever hope to achieve your lofty goals you must accept that distinction. Remember,* the Morphling continued in less accusing tones. *Your Celestiality is the source of your phenomenal abilities, but the Divine essence the Almighty infused within the Mortal soul is your greatest strength. Do not neglect yours.*

"Consider me properly chastised," Lie snapped. "Now was there something in particular you wanted, or did you simply feel the need to exercise your maternal muscles?"

The Seers have discovered that the former Celemor, Caleb is currently seeking an audience with your father, Kaela announced, unperturbed by the animosity radiating from her mistress. Long association with Lie's volatile nature had rendered the Morphling immune to the Halfling's petulant outbursts.

A thoughtful frown covered Lie's face as she considered this information. "Where is the hapless fool?"

At present he is his waiting in the Courtyard of Reflection.

"How long has he been there?"

From what I understand, several days; your father has yet to acknowledge him.

Lie released a disgusted snort. "He will. The winged twit thrives on dramatic encounters. Now what could Caleb want with him?"

Perhaps he seeks counsel on the new Halfling and her purpose within the Creation, Kaela speculated.

"You're probably right. From what I've observed of my Celestial cousin, she's not even aware of her true heritage. She believes she's merely a Harbinger as does her guardian."

That is a most unusual move on the Archangel's part. What advantage is there to leaving a Halfling ignorant of her status within the Hierarchy?

"Nina's lack of knowledge has severely limited her Celestial abilities, which in turn has kept her from notice by the more prominent members of the Hierarchy."

A ripple of surprise flowed through Kaela's mental voice. *The Archangels wanted to hide her. But to what end?*

Lie frowned. "That's the question that needs answering. Have the Seers continue to monitor Caleb and inform me the moment my father deigns to acknowledge him."

Thy will be done. And what new chicanery are you planning within Mortalia? Kaela asked sensing a hint of mischief in her Mistress' aura.

Lie chuckled. "I think it's time our dear Nina had a crash course in Celestial genealogy."

A touch of concern flowed from Kaela. *Take caution, dear one; if Nina is the recipient of special consideration the Archangels may not take kindly to your interference.*

Lie grinned. "Such is my nature. But fear not, Kaela; my interactions with Nina will be...discreet."

Of course they will.

The Morphling's final comment, and the wave of suspicion that flowed from her mind, brought another smile to Lie's face as she returned her attention to the scene being played out within the Window.

Endurance

Chapter 32

The swirling haze that was common to Sublimia's erratic environment coalesced into a vaguely humanoid shape then quickly dissipated. The brief phenomenon went unnoticed by the peculiar Celestial hovering silently above the circular depression known throughout the Realms as the Courtyard of Reflection.

Ages ago the Celestial had been mortal; a simple shepherd named Caleb who roamed with his herd across the grassy plains of the Sinai Valley eking out a modest existence for himself and his family.

The life of a Sheppard was not an easy one, but Caleb was content, comforted by his belief that this was the path that the God of Abraham had chosen for him. But that faith was shattered by the crushing hand of the Egyptian empire sweeping across the country. Caleb's wife and three daughters had been snatched from their tents by the Pharaoh's hosts while the enraged Sheppard was left to die from the multiple stab wounds received trying to defend them.

As he lay there bleeding in the sand and praying for an end to his suffering, a glowing apparition appeared in the air before him. Caleb took heart that his journey to Heaven was underway, but such was not the case for it was not God or one of His angels hovering before him. It was the Celestial being named Iblis; an Archangel who had long since relinquished his prominent position within the Divine Watch, forever separating himself from the Almighty and His Tenets with the establishment of the city of Hell.

It was Iblis who first opened Caleb's eyes to the truth of the world around him and the politics of Heaven and Hell; a revelation that would set in motion a chain of tumultuous events culminating with Caleb's transformation into his current dichotomous state.

But that was in the past. Caleb, or Dichotomy as he now preferred to be called, was more focused on the future; particularly that of the Harbinger Nina and her Celemor guardian, Gabriel.

Two Mortal years had passed since Nina's initial Emergence, and though her Celestial prowess continued to grow as did her popularity among Earth's religious subcultures, her Divine purpose had yet to be revealed.

Generally speaking, once a Harbinger's abilities emerged, whatever Divine addition to the Tenets they were called upon to deliver was done so swiftly. Dichotomy was hopeful that the reticent Raphael could answer some of their questions.

The blended being had communicated their request to the semi-sentient Mist swirling about the Courtyard, knowing that it in turn would alert the Archangel of their presence. As of yet, a response to their entreaty had not been forthcoming, but such was often the case when dealing with the upper echelons of the Hierarchy.

Ages ago, the solemn Archangel had stood proudly beside his brothers amidst Heaven's gleaming spires. But the harsh treatment of Lilith, one of the first Mortals to walk the Earth and later Raphael's consort, following a disagreement between her and members of the Watch planted the seeds of doubt in Raphael's mind about the correctness of the path set for humanity. The near destruction of all life on Earth during the Great Flood allowed those seed to sprout, prompting the disillusioned Celestial to remove himself from the convoluted politics of the Watch and take up residence within Sublimia's erratic border.

Dichotomy just hoped that Raphael's curiosity would prompt him to heed their call before it was too late for them to put whatever information they learned to good use.

Their protracted wait came to an abrupt end with a sudden flash of light heralding the appearance of a tall, winged male. The hovering being regarded Dichotomy through piercing blue eyes, his muscular body unaffected by the harsh winds whipping his long silver hair across his face.

"Greetings Caleb," the Archangel finally spoke. His deep voice reverberated throughout the Courtyard as he settled to the ground. He fanned his immense wings out to their full expanse then collapsed them neatly against his broad back as he folded his arms across his bare, muscular chest. "I hear the two of you have been looking for me."

"We have," Dichotomy said after according the Archangel a respectful bow.

"What is it that you want?"

"Some insight as to the reasons behind the Harbinger Nina Delcielo's recent Emergence."

"Emergence?" Raphael's left eyebrow arched upward while his hands dropped to the braided lariat secured around the waist of his white loose-fitting trousers, its color and texture identical to that of his flowing mane. "I'd say it was more of an awakening."

Dichotomy's form wavered briefly. "We don't understand."

Raphael's eyes narrowed slightly as he studied Dichotomy's face. "No, I guess you don't." He shook his head from side to side. "Poor Caleb, so desperate to distance yourself from the Hierarchy yet still tangled in its deceptive web."

"The Hierarchy no longer dictates our actions," Dichotomy replied stiffly. "Like you we have chosen a life of separation from the structure of the Tenets and the duties of the Watch."

"Yes, but unlike me the personas that reside within your mingled form consistently involve themselves with Watch affairs. Why else would you concern yourself with the likes of Nina Delcielo?"

"The majority of our concern lies not for Nina but rather her guardian," Dichotomy admitted, the dual personas within him struggling to keep the growing irritation out of their voice. Like his brothers, Raphael was quick to take offense with those he considered inferior. "Gabriel's time with Nina has far exceeded that of a normal Task of this nature, as has the revelation of the Harbinger's purpose."

"Ah, but that's the problem," Raphael shot back. "Nina is not a Harbinger, at least not in the traditional sense of the word."

Once again Dichotomy's form wavered with uncertainty. "If she's not a Harbinger then what is she?"

Raphael's wings twitched against his back. "The daughter of my brother Michael."

The Archangel's revelation washed over Dichotomy like a tidal wave, causing his form to morph rapidly between the male and female halves of his personality. It took the Celestial several seconds to regain their composure at which time their features coalesced once again into those of Dichotomy's Pre-Celestial Mortal form. "Are you saying that she's a *Halfling*?"

A devious grin parted Raphael's full lips. "Yes, but unlike any that has existed in the history of The Creation do to her Mortal lineage."

"How so?"

Raphael's wings gave another shudder. "Unbeknownst to Michael at the time of his...indulgence, the Blood of Abraham flowed through Nina's mother's veins and was subsequently passed into those of the child they conceived. Nina is a totally unique creature with the bearing, temperament, and soul of a Mortal coupled with a Divine might that, once fully developed, could rival that of The Almighty Himself."

Dichotomy was stunned. Dalliances between Celestials and Mortals were common but were governed by a rigid code of conduct. In the history of The Creation such a thing had never occurred. "But...how is that possible, and why would The Almighty allow such a being to exist given his ban on the blending of certain Mortal bloodlines and the potential threat said being might someday pose?"

"Only He can answer that question, but I would assume it has to do with her current position in the infrastructure."

"Which is," Dichotomy pressed when Raphael failed to elaborate.

"Nina's purpose is to disrupt Earth's fragmented religious structure to the point where it implodes. Only then will the Mortals be tenable to the reintroduction of the Divine Truth."

Dichotomy's form wavered again. "Are you saying that her purpose is the same as that of...the Son?"

"Not quite," Raphael stated. "The institution of Christianity was The Almighty's attempt to clean up the distortions of the Journals perpetrated by the unrighteous; to gently redirect Humanity back onto their preordained path. Unfortunately, Mortalia's spiritual malaise has progressed too far for such niceties. This time there will be no subtlety in the matter. Nina is the Harbinger of what could potentially become the Final Reclamation."

Dichotomy's eyes widened. "Final...but that would mean..."

"That the Last Rising is upon us," Raphael finished the distressed Celestial's sentence.

The Courtyard was silent for several minutes while Dichotomy slowly digested Raphael's disclosure. The Last Rising...? Just the thought of it chilled the blended being to his core.

"And what is to become of Nina once her Task is complete?

A solemn look consumed Raphael's sharp features. "That depends on her. I would assume that once this Divine undertaking is complete, she will occupy a position of significant authority in the New Order; providing she's up to the Task. Or to put it in a more direct term: She will either restore the Balance or be consumed by the coming conflagration; a fate similar to that of He whom you once held so dear."

"What?" Dichotomy's shout reverberated throughout the Courtyard. "But...why? Why must she suffer the same fate as Christ?"

Raphael's expression softened. "You of all people should know that the Mortals define their existence through their struggles, and the sacrifice of their heroes. Such is the way of their world."

"No!" Dichotomy screamed, thinking of the anguish such an event would cause Gabriel, and Nina whom the blended being had also grown quite fond of. "We will not allow our friends to suffer the pain of such martyrdom!"

Raphael favored the enraged Celestial with a stern look. "Such may be her destiny, Caleb."

"Then we will do all within our power to change it!"

"I know you will," Raphael whispered in the wake of Dichotomy's abrupt departure.

The Archangel allowed his gaze to range over the Courtyard for a moment then a regretful sigh escaped his lips. "I do not like this game you've initiated," he uttered softly. "Such manipulations on your part are what led to Caleb's fractured state, and my subsequent abandonment of the Watch."

I know, my son, The Almighty's voice echoed through the Archangel's mind. *But such duplicity is necessary for my Mortal children to achieve their true potential. The time has come for them to take their rightful place amongst the Realms as the Shepherds of the Balance, but to do that their metal must be tested. The turmoil wrought by the current Reclamation will provide that test.*

As Raphael pondered the ramifications of The Almighty's words a slight flutter impinged upon his awareness.

The Archangel's eyes flared briefly, and the surrounding Mist began to undulate, taking on a humanoid shape. "It is impolite to eavesdrop," he coldly told the ethereal being now quivering before him. "I suggest you and your kin remember that. The next time I catch you meddling in my affairs my reprimand will not be tempered with mercy."

"My apologies Raphael," a wispy voice replied. "Such a transgression will not happen again."

"For your sake let's hope not."

The form coalesced once more as the Archangel released his hold over it then completely dissipated.

"I'm afraid word of your true intentions for Mortalia will soon spread to dissident ears, Father," the Archangel ground out. "I sensed my daughter's taint upon that creature."

Worry not, my son, the Almighty replied and Raphael was surprised by the satisfaction in his Creator's tone. *Lillian's involvement was expected, and, as you know, necessary.*

The feeling of unease that had resided in the pit of the Archangel's stomach ever since The Almighty had made him privy to the true ramifications of The Rising increased two-fold. "I've never been overly thrilled with *that* situation either."

I know that as well, but such has become her fate. And though your heart has always been saddened by the road she now travels you must never forget that she was the one that chose it. Such decisions are never without consequences.

The Almighty removed His presence from Raphael's mind, leaving the Archangel alone in the Courtyard to ponder the significance of his daughter's involvement in the upcoming cosmic events.

*

Lie dismissed the formless Seer with a curt nod then contemplated his report. The revelation of Nina's position as well as the Almighty's intention to initiate the Final Reclamation was unexpected; especially given the fact that her father appeared to be a prominent player in this unfolding drama as opposed to that benevolent fool,

Michael. Usually such Creation-changing events fell under his providence.

Her thoughts turned to The Rising. Long ago, before their relationship had soured, Raphael had shared with her the workings of what was essentially a battle between the forces of Chaos and Order that permeated the Realms. The Final Reclamation was the culling of the various races of the Creation to prepare them for that event. Those deemed worthy would be allowed to continue in their evolutionary advancement within Mortalia's new infrastructure while those found wanting would be forever expunged from the Creation as the Realms progressed to their next evolutionary stage in the Reality left behind following the Rising's wake. Left out of that disclosure was the prominent role the misbegotten inhabitants of Earth would play in the upcoming Diaspora.

Lie's pulse quickened. For centuries she had sought various ways to punish those wretched curs for the numerous indignities both she and her mother had suffered at their uncaring hands. Engineering their expulsion from The Creation would be the ultimate vengeance.

How to proceed was the question. The glimmerings of an idea began to take shape in the Halfling's mind, and she took a moment to mull it over. Such an audacious undertaking would take careful planning, a core of trusted allies, and a significant source of power.

The first was Lie's providence, as for the second and third: A cunning smile parted the Halfling's lips as she considered how best to obtain those as well.

Chapter 32

"And how long have you been having this dream?"

"It started the day after the incident at the Fox."

A look of consternation appeared on Shift's face. "Gabriel was correct in his assessment of this being a psychic transference, and your description of the being in your dream fits that of one of the Archangels. The question now is why has this connection been forged?"

Nina shrugged. "That's why I asked you to come over. Gabriel thought that you being a Morphling might allow you a different perspective on the whole thing."

Shift cast her eyes at the Celemor leaning casually against the wall. "Your faith in my deductive abilities is flattering."

Gabriel smiled. "I give credit where credit is due."

Shift accorded him a nod of thanks then extended her hands toward Nina. "Come, my friend. Let us attempt a partial transference of our own so that I might gaze upon the residuals of your dream."

A look of unease settled on Nina's face as she gingerly took hold of the Morphling's hands. "It's not going to hurt, is it?"

Shift chuckled. "Not at all; in fact, you probably won't feel a...Oh!" the Morphling gasped from the surge of energy she received from Nina when their hands made contact.

"Shift!" Nina quickly reached forward to steady the staggering Morphling while casting concerned eyes to Gabriel who had also stepped up.

"I am uninjured," Shift quickly assured them both. "Your body crackles with energy, Nina. It caught me off guard."

Nina breathed a sigh of relief. "Were you able to pick up anything before my mind got to hot?"

Shift smiled at the curious Mortal that she had grown to deeply respect over the past several months. "The man in your dream is the Archangel Michael."

"Michael?" Nina turned troubled eyes to Gabriel. "Now why in the world would I be dreaming about him?"

"Well, you have been reading his Journal."

"Hell, I've been reading that thing for two years and I've never had dreams about him before. Why should it matter now?"

"It matters because your connection to the Archangel is more visceral than you realize," Dichotomy's voice boomed as the Celestial appeared in the apartment amidst a flash of light, startling Nina and the others.

"The two of you thrive on dramatic entrances!"

Nina's exasperated cry brought smiles to the faces of Gabriel and Shift. Dichotomy however was not amused.

"Forgive our intrusion, Nina but there is much we need to discuss with you."

Nina's stomach tightened with apprehension. "Concerning what?"

"Your true heritage," the blended Celestial answered then proceeded to tell Nina and the others all they had learned from Raphael.

"That definitely explains the dream," Gabriel broke the shocked silence that filled the apartment when Dichotomy had finished.

"Indeed, it does," Shift said placing a gentle arm around Nina's trembling shoulders. "Are you alright?"

"Actually, I'm not," Nina declared, turning haunted eyes to Gabriel whose hand also rested on her shoulder. "Can this truly be real?"

"I'm afraid it is, Nina," a soft voice echoed from the nimbus of white light appearing before them, coalescing into the winged form of the Archangel Michael.

"Oh my God," Nina gasped while Shift and Gabriel immediately accorded the Archangel a respectful bow.

Michael returned the courtesy then focused his attention on Nina.

"Then...it's true?" Nina managed to ask, still staring at him in shock and awe. "You really are my...my...father?"

"I am," Michael acknowledged with a slight nod. "Though it is not the way I intended for you to learn the truth." The Archangel turned disapproving eyes to Dichotomy. "You overstep your bounds, Caleb."

"Why?" Nina snapped, anger replacing amazement. She broke free of Gabriel and Shift's supportive embrace and took an angry step toward Michael. "Because they," she jabbed a finger at Dichotomy, "had the decency to tell me the truth about who, and what, I am? Why didn't *you* do it?"

The damn that had been holding Nina's emotions in check burst. Tears sprang to her eyes as the resentment she had nurtured for so long poured out of her trembling body. "All my life I've been searching for my father, wondering why he abandoned me! Why the hell did I have to find out I'm some freak child of a stupid Angel from anyone other than *you*?"

Michael stared at the seething woman...his daughter...and a feeling of regret settled heavily onto his broad shoulders. When he spoke, his voice was filled with compassion. "There were so many times I wanted to make you aware of your true heritage, Nina; to...embrace you as a proper father should."

Nina's anger subsided somewhat when she took note of the genuine regret in his voice and manner. "Then why *didn't* you?"

Her burning entreaty pierced Michael's heart. He favored her with a mournful look. "Keeping you ignorant of your heritage was the only way to for me to ensure that you would have a normal life."

Nina released a disgusted snort. "And how's that plan working out?"

A regretful sigh escaped the Archangel's lips. "Not as well as I would have hoped."

Nina studied his face, easily identifying her own features in his as she tried to reconcile this bizarre turn of events. Her father! The man she had spent her entire life trying to find was now standing before her, and he was a freaking angel! She tried her best to hold on to the anger she had held in her heart for so long, but it was no use. The sheer wonder of the moment eventually took over.

She breathed a heavy sigh, the last vestiges of resentment draining away as she stared into the eyes that were so much like her own. "I'm trying very hard to hate you right now," she admitted with a resigned sigh.

A slight smile creased Michael's lips and he took her hands gently in his. "And you have every right to, but I do hope you can find it in your heart to forgive me..."

Michael's words were cut short by the sharp slap Nina dealt his face.

"That's for leaving me in the dark about who and what I am," she responded to the stunned expressions from everyone in the room, the most poignant being the one on Michael's face. "And this is for finally showing up," she cried, tears once again springing from her eyes as she threw herself forward and wrapped her arms tightly about his muscular form, Michael eagerly returning her embrace. Both were surprised at how natural it felt.

"Miguel Delcielo," Nina uttered, her head still lying against the sculpted muscles of his chest. "Michael of Heaven; now I see why mom never wanted to talk about you!"

A wistful sigh escaped the Archangel's lips. "Evelyn Sanchez truly was an amazing Mortal."

Nina pulled away so she could see his face. "Who was she; to you, I mean?"

A tender smile played at his lips. "Originally she was just another Mortal whose tireless efforts on behalf of those around her caught my attention." He brought his eyes down to meet Nina's. "But over time she became much more."

Nina took note of the tenderness in his voice. "Did you...love her; the way a man loves a woman?"

A soft glow issued from the Archangel's eyes, and he pressed his lips softly against his daughter's forehead. "See for yourself."

Nina gasped as a kaleidoscope of images assaulted her mind. They were images of her mother, but she looked...different. She looked younger...Nina gasped again. This was her mother as a young woman!

She watched in silent wonder as the story of her mother's life played out before her: Her work as an Army medic during various campaigns around the globe followed by a promising career as a medical researcher when she returned to civilian life. A bought with breast cancer at age thirty-two that left her bed-ridden, awaiting the release of death; the appearance of the winged Michael at her bedside telling her that the Lord at taken notice of her work on Earth and that she still had much to do; glimpses of the unexpected relationship that developed between her and the Archangel shortly after her miraculous recovery and subsequent release from the hospital.

The images changed to various shots of Nina as a child from what appeared to be an aerial view. Her pulse quickened when she realized that these images told the story of the Archangel's silent vigil over his intrepid daughter from the crystal spires of Heaven. The torrent of visual vignettes played on for several seconds before finally culminating with an image of her mother's entrance into the city of

Heaven's Pearl-encrusted gates following the horrendous automobile accident that had claimed her life.

"Why did He take her," Nina whispered, tears of both joy and sorrow flowing freely down her flushed cheeks. "Why did God take her away from me?"

Michael enveloped his daughter's mind and body with a wave of compassion. "I've yet to learn the reason behind my His decision, but rest assured her soul will forever reside in a place of peace and honor in Celestia."

Nina could sense the truth of his words through the psychic rapport that she realized now existed between them. That same connection also allowed her to extract the other reason for the impromptu visit. "You're here with bad news."

A regretful sigh escaped Michael's lips. "I'm afraid so, my child. Events have recently transpired that I fear will introduce a fair amount of turmoil into your life, and your tutelage is incomplete."

Nina reluctantly disentangled herself from his embrace. "Tutelage in what?"

"The use of your Celestial abilities; as Caleb explained earlier, your dual heritage makes you unique, and there is much you need to learn in order to reach your full potential."

"Can't these guys teach me what I need to know?" Nina indicated the silent forms of Gabriel, Shift, and Dichotomy, now standing in a protective semicircle around her.

Michael spared the trio a brief glance then gave a negative shake of his head. "Powerful and wise your comrades and guardian may be, but they are woefully ignorant to the ways of Halflings, let alone one such as you. For that you will need a guide thoroughly versed in such matters."

Nina regarded her father through suspicious eyes. "And just who might that be?"

A touch of humor appeared in the Archangel's eyes. "Your sister," he said then abruptly vanished, only to be replaced by a dark-skinned Mortal woman approximately Nina's age, her brown eyes and attractive features somewhat familiar.

"And you are?" Gabriel asked taking a protective step in front of Nina.

"Like Michael said," the woman spoke, a mischievous smile tugging at her thin lips. "Nina's sister; half-sister if you want to get technical."

Nina stiffened as the familiar timbre of the woman's voice brought instant recognition. *"Misses Watson?"*

Willimena inclined her head toward Nina. "The one and only; now I suggest you all get comfortable." Her gaze widened to include Gabriel, Shift, and Dichotomy's glowing form. "The story I'm about tell you may take a while!"

Chapter 33

Mistress?

"Yes Kaela?" Lie answered her handmaiden's call; her attention focused on the startling events playing out in Nina's apartment.

The Seers have just come across a unique situation involving one of Nina's contemporaries that might be of some interest to you.

"Which one?"

The Priest.

A spark of excitement flowed through Lie's body. She and Father Griffin had had dealings in the past though she doubted if the fledgling priest knew that it was Lie who had secretly helped him expunge the demented Demonstrative from a beleaguered Mortal whelp named Katy. "Show me," she commanded, watching eagerly as the image in the Window reconfigured itself.

*

"My God," Tyree whispered as he poured over the faintly luminescent pages of the Journal. "Everything we've been taught...everything I believed in...it's all a lie!"

"What's the matter, Father," a raspy voice sounded from the office's doorway. "The story you're reading not to your liking?"

Tyree jerked at the unexpected appearance of the two men entering his office. One was tall and muscular with auburn hair tinged with gray while the other was short and stocky, the muted light of the office reflecting from his bald head. "And who might you be?" the Minister asked.

"Associates of Bishop Dresden," the taller one answered drawing another startled look from Tyree. "I'm Malakai and this is Joey."

"How did the two of you get in here?" Tyree asked a feeling of unease settling upon him as he took note of the hostility radiating from the man's eyes.

Malakai released a contemptuous snort. "The locks on your front door are a joke. You really should invest in a more secure entry."

"Apparently I should," Tyree grunted regretting his steadfast refusal to the Vestry's idea of hiring a security team to patrol Saint Christopher's grounds during the afterhours. "How may I help you gentlemen?"

Malakai nodded toward the Journal. "I'm afraid we're going to need that book."

Tyree stiffened, his eyes flicking briefly to the Journal. "And for what reason do you require it?"

"Let's just say we're with the religious preservation department of the *Presbyterii*," Joey responded, his raspy voice sending additional shivers down the Minister's back.

The two men had to be members of the Neutralizers that Cara had warned him about. The fact that they were currently standing in his office inquiring about what could very well be the most significant religious tome in history did not bode well. "You didn't answer my question," Tyree stalled while he contemplated his next move.

"Cardinal Dresden is very interested in what that book contains," Malakai clarified as he and Joey moved further into the office. "After all, it is the job of our Elders to ensure that no heretic ramblings be allowed to influence the minds of the faithful."

A fine bead of sweat broke out on the Minister's forehead. "The book is not mine to give, gentlemen so I'm afraid I won't be able to honor the Cardinal's request."

"Look, priest, we need that book," Joey snapped, his lips drawing back into a feral smile. "Now why don't you just hand it over, and we'll be on our way; no fuss, no muss."

"If it's no fuss you want then maybe you guys had better take off," a feminine voice rang out.

The attention of all three men was drawn to the office's door where Cara now stood, her prized nine-millimeter Beretta trained on Joey and Malakai.

Malakai shook his head from side to side. "Bad move, Car. You know what happens to those lost souls who turn their backs on the Cardinal's orders."

"All too well but in this case I'm gonna have to take my chances. Come Father." Cara jerked her head at Tyree. "Let's get you and your glowing book to a place that's a little less hostile."

Tyree didn't know what miracle had brought the burly woman to his aid, but now wasn't the time to question such divine providence. He quickly gathered up the Journal and began making his way toward her. As he moved past Malakai, the man's arm shot out and his hand tightened painfully on Tyree's shoulder.

Before the Minister could react, a thunderous rapport filled the office and Malakai staggered back, frantically clutching at his throat.

"Oh my God," Tyree gasped when it finally dawned on him that the man had just been shot.

"Come ON, Father!"

Cara's urgent call broke the Minister's shocked paralysis. He moved hurriedly toward the office door while Cara kept the gun trained on Joey who was easing the wounded Malakai into one the chairs in front of Tyree's desk.

"You know it's not over." Joey's voice caught Cara before she backed out of the office, and the two locked eyes. "No one betrays the Elders; No one!" The feral smile reappeared on his face. "I'll be coming for you, Car; *real soon!*"

For Cara, the seething fury radiating from the Neutralizer's steely gaze gave mute testament to the line she had just crossed. Neutralizers were relentless when it came to accomplishing their assignments and none more so than Joey. Cara knew that her sadistic former colleague would hunt her until the End of Days and no matter how far she ran would eventually find her.

"I know you will Joey," she said, a note of resignation in her voice. "And that makes my next decision a lot less difficult." She sighed then squeezed the trigger three times, putting all three bullets in the man's chest.

Joey slumped to the ground, and Cara turned the gun on Malakai.

"Don't," Tyree's soft voice reached her ears at the same time the Minister's trembling hand rested atop her arm. "He's already down. Let's just...let's just get out of here!"

Cara maintained her position for another moment then returned the Beretta to the holster strapped under her shoulder. "Okay," she whispered, and followed him out of the office without a backward glance.

The two quickly made their way to Cara's waiting Stratus, parked on the street in front of the church behind Joey and Malakai's Durango. They jumped in and Cara engaged the engine, shifted the car into drive, and sped away.

"Where are we going?" Tyree asked as they merged smoothly with the evening traffic.

"To Quinlan and Sander's place," she answered keeping her eyes on the road. "I'm hoping they'll be able to help us out of this mess."

"Ah." Tyree shut his eyes and pressed further into his seat; the memory of Joey's body being riddled with bullets playing repeatedly in his mind. "Did you have to shoot him?" he asked after they had been driving for a while.

"I couldn't let Malakai get the upper hand."

"I'm not talking about Malakai," Tyree snapped.

Cara's hands tightened on the steering wheel. "Joey was a killer, Father, and a sadistic one at that. There's no telling the lengths he would've gone to satisfy his thirst for vengeance. He had to be stopped."

"Granted," Tyree said opening his eyes. He studied the woman's sullen frown reflected in the Stratus' windshield. "But did you have to kill him?"

The light in front of them turned red and Cara brought the car to a gentle stop. "Yes, I did," she said after a brief pause.

"But...*why?*"

Cara cringed at the anguish in the Minister's voice. "Because it's what the Elders trained me to do," she answered softly.

Tyree studied her reflection for another moment then averted his eyes as she accelerated when the light changed. He looked down at the Journal resting in his lap, and tendrils of apprehension wrapped around his shoulders. Tonight's brutality was probably just the beginning. Of what he didn't know, but he suspected things were about to get a lot worse.

*

Malakai knew he was dying.

Cara's shot hadn't completely severed the carotid artery when it struck, but the gaping hole it had left in his throat was enough to allow the majority of his blood to flow freely from his body. Already he could feel the numbness in his hands and feet spreading throughout his extremities; a sure sign that he was going into shock.

He heard a gargled cough to his left and managed to shift his position over in the chair just enough to catch a glimpse of Joey, lying in the pool of blood being continuously fed by the holes in his chest. As a former Marine, Malakai had seen enough gunshot wounds to know that his friend's were fatal. A part of him wished Cara's aim had been a bit more proficient. A clean shot through the heart would've been preferable to Joey suffocating as his lungs filled with blood.

Sitting there waiting for darkness to claim him, Malakai couldn't help but marvel at the way his life was ending. Him: one of the *Presbyterii's* most efficient Neutralizers, survivor of numerous campaigns in the Middle East, and a slew of equally hazardous assignments for the Elders, brought down by a single bullet fired from the gun of one of his own! Such an ironic demise belonged in a Hollywood melodrama.

The wounded man tried to chuckle at the sheer injustice of the whole thing, but the laugh quickly turned into a choking cough. A slight movement drew his attention toward the doorway, and his eyes widened as a nimbus of bright light materialized in front of him.

I guess this is it. The angels come to take me away.

Malakai had no doubt in his heart that his soul would find its way into Heaven. Hadn't he spent the past ten years of his life eliminating threats to God's holy plan? There was a war of the spirit raging throughout the world, and all wars resulted in bloodshed. Like the noble clergy of the Inquisition, his was a mission of Christian purity, and he had done all he could to see that mission carried out.

The light coalesced into a woman, and Malakai gasped in amazement for she was the most beautiful woman he had ever seen. Her skin was ivory, her body tall and lean. A heavy mass of platinum hair was braided into a single thick pleat that hung past her waist. Her eyes, the color of the purest emeralds were fixated on his, and a slight smile curved her sensuous lips.

"Who...who are you?" Malakai managed to croak.

The woman's smile deepened. "I am Lie, daughter of the Archangel Raphael."

"Are you here to...to take...take me to Heaven?"

Lie kneeled before him and placed a gentle hand against his cheek. "No, my dear Malakai; I'm here to show you the Truth."

Malakai groaned as a wave of energy enveloped his body infusing every fiber of his being with a profuse heat unlike anything he had never known. He felt his strength returning and his wound began to heal. A kaleidoscope of images surged through his mind as Lie laid the truth of the Creation before his burning eyes.

When she was done, she removed her hand and stepped back.

"It's all...it's all a lie," Malakai whispered, a look of horrified betrayal on his face as he rose shakily to his feet. "Everything the Elders told us...everything I've ever believed about God and the church; it's all a *LIE*!" His fists were clenched so hard that his nails drew blood as they bit into his palms, but the anguished man paid the wounds no heed. "I've been such a fool," he whispered, his shoulder's sagging in defeat.

"No, you haven't." Lie's soothing reply caressed his ears as she reached out and cradled his face with her hands. "You've simply been misled by a God who takes pleasure in fomenting games of deceit and confusion throughout the worlds that He, Himself created."

Malakai was silent as he considered her point. He focused on Joey's twitching body then turned haunted eyes back to the Halfling. "Why did you save me?"

Lie favored him with a cunning smile. "Because I have need of you Malakai: agent of the *Presbyterii*. I've grown tired of the manipulations of the Hierarchy and wish to see it and all those connected to it fall. A man with your particular skills would do well for what I have in mind."

Malakai considered her offer for a moment then turned away to kneel beside Joey's pale form. "Same mud, same blood," he whispered thinking of the numerous adventures he and his friend had shared over the years, first as Marines then later as Neutralizers. He laid a hand gently atop the still man's forehead then shifted his gaze back to the waiting Lie. "Can you save him the way you did me?"

"I can do that and more, as you will soon come to see," she assured him, her eyes glowing softly in the dim light. "

Malakai easily sensed the power radiating from this green-eyed temptress, filling his shattered soul with a new sense of purpose. His lips parted in a grim smile. "Then consider us your servants!"

Chapter 34

The atmosphere in Nina's apartment was thick with anticipation as Willimena began her tale.

"My true name is Aken'ama. I was born in Egypt at the start of the nineteenth dynasty." Willimena smiled at the collective gasp her revelation drew from her audience. "My mother was Aken'sohep, the thirty-seventh daughter of Ramses the Second."

"And I thought you were old," Nina chided Gabriel who responded with an overly hard squeeze of her hand drawing a yelp from her mouth.

A smile briefly touched Willimena's face for the young couple's antics. "Unlike her sisters, mother had no interest in the intrigues of the Egyptian Aristocracy. Her love was for the stars, and she spent the majority of her time in the astrological archives, devouring the knowledge contained in the countless scrolls gathered by various scribes throughout the ages.

It was during one of her daily sessions that she came across a sealed box made of gold and devoid of any markings or inscriptions. Curious as to its contents she struggled for hours trying to break the seal. Eventually she did."

"Well, what was in it?" Nina demanded when Willimena failed to elaborate.

"A copy of our father's Journal."

Nina blinked. "That book really gets around."

Her quip elicited a spattering of laughter from the others.

"Indeed, it does, child. Mother wasn't sure if it was a sacred tome or the ramblings of a delusional scribe, but she was no fool. She knew that possession of such a book could potentially hold deadly consequences for its bearer, so she mentioned it to no one while she diligently set about learning its secrets."

"And she was actually able to make sense of the whole thing?" Nina asked.

A mischievous gleam appeared in Willimena's eyes. "Father became her guide," she said, drawing a second round of startled cries from her audience. "Michael, attuned as always to the handlers of his Journal, had taken notice of her efforts and decided to meet the intriguing young mortal who had taken such a keen interest in his words."

Nina released an awed whistle. "I'll bet that was a memorable encounter."

Willimena beamed. "It was the one that eventually led to my conception."

"And speaking of which," Shift interjected. "As a Halfling your Celestial aura would be considerable, yet the lack of any mention of you indicates that your existence is unknown to the majority of the Creation. How have you managed to remain anonymous for so long?"

Willimena's voice took on a somber tone. "After I was born Father shielded me. He didn't want me to have to endure the negativity Halflings are often subjected to while he tutored me in the Ways of Divinity. Once I achieved a higher degree of control, I was able to conceal myself by transferring the bulk of my Celestial energy into a sentient Vessel."

Nina's left eyebrow arched upward. "What in the world is a...'sentient vessel'?"

"Celestials adept in the manipulation of the energy within their body can create a lower life form to contain that energy. Such transference drastically reduces the initiating being's Celestial imprint throughout the Creation's collective conscious; similar to what Morphs do in the formation of their various veils." she nodded at Shift.

"Creating veils to confuse the senses is one thing," the Morphling declared. "Creating an independent entity is magnitudes above what I am capable of."

"That's only because you lack the proper training. In actuality it's not that difficult a task. Caleb managed a similar feat during the mending of his fractured psyche."

Dichotomy's form wavered. "You are aware of our history?"

"I make it a habit to keep abreast of all Celestials whose actions impact the Creation or the lives of those whom I hold dear." Willimena favored Dichotomy, Gabriel, and Shift with an approving grin. "The three of you, and your mate Darius," she addressed Shift, "have done extremely well supporting Nina."

Gabriel released an amused snort. "The same can be said of you and the Little Angel Foundation."

The smile on Willimena's face broadened. "So, you've uncovered my secret!"

Gabriel smiled in return. "I have. And judging from his absence by your side I would have to assume that the LAF's namesake was your Vessel."

"Aren't you the clever one," Willimena exclaimed. "It's easy to see why the solemn Omen holds you in such high regards."

"Wait!" Nina cried. "Are you saying that Angel wasn't a real dog?"

"Not in the Mortal sense of the word."

"But...how is that possible?"

Willimena gave the perplexed woman's shoulder a reassuring squeeze. "Worry not, dear sister; many of your questions will be answered during our Sojourn."

Nina jerked away from her touch. "Sojourn; what Sojourn?"

"The one you and I must embark upon if you are to achieve your full potential."

Nina turned frightened eyes to Gabriel then back to Willimena. "But I don't understand. Where are we going?"

"To a place more suitable to the Task ahead of us," the Halfling stated giving the living room and surrounding apartment a cursory look.

Nina held tightly to the Celemor's hand. "What about Gabriel?"

"Gabriel's Task is now complete," Willimena gently informed her, infusing as much compassion into her voice and manner as she could. Centuries of watching loved ones grow old and die while she remained the same allowed the Halfling to empathize with her sibling's pain.

"The time has come for you to venture forth on your own, Nina, although..." Willimena paused, an idea forming in her mind as she gazed upon the young woman's distraught expression. "Father didn't exactly specify that your Celemor's presence was forbidden during this process."

Nina brightened instantly. "Then...he can come with us?"

"I see no reason why not," Willimena said then steadied herself as Nina wrapped jubilant arms around her.

"Wait a minute," Nina suddenly exclaimed releasing her hold on Willimena. "What am I talking about? I can't go traipsing around the universe on some holy journey. I've got the Centers to run!"

"A dilemma that can easily be rectified," Shift said, her eyes glowing softly while her body morphed into an exact image of Nina.

"Now that's creepy," Nina uttered staring in amazement at her own self.

Shift/Nina smiled. "I know having yourself duplicated can be unsettling. But in this case, it's a necessary discomfort. You are a Halfling, Nina, and if what Caleb says is true, you are destined to become one of the most significant beings in the Creation. For that you must be properly schooled in the ways Celestiality, and I will be your stand-in for however long said training will take."

"And you're willing to make that type of sacrifice on my behalf?" Nina was still awed by the fact that such immensely powerful beings were showing her such deference.

Shift/Nina's expression turned solemn. "Lord Iblis promised you that he and all those who serve him would do whatever it takes to see your purpose fulfilled. Now that we have a clearer understanding of what that purpose is, I and those who serve with me will do whatever it takes to make that happen."

The apartment was silent as Nina's gazed touched on the faces of everyone there, coming to a final rest on Willimena. "And where exactly are we going?"

"Nirvana."

Nina stiffened. "I'm actually going to...Heaven?"

"To the city itself, no; our Sojourn begins at father's Sanctuary. But worry not," she said in response to Nina's disappointment. "You will have ample time to explore the marble spires of your other...hometown."

The Halfling's quip brought a smile to Nina's face, and she set about detailing Shift on the pertinent details of her life while all the time marveling at her circumstances. Once again, her world was about to take a drastic turn; whether or not it would be for the better remained to be seen.

"Well...I guess that's it," she announced a few hours later when everything was set. "Can anyone think of anything I might have overlooked?"

Gabriel smiled. "I can think of three: Tyree, Tony and Maria."

"My God you're right," Nina cried, aghast that she hadn't even considered the impact her leaving would have on her friends. "I doubt if you could fool them for long," she directed at Shift.

"It depends on their familiarity with you."

"Tony and Maria are basically my surrogate parents, and Tyree and I have known each other since we were toddlers."

"Then deceiving them could prove difficult," Shift admitted.

"Why fool them at all?" Dichotomy interjected. "The priest already knows a portion of the truth, and from what we've observed of your interactions with the winsome Scavelli's, we are certain they would accept your new stature with their typical aplomb."

Nina regarded the blended Celestial through narrowed eyes. "You've been keeping tabs on me too?"

"Not you per say." Dichotomy's eyes rested briefly on Gabriel. "Your guardian is one of the few beings within the Creation that we call friend. Our sight is often upon him and you by association."

Nina turned to Gabriel. "What do you think I should do?"

"I agree with Dichotomy; particularly about the Scavellis." A sparkle of humor lit the Celemor's eyes. "From the questions Tony's been putting to me I think he's beginning to suspect that I'm more than what I appear to be."

Nina laughed. "Yeah, you're probably right! Okay, let's go for it. We'll tell Tony and Maria first then we'll link up with Tyree. Will you guys come with us?" She focused on Shift, Willimena, and Dichotomy. "I've a feeling we're going to need all the evidence we can produce when we spin this tale."

"Of course," Willimena said while Shift, having reverted back to her Sheila persona, acknowledged Nina's request with an affirmative nod. Dichotomy also agreed, and the five Celestials appeared a moment later by way of teleportation on the front porch of the Scavelli's cozy ranch, located in the upscale Detroit suburb known as Grosse Point.

"Well hello people," a surprised Tony greeted the unexpected mob at his front door. "What's going on?" he asked after ushering everyone in to the stylish home's traditionally furnished front parlor where he and Maria had been watching television.

"I'm afraid I've been keeping a few secrets from you guys," Nina confessed as Gabriel and the others formed a semicircle behind her.

A look of concern appeared on Maria's face. "Nothing bad I hope,"

"I'll let you be the judge," Nina said then related to the couple everything that had taken place over the past two years, including her recent discovery of her Celestial parentage and the Sojourn that she was about to take. "And that's basically where we are now," she finished. "Well...what do you think?"

The parlor was quiet for several minutes as the Scavelli's tried to absorb her amazing tale. Finally, Tony released a low chuckle. He turned to his wife while pointing an accusing finger at Gabriel. "I told you there was something peculiar about that boy."

"Oh, hush," Maria told her husband as she rose to embrace Nina. "You poor dear," she cried clutching her surrogate daughter tightly against her heavy bosom. "Why didn't you tell us from the start what was going on?"

"I figured you guys would think I was crazy," Nina admitted as she happily returned the plump woman's embrace.

"You know better than that!" Tony snapped. "There's nothing you could *ever* tell us that would cause us to not support you." He wrapped his muscular arms around the two most important people in his life while Gabriel and the other's looked on in respectful silence.

Their embrace might have lasted forever had Nina's cell phone not rang.

"It's Tyree," she said excitedly then pressed the answer button. "Hey bud! I was just about to..." Nina's smile faded rapidly as Tyree told her of the events that had transpired at the church. "And where are you now?"

"We're with Quinlan and Sanders at their apartment," Tyree's voice echoed from the speaker after Nina switched the phone to loudspeaker mode.

"Hold on a sec, Ty." Nina turned apologetic eyes to the Scavelli's. "I need to bring Tyree up to speed on this so I'm afraid I've got to go."

"Nonsense," Maria spat. "It sounds to me like you guys need to have a major pow-wow, and you can do that out back on the deck while I stir up some dinner."

"We can't impose on you guys like that," Nina began but Maria quickly waved her into silence.

"Of course you can," the plump woman charged with a snort. "Now go fetch the rest of your friends while I get started with dinner. Light the fire pit love," she barked at Tony. "It gets kind of chilly back there." She accorded the others a brief nod then stomped to the kitchen, murmuring to herself the entire way.

Nina stared after her in concern, and Tony placed a reassuring hand on her shoulder. "Don't fret, Nina. You know cooking is how she relieves stress. Now call your friends and give them the address so they can get here by the time she gets everything ready."

"That won't be necessary Tony," Nina smiled then looked pointedly at Gabriel. "Would you be so kind?"

"Damn!" Tony spat as Gabriel promptly vanished from the room only to appear several minutes later with Tyree, Cara, Quinlan, and Sanders, all of whom were looking a bit queasy from the unnatural mode of transportation.

"This is definitely going to take some getting used to," Tony muttered as he ushered everyone from the crowded parlor back to the large, screened-in deck built off the back of the house for what promised to be a memorable meal!

Chapter 35

"Still no word from Malakai?" The hopeful expression on Cardinal Tullis' face turned into one of concern when he received Cardinal Dresden's negative reply.

"I've not heard from him or Joey since I ordered them to retrieve the harlot's book from Griffin."

"You think they ran into trouble?" Cardinal Gianni spoke up, the tone of his voice reflecting his uneasiness with this whole affair.

Shortly after dispatching Malakai and Joey on their mission of confiscation, Dresden had called an emergency meeting of the Elders at his private villa in Rome's sprawling countryside. None of them had been particularly pleased with their fellow's course of action but were now eager to see the results.

"Ordinarily I would say that those two could handle just about anything thrown at them," Dresden said. "But given the fact that the heretic routinely associates with other-worldly beings I fear they may have been compromised."

"Shot and nearly killed would be a more accurate description of what happened," a deep voice rang out from the nimbus of bright light appearing on the villa's patio where the four Elders were gathered.

"God in Heaven," Tullis cried, clutching the silver crucifix hanging from a chain around his neck with trembling hands, the other Elders reacting in a similar fashion as they backed away from the glow that rapidly coalesced into three humanoid shapes.

"Malakai," the soft-spoken Cardinal Milan gasped when the light had faded.

Malakai's lips curved into a sinister smile. "The one and only." He raised his hands toward the unfamiliar woman standing beside him, who was radiating with an unearthly beauty that sent a sliver of desire through the chaste bodies of all four Cardinals. "Elders of the

Presbyterii, I would like you to meet Lie, daughter of the Archangel Raphael, and revealer of Truth."

"And what truth do you bring us?" Dresden asked the glowing woman, his constitution stronger than that of his quivering fellows.

Lie's full lips parted in a sensuous smile that sent another jolt of desire through the Cardinal. "That of the world around you and the God you so selflessly serve," she told them while bombarding their addled minds with the same revelation she'd given Malakai and the now fully recovered Joey.

"No," Tullis whispered his body trembling when the transference was complete. "This can't be real." He turned horrified eyes to his fellow Elders, praying that one of them would put an end to this obvious nightmare. "It can't be!"

"I'm afraid it is, gentlemen," Lie's soothing voice penetrated the haze of shock and confusion encompassing the Elders' minds. "The book you so eagerly sought is in actuality a written account of the Creation's history authored by the Archangel Michael. Had you been allowed to read it you would have discovered that which I just revealed to you for yourselves."

"But...why?" Milan's anguished cry echoed the feelings of confusion and betrayal mirrored on the faces of all the Elders. "Why would God perpetrate such deception?"

Lie approached the trembling old man and placed a gentle hand against his cheek. "Because such is the Almighty's nature," she said, the soothing tones of her voice washing over him. "Our Creator is a callous one."

"NO!" Tullis shouted. "God is not callous! He is almighty and it is not our place to question his judgment or his actions."

"Meaning what, exactly?" Gianni's despondent voice broke the bitter silence following Tullis' proclamation.

Tullis turned resolute eyes to the portly Cardinal. "The Manifestation of Nina Delcielo: The message of religious freedom that she's been spreading throughout the masses seems to indicate that our Lord has decided that we as a species are now ready to know this...this *Truth*. And if that *is* the case then we Cardinals have an obligation to support this Divine effort."

"You're a fool, Calvin," Dresden's steel voice cut through the air of speculation that formed after Tullis' impassioned speech. "The evidence was just laid bare before you, yet you still refuse to see the truth."

Tullis regarded Dresden through narrowed eyes. "And what truth do you speak of old friend?"

The Cardinal's expression hardened. "The God we've sacrificed for, and devoted the greater part of our lives to, is nothing but a puppeteer making us dance to whatever whimsical tune he calls out while the rest of the universe, this so-called Creation, laughs at our collective stupidity!"

The courtyard was silent while the Elders considered the ramifications of Dresden's words.

"And what would you have us do," Milan's tenor broke the silence as he focused his attention on Lie.

Lie assumed a central position amongst them all. "I would have you be free of the Hierarchy's meddling."

Gianni appraised the Halfling through calculating eyes. "And why are you so willing to help us? You're the daughter of an Archangel. How does Earth's spiritual position or any of our positions within this new world you've shown us benefit you?"

Lie's expression hardened and her voice turned bitter. "Because I am half Mortal and have also suffered at the hands of the Hierarchy. The progeny of Raphael I may be, but I am also the daughter of the Mortal Lillith." Her revelation sparked another startled reaction in the Elders, and she released a disgusted snort. "I see you've heard of her."

"According to certain beliefs, Lillith, and not Eve, was Adam's first wife," Gianni's awed voice penetrated the stunned silence that had once again descended over the patio.

Lie favored him with a knowing look. "Those beliefs are partially correct. In actuality the Almighty quickened *several* Mortal couples during the Starting time. Lillith and Adam were always considered the Primes, but her disagreement with the Almighty's Tenets in regard to Humanity's path led to her banishment and subsequent vilification by her peers and their successive generations."

Lie paused as the anger she had nursed for so long over her mother's fate threatened to overwhelm her, and now was not the time. She needed her wits to bring to fruition the audacious plan that had taken root in her mind during her first encounter, and subsequent conversations, with the wounded Malakai. With a conscious effort, she calmed her mind and resumed her oration.

"It was the Archangel Raphael who took pity on Lillith's plight and befriended her. Their dalliance led to my birth, but the continued persecution mother received from the Mortal populace, and the callous indifference of the Hierarchy, completely shattered her soul. When the time came for her to end her Mortal life she rejected my father's offer of a place in Heaven by his side, choosing Dispersion instead of Eternity."

Lie paused again, but this time when she addressed them her voice was cold, her eyes blazing with Celestial fire. "My mother's story is but one of countless other tales of woe that have come as a result of the Almighty and his precious Hierarchy's relentless attempts to maintain the so-called Balance; regardless of how many lives they destroy along the way. I aim to see this era of indifference to the lesser beings of the Creation ended!"

"Then I now stand with you," Dresden announced drawing startled cries from the other Elders.

"Have you lost your mind, Carl?" Tullis ground out. "We are sworn to uphold the laws of the Father Almighty, not some bitter offspring of an Archangel!"

"Indeed!" Gianni seconded, his rotund belly shaking with his indignation.

"They're right Carl," Milan chimed in, grabbing Dresden's arm. "The Pope must be made aware of these developments. As leaders of the Catholic Church, we must begin the process of reeducating the masses as to their Lord's true purpose for them!"

"But that's just it!" Dresden yanked his arm free of Milan's grip. "We don't *know* His plan! And from what we've just learned, it's clear that we probably never will. I refuse to continue my service to a bunch of...creatures who can't even afford me the dignity of telling me the truth about who I am and where I come from!"

"But you don't know her plan either." Tullis jerked his thumb at Lie. "Who's to say she's not toying with our sensibilities? Her very name suggests such duplicity."

"My given name is Lillian, Cardinal Tullis," Lie harshly interjected. "I chose 'Lie' to reflect my ambivalence toward the Tenets. There is much you have yet to learn of the world around you, but I'm sure once you have a complete overview of the Creation and it's minders you'll think differently."

"I'm afraid I won't," Tullis declared, drawing himself up straight. "Hearing you speak has convinced me more than ever that God truly does have a plan for us, and we must endure in our faith of that plan; even if we don't know what it is!"

"Agreed," Gianni's solemn vow was followed quickly by Milan's fervent pledge.

Lie studied the resolute trio for a moment then released a resigned sigh. "I laud your commitment, Elders but I'm afraid your position puts you in direct conflict with my goals."

Lie's statement drew an indignant snort from Tullis. "I guess it does."

"Then I'm afraid the three you shall reap the rewards of your righteous harvest." Her gaze fell upon the silent Malakai and Joey. "Gentlemen, if you would be so kind..."

"It would be our pleasure, Mistress." Joey's his raspy voice sent a chill down Tullis' back.

The Cardinal opened his mouth to speak, but before he could utter a word bolts of Celestial fire leapt from Joey and Malachi's outstretched hands, engulfing the three Elders, and quickly reducing their writhing bodies to piles of smoldering ash.

When it was done, Lie looked pointedly at Dresden, his face pale with shock. "Now you know the stakes of the game you've chosen to play, Carl Dresden," she spoke in a low voice. "Are you still with me?"

Dresden compressed his lips into a grim line, a pang of sympathy stabbing at his heart as he stared at the ashes of his of fellows. "The hand that serves the Lord must sometimes be dipped in blood," he grated out through clenched teeth, turning hard eyes to Lie. "But the Lord has shown Himself to be undeserving of such devotion. So, my hand now serves you!"

*

Standing before the Apex's Window, the Archangel Michael studied the scene unfolding on the wooden deck of the Scavelli home, and a smile of paternal pride split his face. He was less optimistic about the events that had just transpired between the offspring of his brother Raphael and the Mortal clergy; several of whom now lay dead, their souls a flutter against the Archangel's awareness as they Transitioned into the Afterlife.

"It seems Lillian grows bolder by the century," the Archangel Gabriel's baritone voice sounded as he glided purposely into the spherical chamber that housed the Window. "Now she actively aligns herself with Mortals in direct defiance of Father's will."

"The situation is a precarious one," Michael said, giving his brother a nod. "Perhaps I waited too long to instigate Nina's tutelage."

"At the time, you thought what you were doing was best, and it might well have been had you not forgotten one important factor."

Michael's left eyebrow arched upward. "And that factor being?"

Gabriel's wing gave a slight flutter. "The lives of every being within The Creation are subject to His will."

Indeed, they are, The Almighty's voice sounded in the minds of both Archangels. *And it is a burden I gladly bear.*

"Forgive me if I seemed...doubtful, Father," Michael quickly offered.

You've done nothing warranting forgiveness Michael. Lillian's actions have become aggressive of late as have those of other key beings throughout the Realms, but such is to be expected given the fact that the convergence of Chaos and Order is upon us. However, there is no need to fear. Nina is more than ready for the Task at hand. In fact, she was engineered for it.

A look of confusion consumed Michael's features. "Engineered...I don't understand."

I've always known that the day would come when Chaos would overcome the Order I've struggled to maintain throughout the millennia, and when that time came, the Realms would need a champion to properly unite and shield them against its influence. Nina will be that champion for she is a creature comprised of the necessary blend of Divinity and Morality.

"The necessary blend...?" Michael's wings whooshed open as realization hit him. "Nina's Mother...that's the reason I didn't sense the minute Traces of The Blood within her," he exclaimed. "You suppressed my senses!"

And enhanced your attraction to her.

Michael was stunned by The Almighty's admission. "I've always wondered why you never levered any censure upon me for Nina's birth. You manipulated my senses as well as my affections!"

I did what was necessary to ensure the Creation's survival, The Almighty responded sternly. *Lie became Chaos's advocate ages ago and has proven herself well suited to the role. The growing rate of the Mortals disassociation from the Tenets has allowed its influence to grow. Given the Realms current fractured spiritual state The Creation could very well slip into the Chaotic state I have fought to hold at bay.*

"But while all the games and Divine intrigue?" Michael finally voiced the question that had plagued his mind his entire existence. "You are The Almighty; why can't you just quash the spirit of Chaos once and for all?"

Because to do so would rob the Realms of the fundamental element that is essential to ALL living beings: The power of Choice. That is why Nina's Task is so essential. The Races of the Realms must choose between her position and Lie's, and the outcome of that choice will decide the Fate of The Creation.

"But she has not been properly trained to assume such a glorious position," Michael protested, his fear for Nina overshadowing his shock at the Almighty's actions.

A failing I'm confident will shortly be rectified, The Almighty replied. *Is that not the reason you entrusted her tutelage to Aken'ama?*

"I did that in response to Lie's continued interest, and the ripple of awareness I've begun to sense in other notable Demonstratives throughout the Realms. Had I known the true role you intended her to play I would've long since removed the blinders of ignorance from her mind about her heritage."

Worry not Michael, The Almighty soothed. *Lillian's actions are both expected and necessary, but Nina's abilities will easily see her through the trials ahead.*

"And what if Nina fails in her Task and the Realms succumb to Lie's influence.

A deep sadness filled the Almighty's presence. *Then I will have no choice but to unleash the Horseman and bring the Races to heel in order to ensure their continued existence.*

The contact was broken and Michael turned troubled eyes to Gabriel. "I'm afraid I do not share Father's confidence on the outcome of this matter; particularly in light of this new insight."

"That's because your affection for Nina has eroded your objectivity," The Bringer of Death cajoled his brother.

"My feelings for Nina notwithstanding, this situation just became a lot more complicated," the Keeper of Benevolence angrily fired back. "Perhaps if you had ever deigned to sire a Mortal child you would understand the anxiety that I currently feel."

"Such twaddle is the very reason I avoid such dalliances," Gabriel gruffly returned as he leapt gracefully through the Window's borders. "Retaining an emotional detachment is best when dealing with Mortals; especially the Humans," his disembodied voice echoed through the shimmering expanse.

Michael released a frustrated sighed.

Gabriel's steadfast refusal to see the inhabitants of Mortalia as anything other than children to be led would never allow him to empathize in matters such as this. But there was one Archangel who could relate to Michael's ambivalence. Perhaps it was time to reestablish communication with the reticent Raphael; particularly since his daughter was also involved. Maybe together they could discover a way to bring about a conclusion to this simmering conflagration with minimal damage to either of their progeny. Or at the very least contain the coming inferno.

Chapter 36

Celestial society was divided into two primary categories; those that subscribed to the Almighty's Tenets and those that, for whatever reason, did not. Generally speaking, Celestial's that chose to live apart from their Creator, while not living in accordance with his doctrines, still acknowledged his authority and accepted the limitations in regards to Celestial interaction with Mortalia.

The large group of beings gathered on the black-grass plains of Sublimia's Infinity Basin were of the group who not only resented the Almighty's authority but actively sought ways to circumvent it. To the Hierarchy, these sordid beings were known as Demonstratives; to the inhabitants of Mortalia aware of their existence, the name ascribed to them was far less flattering: Demons.

"My fellow Demonstratives," Lie's voice rang clearly across the plains. "I've summoned you all here to share with you a bit of information that I've recently stumbled upon that could potentially alter our dismal standing within the Creation."

"And that information being," the Morphling known as Kiyan spoke up.

Lie favored him with a mischievous grin. The Morphlings of Kiyan's tribe were known for their vicious natures as well as their impatience. "Another Rising is upon us!"

Murmurs and grunts of surprise and consternation circulated through the crowd. "And how did you learn of this?" Chton, leader of the Celestial shadow race known as Wraiths called out.

"My methods of discovery are irrelevant," Lie replied. "What matters now is how those of us who have grown tired of living under the Hierarchy's heel can put the upcoming Creational turmoil to use."

Lie then explained her plans to the listening crowd, reveling in the positive psychic backlash she received as their skepticism turned into eager anticipation.

"And how soon can you set your scheme in motion," asked Chton above the excited murmurs.

Lie favored him with a cunning smile. "I already have."

"You do realize that if you wish to counter the power of the Hierarchy you will need one of the Talismans, and a Mortal to channel its energies," the Wraith pointed out.

"I do and the Talisman has already been located, as has the Mortal for the Task of wielding it."

Chton's shadowy form wavered for a moment. "Mortals are a capricious lot. Are you sure your chosen can be trusted to carry through?"

"Without a doubt," Lie assured him. "The Mortal I've chosen is an Elder of that foul group of misguided zealots known as the *Presbyterii*."

Chton's glowing feline eyes widened at the news. "Do tell! And how did you manage that? Past dealings with that lot have shown them to be particularly devoted to their skewered version of the Tenets."

"I simply revealed the true nature of the Creation and Humanity's place in it. The Mortal's anger over what he considered to be an inexcusable betrayal by the Almighty did the rest."

Chton released a pleased hiss. "As always you prove yourself worthy of our respect, Child of Chaos!"

Lie smiled at the title that the various beings inhabiting the Creation had long ago ascribed to her. "Then I will work hard to ensure that I do not lose it!"

*

Standing amidst the various Celestial races that made up the Demonstratives, the Morphling Drift was careful to display the same enthusiasm as those around her as she casually moved away from their ranks.

Like her sibling, Shift, Drift's loyalties were to Iblis, and it was he that had assigned her the Task of keeping abreast of significant events throughout the Sublimian subculture.

If left unchecked, Lie's ambitions could shatter the very stability of The Creation and the Lord of Hell had to be warned. The Morphling just hoped that her warning would not come too late!

*

"This place is incredible!" Nina's awed cry reverberated around the immense crystal dome that was the central hub of the Archangel Michael's personal Refuge.

"It is at that," Willimena enthusiastically agreed. "It's been several centuries since my last visit, but the sight of this place never ceases to amaze me. Truly this is one Raphael's more distinctive designs."

Nina glanced sharply at the Halfling. "The Archangel Raphael?"

"The one and only; he's favored above all other Celestial Architects by the Almighty. Many of Mortalia's more prolific structures can be attributed to him; particularly on Earth."

"Gabriel did tell me that he's the one that built Stonehenge."

"Bah," Willimena spat. "That pile of rectangular rocks is hardly an indication of Raphael's creative genius. For a true example of his talent, you need look no further than Egypt's Giza Plateau."

Nina's mouth dropped open in astonishment. "He's responsible for the Great Pyramids?"

"In actuality the Majority of Ancient Egypt's architectural splendor can be attributed to Raphael," Willimena said with a sigh. "Had it not been for the...insurrection which cost them The Almighty's favor they would've been Mortalia's greatest civilization."

A puzzled frown appeared on Nina's face. "What insurrection; their making slaves of the Israelites?"

"The fate that befell the Children of Abraham, your guardian's people," Willimena inclined her head toward the Celemor, "was a planned subjugation orchestrated by the Watch to temper their collective spirits. The insurrection I speak of is the Ancient Egyptian's deification of Raphael and other members of the Watch who frequented Earth in those times."

"Before God put a stop to all the heavenly travel," Nina smiled. "Gabriel and I touched on this subject a while back," she responded to the puzzled look Willimena directed at her. "Plus, the 'Ban' as Mich...our father," she corrected with a shy smile, "called it is mentioned a few times in his Journal."

"And who says you're not a reader," Gabriel teased then hissed in pain from the shock he received at the end of the punch Nina gave him.

"Well, that's new," Nina exclaimed, starring at her hands which were now glowing softly in the dome's muted light. "How the blazes did I do that?"

"Here on Nirvana the dampeners that limit a Celestial's ability in Mortalia are not present," Willimena explained. "As that daughter of an Archangel you have in a sense come home, Nina, and your body knows it."

"Wow," Nina whispered, still studying her hands. "So, what else can I do?"

Her question was answered by the crackling of the energy field that engulfed Willimena as she launched herself gracefully into the air.

"That, my dear sister, is what we're here to find out!"

Chapter 37

"What exactly are these Talismans that have been repeatedly mentioned throughout this section?" Dresden asked pausing in his study of the weathered scroll laid out across the large oak table situated in his villa's dining area.

"They are the various items used by Harbingers and Prophets throughout Mortalia's history during the implementation of their respective Tasks," Lie answered the Cardinal whose easy acceptance of the arcane situation he now found himself in had greatly impressed her.

"And what is it about these artifacts that make them so...significant?"

"The Almighty infused each of the Talismans with a portion of his Divine Essence, granting the wielder access to His Celestial might."

"Well, if that's the case why haven't you or others of your particular...disposition used one of these conduits of power to better advantage?"

Lie released an amused snort. "Only those born of Mortal blood may wield a Talisman."

"You are half Mortal," Dresden pointed out.

"I'm also the daughter of an Archangel. The energy contained within the Talisman is anathema to all Celestials save for the Horseman and the Almighty."

"In other words, God booby trapped the things so that none of you could abuse their power."

Lie smiled. "Quaintly put but accurate, this is why I need your help in accomplishing my goals."

"I think there's a little more to it than that."

Lie's left eyebrow arched upward. "Meaning what?"

"Meaning that if a Mortal was all you needed, Malakai or Joey would've easily sufficed. Why did you specifically target the Elders?"

Lie studied the cunning Mortal. Dresden *was* a key component to her plans, but she had hoped to keep him from discovering that. Unfortunately, the wizened Mortal possessed an unusually shrewd mind. "Actually, it was you I wanted," she confessed, deciding that honesty might indeed be the best policy in this instance. "The other Elders, had they been amenable would've held prominent roles in the New Order, but their participation wasn't required."

A chill ran down Dresden's spine at the memory of his fellows' demise. "Obviously not; and what makes me so special?"

Lie accorded him a respectful nod. "Your ability to see beyond the lies of your existence; long have I watched Earth's more prominent spiritual leaders. You are unique among your peers in this regard."

A lopsided grin appeared on Dresden's face. "Why, because I willingly abandoned all that I once believed in and attached myself to *your* cause?"

Lie's expression turned tender as she leaned across the table and placed a gentle hand against his cheek. "Yes. Your unwavering devotion to what you feel is just, coupled with your charisma and ability to affect change, make you a valuable asset."

Dresden savored the feel of her warm hand pressed against his flesh, invoking feelings of desire within his aged body. He swallowed hard several times, sternly forcing his mind away from long abandoned matters of the flesh. "And what happens when my...value runs out?"

Lie reached up and drew his face closer to hers. "I don't foresee that day coming."

The Cardinal's pulse quickened at the feel of her soft hands against his weathered skin. "What are you doing?"

Lie's lips parted in a sensuous smile. "You cannot hide your emotions from me Carl Dresden," she purred. "For most of your life, you've remained chaste in accordance with the mandates of your faith, but I sense the stirrings of your soul; the desire my touch has sparked within you."

"N-no," Dresden whispered as her lips moved closer to his. "I'm a Cardinal of the Catholic Church..."

"Who now knows the truth of the world around him," Lie interrupted. "Your celibacy was a requirement of the lie you once held dear, but your eyes are now open. The time has come for you to quench the burning thirst of your flesh."

"No...this is...wrong," Dresden muttered, but the Halfling silenced his protest by pressing her lips firmly against his.

He tried to resist but in the end the needs of his body won out. With a display of strength and agility belying his sixty-eight years, the Cardinal swept the Halfling into his arms and laid her muscular body atop the table with no regard for the scrolls rolled out upon it.

He fastened his lips upon hers for several seconds, savoring their delightful taste then pulled away; his groin hardening with an urgency he hadn't felt in decades. "What have you done to me you green-eyed witch?"

"Set you free," Lie whispered, surprised at her sudden eagerness to feel him inside of her. Many were the Mortals lovers she had taken over the centuries, but none had ever resonated with her like this. She deftly undid his pants and shoved them down his narrow hips. "You may thank me if you like."

Using his knees to spread her sinewy thighs apart, Dresden levered himself into position and did just that!

*

The wave of passion created by Lie and Dresden's spirited mating reverberated through the Crossroads that bound the Realms of The

Creation together. Amidst their nebulous substance, a sense of satisfaction flowed through the convergence of energy that was The Almighty.

"I see your plans are preceding accordingly, Father," a voice sprang from the spattering of Celestial matter coalescing into a feminine shape.

Yes, it is, Twilight; though there is still much that must be set into place.

"I still say you're taking a big risk with your manipulations."

A ripple of impatience manifested itself in the Almighty's tone. *As the embodiment of Celestial Energy, you above all others know the danger that approaches. My 'manipulations' are necessary if the Realms are to survive.*

Though The Almighty's fervor did manage to dampen Twilight's anxiety for the Creation's impending fate it did not totally remove it. "I hope you're right, Father," she said as her shape began to dissipate. "For all of our sakes!"

As do I, The Almighty's fervent wish echoed through the ether.

Chapter 38

A massive ball of energy blazed in the skies above Nirvana's Silken Mountain Range. So great was its brilliance that even the members of the Angel Legions, long accustomed to such displays, watched in awe from the windows of their lofty aeries riddling the numerous peaks.

"She's adapting to her powers far quicker than I would've imagined," Willimena remarked to Gabriel, their eyes focused on the hovering Nina effortlessly manipulating the swirling mass of light and fire she had created.

"Her rapid growth reflects the effectiveness of your teachings."

Willimena waved the Celemor's praise aside. "I only taught her the basics. I believe her phenomenal progress is due to the unique manner of her creation."

Gabriel focused sharply on the Halfling's face. "What do you mean?"

"Look at her." Willimena nodded toward Nina. "That conflagration could easily obliterate half the life on Nirvana, yet she wields it with the casual expertise of one of the Horseman. Already her power dwarfs yours *and* mine. At the rate she's going I fear that my sister's abilities will soon overshadow those of our father."

"And this concerns you?"

Willimena gave him a sideways glance. "As much as it does you, Celemor, even though you've tried to hide it."

Gabriel grimaced. "Apparently not well enough."

Willimena smiled. "We Halfling's see deeper than most. And since we've both given voice to our fears, let us attempt to qualify them."

Gabriel's features twisted into pensive frown. "I'm just wondering what the endgame is to all of this," he said as he watched Nina execute a series of complex aerial maneuvers with the group of angels that had decided to join her in the air once she had dispersed the energy sphere. "I get the feeling she's being primed for battle, but with whom and for what reason?"

"Your thoughts mirror mine," Willimena said smiling in spite of herself at the high-flying antics of Nina and the Angels. "I've questioned Father repeatedly on the matter and he's yet to satisfy my curiosity."

Gabriel grunted. "I don't like it when the Archangels initiate these cosmic games. It usually doesn't turn out well for the players."

Willimena placed a gentle hand atop the Celemors heavily muscled forearm. "Then you and I must do our part to ensure that our beloved Nina is duly prepared for whatever they have in store."

Gabriel nodded in solemn agreement and the two of them refocused their attention on Nina still happily frolicking in the air.

*

Lie was troubled.

Initially she had mated with the Mortal Dresden thinking it would further bind him to her cause. But in the weeks since their initial coupling, and the several other encounters they had shared, she had begun to feel an uncharacteristic attachment to him.

The Halfling pondered her feelings as she watched Dresden dole out instructions to Malakai and Joey for their upcoming trip to Egypt. The time had come to recover one of the ancient Talismans. This was a key part of her plan yet Lie was anxious for their meeting to conclude so she could have her lover all to herself. What was wrong with her?

Perhaps you'll find the answer to that question when you admit to yourself that the good Cardinal has managed to ensnare you, my dear one, Kaela's voice echoed unexpectedly through her mind.

Nonsense, Lie dismissed the Morphling's notion. *I am the Creation's first Halfling, the Child of Chaos. What possible attraction could this aged Mortal hold over me?*

One that makes your half-Mortal heart flutter every time you gaze upon him, Kaela stated. *You've always denied the emotional aspect of your psyche, but the time may have come for you to acknowledge it.*

I've had numerous Mortal lovers over the centuries, Kaela.

You've had numerous toys over the centuries; playthings to satisfy the inherent lust that beats in your heart. Dresden is the first Mortal to actually stimulate you on an intellectual level as well as physical.

I cannot deny that he has sparked something within me, Lie replied, a slight flush coloring her cheeks at the affectionate wink the Cardinal gave her when their eyes met. *Never before have I encountered a Mortal with such confidence in his abilities or station. My life stretches across Earth's entire history yet when I gaze into his eyes it's as if I'm the child. I know he senses my...vulnerability yet he takes no advantage of it. Nor does he seek to assert his control over me which is generally the case with Mortal males.*

That's because he has embraced you for who you are and not what you are, said Kaela.

And who exactly am I, Kaela?

The daughter of a passionate Mortal woman and an equally intense Archangel; their blood fills your veins as does their wants and desires. Perhaps it is finally time for you to address those needs; to know the pleasures of communing with a kindred spirit.

Lie considered Kaela's words while studying the Cardinal's chiseled profile. "And you think Dresden is that spirit?" she whispered.

What I think is irrelevant, dear one. What matters is what you think.

In truth I cannot say, Lie slowly admitted through the privacy of their mental rapport.

Then discovering this particular truth should also be among your top priorities, the Morphling suggested, and Lie found herself once again in agreement with her Handmaiden's sage advice.

*

Iblis' gaze ranged across the onyx towers and quartz structures that made up the City of Hell's distinct skyline. Normally the view of his domain filled him with a sense of contentment, but today he felt only apprehension in light of the disturbing message he had just received from Silas.

"And you're sure of this?" he asked the Morphling hovering silently beside him.

"The report came from Drift herself," Silas confirmed. "After her discovery of Lillian's recruitment of other Demonstratives, she felt it best to remain close to the key elements of the cabal in the hopes of uncovering any further information that might prove useful."

Iblis frowned. "Well, she certainly accomplished that. The thought of Lillian acquiring one of the Talismans is even more disturbing than her collaboration with Chton and his ilk."

A look of disgust appeared on Silas' narrow face. "The Wraiths have always been a bothersome lot."

"That they have, my friend! Did Drift give any indication as to which Talisman Lillian's targeted?"

"No but considering her father's connection to Egypt, I would hazard a guess that she'll be going after the Staff of the Prophet Moses."

"Yes, that would follow; particularly if she intends to use her Mortal puppet, Dresden, as a figurehead to recruit other Mortals to her venomous cause."

Silas pursed his lips. "That's the other note of interest in Drift's report. She believes that Dresden is far more to Lillian than a simple herald."

Iblis looked sharply at Silas. "What do you mean?"

"Your worrisome niece seems to have taken a curious liking to Dresden, to the point of even deferring to his judgment on certain matters."

Iblis' folded wings twitched at the news. "Are you saying he's become her...paramour?"

"From what Drift indicated it's quite possible."

"Interesting," Iblis whispered while mulling over this unexpected development. Dalliances between Mortals and Celestials, though generally frowned upon by The Watch, were quite common, but Lillian's profound distaste and contempt for her Mortal kin made his Morphling spy's observation astonishing to say the least. "Out of curiosity, how has Drift been able to maintain such a close scrutiny of Lillian's activities?"

A wicked grin appeared on Silas' bony face. "Lillian and her sycophants have taken refuge in Dresden's remote country domicile. The dwelling's substantial size requires a staff of domestics which has afforded Drift a suitable supply of subjects to mimic."

Iblis smiled. "And Lillian hasn't sensed our cunning Morphling's presence?"

"Not at all," Silas confidently assured his Master. "Drift's manipulation of the deceptive Veils we Morphlings generate is equal to her sisters and nearly as adept as mine."

"Let's hope it remains so. At the moment she's my primary source of information."

"For Darius' group as well," Silas amended.

Iblis nodded in agreement. "And how does my dutiful Desomor plan to counter Lillian's initiative?"

"He and Shift have already recruited a cadre of Nina's familiars to undertake a foray into Egypt where they will attempt to make contact with Khaleed, the Talisman's Guardian."

"Good. Though considering who they're up against, they may require additional support. Send Mayhem to join them. Her history with Khaleed, and penchant for violence," Iblis added with a smile, "may come in handy."

"As you wish." Silas accorded his master a respectful bow then withdrew from the office. The Morphling was less than pleased with involving that platinum-haired witch, but he knew better than to argue with his Lord on the matter. Hopefully the volatile nymph had learned her lesson from the Azreal debacle. If not...Another smile curved Silas' lips. He always enjoyed hearing that upstart Desomor scream!

Chapter 39

"Where in the hell *are* we?" Malakai exclaimed when the glow of Lie's carrier nimbus faded.

"Offhand I'd say the desert," Joey remarked dryly letting his gaze sweep across the sandy landscape. The outline of numerous structures was just visible on the horizon.

Lie grinned at his pun. "We are at the city of Memphis' southern border. The Guardian lives in an isolated villa just over those dunes."

A sour look crossed Malakai's face as his eyes scoured the barren landscape. "Then what are we waiting for? Let's grab this holy stick so we can get out of here. This place reminds me to much of Kuwait."

"Yeah, it does," Joey agreed. "But at least this time we don't have to worry about sweating our butts off, now that our bodies are all powered up."

Malakai's frown deepened. "Powered up or not I'll still be glad to leave."

"Patience, Malakai," Lie soothed. "The Celemor to whom the Staff's location has been entrusted has been guarding it for centuries. Rending that secret from him may prove...challenging."

Joey flashed the Halfling a cocky grin. "I thought that's why you brought us along."

Lie gave his head an affectionate pat. "It is indeed, my pets. Come," she gestured with her hand in the direction they needed to go. "Let us be about our business before The Watch takes notice!"

*

The vibrant mosaic produced by the setting Egyptian sun brought a smile to the face of the tall broad-shouldered man kneeling in the courtyard of a modest clay dwelling. A small fire blazed in the metal brazier resting in the sand before him, the light from the flickering flame becoming more prevalent in the rapidly darkening sky.

To the people of Memphis, the old hermit known as Khaleed was a curious enigma; always quick to lend a helping hand to those in need yet fiercely protective of his privacy. On those rare occasions that he did socialize, those in his company were often struck by the air of profound loneliness surrounding him, and even more so by the weariness reflected in his dark brown eyes.

As he watched the stars make their evening appearance, Khaleed's mind drifted back, as it often did, to his life as a simple farmer; one of thousands freed from Egypt's crushing grip following the Exodus.

One night, after imbibing to freely of the wine celebrating the Israelite's final victory over the Canaanites, Khaleed found himself the recipient of a Celestial visit. At first, he thought the glowing, winged man appearing before him was a product of his drunkenness. That notion was quickly dispelled by the apparition's introduction of itself as the Archangel Michael.

Michael then revealed to the awestruck Khaleed the Truth of the Creation, and the farmer's place within the Celestial fraternity known as the Divine Watch due to the Blood of his ancestor Abraham; a bonding that made him part of an elite strain of Humanity labeled Celestial Mortals by the Members of The Watch.

Michael awakened the dormant energy within Khaleed then subjected him to a brief but thorough tutorial in its use. When he was satisfied with his pupil's proficiency, the Archangel charged the fledgling Celemor with the Task of guarding the secret location of the Staff of Moses. Michael had procured the Talisman from the Israelites after Moses' death and hidden it away so that it's power could not be abused by the unrighteous.

A sudden flutter impinging upon his awareness interrupted Khaleed's musings. He focused on the sensory input, and a knot of apprehension formed in his stomach.

For three and a half Millennia, he had successfully kept the location of the Staff hidden from those who sought its power. Something told him that keeping it from the Celestial whose aura now resonated within his mind would prove to be his greatest challenge to date.

The air and sand around him began to stir, and Khaleed sighed. He suspected that this sunset, one of the most beautiful Egypt had ever produced, could be the last one he would view through Mortal eyes.

"I see you're still staring at the sky hoping for enlightenment, Khaleed," a sultry voice rang out from the nimbus of white light materializing above the desert floor.

Khaleed focused narrowed eyes on the muscular woman and two burly men that stepped from the light's core. "I found enlightenment centuries ago, Lillian. A pity the same cannot be said of you."

A cocky smile creased Lie's face. "Oh, but I have. And to show you how...enlightened I've become, I'm going to ask you politely for the Staff's location as opposed to having my companions here beat it out of you."

Khaleed released a contemptuous snort. "Not in this existence, Halfling."

"Suit yourself." Lie gave her henchmen a sharp nod and they started to advance toward the still seated Guardian.

Khaleed studied the approaching duo through glowing eyes. Both walked with the calm swagger of trained warriors, but the subtle shifts in the shorter man's weight as he glided across the uneven sand marked him as the more adept fighter. The bigger man, clumping forward with the finesse of a rhino, appeared to be more of a brawler.

Not that it mattered. During his centuries of life, Khaleed had mastered several forms of Martial Arts, with a particular fondness for the ancient Egyptian fighting system, *Sebak-Kah*.

While the menacing duo's physical prowess posed no threat, the residual swirls of Celestial energy he detected did give the Celemor pause.

Khaleed probed deeper into their auras, his concern lessoning after the completion of his analysis. "I would hazard a guess that these ruffians were Touched by *your* hand, Lillian." His voice was laced with disgust. "You're obviously not as skilled at this sort of thing as your father."

"You just signed your death warrant," the shorter man growled, shifting his weight to his rear leg while cocking his front foot high to deliver a stomping kick.

Khaleed maintained his position until the charging man was fully committed then rolled swiftly to his left. He fired a sharp kick into the knee of the man's balancing leg and was rewarded by the snap of breaking bones.

The man howled in pain, his body crashing to the ground in a shower of sand just as Khaleed hit him with a bolt of Celestial fire, the heat from the blast fusing the surrounding ground into glass.

"NO!" the man's partner roared, springing forward to engage the still grounded Celemor.

Again, Khaleed waited until his opponent was fully extended then leaned back causing his charging adversary to stumble, grasping hands falling short of his target's throat.

In a blur of motion, Khaleed deftly grabbed the man's wrists while tucking his own knees against his chest. He slammed both feet into his attacker's sternum, and pulled his arms upward, flipping him onto his back.

The air whooshed from the assailant's body as he hit the sand, and Khaleed quickly reversed positions, snaking an arm around his neck. With grip firmly in place, the Guardian twisted his torso, stretching until the muted crunch of snapping vertebrae sounded in the air. The man's body gave a massive spasm then went limp.

Khaleed, breathing easily after his exertions released his hold, his eyes focused on Lie as he rose smoothly to his feet. "I told you these two were of inferior quality."

"Their names are Joey and Malakai," Lie remarked, her eyes glowing softly. "And I thought their performance was exemplary."

It was then that Khaleed noticed the peculiar tingling at the base of his skull. Realization of what the Halfling was doing trampled over him like a herd of stampeding camels. He took a menacing step toward Lie then screamed in agony from the numerous bolts of Celestial lightening that slammed into his body, searing his flesh and forcing him to his knees.

"Turnabouts fair play, old man," a raspy taunt sounded in the beleaguered Guardian's ears.

"But...who...?" Khaleed gasped. The answer quickly became apparent as the man he had incinerated casually stepped into view, his charred skin regenerating before the Celemor's pain-ridden eyes.

"I guess we're not has cheaply made as you thought," Khaleed's second opponent chimed in, his voice accompanied by a chorus of popping joints as he twisted his head and neck back into their proper position. "Ta-dah," he said with a smirk then slammed a booted foot into the Guardian's chest. The kick connected with a sickening thud, fracturing Khaleed's breastbone as it knocked him onto his back."

"Fool," Lie spat, squatting beside the fallen Guardian. "I am the progeny of an Archangel; one of the most powerful beings in the Creation! Did you truly believe Mortals Touched by my hand wouldn't be up to the challenge of taking down a lone Celemor?" Her mocking laugh echoed through the courtyard. "I knew that you would never willingly reveal the Staff's location, and your mental defenses were too strong for me to pry the information from your mind." The Halfling leaned closer until her lips were barely an inch away from his. "But if something were to distract you, cause a break in your concentration..."

A look of horror consumed Khaleed's face. "No," he whispered, and Lie's full lips curled into a malevolent smile.

"Yes, you devout simpleton. Your valiant efforts were for naught. The Staff and all its glory will soon be mine!"

"But you can't...can't...wield it," Khaleed wheezed, his injuries making speech increasingly difficult.

"Nor do I intend to," she assured him sweetly. "But you need not concern yourself with such trivia." She brushed her lips gently against his, her smile deepening at his revulsion.

Several muted explosions drew their attention and Khaleed, wincing in pain, managed to shift his head just in time to see the roof of his once stately home collapse upon itself.

"There," the man who had kicked him chortled, his eyes and hands glowing softly in the darkening sky. "Place was a little to prim and proper for my taste."

The other man chuckled, and Lie flashed them both an approving grin before refocusing her attention on a despondent Khaleed. "Farewell Celemor," she said, rising nimbly to her feet. A nimbus of light formed around her and her henchmen. "May the skies continue to bring you enlightenment!"

The nimbus flared brighter then disappeared, leaving a battered Khaleed alone to contemplate the dire consequences of his failure.

Chapter 40

"That definitely takes getting used to," Cara cried, her body trembling as she tried to calm her rebelling stomach.

Sanders, a bead of sweat dotting his pale forehead nodded in grim agreement while Quinlan, making no attempt to preserve his dignity, vomited violently onto the sand.

Dichotomy accorded them a sympathetic smile. "Fear not my friends. Traversing the Crossroads can be unsettling for Mortals, but your feelings of disorientation will quickly pass."

"Define quickly," Quinlan muttered after taking a swig from his canteen to rinse the taste of bile from his mouth.

"Depends on how tough you are, Q," Mayhem snickered, shooting the Seeker a teasing wink which brought a slight flush to the man's pallid face.

Since her glowing arrival on the Scavelli's deck, Mayhem had flirted shamelessly with all the males to the point where Maria had threatened to rearrange the trollop's face with a butcher knife if she didn't behave; particularly where her husband was concerned.

An amused Mayhem had respected the aggravated woman's request which left Tyree, Quinlan and Sanders as fair game for her ploys.

Neither Tyree nor Sanders paid her any mind, but the same could not be said of Quinlan. He was clearly uncomfortable in the face of such pronounced sensuality, and thus became the focus of Mayhem's efforts.

"Physical fortitude has little bearing on the effects of a Celestial transition," Dichotomy intoned. "Simply put: the Mortal form is not conditioned for such trauma."

Mayhem's eyes gave an exasperated roll. "I was kidding, Caleb," she grumbled as she positioned her hand over the three shaken Mortals. The Desomor closed her eyes for a moment and a field of light encompassed Cara, Quinlan, and Sanders. "There," she said when the glow had faded. "That should help."

"Wow!" Cara exclaimed, flexing her arms and shoulders. "I feel great and... taller." A look of trepidation crossed her face when she noticed that her cargo pants seemed looser and shorter.

"What did you do to us?" asked an equally shaken Sanders as he studied his hands and arms. "I feel...stronger!"

Mayhem shrugged. "I simply gave your body a Celestial boost and corrected a few...defects in your DNA."

Quinlan's jaw dropped open. "You did what?"

"She enhanced your physical forms to the peak of human perfection," Dichotomy explained to the amazed Mortals, turning disapproving eyes on Mayhem. "You know such alterations are forbidden by the Tenets without the consent of The Watch!"

"Spare me the lecture, Caleb. Considering whom we're up against, and the stakes of this little sojourn, we're going to need every advantage."

"We still say you overstep your bounds," Dichotomy grumbled but made no further protest.

"So, what's our agenda?" Cara asked reveling in the incredible feeling of strength surging through her limbs as well as her body's new lean musculature.

"First we find the Guardian amongst the rabble in that town, and warn him of the impending danger," Mayhem answered casting her gaze over the sprawling village that lay at the base of the sandy ridge they had arrived on. "I just hope we're not too late."

*

"So much for that dream," Mayhem uttered as she and the others stood before the demolished remains of what had once been a modest home situated in a clearing at the village's isolated northern edge.

"You think Khaleed survived?" Dichotomy's terse question reached the Desomor's ears as she surveyed the wreckage.

"Only one way to find out," Cara spoke up before Mayhem could answer, muscling her way through the collapsed timbers of the doorway and entering the sagging home.

Mayhem smiled. "I like her spirit. Stabilize the structure as best you can Caleb while the rest of us search the rubble."

Dichotomy stretched out his arms toward the ruined house, and a haze of light engulfed the structure. "Go; we will hold it in place."

"Come," Mayhem called to Quinlan and Sanders as she started toward the house. The Seekers exchanged apprehensive looks with one another then followed the Desomor inside.

"I found him!" Cara's voice rang out from the rear of the home and the others quickly pushed their way through the debris of clothes and broken furnishings.

They found Cara outside in the rear courtyard kneeling beside a prone Egyptian male.

With everyone safely outside, Dichotomy released his hold on the sagging structure and joined them in the courtyard.

Mayhem took one look at the fallen man's charred body and swore softly. "I wish our reunion could've been under better circumstances Khaleed," she spoke as she knelt beside him.

Khaleed managed a slight grin. "Ever the compassionate one eh, Margaret?"

A spark of humor briefly lit Mayhem's eyes. "It's been centuries since anyone's called me that." She placed a gentle hand against his cheek. "What happened here?"

Khaleed's brown eyes filled with hatred. "Raphael's miscreant daughter showed up with a couple of her goons demanding to know where the Staff was hidden," he ground out, his voice wispy, his breathing labored. "I told her no. You can guess the rest."

Mayhem released a disgusted snort. "Indeed, I can. Did that green-eyed bitch get what she was after?"

A defeated sigh escaped Khaleed's ragged lips. "The foul wench pulled what she needed from my mind while I was busy fighting her henchmen." His voice was growing fainter. "I'm sure she's already at the Sphinx searching for the entrance to the Staff's chamber."

Quinlan and Sanders jerked in surprise, and a startled gasp escaped Cara's mouth.

"It's hidden in the Sphinx?"

Khaleed managed another half-smile. "It seemed like the perfect place seeing as how Raphael's the one that crafted both it and the effigy."

Quinlan's eyes grew wider. "What?!?"

"These Mortals are woefully ignorant of Egypt's true history," Mayhem said smiling at the look of irritation that flashed across Quinlan's face. "Worry not, Seeker. When this is over, I'll personally give you a full account of this land's history, along with anything else you want." She gave him a seductive wink at which Quinlan blushed.

"In the meantime, we have work to do," the Desomor continued briskly, focusing once again on the battered Guardian. "I noticed your body isn't healing Khaleed. Are your injuries that severe?"

A faint smile played on Khaleed's lips. "Nothing I couldn't handle...if I wanted to."

Mayhem gave him a puzzled look. "Then why...?"

"I'm *tired* Margaret," the Guardian said and the Desomor winced at the overwhelming fatigue she sensed in him. "I've carried this burden for over three thousand years. I'm more than ready to make the Final Transition to Celestia; particularly in light of the turmoil I foresee on Mortalia's horizon due to my failure."

Mayhem studied his burned face, and the memory of their first meeting flashed through her mind.

It was Khaleed that had initially befriended the bitter woman after her initiation into Celestiality; taking the time to teach the former member of a Salem Coven, rescued from a burning stake by Iblis, the finer points of her new life. The two formed a curious bond and despite Margaret's, who adopted the name Mayhem to reflect the state of Earth's fractured spiritual infrastructure, continued devotion to Iblis and his Doctrines, the two remained close.

She placed a gentle hand atop his forehead. "I understand, my friend. May your time in Heaven be forever sweet."

"And may your life in Hell be equally fulfilling," Khaleed responded. He flashed the Desomor one last smile then closed his eyes. Moments later, his body went lax.

"Farewell Guardian," Dichotomy whispered to Khaleed's spirit shifting through the Crossroads.

A soft glow emanated from Mayhem's eyes, and a wreath of Celestial fire engulfed Khaleed's body, reducing it to ash.

"So I take it we're heading to the Sphinx to look for the Staff?" Cara spoke after the flames had died out, and Khaleed's remains were scattered across the sands by the desert winds.

Mayhem's eyes flared brighter. "And to seek *vengeance*," she roared, disappearing along with the rest of the team amidst a flash of blinding light.

Chapter 41

"This place is amazing!" Dresden's awed cry echoed through the night as he gazed up at the Sphinx's imposing bulk. "Though I can't say the same for your methods of transportation," he added grimly, still feeling the aftereffects of his Celestial jaunt to Egypt.

"Why don't you let the Lady juice you up like she did us," Malakai suggested according Lie a respectful nod. "Then you wouldn't feel the effects at all."

Lie gave the disheveled Cardinal's shoulder a comforting squeeze. "Carl must remain un-Touched if he is to wield the Staff. Now then," she turned her attention to the Sphinx. "Let us see if we can put Khaleed's information to good use."

Dresden stood back while Lie, Joey, and Malakai began to search the monument's massive, front left paw which, according to the information stolen from Khaleed, was the location of a hidden entrance to the secret underground chamber that held the Staff.

A brief sandstorm, created by the Halfling's deft manipulation of the local winds, had cleared the area of the spattering of locals and tourist, allowing Lie and her henchmen to search unimpeded.

Their efforts quickly yielded results, and the fitted stone that made up the entrance was revealed. Time and the desert had long since eroded the mechanisms that once operated the ingenious door, but a blast of Celestial lighting from Joey took care of the problem.

After allowing fresh air to circulate, the four explorers carefully made their way into a dank, narrow passageway; Lie's glowing form providing light for Dresden to see.

An hour of steady travel brought them to the chamber's entrance, but the way was blocked by a massive, rectangular stone wedged tightly in the entryway. Joey and Malakai set about investigating the ornately carved slab while Dresden took a moment to study the artwork carved into the corridor's surrounding walls.

"A pity the other Elders are not here to witness this," he lamented sliding his fingers across the various symbols and hieroglyphs. "Like me, Calvin was an Egypt enthusiast. A detailed study of this place would have brought him great pleasure."

Lie took hold of his free hand and gave it a gentle squeeze. "I empathize with your remorse, but their fate was of their own choosing."

Dresden returned the gesture. "I know, Lillian." The Cardinal smiled at the shy expression that always appeared on the Halfling's face when he used her birth name.

As their relationship progressed, Dresden had quickly decided continual usage of Lie's self-proclaimed title just wouldn't do, stating that is was hardly a fitting name for such an amazing woman.

For Lie, such consideration along with his frequently expressed accolades of adoration were a source of great pleasure, and her attraction to the wizened Mortal continued to grow; much to the delight of the ever-watchful Kaela.

"It's just such a waste," Dresden remarked, drawing Lie's attention guiltily back from her musings.

"What is?"

Dresden nodded toward the stone. "Hiding these Talismans away; such power could've easily righted the wrongs of this world. I just can't understand why God wouldn't *want* us to use it?"

Lie's green eyes filled with compassion. "The same reasons he's refused to reveal the Truth of the Creation to your kind and banned the majority of my Celestial kin from Mortalia's borders. He doesn't feel the Mortals of Earth are mature enough to handle such burdens."

"And yet according to the ancient scrolls we're the so-called Vanguard Race of this Realm." Dresden's voice took on a mocking tone as he pantomimed a pair of quotation marks with his fingers. "Puppet Race would be a more apt description."

"That's what we're trying to change," Lie soothed as she leaned closer and kissed him softly on the cheek. "Once we have the Staff we'll be able to stand on an even footing with The Watch, and force concessions concerning the governing of the Realms."

A thoughtful look appeared on Dresden's face. "Is the Staff really that powerful?"

"In the right hands it can be."

While Dresden pondered the significance of her statement the air reverberated with Malakai's triumphant shout.

"I think we've figured this rock out!"

Lie and Dresden quickly made their way to the entrance where Malakai and Joey were waiting, their bodies braced against the offending block. "Alright Joey we need to apply even pressure on each of these ankhs." Malakai indicated the ancient symbols of life carved in sharp relief at each of the slab's four corners. "You ready?" Joey nodded ascent and the two men placed their hands and feet on the appropriate spots. "We push on three; one, two, THREE!"

A soft glow formed around their bodies as they leaned hard against the stone's smooth surface. For several seconds nothing happened then, with a loud groan, the massive stone slid in several inches, and crumbled into a thousand pieces.

"What the hell?" Malakai cried, shielding his eyes from the sudden shower of dust and debris.

"Must've been some type of pressurized seal," Joey commented fanning the clouded air with his hands to get a closer look at the slab's remains. "It looks like this block was made out of mortar." He ran a hand over the cut stones that made up the door's jamb. "I'll bet the weight of the Sphinx kept the slab compacted. Once that pressure was removed it couldn't handle the expansion and broke apart."

"Looks like all that time watching the History Channel paid off," Malakai teased.

"Knowledge is power," Joey grinned back unperturbed. His obsession with documentaries on ancient cultures had long been a source of ribbing from his colleagues. "I'm just wondering why they didn't use granite for this door. That's how the ancient Egyptians usually sealed these secrets rooms."

"Granite would not have allowed them to set their clever trap," Lie announced.

Joey focused sharply on her. "What trap?"

"The one Khaleed managed to keep hidden during my probe." The Halfling nodded toward the slab's remains. "Take a closer look at those fragments. This construct was permeated with some type of toxin."

Joey gazed upon the rubble with increased respect. "It's probably Lye," he speculated. "The ancients were fond of corrosives, and from what I hear," he gave his Mistress a mischievous wink. "Lye's pretty damn lethal."

The Halfling chuckled. "You heard correctly,"

Dresden gave the entryway a dubious look. "Is it still potent?"

Lie shrugged. "Probably, but you needn't worry." The glow about the Halfling's eye intensified, and a field of light surrounded the Cardinal. "This shield will filter any toxins from the air around you."

"What about them?" Dresden nodded at Joey and Malakai.

Lie grinned. "The Celestial energy in their bodies protects them from earthly poisons."

"The dynamic duo at your service," Malakai quipped flexing his arms and chest."

Lie's grin deepened at his foolery. "Indeed, you are. Now if you would be so kind as to lead the way." She indicated the chamber's dark entry.

Malakai snapped her a cocky salute then stepped through the doorway. "Damn this place is huge!"

The dusty hall they entered was easily the width and height of a college gymnasium. Increasing the glow of their bodies filled the room with an ethereal light, and Malakai released an awed whistle at the sight that greeted them.

"Somebody sure had a lot of time on their hands," he whispered, and Joey nodded in stout agreement.

The interior walls were covered with thin sheets of dark granite; numerous hieroglyphs, symbols, and pictographs inscribed on their surface with meticulous precision. A closer inspection revealed the carvings to be a visual telling of not only Egypt's rich history, but that of several other ancient cultures as well.

For Dresden, a professed student of history, the carved sheets represented the find of a lifetime. "Look at all of the varying languages," he uttered as he moved from sheet to sheet. "Aramaic, Egyptian, Latin, Greek, and... oh my!" He ran his fingers over a vertical row of angular characters. "This is Angelic script!" Similar rows of lettering seemed to bisect each panel, separating the various writings into specific groups.

"That is the Tongue of Celestia," Lie informed him after examining the carvings. "I suspect at one time this chamber served as a teaching hall.

Dresden turned startled eyes on her. "For whom?"

"The ancient Mortals of this region; if you notice here," She indicated a section of the wall further down. "These carvings are a visual representation for the raising of the Great Pyramid. The Celestian script underneath gives a written account along with its translation into the Mortal tongues relevant at the time of this chamber's inception."

Dresden's awed gaze touched briefly on each panel traversing the chamber's length before resetting on Lie's expectant face. "Was that sort of thing common back then?"

"Extremely; though I am not familiar with this particular hall, I do know that there are numerous other structures very similar to this one where my Father and his Brothers used to instruct their chosen Mortal Scribes. That is how the land of Pharaohs came to be built with such splendor. Of course that was before The Almighty's ban on such interaction," she added sourly, thinking back to the chaos said decree caused among Earth's fledgling populations.

Dresden made no reply as his eyes continued to devour the tablet's offerings. The wealth of knowledge they represented was staggering, and the Cardinal once again found his ire rising toward God for his callous treatment of the Human Race.

How many men, like himself, had devoted their entire lives to the propagation of what they thought was His way? How many selfless historians and archaeologists had wasted their time and resources scrambling around the world trying to piece together Mankind's fragmented history from bits of antiquated scraps, when it was already neatly recorded in halls like this? How many innocents had perished, and were continuing to perish, in the name of religious doctrines and ideas whose very foundations were predicated upon a universal lie?

This ruthless manipulation of the Human race, of *all* Mortal races, must stop! Dresden was glad that his eyes were finally opened, despite the cost of that awakening. The death of the other Elders still weighed heavy on his heart, but he would ensure that their sacrifice would not be in vain!

"Is this the prize we're after?" Joey's raspy voice sounded from the far end of the chamber where he and Malakai were standing in front of a shaft of white light that ran from floor to ceiling, creating a narrow, illuminated column.

Lie's gaze fell upon the long cylindrical object floating within the light's confines, and her pulse quickened. "It is indeed!" She propelled herself and Dresden to the other end of the chamber.

"I thought it was made out of wood," Malakai noted the Staff's silvery finish when the four were together again.

"This is the Staff's original form," Lie explained, her green eyes glowing with excitement. "Once paired with a Mortal, a Talisman reconfigures itself to the wielder's specifications."

Joey turned incredulous eyes on her. "Are you saying that thing's *alive*?

"It does contain a degree of sentience. I wouldn't do that if I were you!" Lie's warning halted Malakai just as his fingers were about to penetrate the shaft's pulsating mass. "The Staff and the field surrounding it are anathema to all Celestially Touched beings, save for the Almighty and his Horsemen."

Dresden swallowed hard, his heart rate increasing as he took a tentative step forward. "I guess that's my cue." He took a deep breath, and slowly pushed a trembling hand into the shimmering column. He took firm hold of the Staff and cried out at the surge of energy that tore through him.

Years melted from his face as the energy permeated every pore of his body, eradicating the debilitating effects of age, giving him the look and bearing of a man in his prime.

Dresden's mind underwent a similar catharsis, his awareness expanding geometrically as the secrets of Existence were laid bare before him; making him feel small and insignificant in the face of the swirling mass of life, energy, and matter that was...The Creation!

"It's....it's so vast..." he muttered when the metamorphosis was over.

"Are you alright, Carl?"

An incredulous smile lit Dresden's face. "I'm better than alright, my love!" He drew the Staff from the column and held it aloft; the light generating from its gleaming surface casting eerie shadows throughout the chamber. "I now understand your reverence for this treasure. With this we can wake the world from its collective ignorance and change the course of Human history!"

"Such decisions are not yours to make!"

The hard voice ringing from the chamber's entrance instantly drew their attention to the remains of the doorway where Dichotomy, Mayhem, and their Mortal companions stood waiting.

"Looks like Khaleed called for backup," Malakai said with a chuckle as he and Joey moved to intercept the interlopers. "Hey Cara," he greeted his former colleague when he recognized her amongst the group.

Cara froze, her eyes nearly popping from their sockets. "Mal... Joey...But...how? I shot you!"

Malakai's sinister cackle echoed through the chamber. "Yeah, you did! Lucky for us we made a new friend." He jerked his head in Lie's direction. "She fixed us up and gave us a job."

"One more suited to our talents," Joey's raspy voice chimed him, his even white teeth bared in a feral smile.

"Since when does being a sadistic bastard require talent?" Cara spat, her sinewy muscles tensing as she readied herself for combat.

Quinlan and Sanders took up flanking positions beside her, and Malakai released a hearty guffaw, pointing his thick index finger at the two Seekers.

"Well look who it is; Sandy and Quintessa! You pansies ready to get your hands dirty?"

"Do not let them goad you," Dichotomy cautioned his seething companions. The blended being turned his baleful glare on Lie. "Curious company you're keeping these days, Lillian."

"One could say the same of you, Caleb," Lie retorted with a nod at Mayhem. "I see you've even recruited my uncle's favorite pet."

The Desomor's eyes narrowed to slits of Celestial fire. "This pet is about to tear you a new one for what you did to Khaleed, bitch!"

"I doubt that," the Halfling snapped, the glow about her eyes intensifying as the two groups slowly converged on one another.

"ENOUGH!" Dresden's cry halted everyone. "This bickering is pointless!" He focused on Cara and the Seekers. "I trust your new allies have made you aware of the Truth about our world?"

"They have," Cara replied not taking her eyes off her opponents.

"Then why do you persist in supporting the cause of such a callous lord; one that would leave you ignorant of your true purpose and position in the universe while he and his angels sit arrogantly on high, laughing as we dumb Mortals strive to adhere to the stifling doctrines of a false faith?"

"The Almighty is *not* arrogant," Dichotomy's angry cry echoed through the chamber before Cara, or the Seekers could respond. "Nor is he callous!"

Lie released a bark of laughter. "So speaks the Creation's primary puppet! Look at you Caleb: from Desomor to Celemor to Celestial abomination. Your entire life is testament to the sordid games the Almighty continually inflicts upon his so-called children!"

"NO!" Dichotomy screamed, his form wavering. "We are what we are because of the choices *we* made!"

"You are what you are because of the choices that were made *for* you!" Lie fired back. "All of you are!" She focused her sizzling glare on Mayhem and the three Mortals. "Each of you standing here once structured your lives in accordance with the Mortal interpretation of those putrid Tenets, sacrificing much in the process; and for what? Your whole belief system is based on a lie; one that your creator could've easily clarified but chose not to!"

The Halfling's expression softened, and her voice took on a seductive lilt. "Why not join us? We have an opportunity to free the masses from the sham of their reality; to show those who would sit in power and judgment over us all that we have the right to forge our *own* destinies based on *our* designs. No longer need we bow down to the whims of a fickle Creator."

"But at what cost?" Cara asked, abandoning her defensive posture, and turning her full attention on Lie. "What you say about God and his deception is true, and I won't deny the betrayal I felt when I found out. But I don't believe he deceived us out of spite; nor do I believe he intends for us to remain ignorant."

"But Cara," Dresden entreated, taking a step toward her. "How can you possibly say that after everything you've seen and heard?"

"Because of Nina," Sanders' deep voice intoned before Cara could respond.

Dresden turned hard eyes on him. "Nina?"

"Her entire message is one of self-actualization and looking past the restrictive borders of religious doctrines in order to forge a more personal relationship with God." Though he spoke passionately, the Seeker's eyes remained locked on Joey and Malakai's subtly shifting forms.

"Originally, you and the other Elders labeled Nina as a heretic," Cara pressed. "You said her stand on organized religion went against everything the Church stood for, but I think it's just the opposite. I think God's using Nina to gradually usher in a new age of understanding."

Lie favored the impassioned woman with an approving grin. "Nicely reasoned, Mortal, but your argument is mired in your naive perception of the Creation. True, the daughter of Michael has sparked a Reclamation among your brethren, but to what purpose? When last I checked, my Kinsman's life was in turmoil over her radical proclamations. If the Almighty truly wishes to reveal the Truth, and Nina is his herald, why put her through such duress? For that matter why must any Mortal endure the humbling ordeals associated with their belief of Him?"

"To Heaven with this chitchat," Mayhem bit out, tendrils of Celestial energy swirling about her body. "Whatever the Almighty's plan is I'm sure it doesn't involve you grabbing hold of that Talisman. So why don't you just put the Staff back before we send you and your lackeys to join Khaleed in the Afterlife!"

Lie's eyes widened at the news. "So, he chose to die, did he? It's just as well. Living with the shame of his failure would've eventually killed him anyway."

Her cruel jibe pushed Mayhem over the edge.

"Time to die, bitch," the Desomor snarled, and a bolt of energy leapt from her hands.

The beam sliced through the air toward Lie's group only to impact harmlessly against the glowing shield that sprang up around them. An infuriated Mayhem raised her hand to deliver another salvo, but a second field formed around her and her companions, instantly paralyzing them.

"The knowledge contained in this chamber is too valuable to risk losing during a senseless battle," Dresden's stern voice penetrated the confines of the glowing prison as he favored them all with a paternal look. "It's obvious that none of you have the fortitude to break the chains placed around your souls by an indifferent deity. Fortunately, I have transcended such hindering notions."

Dresden raised the Staff, and a nimbus of white light sprang up around him and his companions. "I sincerely hope that the next time our paths cross your perspectives will have changed," his voice sounded just before he and his cohorts disappeared.

The moment the residual glare of the carrier nimbus faded; the restrictive field of light dispersed.

"Well, that didn't go as planned," Sanders quipped, his comment drawing a disgusted snort from a still fuming Mayhem. "So what do we do now?"

"We wait for them to make the next move," Dichotomy answered, the uncertainty in the Celestial's blended voice reflected in the faces of the others. "And pray that Nina will be there to stop them!"

*

A shiver traversed the large wings of the Archangel Michael as he stood before the Apex's Window, observing as Caleb transported his group from the chamber.

The Almighty's decree had prevented him from stopping the theft of the Talisman, just as it kept him from aiding Khaleed during his lopsided battle with Lillian and her ruffians. A pang of regret still lingered in his heart for the Guardian's Mortal passing. Khaleed had been an exemplary Member of The Watch. His presence on Earth would be sorely missed.

"Exactly how long are we to watch Lillian's twisted schemes unfold before we intervene?" Omen demanded as he emerged unceremoniously through the Window's shimmering expanse.

"Until the Almighty says otherwise," Michael curtly informed the angry Overseer.

"But she now has access to the Talisman's unlimited power," Omen protested. "We of The Watch *must* take action before it's too late!"

Calm thy self, Omen, The Almighty's voice echoed sternly through the Overseer's mind. *Lillian's actions are in accordance with my plans.*

"I meant no disrespect, Creator," Omen immediately humbled himself. "It's just that I fear The Watch's ability to route the Halfling should her intentions prove nefarious."

The Rising is at hand, Omen, and the resolve of my Earthen children must be tested. It is Lillian's destiny to provide said test.

"And what if the Mortals of Earth fail you, my Lord?"

Then my faith in their resilience and potential will have been misplaced, The Almighty responded. *In the meantime, no Member of The Watch is to render aid to the Child or her allies beyond that which Michael has already initiated.*

The glow around Omen's eyes intensified for a moment then dimmed. "As always we are yours to command, my Lord." The words of acquiescence left a bitter taste in the Overseer's mouth.

The Almighty's presence lingered in his mind for a moment longer then was gone.

"I know the affection you have for Gabriel and his friends," Michael's voice halted Omen as he prepared to exit the Chamber via the Window.

"Then you also know the fear I have for him and the Mortals of Earth in general. Something's not right, Michael. A Reclamation that we of The Watch are forbidden to intercede in. It just doesn't make sense."

A troubled look appeared on Michael's face. "I'm inclined to agree with you. I am unsure as to what strategy Father has chosen to implement, but there is one thing I *am* sure of." Michael's hazel eyes bored into Omen's hooded features with an intensity greater than any the Overseer had ever glimpsed from his Superior. "When the time comes for Nina to play her part in this unfolding drama, she *will* be ready!"

Transcendence

Chapter 42

A massive column of water erupted from the Trinity River's glistening expanse, followed immediately by a second and a third. The liquid tendrils grew in height until they were easily a hundred feet tall then began weaving in, out, and around one another in an intricate pattern that sent the numerous dolphins circling the undulating trio into a joyous frenzy.

Hovering slightly above the columns, an amused expression etched across her face for the dolphin's exuberance, Nina marveled at how easy performing such feats was becoming in the wake of her recent lessons on molecular manipulation.

That particular lecture had been given by her Father with whom Nina had grown increasingly close as her Celestial tutelage continued.

"Manipulating matter is relatively simple once you understand the principles of molecular interaction," The Archangel explained during one of their sessions. "Then it's just a matter of imposing your will upon the required number of molecules to achieve the desired effect."

To demonstrate his point, Michael brought his power to bear on a group of small islands resting just off Heaven's eastern shores. Nina watched, admiration for her father's awesome might plastered on her face, as the countless tons of land and vegetation broke free of their earthly base, reassembled themselves into a singular expanse of land, and settled gracefully back into the roiling waters.

"Bravo, Dad," Nina gushed, and a slight flush colored the Archangel's cheeks. He was still unused to the numerous Mortal terms of endearment she often peppered their interactions with.

More lessons taught by varying Members of The Watch followed; including one helmed by the sullen Archangel Gabriel in which Nina learned to properly interact with the numerous spirits inhabiting Heaven's boundaries.

"There are certain Protocols that must be adhered to when conversing with Denizens of Heaven; particularly new arrivals from Mortalia," The Bringer of Death dutifully informed his familial charge in his sonorous voice. "A Mortal's integration into the Divine infrastructure after their Transition to the Afterlife varies depending on their Race's degree of Creational understanding. As a prominent member of the Hierarchy you must understand and respect those differences in order to interact accordingly."

The Archangel's overbearing attitude frequently got on Nina's nerves, but she bore it in stride. Her unflappable stoicism and eagerness to learn proved to be just the flame needed to thaw Gabriel's icy reserve, and a bond of mutual respect was formed between them. In fact, The Bringer of Death was so impressed by Nina's progress he presented her with a gift at their sessions' conclusion.

"Your skills of communication have developed rapidly Nina," Gabriel remarked as he and his charge strolled through one of Heaven's sprawling residential areas. "Such diligence should be rewarded."

Nina spared the Archangel a puzzled look then cast her eyes over Heaven's cityscape; struck as always by its divine splendor.

In form and fashion, Heaven reminded Nina of an artist's rendering she'd seen at the Detroit Institute of Art on how ancient Egypt might have once looked which made sense given the influence the Archangel Raphael was reputed to have had on Earth's ancient civilizations.

Their steps took them to the front courtyard of one of the numerous spherical constructs, or domiciles as they were more commonly called, arrayed in a neat order that ran the length of the street they were on; their polished marble surfaces reflecting Nirvana's sun's golden radiance.

Such areas could be found throughout Heaven's borders for these where the homes for those souls that chose to dwell within the city proper.

Gabriel lightly knocked on the door then stepped aside, a mischievous smile playing at his lips. Nina was about to question him but the domiciles front entry cycled open. She took one look at the petite Latino woman that greeted them and froze, her mouth making an "O" of astonishment.

"Hello, baby," the woman beamed, tears streaming down her cheeks. "I've been waiting for this moment for so long!"

Still in shock, Nina responded the only way she could; she collapsed into her mother's waiting embrace. After what seemed an eternity, the two separated. Nina's mother motioned them inside, but Gabriel declined, stating that this time was theirs and he had no wish to intrude. He accorded them a respectful nod then, with a mighty flap of his elegant wings soared up into the evening sky.

Nina and her mother barely took notice of his exit as they made their way into the modest dwelling. Nina was shocked at the home's interior for it was an exact replica of the home in she had grown up in, even down to the little oak cabinet the two of them had restored to hold the various souvenirs they had collected from their yearly vacations.

"It feels like I've stepped back through time," Nina whispered as she picked up the ceramic saltshaker fashioned in the shape of a palm tree that her mother had purchased during their trip to Palm Springs. "Or a dream," she added with a sigh as she replaced it back on the shelf besides its matching counterpart.

Evelyn Sanchez smiled at her daughter's wistful tone. "The true 'Heaven' is as much a state of mind as it is one of being. Once you Transition to the Afterlife, your surroundings tend to reflect the period in which you were most happy during your Mortal life." Evelyn took hold of her daughter's hands. "For me that was watching you grow into the amazing woman you've become."

Once again Nina was overcome by emotion as she and her mother embraced one another again. There were so many things she wanted to say but the words just wouldn't come out.

For Evelyn, her daughter's verbal failing was of little concern. The time for talk would come soon enough. For now, she was content to once again hold her in her arms.

Their joyous reunion lasted well into the night and was the first of many such visits to come as Nina's tutelage continued.

Per her request on his behalf, her father begrudgingly granted Gabriel a similar boon and the joyous reunion between the Celemor and his family sparked a wave of happiness that reverberated throughout Celestia.

At first Nina feared that Gabriel's contentment would prompt him to abandon his Celestial post *and* their relationship, but her worries were quickly quelled; surprisingly by Gabriel's wife Clarissa.

"Gabriel and I had our time," Clarissa offered sensing Nina's trepidation during their introduction. "And though it was cut short I cannot fault him for moving on. Besides," Clarissa's brown eyes shifted to her husband chatting away with their daughter, now a grown woman as a result of the realization of her spirit's potential after her transition to the Afterlife. "Gabriel sacrificed his freedom so that my soul could dwell with our daughter's in this wondrous land! Knowing that he has finally found another to love will allow my spirit to rest easier, particularly now that I know the identity of my successor."

Nina blinked in confusion. "Why is that?"

Clarissa's eyes sparkled with mischief. "The fact that it took The Child of Order to take my place in his heart gives mute testament to the hold *I* once had over him!"

Nina's enjoyment of Clarissa's pun was slightly overshadowed by her unease at the woman's choice of words, wondering what could have prompted her to use such a presumptuous title.

She had often entertained similar feelings toward her own name but given her Celestial parentage she now understood her mother's clever play on words. Clarissa was privy to none of those facts which made her choice of labels all the more confusing.

As time progressed so did Nina's abilities; to the point that her Celestial prowess now surpassed those of the majority of the Members of The Watch. Nina had long since accepted the fact that she was an integral part of some Divine scheme, yet she still had no clue as to what said scheme was.

'The Child of Order,' Clarissa's words echoed through her mind yet Nina still was no closer to understanding what they meant, despite the fact that she sensed her "training" was nearly complete. Just what exactly was she supposed to do with all this new-found Celestial might? It was a question that constantly plagued her mind. Even now amidst the spray of her liquid lariat, she continued to ponder the significance of it all.

She had broached the subject with Willimena and their father, but neither of them had offered much insight. She considered seeking the advice of the Overseer Intuition with whom she had formed a friendship but had thus far refrained from doing so. She wasn't sure if it was because she feared being chastised by her father when he found out she had sought answers apart from him, or that said answers might prove to be one more thing that she wasn't ready to hear.

I would say the latter assumption is the most accurate.

Nina cried out at the deep voice echoing through her mind; the twirling columns dispersing as she lost her hold over their watery forms. "Who...who said that?"

The air before her began to shimmer, and Nina inhaled sharply as the Trinity River and Nirvana's blue sky were abruptly replaced by an enormous cloud composed of swirling colors, the varying patterns of their vibrant hues bringing tears to her eyes.

The undulating mass enveloped her, but the buffeting winds Nina expected to encounter were absent. Like the eye of a hurricane, the cloud's center was calm, its interior filled with a slowly pulsating light.

"What is this place?" Nina whispered for fear that her voice might disrupt the new location's serenity. "It's...beautiful!"

As is the soul radiating from within you, the voice intoned.

Nina swiveled her head from side to side, searching for the voice's owner. "Who...who are you?"

I am known by many names throughout the Realms, though my Celestial children refer to me as Father.

The color drained from her face. "Father...you mean as in...*God?!?*"

I have been called that as well. There is no need to fear, child, The Almighty replied when Nina began to tremble. *You are here because the time has come to answer the numerous questions brimming within your mind.*

Nina inhaled sharply trying her best to muster her thoughts in the face of The Almighty's blazing presence. "Does that mean I can...um...speak freely?"

You may.

A surge of adrenalin poured through Nina's veins as she made ready to voice the one question whose answer she so desperately wanted. "Why did you take my mother from me?"

A wave of compassion touched the Halfling's mind. *The Task set before you is great, Nina. In order for you to fulfill it your fortitude and self-confidence must be firmly established. Continued attachment to your mother would've hindered that process.*

Nina balked at The Almighty's words. "'Attachment'? I *loved* her. She was my *Mother!*"

No, she was the Mortal chosen to rear you, The Almighty responded firmly. *As a genuine Child of The Creation you are connected to all beings, not just a single Mortal woman.*

"And you think that shit matters?" In the back of her mind Nina knew that given the fact that it was God she was addressing, her lack of respect was practically criminal, but at the moment she didn't care. Her disgust and anger took precedence.

"Whatever type of heavenly or universal freak I may be, I was raised as a Mortal with Mortal feelings! Maybe if you would've climbed off your high cloud and told me the *truth* about what I am from the start I wouldn't have been so torn up about the whole thing, but you didn't, did you? You left me in ignorance my entire life, and now you expect me to just...accept that it was all for some 'greater good'?" Nina released a disgusted snort. "Well, I'm sorry to disappoint you, but right now I don't feel 'great' and I sure as hell don't feel 'good'!"

Another spate of compassion enveloped Nina's mind. *Believe me when I say that I understand your ire toward me and your situation, Nina, but all that has befallen you was necessary. As I said before, your Task is monumental and will require all of the considerable attributes you have acquired as a result of your spiritual and emotional tempering.*

Despite the pronounced sense of importance The Almighty's words conveyed, Nina was still determined to hold on to her anger. In the end, the continuous wave of reassurance radiating within the swirling expanse, coupled with her curiosity, proved to be the greater force.

"If you say so," Nina uttered after releasing a resigned sigh. "So, what exactly is this big Task?"

The Almighty paused briefly before answering. *The spiritual Reclamation and eventual Unification of* all *the Races throughout The Creation.*

Nina blinked. "I see. And why is all of this so important?"

A wave of energy rippled through the cloud. *A definitive cohesion of the Races is the only way to stave off the coming destruction of the Realms.*

"Wonderful," Nina uttered in a small voice, her shoulders sagging as she realized that once again her life was about to change; though this time she was fairly certain that it would not be for the better. "Something tells me you'd better start this tale from the beginning," she sighed.

As you wish, The Almighty intoned as Nina settled her mind and body as best she could in preparation for what was sure to be a monumental disclosure.

Chapter 43

For the Celemor Gabriel, being reunited with his long deceased wife and daughter was truly one of the happiest moments of his life. Knowing that their time together was limited, the three of them had taken advantage of every moment; exchanging tales with one another of all that had happened during their century long separation.

Of greatest relief to him was his family's complete acceptance of his relationship with Nina.

"As I told her during our introduction," Clarissa remarked as she and Gabriel strolled lazily along the white sands of Heaven's Eastern shores. "Our time has passed and though our end was tragic, I do not begrudge you the life you've led nor the decisions you've made in the wake of Gaby's and my passing. Though I must admit my heart has often been heavy knowing the sacrifice you made so that I might enter this glorious place."

Gabriel stopped and turned Clarissa's body so that they now faced one another. "I don't ever want you to feel bad or guilty for the decision I made. Knowing that your soul would forever be at peace was worth it."

Clarissa placed a gentle kiss against his lips, savoring their familiar taste and feel. "You're taking on the mantle of Celemor on my behalf was still the greatest declaration of love a woman could ever receive; and one that I hope you will not have to repeat."

Gabriel gave his wife a puzzled look. "What makes you think that I will?"

"Because of Nina; she is the Child of Order and thus destined to do great things, but I fear that such a burden might ultimately destroy her."

Gabriel took hold of Clarissa's hands and gave them a reassuring squeeze. "That's why I'm here; to keep her safe."

"But that Task ended when she arrived in Celestia," Clarissa pointed out. "It was only through the Archangels' graces that you've been allowed to remain here with her as well as spend time with us."

Gabriel's left eyebrow arched upward. "You seem to know a lot about my comings and goings."

Clarissa laughed, jerking her head at Gabriella who was frolicking happily in the water with a pair of dolphins. "You can thank her for that. Her aquatic friends are the most notorious gossips!"

"So, I've heard," Gabriel muttered a bemused smile on his face as he watched his daughter execute an intricate flip above the waves, her tall, sinewy frame a sharp contrast to the image of the cherubic toddler stored in his memories. "And have her...advisers revealed what Nina's true Task is?"

Clarissa frowned. "No, they haven't but judging by their recent chattiness and the overall sense of excitement that seems to be running through Heaven's populace, I get the feeling that that's about to change."

"Meaning what, exactly?"

"Meaning that Nina's time in Celestia is coming to an end," a silvery voice rang out as the Archangel Michael swooped down on their position coming to a gentle stop atop the white sands. "I do apologize for this intrusion, Gabriel, but there is much you and I need to discuss in regard to you and my daughter's return to Mortalia and the fulfillment of both of your respective Tasks."

The Archangel's peculiar courtesy ignited a pyre of apprehension within Gabriel. "And said Tasks being?"

A look of disgust consumed Michael's normally stoic features. "To prevent your kind from falling prey to the machinations of that insufferable cur, Lillian, and her band of Dissident filth!"

Gabriel was stunned by Michael's outburst, and even more so by the hostility radiating from him. Normally such spiteful declarations were the providence of the Bringer of Death. "Has something happened on Earth?"

Michael sighed. "I'm afraid much has transpired these paths several months."

Gabriel, Clarissa, and Gabriella who had joined her parents after the Archangel's sudden arrival, listened in shock as he related to them the tale of Lie's organization of the Demonstratives and subsequent acquisition of the Staff of Moses.

Gabriel shuddered at the thought of one of the Talismans in the hands of a miscreant like Lie. "Have they made any demands of or threats against the Hierarchy?"

Michael's jaw tightened briefly. "None as of yet, but I'm sure it's just a matter of time before they do which is why I am here. Your service to The Watch, particularly your stewardship of my daughter, has been exemplary; in spite of the contempt with which you hold us."

Gabriel flinched as Michael's barb hit home. He opened his mouth, but the Archangel cut him off before he could speak. "You need offer neither explanation nor apology, Gabriel. Omen and I have often spoken of your dissatisfaction with your Celestial post due to the..." Michael's eyes flickered briefly to Clarissa and Gabriella, "conditions of your service; a contract that I am here to amend."

Gabriel regarded the Keeper of Benevolence through narrowed eyes. "In what way?"

"By releasing you from your obligation to The Watch and assuring you that, regardless of your answer to what I am about to ask, you no longer need concern yourself with Clarissa's well-being. Her place in Heaven is secured."

The joy that Gabriel should have felt at Michael's proclamation was overshadowed by the ominous double entendre. "And just what is it that you are about to ask me."

Michael leveled serious eyes on him. "That you remain a Celemor."

It took a stunned Gabriel several minutes to digest the fact that after a century of forced Celestial vigilance he was now being asked to remain at his post. "Not to be disrespectful," he began when his tongue thawed enough for him to speak. "But why in the Realms would I want to do that?"

Having anticipated the Celemor's reluctance to stay Michael had already prepared a reason that he hoped would garner his support. "Because of all the Celemors that have ever served us you have been the most diligent in carrying out your Tasks, and your dedication and experience is something Nina desperately needs if she is to succeed in hers."

Gabriel was annoyed at the Archangel's use of Nina as bait to entice him to remain under the heel of the watch, but he couldn't blame him. It was obvious that despite his customary Celestial aloofness the Archangel cared very much for her.

Gabriel was torn. What Michael was saying about Nina's need of his abilities was true, yet how could he leave his family now that they were finally reunited? Of course, the same argument held true for Nina and not just because of his position as her guardian. Oddly enough the time spent with his family had shown the dutiful Celemor how much he had truly come to love his unique charge. And now that the situation was changed, how could he possibly leave her?

His troubled thoughts were interrupted by the feel of Clarissa's hand on his chin turning his face toward her. "I see the turmoil in your eyes, my love, but this is something that you must do. Nina *needs* you and I'm not just talking about your Task as her guardian, and you need her," she added, a tender smile curving her lips.

A wave of guilt consumed Gabriel as the truth of his wife's words hit home. "But what about *your* needs?"

Clarissa chuckled. "You have already provided for my needs in the most amazing way." She waved her hand in the direction of Heaven's gleaming skyline. "This is a different place and a different time. I've no doubt that the love you once had for me is still strong, as is mine for you, but I am your past. Nina is your present and future."

Clarissa's words produced a flood of relief within Gabriel. "Thank you," he whispered then shifted his gaze to his daughter. "And what's your opinion about all of this?"

Gabriella flashed her father a proud grin. "Mother and I have long since accepted the fact that even though you still love us, you are *in* love with Nina. I also feel that Michael is correct in his estimation of her need of you. If even half of what the dolphins have told me about Lie is true then the sanctity of the Realms is indeed at stake, and we must do our best to support Nina in her efforts to stop whatever insanity that psycho Halfling has planned."

Gabriel focused sharply on his daughter's face. "*Our* best?"

A mischievous grin tugged at Gabriella's lips. "You're not the only Leyr skilled in the art of Celestial deal-making."

"And just what does *that* mean?"

Gabriella gave her father a saucy wink. "It means that when you return to Earth, I'll be coming *with* you."

"That is one of the other matters that you and I must discuss," Michael interjected into the stunned silence that followed Gabriella's announcement. "It seems that shortly after Clarissa and Gabriella's arrival in Heaven that conflicted sack of Celestial confusion, Caleb, took it upon himself to befriend them; often relating to them the details of your various Tasks."

Once again Gabriel found himself gaping in amazement at the Archangel's words. "But...why?"

A look of annoyance flickered briefly across Michael's face. "I suspect it was to reassure them in regard to your well-being in much the same manner he would often reassure you as to theirs."

Gabriel pinned his wife and daughter with a hard stare. "Why didn't you tell me that Dichotomy had been giving you a running account of my activities these past several decades?"

"He or rather 'they' made us promise not to," Clarissa responded calmly in the face of her husband's sudden hostility.

"I only recently learned of their interactions myself," Michael noted, surprise still swirling in his mind over the unexpected visit he had received from the former Celemor earlier that day, and the unusual request the blended duo had made on Gabriella's behalf. "It seems that the stories of your exploits have inspired your daughter." Michael favored Gabriella with an approving grin. "She has requested that she be allowed to Transition back into Mortal form so that she can assume the mantel of Celemor and stand beside you in the coming conflict; a request that has been approved."

"The hell it has," Gabriel snapped, his eyes flashing with Celestial fire. "You've got some nerve, Michael! First, I'm coerced into being The Watch's lapdog and forced to adhere to a bunch of cockamamie rules about who lives and who dies. Then after a century of service you *release* me from that bond only to press me into service again by dangling Nina's fate in front of me, and now you tell me that the daughter whom I'm only just now beginning to know, is about to be thrown back into the fire with me? And how is that even *possible?*"

Gabriel stabbed a finger at Gabriella though his eyes never left Michael. "She died, Archangel; they both *died!* And I mourned their deaths for over a hundred years despite the fact that I knew they were in Heaven! How *dare* you ask for more of my family's blood? Enough has been spilled already!"

"*He* didn't ask," Gabriella leapt to Michael's defense, placing herself between him and her furious father. "I did; this was *my* decision!"

Gabriella's words caught Gabriel up short, and he turned stunned eyes to her. "But why, Gabby; you've obviously heard about the life I've been forced to live and the hardships I've had to endure. Why would you choose to subject yourself to that?"

"You said the words yourself," Gabriella replied stepping closer to her father. "My entire afterlife I've only *heard* about you and the type of man you are, both from mother and Caleb. That's just not enough anymore. I want to *know* who my father is, and fate has presented me with this opportunity to do so."

As Gabriel took note of the burning entreaty in the eyes of this *woman* who had once been his little girl, his anger began to fade, though not his feelings of trepidation. "I still think that this is a bad idea, but I suppose watching your children follow their own path is a part of parenting that I must work on." A look of joy suffused Gabriella's face and she threw herself into her father's waiting arms hugging him tightly. "I just hope I'm able to live up to the sterling image you have of me."

"You already have," Gabriella assured him.

Gabriel's eyes sought those of his wife. "Are you okay with this?"

"Gabby has been my constant source of joy for over a century," Clarissa beamed at them as she joined in their embrace. "I think the time has finally come for her to look after her father now."

Gabriel gave both of them another squeeze then focused his attention on a waiting Michael. "Alright, Keeper of Benevolence; we're in. What happens now?"

The Archangel's relief was obvious as he answered Gabriel's question. "We wait for The Almighty, who is currently holding council with Nina, to decide on the proper time for you to return to Mortalia and hopefully put a stop to that troublesome Halfling's meddling once and for all!

Chapter 44

The authority of The Almighty's tone settled heavily in Nina's mind as she listened to the story of The Creation's beginning.

In the Beginning of all Beginnings there was the Event, a molecular cataclysm that spawned all that exists, including myself.

For millennia untold I existed without corporeal form, in a state of contemplation and discovery as the universe around me continued to develop. Over the eons I watched as the multitudes of copious vessels of energy surrounding me evolved into the various forms of life that currently span the expanse that is our current Reality.

It was through my meditations that I discovered that not only was I intrinsically connected to the universe but through force of will, and the channeling of the molecular or Celestial *energy that permeates all in existence l could control the development of that which surrounded me. I also discovered that I was not alone in this respect.*

Nina's shoulder's straightened as she jumped on The Almighty's statement. "You weren't?"

No. Two others had also risen during Reality's birth; their essences far more ephemeral than mine but both nearly as influential in terms of shaping our world. One was structured in its thinking, promoting a sense of Order in all that it touched while the other was the complete antithesis, giving rise to disruption and random destruction on a cosmic scale. Where one was light the other became darkness, and while one's primary purpose was to instill order and continuity in the ever-changing expanse surrounding us, the other's was to foment that which it had taken as its namesake: Chaos.

"Amazing," Nina whispered. "Are they more powerful than you?"

In terms of raw ability and cognitive facilities, no. Nor are they able to manipulate the physical properties of that which is Reality. Their power lies in the manipulation of the ephemeral, or spirit as you Mortals would term it.

Nina's brow furrowed with consternation. "But I don't understand. If your abilities are greater, why don't you just destroy Chaos?"

As I said before, in all things there is duality, a balance. Within that which you know as The Creation, Order and Chaos provide that balance, or rather they used to.

Nina's eyes narrowed. "What does that mean, exactly?"

As the Races matured so did their need for understanding of that which is around them.

"And this is a bad thing?"

A twinge of apprehension flowed through The Almighty's aura. *It can be. The need for understanding, or 'search for truth' as I have heard it termed can often lead beings to the discovery of potentially dangerous matters which they are not yet ready to handle. This is particularly true of your kindred on Earth.*

Nina's eyes widened with surprise. "But what's wrong with that? On Earth there's a saying: 'The more you know, the further you go'. I would think that you'd want that for us, especially since Humans are supposed to be the Vanguard Race."

It is true that knowledge is power, but it can also be dangerous if the receiver is unprepared for it as evidenced by another of your quaint Mortal euphemisms: Absolute power corrupts absolutely. It is in situations like these that Chaos asserts her control, often to disastrous effects.

"Such as?"

All you need do is look to Earth's recent history, The Almighty intoned. *There are countless examples, one of those I believe you once questioned your Celemor guardian about.*

Nina searched her memory for said reference and her eyes went wide. "You mean...the Holocaust?"

A pang of regret flitted through The Almighty's aura. *I do. You once asked Gabriel why I would allow such an atrocity to happen when in truth it was not I who allowed it but rather those involved who fell victim to Chaos's corruption of the one force I dare not control; one inherent to all Mortals but Mankind in particular: the power of Choice.*

Nina stared hard at the swirling mass, a look of disbelief on her face. "Choice?"

Yes, Choice; something that should've been a great boon for all Mortals but instead became, what your kind term, a double-edged sword.

Nina's eyes lit with understanding as she recalled an entry, she had read in Michael's Journal dealing with Humanity's beginning; a tale that differed greatly from its counterpart in the biblical book of Genesis. "You're talking about Adam, Lillith, and the other First Ones aren't you; where we first gained awareness of right and wrong?"

I am. That was a lesson that was prematurely given.

"Why is that? When you created us, didn't you want us to eventually become self-sufficient?"

I'm afraid that is another misconception that has been perpetuated through the ages.

Nina was surprised at the sudden apprehension she sensed in The Almighty's voice. "What, that you wanted us to grow up?"

No, that I am your creator.

Nina stiffened. "Are you saying that you *aren't*?"

Not in the manner that you perceive. As I said before I am merely one of the oldest beings spawned during the Event, and as such have taken it upon myself to guide the other Races in their evolution; occasionally modifying certain Castes to better serve The Creation as a whole. It was for this reason that I separated it into three distinct Realms. It was my intention to bring into being a rank-and-file system that would be beneficial to us all; one that would lessen the potential for the Catastrophic end I mentioned earlier.

"In what way?"

Both forces are essential to Creations overall development. Without Chaos, Order leads to stagnation; without Order, Chaos leads to annihilation. It was for this reason that I... seeded the Human Race with a portion of my Divine intellect, so that when the time came, you would be able to differentiate between the two and lead the less enlightened Races. But such maturity does not come without careful nurturing which is why I have allowed Mankind to develop as it has; so that you would slowly develop the traits required to lead.

Unfortunately Lie and her sycophants, including the Mortal that has taken possession of one of the Talismans, refuse to accept this universal truth. They see my Tenets and the steps I've taken to propagate them as outright manipulation and subjugation of the Races. It is up to you to show them the flaws in their logic and hopefully steer them from their disastrous course.

Nina made no further comment as she struggled to process The Almighty's revelation. True, she had never subscribed to Earth's various religious doctrines, but she always accepted the fact that there was a Supreme Being in charge of it all. For her to have just discovered that there were actually *three* and that two of them were working at crossed purposes was a lot to digest even with the newly expanded parameters of her mind.

"So why is uniting the Realm so important and how exactly am I supposed to do it?"

Chaos' influence is most potent amidst times of disharmony. A unified Creation will be less susceptible to its machinations, giving Order a chance to assert its presence as well, thus restoring the Balance. But for this to happen, you must counter the flood of misinformation being fed to Humanity by Lie and her minions.

Nina released a resigned sighed. "Lucky me; and what if I'm unsuccessful in this...Task?"

A sense of profound regret permeated The Almighty's aura. *Then I will have no choice but to unleash the Horseman; a quartet of immensely powerful Celestials that I engineered for the sole purpose of restoring the Balance by whatever means necessary, even if that means expunging entire Races from The Creation.*

Nina swallowed hard. "And I take it that would be a very bad thing."

Calling the Realms to heel in such a way would essentially rob The Creation of Choice, and Hope. Reality would continue but it would be a bleak one indeed.

"Yeah, I guess it would," Nina uttered after releasing a resigned sigh. "It looks like I've got a lot of work to do in order to keep things from coming to that."

A hint of humor colored Almighty's tone for the disparity in Nina's voice. *Worry not, child. I have long foreseen such an occurrence which was why I charged Michael with the Task of engineering a being who would one day become Realities champion. That being is you, Nina, and your abilities have far surpassed even my expectations. They will stand you in good stead during the coming confrontation. All that remains is your final transformation.*

Another knot of apprehension formed in the pit of Nina's stomach. "Transformation into what?"

That which you were always meant to be. As I said before, there must always be a balance. The Child of Chaos has already made her presence known. It is now time for The Child of Order to do the same!

The Almighty's proclamation thundered through Nina's mind, and a nimbus of blinding light formed around her body as The Creation's principle being reached deep within her essence triggering the final sequences of her unique genetic code.

The nimbus flared even brighter, and a cry of alarm escaped Nina's lips for the sudden pain as her body began to change...

Chapter 45

"My fellow Demonstratives," Lie's voice rang out garnering the attention of the multitude of beings gathered across the vast plains of the Sublimian wasteland known as the Gardens of Luna. "You have all met he whom I claim as equal." She indicated the softly glowing form of Dresden standing beside her. "And you have all bore witness to his mastery of the Talisman he now holds."

A slight rustling echoed across the Gardens as the eyes of several thousand beings flicked briefly to the gleaming staff the former Cardinal was holding firmly in his left hand.

"With his power now supporting us we need not fear the reprisals of The Watch as we implement our strategy." The Halfling's gaze settled on the sullen face of Chton, the dark crimson of his eyes an indication of the Wraith's excitement. "To you and your ilk goes the honor of the first salvo, Chton," Lie shouted above the roaring cheers her proclamation evoked from the masses. "The Realms have suffered the stifling taint of those putrid Tenets for long enough. Let the Era of Chaos begin!"

Once again Lie's words were met with a roar of approval from the crowd with the exception of the Morphling who quietly separated herself from the main throngs.

Drift's mind was racing with anxiety as she made ready to depart the gathering. The details of Lie's plans had been passed to her master some time ago; all that had remained was the moment said action was to commence.

"And now that you have that information what will you do with it," a deep voice sounded as Dresden materialized before the startled Morphling, Malakai and Joey beside him. "Will you run back to your master's bland tower and report it in the hopes that he and his loyal sycophants can mount some type of counter-offensive?"

Drift quickly dropped into a defensive posture as Malakai and Joey assumed flanking positions around her.

"There is no need for that," Dresden interceded waving the others away as he stepped toward the scared Morphling. "We are not enemies Drift, which is why I have allowed your continued presence among us." Dresden smiled at the startled look that consumed the Morphling's features. "Yes, I've been aware of you ever since my Celestial elevation."

"But why...?"

"Did I allow you to continue in your subterfuge?" Dresden finished the Morphling's question. "Like I said, I am not your enemy, nor is Lillian." He accorded the Halfling materializing beside him an affectionate smile. "In fact, I had hoped that continued exposure to our plan might help you to see the logic of it." Dresden studied Drift's face for a moment then released a resigned sigh. "But I can see by the defiance in your eyes that such is not the case; despite what you have learned you still do not understand why the coming revolution must happen, nor I would hazard will your master. Go," he commanded waving his hand toward the sky. "Go and report to Iblis all that has transpired here today. My offer of an alliance between our respective forces still stands, but know this," Dresden's eyes blazed with Celestial fire. "Though we have no wish to harm you or any of your compatriots, my mistress and I will tolerate no interference and will take whatever steps necessary to ensure the success of our plans."

The ominous tone of Dresden's voice sent an additional wave of unease through Drift's formless body. "I will convey your offer to my master and your warning," she replied, her voice shaky. The Morphling then accorded Dresden and Lie a brief nod and promptly vanished.

Lie studied the spot where Drift had been for a moment then turned questioning eyes to her mate. "Are you sure it's wise to let her go, my love?"

"I am," Dresden assured her speaking loudly so that his voice carried to those that had gathered in a loose circle around them. "The one thing that I have learned during my recent meditations is that the entire structure of the Realms is predicated on Choice. For us to force others to our way of thinking would make us no less vile than those we seek to supplant. That is why the Task given to the Wraiths is so vital. My people must be shown the *truth* of the universe around them so that they may choose whether or not they wish to continue living the lie."

Lie pondered his reasoning for a moment. "And what of those who refuse to accept it?"

Once again Dresden's eyes flared and a stern look consumed his features. "Those that choose not to follow us will serve no purpose in the new order and will be expunged from the coming utopia, physically *and* spiritually. Lenience toward dissenters is a trait of The Almighty that I do not share."

Chapter 46

As one of Detroit's premier caterers the Scavelli's had attended numerous social functions and gala events over the years, but even the most spectacular of those paled in comparison to the small gathering currently taking place on their screened-in deck.

After receiving Drift's dire report, Darius had called a meeting of Nina's allies at Toni and Maria's spacious home which had become the unofficial headquarters of the group much to the delight of the winsome couple. However, the Scavelli's joy over their inclusion into what Tony had termed the Cosmic Calvary was taken to a whole new level with the appearance of the *special* guest the Desomor had summoned.

"Dresden's calm reasoning gives further proof of his rapid adaptation to the Talisman's power," Iblis intoned after Drift had completed the retelling of her tale. "Of course, given the fact that Humankind was specifically bred for that very purpose I would've been surprised if he hadn't."

"What do you mean by 'bread for that purpose'?" Tyree asked, a slight flush rising to his face as the fact that he was addressing not only an angel but the so-called Devil himself once again threatened to overwhelm him.

"The Almighty engineered your kind using a template of His own divine self," Iblis explained pressing his wings tightly against his back so as not to disrupt the deck's furnishing as he shifted his attention to Tyree. "It is the reason Mankind is held in such high regards by Members of the Hierarchy. It is also the reason Lillian seeks to subvert your collective spirituality," he continued to the room at large. "As the Creation's vanguard race, humans are destined to lead the other inhabitants of this Realm to a higher level of spiritual and intellectual awareness."

"You mean once we grow up," Tyree interjected having learned a great deal on how the majority of the Celestials regarded Mankind.

Iblis favored the minister with a paternal smile. "Yes, although considering my Father's initiation of this process I would suspect that your 'growing up', as you termed, it is progressing to His satisfaction."

"Is that why Lillian or Lie is so determined to convert us to her cause?" Cara asked, the slight tremor in her voice an indication of the internal struggle she was having trying to reconcile all she had been taught about the devil with this magnificent winged being standing before her.

"It is. Lillian knows that, given your stature amongst the other Races of Mortalia, Mankind's disassociation from The Almighty and his Watch might prompt others to do the same which could lead to the destabilization of the Divine Order, an event that would be catastrophic for The Creation as a whole."

"Excuse me for saying this," Tony spoke up in a tentative voice. "But isn't what Lie and this Dresden guy doing similar to what you did when you walked out of Heaven?"

Iblis looked upon the stocky Mortal with increased respect. "Such an astute observation does indeed signify your Races intellectual evolution."

Tony shifted uncomfortably in his chair. "Uh...thanks; I think."

Iblis smiled. "You're quite welcome, and in answer to your question: To some degree what Lillian is planning *is* similar to what my brethren have termed my Idealistic Revolt, though our intentions are vastly different. I only sought to question the effectiveness of the Tenets in the hopes of amending them. Lillian and her ilk wish to abolish them completely."

"Which is what we must help Nina to prevent upon her return," Dichotomy intoned, the other murmuring their agreement.

The Lord of Hell experienced a pang of regret as he gazed upon the former Desomor's blended form, knowing that he was in part responsible for the chain of events that resulted in Caleb's bizarre transformation. But such reflections were best left for another time. At the moment their primary concern was Lillian. "Indeed, it is, Caleb."

"When do you think we'll start noticing the effects of these Wraith things?" Quinlan asked, his gaze shifting between the five Celestials.

"I would hazard a guess that it will be fairly soon," Shift spoke up in the thoughtful silence that followed the Seeker's question. She had reverted to her true form for the meeting; a process that still astounded Tony and Maria despite the fact that they had witnessed the transformation numerous times over the past several weeks. "Dream weaving is the most effective way to manipulate the Mortal masses and Chton's lot are particularly effective at invoking the chaotic scenarios that Lie is calling for."

"They most certainly are," Iblis agreed with a snort. "That is why we must all do our best to mitigate the effects of their tampering until Nina's return, at which point we will then take the fight to them," he added, his wings twitching in response to his aggravation.

"And speaking of which," Mayhem interjected as she shifted to a more comfortable position on the ornate oak bench beside Quinlan to whom she had taken a genuine interest in, much to the Seeker's delighted surprise. "Have we any estimates on when the chosen one will be making her return?"

As usual the Desomor's remarks were met with a smattering of chuckles from the others who had gotten used to her acerbic personality; though Maria still kept a butcher knife handy and would brandish it whenever the hussy's attentions were focused overly long on Tony.

"From what Silas has learned from his sources, I would say that Nina's tutelage in Celestia is drawing to a close."

Iblis's reply elicited a chuckle from Mayhem. "I take it old grim-face has been swimming with the dolphins again?"

"Their chatter is often useful," Iblis smiled in return. "At any rate I want you lot to remain vigilant while I return to Hell and continue to prepare as best I can for the coming struggle. Mister and Misses Scavelli," the Lord of Hell addressed the startled couple. "Again, I wish to convey my gratitude for the support and hospitality you've shown my agents since your inclusion into this Celestial debacle. All of you," Iblis's gaze took in Quinlan, Sanders, and Cara, "are to be commended on your ability to rise to this Divine challenge. Clearly does my Father's Grace shine within each of you!"

Iblis accorded them all a final nod then vanished from the deck amidst a flash of bright light.

"Whew," Maria exhaled, her shoulders sagging in relief. "That is one intense individual!"

"Yeah, having wings tends to do that to a person," Mayhem snickered then turned her attention to Darius. "So, what now boss?"

The Desomor shrugged "We do what the master said: We watch and wait."

"Well in that case I'd better get lunch going," Maria proclaimed as she happily made her way to the kitchen. "I hear divine stake-outs can really give you an appetite!"

*

Standing before the dimensional rift known simply as the Window, which was housed within the massive marble pyramid that made up Heaven's Seat of Authority, the Overseer Omen watched the events taking place at the Scavelli home with a growing sense of apprehension.

One would think that a pledge of support from one of the most powerful beings in the Hierarchy would inspire a sense of confidence, yet Omen drew scant comfort from Iblis's involvement.

Never before in the history of The Creation had a being attempted to use a Talisman in any way other than what The Almighty intended, let alone as a weapon in challenge of His authority.

With the awesome might of the Staff of Moses now at his fingertips, the misanthrope Dresden was, for all intents and purposes an almighty being himself. Even considering the power that Nina now possessed because of her Divine heritage, how could she and her allies possibly hope to mount an effective counter-offensive against whatever it was that Lie and Dresden had in store?

Omen was not fool enough to think that the information retrieved my Iblis's Morphling operative was the extent of their scheme.

Nor has The Almighty revealed the extent of His, a silken voice echoed through the Overseer's mind as a sphere of pure Celestial energy appeared in the Chamber beside him.

The sphere reformed itself into shape of a faceless humanoid woman and Omen released a startled gasp. "Twilight!"

"Greetings Omen," Twilight switched to vocal speech, the aura emanating from her glowing form conveying a sense of pleasure as she extended her right hand forward. "It is good to see you again."

"And you as well," Omen replied, his eyes flaring briefly due to the spark of energy he received after touching his open palm to hers in the Celestial Greeting of Equals. "What circumstances have afforded me the rare treat of your company?"

"Your troubled thoughts," said Twilight. "As you know I am directly linked to the Members of The Watch and am therefore cognizant of increased levels of stress, and your levels have been extremely elevated of late."

Omen released a weary sigh. "It's this whole business with Lie; I fear that her acquisition of the Staff has tipped the scales in her favor, yet apparently I am the only one. The Archangels do not appear overly concerned, and I cannot fathom the reason why."

"Perhaps it is because they have faith in The Almighty's wisdom in regard to this matter."

Omen's hovering form wavered lightly. "I have faith, though I must admit it has been sorely tested these past several months. I've also sensed similar feelings from other Celestials."

Twilight laid a gentle hand atop the Overseer's forearm infusing her touch with a spate of soothing energy. She had always held Omen in high regards and did not like to see him thus. A part of her wished she could give him the same disclosure that Nina had received once her transformation to her Ultimate state had been completed as to the *true* nature of the Celestial Caste's relationship to The Almighty, but she knew to do so would be counterproductive. When the time came, *all* of The Almighty's 'children' would be made aware. Till then she would do what she could to offer the pensive Overseer hope.

"Perhaps your having doubts is part of The Almighty's plan as well; to shake the very foundations of Celestial society as well as Mortal so that we may all journey toward a heightened understanding of The Creation and our individual place in it."

The Chamber was silent as Omen considered her suggestion for a moment. "Perhaps you are right, my friend," he sighed. "And if that *is* the case then I will strive to remain resolute in my duties and trust our Creator's plan; whatever it may be."

Chapter 47

Throughout the ages the manipulation of dreams has always been the most effective way to convey The Almighty's decrees to the Mortal masses. To accomplish this, Members of the Watch would often employ the services of Wraiths, a race of Celestials endowed with the unique ability to traverse and manipulate the properties of the nebulous space between the Real and Ephemeral known as the Crossroads.

In terms of Celestia's political structure most Wraiths were considered Demonstratives given the fact that they still acknowledged The Almighty's authority despite their minimal adherence to the Tenets. Then there were the Dissidents, Celestials that despised The Almighty's mandates, often carrying out specific Tasks that were in direct contention with His will.

Most of the atrocities committed throughout Mortalia could be attributed to them for theirs was the power of mental manipulation of the Mortal Races, and they had spent several millennia honing the skills that were currently being called into play against Earth's unsuspecting populace.

A wave of unrest arose across the planet as Mankind was assaulted by dreams and omens showing the fall of what was being portrayed as a false deity, and the subsequent rise of a new religion helmed by two benevolent beings; one male, one female and both pictured with open arms welcoming the teeming masses to their bosoms.

Churches and temples around the world were besieged as millions of people desperately sought the advice of spiritual leaders who were just as, if not more, conflicted as their constituents.

At the height of the confusion, Dresden and Lie began the second phase of their scheme by manifesting their physical selves in areas they deemed suitably open to their new message of spiritual emancipation from an uncaring God.

Occasionally they were met with resistance by the obstinate few that chose to cling to their own specific faith, but for the most part they were joyously accepted by a scared populace who took heart at the appearance of the subjects of their dreams; particularly in light of the distorted truth they were being told.

"Our plan proceeds accordingly, my love," Lie commented to Dresden as he stepped onto the patio of his villa where the Halfling was scanning various news broadcast of their most recent public outing on the television; a technological device she had come to find quite fascinating. "The people are flocking to our cause in droves; even those stubborn zealots of the Muslim faith have begun to accept us."

A pleased smile creased Dresden's thin lips as he also focused attention on the screen. "As I knew they would. The Almighty's influence on the world has waned of late and the masses have been *looking* for something or someone to believe in." He leaned down and placed a kiss on Lie's forehead. "We've simply fulfilled that need."

"But at what cost?"

Lie and Dresden were startled by the booming voice issuing from within the nimbus of white light forming on the deck before them. The light quickly coalesced into the winged form of the Archangel Raphael.

"Father!"

"Daughter," Raphael responded to Lie's incredulous cry before settling his baleful glare on Dresden. "And you must be Carl Dresden; the former *Presbyterii* Elder who now fancies himself a Celestial."

"Not at all, sir," Dresden replied, nonplused by the Archangel's disdainful remark. "I'm simply a Mortal who's been given the opportunity to guide his people to a higher stature within that which you call The Creation."

The deck was silent as the Keeper of the Talisman and the Archangel regarded one another. Finally, a ghost of a smile appeared on Raphael's narrow face. "Well played, Mortal. It is easy to see why my daughter has taken such a fancy to you."

The Archangel's comment was met by another startled reaction from Lie. "You've been monitoring me?"

"As would any father whose child was as prone to mischief as you are."

Lie released a disgusted snort. "And is that why you're here; to call me to task for my aberrant behavior?"

A bark of laughter escaped Raphael's lips. "Such an attempt would be futile, Lillian. You've long since proven yourself beyond my ability to tame. Your will is indomitable. In that respect you and Lillith are much alike."

Lie noticed the slight twitch of her father's jaw after mentioning her mother's name, a testament to the intense feelings he still held for her. It was one of the few things they had in common. "Well, if you're not here to chastise me then why have you decided to grace us with your Divine presence?"

"To hopefully instill a bit of reason in both you and your paramour for this dangerous course you've set."

"And why would our separation from The Almighty and his Watch pose said threat. Carl and I are simply following in your glorious footsteps."

"Hardly," Raphael snapped, his wings twitching with suppressed emotion. "I simply stepped away from the convoluted politics of The Hierarchy. You plan to supplant them."

"And considering their mismanagement of the Realms is that truly such a bad thing?"

Raphael focused glowing eyes on Dresden. "Have a care, Mortal. Powerful and more knowledgeable you have become via the Talisman, but yours are recent enhancements. You would do well to refrain from commenting on that of which you have no true understanding."

"Spoken like the arrogant Celestial you are," Dresden replied, the Celestial energy now flowing through his veins bolstering his confidence in the presence of his Divine antagonist. "The disdainful positions in which you hold us have made the lot of you consistently underestimate our abilities throughout the Millennia."

Raphael regarded Dresden through narrowed eyes. "And just what abilities might you be referring to; a Mortal's penchant for spiritual and moral disobedience, and self-destruction? From where I sit those seems to be your Race's primary pursuits."

Dresden bristled at Raphael's insults. A part of him wanted to unleash his power against the winged buffoon but an inner voice prompted caution. Powerful the Talisman may be but there was still much he had to learn in terms of wielding it. Pitting his fledgling might against that of an Archangel would more likely be an act of suicide than one of defiance. "Say what you will, Raphael; the fact still remains that the Hierarchy's stewardship of us has been a comedy of cosmic errors, particularly the lie of Christianity we Mortals of Earth have been forced to submit to."

Raphael's left eyebrow arched upward. "And you actually believe *your* judgment is greater than that of The Almighty?"

"Is it really so hard to believe? After all, He did christen us the Vanguard Race of Mortalia. Who's to say what we could accomplish as a species if left to our own designs?"

Raphael couldn't help the spark of respect rising in him for the intrepid Mortal. Though he still disagreed with their methods he couldn't fault the logic of Dresden's reasoning, nor could he deny the fact that the Mortal's grievances mirrored his own in regard to The Almighty's Tenets governing Mortalia.

Raphael studied Dresden's resolute face for another moment then shifted his gaze to his daughter. "I'm beginning to understand his reasons for instigating this aggressive campaign." He jerked his thumb at Dresden. "What's yours? Unless I'm mistaken, your goal has always been the demise of your Human kin, now you profess yourself to be their savior?"

A slight flush darkened Lie's ivory features. "For centuries I placed the blame of mother's death equally between Mankind and the Hierarchy. I have since come to realize that my Mortal brethren's forced adherence to the Tenets is the true culprit. That is why Carl and I have taken up this cause; Mortalia needs to be freed of such Divine restrictions. Perhaps then the inhabitants of the Realm will be able to reach their true potential."

Lie's impassioned speech prompted Raphael to regard her in a new light and he was pleased with what he saw. The malice which was once such an integral part of her personality was gone, as was her ambivalence for her dual heritage. His one regret was that such a change had come on the cusp of what could only be seen as monumental rebellion against The Almighty and his Hosts, though perhaps that was as it should be.

Lillian and her compatriots would undoubtedly suffer severe retribution for their actions, but at least their destiny would be one of their own making. In the greater scheme of things, the benefits of achieving such freedom far exceeded the risks.

"The two of you make a compelling case," Raphael addressed the stout couple. "I look forward to watching this particular drama unfold."

Both Dresden and Lie were taken aback by the Archangel's unexpected accolade. "Does this mean we can count on *your* support should the need arise?"

Raphael surprised his daughter again by tenderly taking hold of her hands and drawing her body close to his. "No, it does not. Despite my...dissatisfaction with Celestia's politics I cannot, and will, not lift a hand against The Hierarchy." Raphael took note of his daughter's disappointment, and he took hold of her chin and tilted her head up so that their eyes met. "Nor will I lift one against you."

Lie's expression brightened. "Thank you, father," she whispered, pressing her cheek against his like she did when she was a child, before the politics of Reality erected the timeless barrier between them.

Raphael savored the physical contact for a moment then gently disentangled himself from her embrace. "You're welcome...daughter," he whispered back. He accorded Dresden a slight nod then vanished from the courtyard.

"That went better than I expected," Lie commented when the glow of the Archangel's carrier nimbus had faded.

Dresden embraced the Halfling from behind and nuzzled his lips against her neck. "Indeed, it did, which surprised me considering your father's initial hostility."

Lie opened her mouth to respond but paused when she felt his body stiffen. "Is something wrong?"

Dresden pointed toward the television where the Pope was issuing an unprecedented request for the nefarious duo currently professing themselves to be Mankind's new saviors to attend a gathering of the world's spiritual leaders at the Sistine Chapel, in the hopes of mitigating some of the chaos their appearance had caused.

"I take it you mean for us to honor your Pope's request," Lie said when the story had played itself out.

"Indeed, I do," Dresden confirmed, his eyes glowing with Celestial fire. "Though not for the reason His Holiness expects!"

*

Sitting in Nina's office at the Lafayette Rec Center, Darius, Cara, Sanders, and Shift cloaked in her Nina-persona were also watching the Pope's televised plea.

"Do you think Lie and Dresden will go for it?" Sanders asked when it was over.

A look of consternation appeared on Darius's face. "It's hard to say. On the one hand it would be the perfect opportunity for them to eliminate the competition so to speak but considering the elaborate steps they're taking with the Wraiths I get the feeling that using brute force to achieve their goal isn't part of their agenda."

Cara, who was still adjusting to her body's new proportions, gave her muscular arms a brief stretch. "So, what's the plan, boss; soft and subtle or smash and grab?"

Darius smiled. "Actually, a little of both; I'm curious to see how Lie and Dresden will respond to this collective effort on the part of Earth's primary religions. The two of you will head to Rome where you will *quietly* infiltrate the gathering, after you collect Mayhem and Quinlan from their...date of course."

Cara and Sanders exchanged knowing looks while Shift chuckled softly. "And what shall you and I be doing, my love?"

Darius sighed. "Unfortunately, we have to put in an appearance at City Hall. Nina's scheduled to speak at the meeting the mayor has convened of all community leaders to discuss the current crisis."

Shift sighed. "Another meeting? I must admit my respect for Nina has greatly increased these past few months. I never realized how much of her time was usurped by her philanthropic efforts. That woman's indefatigable."

"Let us hope that same fortitude will carry her through the coming conflict," the blended voice of Dichotomy rang out as the Celestial appeared in the office. "For we strongly suspect she will need it."

"That goes without saying," Darius said after according the newcomer a respectful nod. "I take it the two of you are here for the Rome jaunt?"

"We are. Our power will prove useful should the Vatican situation become untenable."

"Considering the ease with which Dresden dispatched you lot during your first encounter I'm not so sure how much of a difference your addition will make. Not that I'm criticizing," the Desomor added hastily when he sensed the others taking umbrage. "I'm simply pointing out the fact that until Nina returns, we're pretty much outclassed in the power department."

A look of defiance crossed the blended being's face. "Then we will simply have to manage as best we can without her. Besides," Dichotomy continued, a peculiar smile playing at his lips. "All is not as one-sided as it may seem."

Darius's left eyebrow arched upward. "Meaning what?"

"Meaning that we have initiated certain...protocols within Earth's spiritual infrastructure," Dichotomy responded.

The office was silent as Darius and the others took note of the decidedly smug look on Dichotomy's face.

Mayhem released a contemptuous snort. "I take it you don't plan on elaborating on these...protocols of yours?"

"We would prefer to wait for the appropriate moment."

"Well, I just hope that whatever the two of you have up your collective sleeves will have as much of an impact as you seem to think it will," Darius stated.

A solemn look consumed Dichotomy's features. "As do we."

Chapter 48

Within the hallowed walls of the Sistine Chapel an unprecedented meeting was underway. Hundreds of Clergy men and women representing Earth's numerous religions had gathered at the bidding of Pope James in the hopes of peacefully confronting the enigmatic duo who were steadily usurping the world's spiritual infrastructure; a hope that was rapidly waning as the hours ticked by with no indication that the two intended to honor the Pope's request.

Hovering above the crowded sanctuary, their presence Celestially masked, Nina's allies quietly observed the nervous throng.

"The natives are getting restless," Cara commented to Sanders, her gaze ranging over the massive crowd. "What do we do if Lie and Dresden decide to opt out of this little holy meet-and-greet?"

Her question was rendered moot by the spectacular arrival of the couple in question. Several of those gathered uttered cries of shock, amazement, and fear while a scattered few possessed of cooler heads, though still awed, regarded the glowing arrivals with more than a hint of skepticism.

"Greetings my fellow spiritual leaders," Dresden's voice rang above the nervous muttering that echoed throughout the sanctuary when the glow faded, and he and Lie's features were revealed.

"Cardinal Dresden," the Pope gasped in open mouthed astonishment. "Is it truly you?"

"It is indeed," Dresden replied giving the shaken head of the Catholic Diocese a respectful nod. "Though I believe *former Cardinal* would be a more apt title."

Standing beside the Pope, Rabbi Horowitz, also an associate of Dresden, voiced his own confusion. "But...what has happened to you Carl?"

Dresden favored his former friends, colleagues, and superior with a paternal smile. "I'm glad you asked." He then launched into a narrative of his startling transformation from dutiful Catholic sentinel into the Divine being now standing before them.

"Shouldn't we be doing something?" Mayhem asked as she and the others observed from their hidden cloaked position.

Quinlan placed a restraining hand atop her shoulder. "Not yet; let's wait and see how the religious masses respond to the load of crap being dumped on their plates."

The Desomor drew the Seekers hand to her lips and placed a kiss in his palm. "As you wish my pet," she said shooting a menacing look at the snickering Cara and Sanders.

"Focus," Dichotomy scolded. "A momentous event is occurring below us and all of our energies should be directed there."

Agreed, Lie's disembodied voice penetrated their startled minds. *Worry not, my friends,* the Halfling continued, her tone laced with humor for the sudden apprehension her presence evoked in her adversaries. *Though you have appeared at these proceedings uninvited, neither Carl nor I bear you any malice. And that being the case, you need conceal yourself no longer!"*

A collective cry of amazement went up from hundreds of throats as Lie deftly removed Dichotomy's Celestial concealment spell rendering them visible to all.

"Fear not my fellow leaders," Dresden called over the frightened voices. "Like my companion and I, the beings before you mean you no harm for they too are part of the greater universal truth that I am about to reveal to you!"

Amidst the numerous looks of confusion Dresden raised the Staff above his head, the resulting flash released from it bringing all conversations to a halt. He then proceeded to reveal to the gathered clergy, much to the surprise of Nina's allies, the true history of The Creation.

"And that is why Lillian and I have initiated this awakening if you will; to free Mankind and the rest of our Mortal brethren among throughout this Realm from the shackles of ignorance and servitude placed around us by a fickle deity and his callous band of Celestial sycophants."

The sanctuary was silent as those gathered struggled to absorb Dresden's incredible tale. Then like a slowly cresting wave voices started to rise as the clergymen began to discuss their former peer's disturbing revelation.

"The man does know how to move a crowd," Sanders noted as he and the others tried to gauge the reactions of the crowd below who had all but forgotten the hovering quintet during Dresden's mesmerizing oration.

Cara released a disgusted snort. "Yeah, the Cardinal's always had a silver tongue. The question now is how will the masses respond?"

"It would seem that we are about to find out," Dichotomy announced as the Pope raised his hands for silence.

"Much has been revealed to us this day," he addressed the crowd when they had quieted down. "And what we have learned has forever changed the spiritual landscape. We now have irrevocable proof of our Lord's existence which means that for the first time, in the history of Mankind, our people can stand united under one faith."

Several cries of "Amen" went up from the assembly as many realized that the Pope's words did indeed ring true.

"The question now becomes," he continued over the din of conversation. "What faith shall we choose?" Pope James turned solemn eyes to Dresden and Lillian. "You propose that our stewardship under God and those you call The Hierarchy has been detrimental to our world and the worlds of the other varied Mortal races that inhabit this so-called Realm."

Another spate of nervous mutterings circulated the sanctuary as those gathered continued to struggle with the fact that Mankind wasn't alone in the universe; a fact that some were finding even more disturbing than the dissolution of their flawed belief systems.

"You also suggest that we as a people stand under your banner as you excommunicate yourself from the Tenets of God and his host, yet I can't help but wonder if the two of you truly understand the magnitude of the folly you are attempting."

Dresden's eyes widened with surprise at the Pope's unexpected response. "Folly, you say?"

"Yes folly," Pope James responded meeting the sudden hostility in the other's gaze with unflinching resolve. "You see today is not the first time that I've heard this incredible tale of our world's beginning."

Dresden's sullen frown turned into one of incredulity. "It's not?"

"No, it's not," the Pope confirmed, his eyes shining with an inner light. "I was recently given access to the most remarkable book; the Journal of the Archangel Michael."

Again, Dresden was stunned. "Have you now; and who was it that gave you this...access?"

The Pope's gaze shifted upward, and a slight smile creased his lips as he pointed to Nina's allies hovering silently above them. "I was recently made privy to the true nature of our world by the Celestial entities that call themselves Dichotomy."

This time it was Nina's allies who were stunned as they turned questioning eyes to their dichotomous friend.

"When the hell did you sit down for a meet-and-greet with the Pope?" Cara demanded, her startled cry drawing the nervous attention of all those gathered.

Dichotomy accorded the Pope a respectful nod. "We approached him at the onset of Dresden and Lie's psychic onslaught against humanity. As the ruling voice of one of Earth's most significant faiths he needed to be made aware of the dire situation The Creation now faces."

"And as well he should've been," Dresden's thunderous voice overrode the sanctuary's excited chatter. "This is why Lillian and I have chosen to come forth at this juncture."

The Pope's eyes flashed with anger. "No, it isn't!" His sharp denial cut through the chatter like a laser. "You've chosen to reveal yourselves in the hopes that such a spectacular spectacle would divert the world's attentions away from the fact that, like so many megalomaniacs of the past, you seek to dominate those whom you feel are now inferior to you!"

Dresden was taken aback by the Pope's vehemence. "You clearly misunderstand our purpose..."

"And you clearly misunderstand just how much was revealed to me," Pope James cut him off. "Like the fact that the staff you carry, the source of your miraculous transformation, was not attained through the normal channels of enlightenment, such as perseverance or self-sacrifice. You took it by force; in much the same way you are now trying to take Mankind's spiritual allegiance!"

"Have a care in the manner in which you address us Mortal," Lic spoke up when a rattled Dresden failed to respond. "Though the manner of Carl's acquisition of the Talisman was not without bloodshed, his intentions were and continue to be honorable."

Pope James balked at the Halfling then turned hard eyes to Dresden. "Honorable," he ground out. "Is this what you call honor; aligning yourself with a creature whose sole purpose for countless centuries has been the disruption of the Mortal Condition; an allegiance that led to the deaths of your fellow Elders and the Talisman's rightful guardian? And now you seek to gain favor with humanity by using demons to invade and influence our dreams while at the same time persecuting God's chosen messenger because her purpose contradicted your personal views of how our service to Him should be. That's not honor; it's tyranny!"

"You really laid it out for the old boy didn't you, Caleb?" Mayhem whispered while she and the others silently watched the drama unfolding at the altar.

"Our observation of James has shown us that he truly is a devout believer of The Almighty's way despite his limited understanding of The Creation's true nature. The world will have need of leaders like him during the chaotic throes of this Reclamation. We felt it would be best if knew the *entire* truth so that he could come to an honest and unbiased decision on how best to proceed."

"Well, it looks like your plan may have succeeded," Quinlan said as he and the others took note of the rising voices in the sanctuary as other spiritual leaders begin to catch the Pope's fever of indignation, the more outspoken ones now directing outcries of anger and hostility toward Humanity's self-proclaimed saviors.

"ENOUGH!" Dresden's bellow reverberated throughout the Chapel's hallowed ceilings as a nimbus of energy formed around he and Lie, repelling several brazen individuals attempting to storm the alter.

"Uh-oh," Cara muttered as she and the others pressed against a similar field that suddenly materialized around their hovering forms rendering them completely immobile. "I think the shits about to hit the fan!"

As usual your observation is quite astute, Cara, Dresden's stern voice echoed in their minds. *As Lillian pointed out, the five of you came here uninvited. In the spirit of cooperation, I allowed you to stay, but considering the unfortunate turn these events have taken, I feel it would be best if these proceedings continued without you!*

Mayhem had just enough time to utter a profane oath before she and the others vanished from the sanctuary amidst a flash of blinding light.

Chapter 49

Dresden waited until the nimbus's glow faded away then focused his attention on the assembly, most of who had been shocked into silence following the abrupt expulsion of the quintet they had begun to look to for protection.

"Lillian and I came here today with hope of mending our world's fractured spiritual state," he bit out, his voice harsh. "But instead of embracing our cause and joining us in the fight against the deity that has turned you into complacent puppets, you have the temerity to take umbrage against us! Clearly, I was mistaken in thinking that any of you faith-driven fools would have the courage and fortitude to do what must be done in order to rid ourselves of the yoke of Divine oppression!"

"As if life under your guidance would be any better," the Pope fired back, fear giving way to indignation as he freed himself from the dutiful priests that were trying to keep him away from the seething Dresden. "You claim to be a benevolent leader yet use spiritual and mental manipulation against the masses to achieve acceptance."

"Which is no more than what The Almighty has done," a thoroughly incensed Lie interjected. "Carl may be new to the ways of Divinity but my life spans the breadth of Humanity's existence..."

"Yet throughout all that time you've failed to notice the one key component in God's stewardship of us," the Pope cut her off.

Lie regarded the wizened Mortal through narrowed eyes. "And this...component being"

"The power of Choice."

"Choice," Lie spat. "Do you truly believe that such power has been granted you?"

"I do," the Pope stoutly declared. "Regardless of how...*limited* our understanding of our world has been up to this point, I still believe in my heart that God did not keep us ignorant out of spite, but rather as a precaution until we became mature enough to truly understand the path he has placed us on."

"Are you truly that naive?" Dresden asked struggling to understand such illogical devotion from the man he had once held in such high esteem. "Considering the familiarity you claim to have already had with the way of the world, how can you see God's so-called plan for us as anything other than bondage on an evolutionary scale?"

The Pope's focused steely eyes on Dresden's scowling face. "Because despite the Lord's ability to *bend* Mankind to his will, he hasn't. He put forth his commandments, or Tenets as the Celestials term them, and allowed us to choose whether or not to adhere to them!"

"Just as He *chose* to eradicate our ancestors with the Great Flood when they turned their collective backs on His mandates," Dresden ground out.

"Granted God's wrath during that time was indeed harsh but He has since made restitution to Mankind for his rash decision in addition to making a pact to never again visit such destruction upon the Earth; a fact that is present even in the Bible's distorted accounts of our universe's history."

"Which is another bone of contention I wish to pick with our so-called God," Dresden charged, his eyes glowing with Celestial fire. "Why has He allowed so many variations of the Tenets to propagate unchecked throughout the millennia? Think of the countless millions that have been and are still being persecuted based on their religious beliefs. If God truly is the almighty deity, you and countless others proclaim him to be, why hasn't he long since revealed the Truth of the Realms and put an end to this madness?"

All eyes were on the Pope as he paused to consider Dresden's loaded question.

"In truth I cannot say why God has allowed the Lie, as you put it, to continue throughout the ages. Despite the knowledge I have recently gained I do not proclaim to be all-knowing in such matters."

Many nervous mutterings were exchanged after the Pope's admission and a knowing smirk appeared on Dresden's face.

"But then I don't have to be," the Pope's confident remark echoed loudly through the sanctuary. "Regardless of the haphazard way we arrived at this critical juncture in our world's history, we have still arrived and in my heart of hearts I truly believe that such is as God intended, and the path he has set before us is the one on which we should remain."

Several cries of "Amen" went up from the crowd following the Pope's stirring words. Dresden stared at his former superior and mentor for a moment then allowed his gaze to range over the crowd, most of whom were once again shouting cries of outrage against he and Lie. He refocused on the Pope and a resigned sigh escaped his lips.

"I see now that there is no reasoning with you, Vincenzo," he spoke softly addressing the Pope by his birth name in much the same way he did when they were classmates at the seminary so many decades ago. "Your faith and that of the majority here, which seem to have sided with you, though laudable is sadly misplaced. The time for change is upon us, and if you and those that follow you cannot accept that then I'm afraid your usefulness has come to an end."

A look of uncertainty flickered across Lie's face at Dresden's proclamation. One of the key elements of their strategy to supplant the Hierarchy was to sway the Mortal clergy to their side. Their influence on the respected masses would greatly aid in the coming transition.

The Halfling turned questioning eyes to her paramour but before she or any of the other clergy could respond, Dresden brought the edge of the Staff down hard against the glistening marble that made up the altar's base, the resulting shock wave created by the blow knocking most of the assembly to the ground.

"For centuries The Sistine Chapel has been a symbol for religious order and authority," Dresden's thunderous voice boomed above the growing rumbling created by the sudden violent shaking of the hallowed church's foundation. "But that age is coming to an end. The time has come for a new Order to arise; one that I had hoped all of you would've been a part of, but alas such is not to be."

Several cracks appeared in the numerous frescoes lining the sanctuary walls as the once magnificent structure began to slowly break apart. Those gathered raced frantically for the exits only to discover that they were all completely sealed trapping them inside the collapsing sanctuary.

The Pope's eyes locked with Dresden's. "In the name of God, Carl, you can't *do* this," he cried fighting to make his voice heard above the horrified screams of the terrified mob surrounding him.

"I'm afraid you've left me no choice," Dresden coldly responded a nimbus of energy forming around him as he held his hand out expectantly to Lie. The Halfling's eyes flickered briefly about the chaotic scene before them but made no comment as she accepted his hand in hers and stood beside him. "Like the callous God you so blindly serve, I too gave you a *choice*, Dresden called out as he and Lie began to fade. "Unfortunately, you chose wrong!"

With a final flash of brilliance, the carrier nimbus vanished leaving the foremost religious leaders on Earth to perish as a loud crack signaled the final collapse of the chapel's famously painted ceiling.

As he watched Michelangelo's masterpiece come crashing down upon him, Pope James closed his eyes and uttered a final prayer. "Father I know not why you have allowed these events to transpire, but my faith in you remains. I pray that you allow my soul and those of my fellows into Heaven's gates this day!"

Sorry, Your Eminence, but your work on Earth's not done yet!

The Pope gasped at the feminine voice echoing loudly through his mind. His eyes snapped open, and he stared in horrified amazement at the tons of plaster and metal suspended above his head.

"In the name of *God,*" he whispered as he and the others trapped with him watched in stunned fascination as the collapse of the sanctuary slowly began to reverse itself like a movie that was now being played backwards.

Within moments the Chapel was completely restored and the Pope and all those gathered within stared in awe at the nimbus of blazing white light now hovering before them. Eventually the light coalesced into three beings: One was a tall athletic woman, her sharp features and dark skin color similar to the tall muscular man standing beside her.

The final being was also female though unlike any the Pope or his colleagues had ever beheld: Prominent cheekbones set in an oval face that was dominated by a set of intense hazel-colored eyes that combined with the mocha color of her skin giving her an exotic beauty that was breathtaking to behold. Like her companions she was also extremely fit, but what completely set her apart from them were the pair of enormous glowing wings protruding from her back.

"Who...who are you?" Pope James managed to croak when he finally recovered from the shock of being saved.

"Fear not, Your Grace," the winged woman spoke, her rich contralto voice carrying easily to the back of the sanctuary. "This is Gabriel and his daughter Gabriella." She indicated her companions. "And like me they have come to aid you during these dark times."

"But...who are *you?*" the Pope asked, a look of incredulity covering his face

The woman straightened her shoulders, and her wings slowly began to fade away as did the glow radiating around her. "I am the daughter of the Archangel Michael and the Mortal Evelyn Sanchez, the Child of Order, and Harbinger of the Final Reclamation!" Her face softened after she finished her proud proclamation, and she favored the Pope with a friendly smile. "But you can call me Nina."

"My God," the Pope uttered leaning heavily against the altar, his whisper breaking the awed silence that had descended upon the frightened clergy in the wake of the miraculous restoration of the Sistine Chapel and the appearance of the three enigmatic beings standing before them.

Nina favored the trembling man with a benevolent smile. "I know this has been a trying day for you, for all of you," her voice echoed across the sanctuary. "Rest assured that you have nothing to fear from neither me nor my companions.

"Then...you're with the other group?"

"Other group?" Nina repeated the query of the trembling member of the Muslim contingent that had spoken, her eyes glowing softly as she quickly scanned the images of the morning's events still fresh in the young man's mind. "It seems the good Cardinal has left our friends in an awkward position," she directed her gaze toward Gabriel and Gabriella after observing the disturbing images. "Can you two mind the chapel while I go give them a hand?"

"We've got you covered," Gabriel assured her smiling at the kiss she blew at him before disappearing in a flash of light.

"That is one dynamic woman."

Gabriel couldn't help but chuckle at the Pope's nervous statement. "You have no idea how true that is, your grace!"

*

"Well that definitely did not go as planned."

Quinlan's jocular comment brought forth a round of disgruntled snorts from his companions as each of them tried in their own way to free themselves from Dresden's energy prison floating amidst the Crossroads ever-shifting mass.

"Yeah, well who knew your former employer had become so adept at channeling the Talisman's power," Mayhem spat as she fired yet another ineffective bolt of Celestial energy at the glowing sphere's impenetrable walls. "The question now is how do we free ourselves from this stupid bubble?"

"Leave that to me," a powerful voice boomed from the nimbus of light appearing besides the captured quintet.

"Nina?" Dichotomy gaped at the glowing winged figure hovering before their spectral prison. "Is it truly you?"

Nina favored the blended being with a maternal smile. "It is."

Cara released an appreciative whistle. "It looks like somebody got a serious upgrade!"

"That's putting it mildly," Nina said marveling at how different the universe around her seemed in the wake of her...Transformation. "But that's a topic for another discussion. Right now, let's focus on freeing you lot."

"Good luck with that one," Mayhem said with a snort. "Whatever this glowing bubble is made off just absorbs our energies."

"Such is the way of static celestial particles," Nina mused. "It would take me a year to explain the theory," she responded to the confused looks of the energy sphere's occupants. "Fortunately freeing you is far less complicated. I suggest you all close your eyes."

Dichotomy and the others did as Nina instructed as the glow about her body intensified to a painful degree. Within moments the glare faded, and Dresden's former prisoners gaped through stunned eyes at the sculpted walls of the Sistine Chapel that now surrounded them.

"Like I said," Cara's awed voice penetrated the shocked silence. "Somebody got a serious upgrade!"

Chapter 50

The frigid winds of Nirvana's arctic region tried their best to dissuade the lone, winged figure from his journey, but the Archangel Michael paid them no mind. His thoughts were on more important matters than Nature's follies.

So much has changed since last I raced these lands, the Archangel mused as he soared across the frozen landscape. In the early days of his eons long existence, he and his brothers had raced one another endlessly across Nirvana's surface trying to prove which of them the keenest flyer.

If only such a contest was the purpose of my visit today, the Archangel thought ruefully as he banked sharply toward the vague towers and shadowy structures that marked the city of Hell's imposing skyline. As always Michael was struck by the similarities to Heaven's awesome radiance, and couldn't help but wonder what would become of both cities given the precarious position The Creation now found itself in.

Perhaps the outcome of this meeting could affect the necessary safeguards to protect the sanctity of both, he hoped as he rapidly approached the massive alabaster edifice known as the Tower of Self, the high seat of Hell's ruler Iblis.

"Welcome, brother," a deep voice echoed through the open archway of the Tower's aerie as Michael landed gracefully in the circular courtyard.

"Iblis," Michael acknowledged the other walking toward him as he folded his wings onto his back.

"It is good to see you again," Iblis said touching his outstretched palm to Michael's in the Celestial greeting of equals. "But considering the Creation's current spiritual disarray I would surmise that this is not a social visit."

"Would that it was," Michael's fervent wish echoed softly. "But I'm afraid the current state of the Realms, particularly the events transpiring on Earth, is the reason I've come."

"Then let's not bandy words. You're here to discover my reasons for aiding your beleaguered offspring."

Michael's wings gave an involuntary twitch. "I am."

A slight smile curved Iblis' lip. "The answer is simple: together we stand divided we fall."

Michael's wings twitched again. "Then you agree with me that Lillian and her paramour must be stopped before they can jeopardize the Balance any further?"

"I do," Iblis announced in a solemn voice. "Although," he added regarding Michael through speculative eyes. "Your presence here indicates that not all of our Celestial kin share our viewpoint."

"On the contrary," a deep voice rang out as the archangel Gabriel swept from the sky, touching down lightly besides his brothers. "Most of the Hierarchy agrees that something needs to be done," he said after giving them both a stiff nod. "The question is: how do we quell this rising flood of disruption without violating the sanctions The Almighty has imposed on our actions."

"A good question indeed," Iblis replied, pleased in spite of the circumstances to once again be in the company of two of his Archian peers. "Come," he gestured towards the aerie's open doors. "Let us retire to more comfortable settings and discuss this matter at length."

Such a discussion need not take place, The Almighty's voice echoed through the surprised minds of the three Archangels. *The events transpiring on Earth are necessary to the restoration of The Balance.*

"But my, Lord," Michael spoke up in the shocked silence that followed The Almighty's decree. "The Mortal Dresden's usurpation of the Staff has..."

Allowed him to achieve the position of Chaotic authority that he must in order to fulfill his destiny during this Rising, the Almighty sternly interjected. *Let it be known throughout the Realms; I will not tolerate ANY interference from the Members of the Hierarchy.*

The Almighty severed the link leaving the Archian trio stunned by the extreme degree of finality in his voice.

"I guess that, as the Mortals say, is that," Gabriel said as he leapt into the air. "It was good seeing you Iblis. Hopefully it will not be another eon before our next encounter." He accorded his brothers a final nod then, with a mighty flap of his wings, soared off toward the distant spires of Heaven.

"I see he hasn't changed over the centuries," Iblis noted as he watched Gabriel's dwindling form.

Michael released an amused snort. "No, he hasn't. Nor does he have a vested interest in how this story plays out."

Iblis regarded his brother through solemn eyes. "You're referring to your progeny."

A slight smile creased Michael's lips. "I am. Against all reason and my own better judgment I have developed strong feelings for Nina. I would not have her suffer needlessly."

Michael's words sparked an idea within Iblis's mind. "I wonder if the same can be said about Raphael. Given Lillian's connection to Dresden, he too has a personal stake in this."

A thoughtful frown creased Michael's brow. "Are you suggesting that we contact our reticent brother and see if together we three can discover a way to...influence the outcome of this Rising *without* disobeying our Lord?"

"Considering what's at stake I would say it's well worth a try. Come," Iblis gestured toward the aerie's open doors. "Perhaps we have something to discuss after all."

*

"It appears Michael and Iblis have reacted just as you thought they would," Twilight said as she observed her Archian kin through The

Window. "Do you plan on putting a stop to this particular scheme as well?"

No, The Almighty's disembodied voice filled the chamber's spherical dimension. *Though they are technically still in violation of my non-interference mandate, I am interested to see what will come of their parlay with Raphael.*

"You mean you're interested to see if you're subtle manipulation of these events will continue to guide this Rising toward your preferred outcome."

Considering how connected you *are to The Creation's overall integrity I would think that you would prefer to not leave things to chance.*

"I would've *preferred* it if the Members of the Hierarchy had worked harder to prevent the current destabilization of The Balance," Twilight replied tartly, her shimmering form flaring brighter with her agitation. "And even though such is not the case, I'm still...uncomfortable with your current course of action."

A wave of compassion enveloped Twilight's mind. *I am aware of your displeasure, but I ask that you have faith in my plan.*

Twilight's form shimmered again. "Unlike the Mortals I have no Choice *but* to adhere to your scheme," she muttered bitterly closing her mind to The Almighty's touch as she returned her attention to The Window, and though He could've easily forced his way back into her psyche, The Almighty respected her pointed request for solitude and withdrew his presence from the Apex.

Chapter 51

"And basically, that's the situation."

The air was ripe with uncertainty as the small group of clergy the Pope had gathered in his office struggled to absorb the words of the Celestial being before them. Nina had reverted to her human form for this meeting but the sense of purpose and power radiating from her chiseled frame gave her an unearthly presence that was breath-taking to behold.

"I must say that's a lot to digest," Cardinal Piazzen, one of Pope James' most trusted advisor's spoke up; his baritone voice shattering the tense silence that had descended over the group following Nina's oration. "To discover that all the doctrines and belief's that have been held sacred for centuries by Earth's various religions are not only inaccurate but have been allowed to perpetuate in order to cover up a universal deception." The Cardinal shook his head from side to side. "It begs the question of 'why.'"

Nina favored the tall clergyman with a sympathetic look. "To put it bluntly; The Almighty didn't feel we were mature enough as a species to accept the truth of our reality or our singular status amongst the other Races; particularly after He witnessed the confusion following the premature Awakening of the First Ones."

"The fact that we truly are not alone in the universe is another topic I find particularly disturbing," Piazzen uttered, his comment met with nods and mutters of agreement from the other clergy.

Nina couldn't help but marvel at the egocentricity of their thinking. The world as they know it had just changed and their primary concern was the fact that Mankind wasn't the center of the universe. She was beginning to understand The Almighty's reluctance to impart the full truth of The Creation. Sadly, Mankind clearly *wasn't* ready. "I'm afraid the world around you is far beyond the scope of your naive assumptions."

"It is indeed," Pope James smoothly interjected when he sensed some of his fellow's taking umbrage at Nina's derisive comment. "But I trust you, fair Nina, shall be our guide through this new spiritual maze?"

"I will certainly try," Nina vowed favoring the Pope with a smile for his deft handling of what could have become an unnecessary bone of contention between her and the clergy. These were *her* people, the very beings she had been chosen to guide and protect. And though her intellect was now countless degrees above theirs, she could not let her newly acquired divinity alienate them. "I would also like to take this moment to apologize if I seem curt," she offered. "My recent transition to my current state has left me feeling somewhat...disconnected."

"The fact that you just apologized to us proves that you're not as disconnected as you think," Piazzen spoke favoring Nina with a look of such profound adoration that she couldn't help but smile. "Given your elevation by God, we must seem like children to you, yet you treat us as equals."

Nina wasn't sure how to respond to the man's earnest observation nor the looks of awe directed at her from the other members of the clergy. "In truth I don't know any other way *to* treat you," she confessed. This whole process, from my initial Emergence to this so-called Elevation, has been like riding a crazy roller coaster that never seems to stop."

"I believe I speak for all my fellow clergy when I say we completely understand," Pope James told her with a warm smile. "In fact, I think we're *all* beginning to share in that feeling." Murmurs of agreement echoed through the office. "The important thing is that now that we are all on the same spiritual page so to speak, we can move forward together."

"We can indeed," Nina smiled. It was easy to see why this gentle, yet outspoken man had been chosen to head the Catholic diocese.

His experience at guiding the masses should prove most useful. "And the first thing we need to do is formulate a plan to counter the false rhetoric currently being spread by Dresden and Lie. Thanks to their meddling the world's collective consciousness is in a fragile state."

"Seeing as how you're all powered up now can't we just beat them into submission?" Cara asked drawing murmurs of agreement from several of the others.

Nina favored the former Neutralizer with an amused look. "Given all that's happened I can understand you wanting to seek retribution against our foes, but we must refrain from using violence."

"If you say so," Cara grumbled not bothering to hide her disappointment. "It just seems like it would be quicker to take those two out of the equation."

"Quicker, yes, but not wiser," Pope James spoke up before Nina could reply. "Despite the fact that Dresden and his companion have used mass spiritual manipulation to garner the following they have, they still provided the masses with the illusion of choice. In order to counter their attack, we must offer the same option only our methods must be pure."

"Exactly," Nina agreed, her respect for the Pope growing another notch. "And given the potential Celestial forces we both can bring to bear such a confrontation would shatter the Balance and lead to the destruction of The Creation."

A look of chagrin appeared on Cara's face. "Point taken; though I still wish we could just shoot them both and be done with it."

Her disgruntled comment drew another spattering of chuckles from the room.

A mischievous gleam appeared in Nina's eyes. "You and me both, Cara; though I doubt The Almighty would be pleased with us if we did." More laughter echoed through the chamber and Nina found herself relaxing more into her new role. "In the meantime, are there any suggestions as to how we should go about debunking Dresden and Lie's propaganda?"

"We could try taking a page out of their book in terms of spreading our own propaganda," Cara suggested.

"Absolutely not," Nina declared stoutly. "I will not subject the masses to more of the Wraith's mental and spiritual manipulations, regardless of the message."

"Who said anything about using the Wraiths? I was thinking more along the lines of social media and the internet."

Nina regarded the former Neutralizer through disapproving eyes. "Please tell me you're kidding."

"I'm dead serious. Social apps like Facebook, Instagram, and Twitter have become the primary medium through which today's world communicates."

"Cara's right," Quinlan agreed. "The internet is also the fastest and easiest way to draw attention to your cause. If a few pics of a champagne glass perched atop Kim Kardasian's nude butt can cause a world-wide frenzy, imagine what a video of you restoring this chapel would've done." Quinlan's jocular comment produced a round of indignant snorts throughout the office.

"Which is rather pathetic when you think about it," Nina said shaking her head from side to side. "Though I do see your point,"

"As do I," the Pope reluctantly conceded allowing his gaze to sweep across the chapel's famed architecture. "Some of my more modern-minded contemporaries have suggested more than once that I allow the installation of a video system within these hallowed walls. Perhaps if I had taken their advice, we would have a recorded document of your miraculous arrival."

"Actually, we do, Your Grace," a light baritone proclaimed as Jamal Hadad, a prominent Imam in the Muslim hierarchy nervously held up his Samsung smartphone. "I know the ban on recording devices within the chapel but given the unprecedented situation we now find ourselves in, I thought it...prudent to have some type of record of these proceedings."

A chill crept down Pope James' spine as he watched the recording of the crumbling chapel and its subsequent restoration followed by Nina and her comrades' glowing appearance. "Utterly amazing," he whispered turning awed eyes to the Imam. "And you were able to record this in the midst of all that chaos?" Jamal responded with an affirmative nod and the Pope smiled. "Then I commend your fortitude, Imam Hadad."

"As do we all," a powerful voice rang out from the nimbus of white light forming in the center of the office that coalesced into the forms of Darius and Shift, the latter in her 'Sheila' persona. "Such evidence will be invaluable if we are to launch a counter campaign."

Mayhem released an irritated snort. "Now you two decide to show up."

Darius favored his fellow Desomor with a teasing wink. "Had I known that you five would've been so ineffectual against Dresden and Lie I would've joined you sooner."

"Your inclusion would have made little difference," Dichotomy's comment forestalled Mayhem's more potent retort. "With the Staff of Moses now in his possession, Dresden's power level far exceeds all of us combined, with the exception of Nina," he added according her a respectful nod."

"Our somber duo is right," Darius said taking note of the extreme levels of Celestial energy radiating from Nina. "I sense a lot of has changed since your sojourn to Heaven; including the addition of a new member to our band of Balance savers," he added taking note of Gabriella. "From your look and bearing I would have to surmise that you are Gabriel's long-lost daughter now returned."

"Gabriella Leyr," Gabriella introduced herself. "And you would be the Desomor Darius," she said shaking his outstretched hand.

"And you Shift, progeny of the Morphling Lord, Silas." Gabriella accorded the Morphling a respectful nod.

Shift's eyes widened with surprise. "Indeed, I am though I'm surprised that fact is known to you."

"The Archangel Michael was very forthcoming with the histories of the beings I might come into contact with during this Task."

"Which means we can cut this meet-and-greet short and get back to business," Mayhem curtly interjected ignoring the looks of disapproval directed at her. "Time is of the essence if we're going to put a stop the madness."

"Margaret is right," Nina said taking note of the slight flush that rose to the Desomor's face at the use of her birth name.

Nina's Transition had expanded the parameters of her mind to the point that the secrets of *all* beings could be laid bare to her if she so chose; an ability that could easily become bothersome she realized as the life-stories of all those around her were revealed to her through a flow of sensory data that took her a moment to stem.

"So, Darius," she addressed the Desomor after regaining her composure. "You are well versed in all things PR; how do we proceed from here?"

"Well, the first thing we need to do is find a better place to strategize," Mayhem said casting an apologetic look toward the Pope. "No offense Your Holiness but this office is a bit cramped."

"Margaret does have a point," Gabriel agreed smiling at the hostile look the Desomor directed at him for his presumptuous use of her name. "We do need a larger base of operations that will also afford us the privacy we need. Fortunately, I know just the place."

"Clawson is the perfect place," Nina cried having plucked the idea from his mind. "I suggest you members of the clergy brace yourselves; the mode of travel you're about to experience can be a bit unsettling to the uninitiated."

Several looks of concern crossed the faces of Pope James and his contemporaries as a nimbus of white light quickly engulfed all fifteen occupants of the office and whisked them away through time and space.

Chapter 52

"How is it we are able to watch these events on this device here while they're happening somewhere else?"

Sanders couldn't help but smile at the look of wonder on Gabriella's face as she stared at the screen of his iPad. On it was the latest video of Nina using her power to help the diligent workers of the EPA's emergency cleanup units contain a massive oil spill from a damaged tanker in the Pacific Ocean.

For the past few weeks several such videos uploaded by Tip's girlfriend Raymonda, whose technical proficiency had been discovered accidently after the two had been recruited by Darius to assume the duties of running Clawson's kitchen. Though shocked by the disclosure received from the Desomor on *true* way of the world, Tip and Ray had eagerly accepted the offer. Given Tip's culinary creativity and Ray's tech skills, the two had quickly become invaluable members of the group staying at Clawson that Tony Scavelli had jokingly named 'Nina's Heaven Squad' during the couple's tour of the ranch.

"Through the use of satellites," the Seeker said also watching the feed. Gabriella arched a questioning eyebrow and Sanders quickly launched into brief but concise description of the aforementioned technology and its numerous applications in modern society.

"This satellite network seems to work very much like the system of Windows the Hierarchy uses to monitor the Realms," Gabriella said, her eyes once again glued to the iPad. "Can you also use these devices for travel as well?"

"I'm afraid Mankind has yet to master that type of technology; at least not yet."

"Mankind has progressed so much since my death."

Sanders swallowed hard. The matter-of-fact way Gabriella spoke of her mortal passing always made him uncomfortable.

The past few weeks with the Celemor had opened the Seeker up in a way he hadn't thought possible. Her youthful naiveté coupled with the boundless wisdom acquired during a century of Heavenly existence made for a potent blend that affected him unlike any woman he had ever known. It was also the source of his discomfort.

Gabriella was a woman who achieved maturity *after* her death. As a result, she never developed the social and behavioral skills usually learned over a lifetime of actually *living,* which sometimes made for awkward moments during her interaction with the group of Nina's allies and clergy now inhabiting Clawson. Case in point: The fact that she was a resurrected being was of no consequence to her, yet to Sanders it was a miracle that he still had difficulty wrapping his head around.

"I know the feelings of affection and protectiveness you've developed for her are difficult to reconcile with the fact that she's a Celestial Mortal capable of incredible feats, but right now your steadfast support and friendship are what Gabriella needs to re-acclimate herself to the human condition," Pope James had counseled after the Seeker had come to him for advice. "And given the fact that her father, another being capable of miraculous feats, and violent ones," the Pope added with a teasing wink, "has given you his blessing in regard to your relationship with his daughter, I suggest that you continue to let your heart and head guide you."

Having been raised in a family that stressed kindness to others helping Gabriella, or Gabby as she insisted everyone call her, find her way came naturally though he had to admit his current situation was a far cry from *anything* he had experienced; both as a kid growing up in Oregon and as *Presbetyrii* Seeker. Still, he had to admit that the bond forming between them filled a void that he hadn't realized was there.

Sanders' experience with the opposite sex was extremely limited, due mostly to his pensive manner and devotion to his faith, but his time with Gabby had opened his heart in ways he never thought possible, and she seemed genuinely interested in him as well. Where all of this was heading, Sanders didn't know, but he was perfectly content to let things developed at their own pace as opposed to throwing all caution to the romantic winds the way Quinlan had with Mayhem; though he had to admit he had never seen his friend happier.

"You're looking mighty tense there, Sandy. Are you alright?" Gabby's voice penetrated his reverie.

"Oh, sure," Sanders assured her wincing only slightly at the nickname she had saddled him with. Yet another change brought about by this Celestial scamp. No one had *ever* gotten away with bastardizing his name, but coming from her the diminutive didn't bother him; at least not too much. "I was just wondering if maybe Nina could use some help," he dissembled. "That spill looks pretty significant."

Gabby Smiled. "Then let's go help her," she decreed, a nimbus of light forming around them as she grabbed Sanders' hands and 'ported them away.

Chapter 53

Dresden's jaw tightened briefly as he watched the YouTube video upload of what the internet was calling "the miraculous restoration of the Sistine Chapel" play out on Malakai's Galaxy Tab's ten-inch screen. For the past several weeks the stunning footage of Nina's restoration of the venerable structure, as well many new clips of her and cadre of enhanced followers performing Celestial deeds in various spots around the world, had dominated the media and internet; with many voices wondering if she had come to oppose the two demi-gods that recently proclaimed themselves the "Leaders of the New Spiritual Revolution" yet thus far had done nothing but spout rhetoric.

"It looks like Ms. Delcielo has managed to go viral."

Malakai's quip drew an irritated snort from the former Cardinal. "She has indeed, though it matters little in the grand scheme of things. The Mortals of this world will yield to my guidance or suffer the repercussions."

"That goes without saying, boss, but sometimes people yield a little easier if you give them something spectacular to yield to."

Dresden's expression darkened as he considered the Neutralizer's suggestion. "Then perhaps it's time I did just that." He gave the tablet's screen a final contemptuous glance then abruptly vanished from the room.

"Is it just me or is the good Cardinal getting more hardcore every day." Joey's raspy voice filled the silent void left after Dresden's proclamation and abrupt exit.

"Man's got a point," Malakai said to Lie. "Ever since Nina 2.0 showed up your man's been wound up pretty tight."

"I'm afraid I have to agree," she admitted trying hard to ignore the sudden ache in her chest as her eyes lingered on the fading glow of Dresden's carrier nimbus. Over the past several weeks she too had noticed the gradual change in her lover's demeanor that seemed to begin during their meeting with the clergy. "If truth be told his current disdain and aloofness mirrors that of certain Members of the Hierarchy though at the moment I can't discern the cause of it."

It is the effect of the Celestial power he now wields.

"Father," Lie gasped at the unexpected sound of Raphael's voice echoing from the nimbus of white light appearing in the room.

"Fuck me," Joey hissed, both he and Malakai dropping instinctively into defensive stances as the light coalesced into the muscular, silver-haired form of the Archangel. "Who the hell is *this?!?*"

"My father, the Archangel Raphael," Lie told her cohorts, touching her raised palm affectionately to the Archangel's.

"Oh," Malakai muttered relaxing slightly. "Sorry for the disrespect but given the company we tend to keep you can never be too careful about folks popping in on you."

The big Mortal's irreverent quip drew a bemused smile from Raphael as he focused glowing eyes on the still apprehensive duo. "It's nice to see you've recruited such stalwart defenders to your cause, daughter," he said taking due note of the significant levels of Celestial energy coursing through their bodies. "Am I right in assuming their Elevation is by your hand?"

Lie smiled. "You taught me well."

"Indeed, I did." He accorded Joey and Malakai a brief nod then turned serious eyes to his daughter. "You're correct in comparing your paramour's disposition to certain Members of the Hierarchy. The power he now wields has indeed elevated him to Celestial status, but such a transition is not without cost. In Dresden's case as his mind continues to evolve, his core dynamic, what the Mortals of Earth call "humanity", will further recede.

Lie's eyes widened with alarm. "But...why?"

"Simply put; his Mortal mind is not adequately equipped to handle such power."

"But I don't understand; other Mortals have handled the Talismans throughout the ages."

"True but the Blood of Abraham coursed through their veins and that seed of Celestiality allowed them to wield the totems unaffected. Such Mortals truly are a breed apart."

The room was silent as Lie considered the ramifications of what her father was saying. The fact that Carl's elevation was slowly robbing him of the qualities that had endured her to him was a matter of great concern. The casual aloofness and cold-hearted disdain Members of her Father's race had always been of particular annoyance to the Halfling; especially given the pain such disregard had caused her mother. In fact, one of the benefits she hoped would be gleaned from her and Carl's disruption of the Celestial status quo was the installation of a more compassionate Seat of Authority throughout the Creation. But now, given Carl's current state of annoyance with his would-be charges, she wondered if such a goal was even still possible. "Is there any way to...reverse his condition?"

Raphael leveled stern eyes on her. "Yes, there is, have him surrender the Staff."

Lie released a disgusted snort. "Of course you would suggest that. I'm quite certain Carl relinquishing his power would make you, the Hierarchy, and The Almighty, *very* happy."

A look of annoyance settled on Raphael's face. "Actually, The Almighty has decreed that no member of the Hierarchy be allowed to interfere with this little coup the two of you have initiated."

Lie's eyes widened with surprise. "He has; what prompted that?"

The Archangel's irritation deepened. "Apparently your insurrection is a necessary evil in the Creation's continued existence."

It took Lie a moment to absorb her father's words. "So...you're *not* here to try and force the issue of Carl's Celestiality?"

A resigned sigh escaped Raphael's lips. "No, I am not."

"Then...why *are* you here?"

Raphael reached forward and stroked his daughter's cheek. "I'm here because I've just had the most...unusual interaction with Michael and Iblis."

Lie blinked. "Really; and what did The Keeper of Benevolence and The Desolate one have to say?"

"Turbulent times are on the horizon, despite all that's happened between us over the millennia you are still my daughter, Lillian. Your fate matters to me. Whatever the outcome of this cosmic game you and your compatriots are playing, I pray you are not adversely affected by it."

Lie placed her hand atop his and gave it a gentle squeeze. "Thank you," she whispered.

Raphael leaned forward and placed a gentle kiss atop his daughter's forehead then pulled away as a nimbus of white light formed around him whisking him away.

"That was intense," Malakai said after the glow of the carrier nimbus had faded.

"It was indeed," Lie replied. "And unusual; my father's not one for sentiment."

"Should we be worried?" Joey asked, and Lie regarded him through thoughtful eyes.

"I wouldn't say worried," Lie told him. "But given the fragile state of Earth's spiritual front at the moment, we should be *aware* of any potential threats to our plans."

"Actually 'worried' might be the better word," Joey commented pointing to the wall mounted television, specifically to the live news feed of the terrifying events unfolding at the Giza Plateau in Egypt.

Standing atop the Great Pyramid, tendrils of Celestial fire radiating from his body, was Dresden; the Staff of Moses clutched in his right hand while above him floated what appeared to be five people, all of them visibly struggling against the unseen hand that held them aloft.

"Oh shit! That's the *President*," Malakai blurted as the camera zoomed in on The Leader of the Free World's distinctive flushed face and blonde comb-over. "What the hell is he playing at?"

"I think the Lady's about to ask him that same question," Joey said at Lie's abrupt departure from the room amidst a flash of light.

"Yeah, I think you're right," Malakai muttered as Lie materialized on the Pyramid beside Dresden, the television's high-def properties clearly showing the agitated expression on her face. "I also think the Celestial shit's about to hit the fan!"

"We should be there to cover her six," Joey ground out, his eyes burning into Malakai's who returned his friend's hostile look with one of helplessness.

"Agreed, but how? I haven't made it to the teleportation section in the new-power manual."

Perhaps I may be of assistance, a familiar voice echoed suddenly in the startled minds of both men.

"Raphael?" Malakai called out, his shock over the unexpected interaction with Archangel mirrored on Joey's face.

Raphael's amusement flittered through the link he had established with the two Mortals. *The Almighty's decree prevents me from helping my daughter, but not you. Dresden's psyche has reached a tipping point. And while I am unsure as to what caused this sudden shift, I am quite certain the two of you should be by your Mistress's side.* Before either man could respond, a carrier nimbus formed around their bodies and teleported them away.

*

Dresden looked upon the throngs of people steadily gathering in the sands before the Great Pyramid, a feeling of immense pride welling up within him. For countless centuries, the world existed in a miasma of confusion and conflict; brother against brother, village against village, nation against nation, and for what; the pathetic pursuit by the few to control the many?

Such madness could only be attributed to the lack of *true* leadership from the so-called kings, queens, presidents and so forth; those misguided, conceited few who dared to think that their vision of what the world should be outweighed those of similar-minded megalomaniacs. Such discord had allowed humanity to exist in a state of constant war since its inception. Add to that the cruel lies of faith and spirituality perpetuated by the world's own so-called Creator, and you ended up with a chaotic mass of feudalism and racism that fueled the body-and-soul-grinding machine trying to pass itself off as the home of Mankind.

Such despair could not be allowed to continue if Mankind were to truly take their place as the Vanguard race, and he, Carl Dresden, former officer of a sham faith in the service of an indifferent deity would usher in the change and salvation that was truly needed!

But at what cost, my love? Lie's voice echoed through Dresden's mind as the Halfling appeared in the air before him. "Can't you see that what you're doing is perpetuating the very chaos we sought to cure?"

"You're wrong, Lillian," the former-Cardinal's voice thundered through the air, drawing the attention of both the masses at Giza and the millions of people around the world watching this incredible drama play out. "These so-called leaders were charged with the care and prosperity of their constituents; they failed! God was charged with the care and prosperity of the children that he created; he also failed! The world is in total disarray and mankind is on the brink of annihilation, but I will set matters right. Through my guidance, all will learn the truth of their existence, and learn to walk a batter path. Through my guidance the arrogant Celestial beings of the heavens will learn to respect those Mortals whose possession of a soul puts them in a category light-years beyond them. Through my guidance and rule, this...Creation shall be brought to heel!"

Lie stared at the Mortal...the *Man*...that had come to mean so much to her, and for the first time in her eons of existence, a touch of fear seized her heart. It was as if the intelligent, stern yet caring person she had come to know, love, and cherish had been consumed by this glowing, insanity-spewing being before her. Her father was right; the power of the Staff had driven Carl completely mad.

"I am not mad, Lillian," Dresden said having read her mind. "What I am is awake! Watching the people's reaction over Nina's exploits suddenly revealed an inescapable truth. The needs of this world and the billions that inhabit it have been ignored for far too long." The intensity of the tendrils of Celestial fire that circled Dresden's body increased as did the volume and power of his voice. "For too long chaos has reigned. For Mankind to achieve all we were created to, order must be restored, and that restoration starts...NOW!"

With a final flare of energy from his outstretched hand, the captive diplomats were sent hurtling toward the ground. A collective gasp was released around the world as Mankind watched in helpless horror as the leaders of the most powerful and influential nations on Earth plummeted to their deaths; followed by an equally all-inclusive sigh of relief as Lie, using her own considerable might, halted their fall then lowered them safely to the sands below.

"You...DARE," Dresden roared at the Halfling whom he trapped in a bubble of light and drew toward him. "You, who first opened my eyes to the truth, who pledged her support and love to our mission, would now *betray* me?"

"It's *you* who is guilty of betrayal, Carl," Lie seethed, her eyes glowing with Celestial fire, her body trembling with rage. "It's you who has lost sight of our goal and become nothing but a tyrant. You who has..."

The rest of her statement went unsaid as Dresden's glowing hand passed through the bubble and connected with Lie's face, the force of the blow so powerful that the barrier holding her shattered, and the dazed Halfling was sent hurtling through the sky toward the Sphynx at an unbelievable speed.

Again, the world gasped, this time in amazement as another flash of blinding light signaled the arrival of Malakai, and Joey atop the famed monument's head. Immediately grasping the trouble their mistress was in, Joey grabbed Malakai by the front of his jacket and hurled in the air just in time for his friend to catch Lie's inert body. Drawing on his own Celestial power, Malakai absorbed her momentum, an agonizing cry torn from his lips as the considerable kinetic energy that he hadn't been able to compensate for coursed through his body, shattering the bones in his chest and shoulders. Even wounded as he was, the former Green-beret managed to land gently atop the Sphinx's head where he collapsed onto his back; an unconscious but uninjured Lie cradled safely in his broken embrace.

"How...how did you two get here," Lie whispered as Joey gently lifted her from Malakai's arms, the bones of which were already mending.

"In a way that'll probably blow your mind," Joey said, channeling some of his own energy into the hand that rested against the bruise on Lie's jaw from Dresden's blow. "Your old man's voice popped in our heads after you vanished, telling us we needed to be with you. Next thing you know, we were."

A tender smile curved Lie's lips, and not just for his terse explanation of her father's unexpected action. She could've easily healed her own injuries, but Joey's gesture, as well as Malakai's daring rescue, had touched her heart; making her realize that she had come to care a great deal for her two loyal henchmen.

"I take it you're chat with his former holiness didn't go as planned."

The Halfling's smile vanished at Malakai's quip. "No, it didn't. And given Carl's considerable power via the staff and current chaotic state of mind, I am quite certain that further attempts to talk him down will also fail."

"Putting an end to his lunacy need no longer concern you, child," Raphael's stern voice rang out as he, Michael, Gabriel, and Iblis appeared in the air above the Sphinx. "We shall take it from here!"

Chapter 54

"And you're sure now is the right time for something like that?"

"I think it's the *perfect* time," Tyree responded to Nina's skepticism for the idea of a global, religious summit he'd just proposed. "Your presence on the internet has reached saturation levels never before seen, and you're a primary trending topic on the majority of the social media platforms. Compared to you, Dresden and Lie are just a blip on the social radar."

"That's all well and good but I'm still not sure that *I'm* ready to put myself out there like that."

"It's what you've been building toward," Gabriel said as he entered the parlor. "Since your return from Heaven and final Elevation you've been on a mission to alleviate the turmoil caused by Dresden's brute-force attempt to capture Mankind's devotion, and Mankind itself has taken notice. Just look at what's happening at the Centers. They've become beacons for those spiritually lost soul seeking to know the Truth about their world and God."

"That's my point," Nina exclaimed, still shocked by the overwhelming throngs of people massed around the Centers praying and chanting, and all of them calling her God's *true* messenger. Amazingly there were no instances of violence considering the multitudes gathered. In fact, it was just the opposite. It was as if her Centers had become the site of numerous modern-day incarnations of Woodstock! "All five locations have become...spiritual circuses for lack of a better term! People lined up for blocks, some even camping on the streets in the hopes that I'll show up."

"All the more reason I say you need to officially declare your purpose, and call Dresden and Lie out," Tyree pressed pounding his right fist into his left palm. "Their holy charade needs to come to an end!"

"I think the Cardinal may have the same idea," Quinlan called out from the kitchen where he, Mayhem, Gabby, and several of the Clergy were gathered around the large, wall-mounted flat-screen television; one of several recently added to the Ranch at Raymonda's insistence that the group needed a more efficient way to monitor the news and internet. "I think something nasty is about to happen in Egypt."

Nina quickly made her way to the kitchen, followed closely by Gabriel and Tyree. She took one look at the screen, and her mouth formed and 'O' of astonishment.

"Yeah, I'd say that's definitely a problem," Tyree muttered, his eyes, like everyone else's glued to the image of a glowing Dresden standing atop the Great Pyramid, and the four, winged beings hovering in the air before him.

"I do believe the Archangels have finally decided to bring that fool to task," Mayhem noted with a satisfied grunt. "And the fact that the four of them seem to have put aside their differences to do so lends weight to how serious this is."

A slight frown creased Nina's brow. "I agree, though I fear their involvement will do more harm than good. The Celestial forces unleashed during such a confrontation would be catastrophic to the Plateau, not to mention the thousands of poor souls gathered there."

"Shall I gather the troops?" Gabriel asked. "Perhaps we could mitigate some of the collateral damage."

"Not this time." The timbre of Nina's voice deepened as she morphed into her full Celestial state; the glow from her translucent wings shining so bright that the others were forced to shield their eyes. "This is something I must attend to alone!"

"Well, that was strange," Cara spoke up in the awkward silence that followed Nina's abrupt departure.

"Not as strange as the restriction she seems to have placed on us following her." The shock in Gabriel's voice was reflected on his face as he tried unsuccessfully to follow the Harbinger. "There's some type of barrier in place around the ranch neutralizing my teleportational abilities!"

"I guess she wasn't kidding when she said needed to handle this mess by herself," Tyree said a knot of apprehension forming in his stomach as the screen showed Nina's glowing appearance in Egypt. "I just hope she's up to the challenge.

Chapter 55

"Stand aside, daughter," Michael's powerful voice reverberated through the air as Nina took a position between the Archangels and Dresden. "The time has come for we of the Archian cast to end this arrogant Mortal's usurpation of this Realms destiny!"

"That's not your Task, father," Nina fired back, her formal address emphasizing the seriousness of the situation. "Despite his possession of the Staff's power, Dresden's current infraction is a Mortal matter, and such transgressions fall on under *my* purview, not the Watch's."

"I answer to neither them *nor* you," Dresden spat, his eyes blazing as he called upon the Staff's energy to prepare for the battle to come. "For too long have my people existed under the heel of Celestial tyrants. That ends *Now!*"

"You overstep, Mortal fool," the Bringer of Death ground out, his thunderous voice causing the multitudes watching from the sand below to cringe in fear; many of them trying to flee the area as the Archangel's drew closer to the implied line Nina had drawn in the air.

"Plus, you dared to lay hands upon my daughter," added a seething Raphael, his massive wings vibrating with suppressed anger. "Such cowardice and abuse cannot go unpunished!"

Nina's gaze darted briefly to the sands below and the carnage the Celestial standoff was causing amongst the people trying to retreat from the plateau, many of them being trampled during the chaotic exodus.

A sudden flash of light drew her attention back to Dresden and the Archangels, and she cringed at what she saw: The Archangels having formed a circle around Dresden were bombarding him with beams of pure Celestial energy, but the protective shield Dresden erected held firm though the strain of keeping his attackers at bay was showing on his face.

Nina watched in morbid fascination as her father and his brothers increased their efforts, the bodies of all four wreathed in Celestial fire as they sought to overwhelm Dresden's defenses. To his credit, Dresden did not waver, calling on the Staff's near infinite power to repel the massive onslaught of energy.

Just as Nina was starting to wonder which side would prove stronger, a sudden rumble filled the air as the Great Pyramid began to vibrate, its ancient stones no longer able to withstand the waves of power coursing through Dresden and washing over it.

Realizing that disaster was imminent, Nina brought her own considerable power to bear. "*ENOUGH!*" The Harbinger screamed as she released a surge of primal energy that washed over the area bringing an instant cessation of all movement, both on the ground and in the air which, consequently, brought the battle between Dresden and the Archangel's to an unceremonious end.

"That's better," Nina's voice echoed softly in the prevailing silence. "I understand your need to oppose Dresden," she sternly addressed the Archangels. "But what none of you took into consideration is the effect such a confrontation would have on the very beings you've been Tasked with protecting." Nina gestured toward the thousands of people immobilized on the ground below. "And you," she directed her harsh gaze toward Dresden. "I understand the anger you feel over the Almighty's deception, and your desire to set our people on a more truthful path, but did you at any point in time stop to truly consider *why* He perpetrated such a deception? Trust me when I say that Humanity as a whole, truly wasn't ready."

Nina put as much sincerity in her voice as she could muster but she could tell she wasn't getting through to him. Fortunately, she had another way of convincing the seething Dresden that what she spoke was the truth.

"I can see it in your eyes that you don't believe me, which is why I've decided to show you what was shown to me during the final stages of my Elevation."

Dresden cringed inwardly, but could do nothing to prevent Nina from laying her hand atop his forehead, however his determined resistance evaporated instantly when the Harbinger's touch brought forth an explosion of images and feelings as his mind and perceptions were expanded exponentially to handle the Truth being laid out before him. With fresh eyes he saw the Creation's humble beginnings and its progression to its current erratic state; with new perceptions he became aware, and now understood, The Almighty's reluctance to fully enlighten the mortal species he considered the *true* watchers of reality. With heightened empathy he shared The Almighty's pain over the failure of His numerous attempts to subtly guide us toward that eventuality for the betterment of *All* beings. And with this new insight came the crushing realization of how he and Lillian had become unwitting conduits for the semi-sentient shadow of Chaos that remained in constant battle with its eternal counterpart, Order; their ruinous actions disrupting the delicate Balance The Almighty had struggled over the eons to maintain, thus putting The Creation at risk.

"My, God," he whispered as Nina drew his battered psyche back from the state of complete Creational awareness, and he began to weep as the weight of his transgressions bore down on him. "I've been such a fool."

A slight smile curved Nina's lips, and she cradled his tear-streaked face in her hands. "No, you haven't. You've been doing what we Mortals have done since the beginning of time: making mistakes. What matters most is what we choose to do once we realize we've made them: keep messing up or learn from them and move forward."

Dresden managed a dry laugh. "Definitely the latter," he said heaving a relieved sigh as Nina released her hold over him and drifted back.

"Deftly handled, my child," Michael said, forgoing all forms of decorum and drawing her close to him. "Your wisdom far surpassed ours this day!"

Nina relaxed into his embrace, savoring the warmth and strength of his powerful frame, as well as the approving energy flowing from the other Archangels. "Thanks dad." She knew that such accolades coming from four of the most powerful beings in The Creation warranted a more prolific acknowledgment, but for the moment, her simple response felt the most appropriate.

"So..." Dresden began, regret for his recent actions still reflected on his lined face. "What happens now?"

Nina reluctantly disentangled herself from her father's arms and took the former Cardinal's hands in hers. "Now, Carl Benjamin Dresden; we gather our respective forces and begin the process of healing our world!"

EPILOGUE

"I take it the time has finally come?"

Nina favored Dresden with what Tony had come to call, her Realm-changing smile. "It has, thanks in no small part to you and your acolytes."

Dresden waved her praise aside. "Please, compared to what you've accomplished these past few years since Giza, our roles have been easy."

Nina's eyes arched upward. "I would hardly call the unification of every religious faction on the planet into a single faith easy, Prime Minister Dresden; particularly in light of the fact Lillian's firm usurpation of control over the Demonstratives kept them from interfering or aiding you in that endeavor," she added according the Halfling standing beside Dresden a nod of approval.

Lie released an amused snort. "Keeping that rabble in line was easy giving the broader powers and authority The Almighty granted me and the other Halflings you swayed to your cause. The real accomplishment was your gaining His approval for the restructuring of the Hierarchy. I still find *that* hard to believe."

Nina laughed. "Actually, it wasn't me that convinced Him that a Reclamation was due for *all* beings, not just the Mortals."

Nina's mind drifted back to those tumultuous months following the events over Giza, and the massive effort Dresden and his newly formed Truth Ministries had undertaken to lift the world from the state of spiritual depression it had sunk into. Using the power of the Staff, which she had insisted he keep despite his insistence that he wasn't worthy of such power, Dresden had reopened the numerous Angelic teaching halls similar to the one under the Sphinx that were stationed around the world. With an army of devout converts at his command and a host of Celemors and Desomors, called upon by Nina, to assist, the newly christened Prime Minister had initiated a spiritual reeducation program the likes of which the world had never seen.

Having watched Earth's transformation from a spiritual and religious miasma into a unified, planetary religion had inspired Nina to suggest a similar overhaul within Celestia's halls of power, and though reluctant at first, The Almighty had eventually agreed that the time for change had indeed come for the entire Creation. Of great pride to Nina was the fact her mother was the one to finally make Him see the light, so to speak.

As the Mortal mother of the second most powerful being in The Creation, Evelyn Sanchez's position within Heaven had been elevated to such that she now had access to every part of the Crystal City including the Apex where, much to her amazement and delight, The Almighty would frequently commune with her. It was during one of those sessions that Evelyn asked Him why, since he had put so much effort into engineering Nina's creation, he didn't heed her advice; a question which led to his acquiescence on the matter of a Celestial restructuring.

"Have you decided which world you're going to establish communication with first?"

Nina blinked as Dresden's question drew her once again from her musings. "Not yet," she admitted with a shrug. "I figured that before I do I need to make sure the thing still works."

Dresden and Lie chuckled as all three cast their gaze on the massive granite slabs before them.

Evelyn's influence had also been monumental in gaining The Almighty's support for Nina's current objective: the activation of the portal at Stone Hinge. With the people of Earth finally united in their beliefs and purposes, Nina felt that the time had finally come to put the famed monolith to the use for which it was intended.

"I'm sure it does," Lie stated with complete confidence in her father's creation.

"Why don't we find out," Tyree's excited voice boomed from the massive carrier nimbus containing him, Gabriel, Gabby, Sanders, Quinlan, Cara, Joey, Malakai, and Dichotomy materializing on the grass beside them.

"It's about time you lot showed up," Nina teased her friends and allies as they formed a semi-circle around her. "I was starting to think you all had chickened out."

"Not a chance," Joey's distinctive rasp carried through the air drawing a few laughs from the others. He and Malakai's inclusion by Nina's group into the fold had been tense at first, but after numerous Celestially enhanced sparring sessions between the various participants, all grievances had been settled and put aside.

"We're all here, love," Gabriel said taking hold of Nina's hands. "It's finally time to see what this thing can do!"

Nina maintained her hold of his hands as she morphed into her Celestial form. "You're damn right it is," she smiled as she brought her power to bear on the slabs of the ancient monolith, all of which had begun to glow. Dark clouds began to gather in the air above as lightning flashed through the sky accompanied by the roar of thunder, while around them the earth began to shake. For a moment Nina feared the ancient slabs would topple, but after a few moments, the tremors subsided as did the gathering storm in the sky.

"Damn," Cara gasped in awe, her sentiment echoed by the others as the gray surfaces of each of the standing slabs began to shimmer and were quickly replaced by scenes of varying landscapes; some similar to Earth, others unlike anything Nina and her Mortal friends had ever seen.

"It looks like the doors are open, people," an excited Nina spoke up in the awed silence that had settled over the group. "Which one do we step through first?"

The Beginning....

Thank you so much for buying my book!
I hope you enjoyed your time in the Realms. If you have a moment, please post a review. Positive or negative, your opinion matters to me.

Also by Art Gulley Jr.

Milton Keynes UK
Ingram Content Group UK Ltd.
UKHW041949291124
451915UK00001B/60